By Julie Brannagh

Catching Cameron
Rushing Amy
Blitzing Emily

Catching Cameron

A LOVE AND FOOTBALL NOVEL

JULIE BRANNAGH

AVONIMPULSE
An Imprint of HarperCollinsPublishers

Excerpt from *Falling for Owen* copyright © 2014 by Jennifer Ryan.

Excerpt from *Good Girls Don't Date Rock Stars* copyright © 2014 by Codi Gary.

EPub Edition MAY 2014 ISBN: 9780062279736

Print Edition ISBN: 9780062279767

JV 10 9 8 7 6 5 4 3

*To Susan Mallery, who wouldn't accept
anything but my very best.
Thank you for everything.*

Acknowledgments

AS ALWAYS, I have lots of thank you's for all of those who gave advice and encouragement while I was writing *Catching Cameron*.

I wish I had the words to express how grateful I am to Sarah E. Younger of Nancy Yost Literary Agency and to Amanda Bergeron of Avon Impulse for all of their help and their hard work on my behalf. Thank you for being such a great team, too.

I would be remiss if I didn't thank the following: the Avon Books art department; Amanda's assistant, Carly Bornstein; Dianna Garcia of the Avon Books publicity department; and Jonathan Baker, my copyeditor, who should get some kind of national award for saving the world from my crimes against grammar and punctuation.

Thank you to Jenn Mueller, amazing sports reporter, for helping me with the research for this book by granting me an interview. I am in awe of what she does every time she steps in front of a TV camera for the Seattle Mariners and the Super Bowl Champion Seattle Seahawks. She's the greatest. If you'd like to learn more about Jenn, please go to www.talksportytome.com!

Jessi Gage and Amy Raby of the Cupcake Crew, Friday is still my favorite day of the week. Thank you for your critiques, your friendship, and all the cupcakes.

Thank you (as always) to my husband, Eric. I could never do this without him. I love you, honey.

The incomparable Mary Buckham helped me write the query letters that got me the gig. She's amazing. If you write, it's worth whatever it takes to get to one of her craft classes, or buy her books.

Once upon a time I met Cherry Adair, and she told me to get my butt in the chair and Write the Damn Book. I've sold four of them, thanks to her. And yes, I am still more afraid of disappointing her than I am of my editor and agent. Thank you!

I'd like to thank current and former Seattle Seahawks for interviews they've given in various forms of media that were a huge help in my research. I'd also like to thank the Legion of Boom for reminding me that it really doesn't matter where you start, it's all about where you finish.

I'd also like to thank Lisa Olson and female sports reporters everywhere. Obviously, my light-hearted book doesn't explore the barriers women still face in reporting on sporting events that the guys in the profession will never have to deal with in their careers. I admire your courage and dedication. Thank you for being role models for an entire generation of little girls who are now being told "you can" instead of "you can't."

Thank YOU for buying my book. I hope you will enjoy it! As always, I'm at juliebrannagh.com, on Facebook, and on Twitter as @julieinduvall. I love to hear from readers!

Go Sharks!

Chapter One

ZACH ANDERSON WAS in New York City again, and he wasn't happy about it. He wasn't big on crowds as a rule, except for the ones that spent Sunday afternoons six months a year cheering for him as he flattened yet another offensive lineman on his way to taking out the guy's quarterback. He also wasn't big on having four people fussing over his hair, spraying him down with simulated sweat, and trying to convince him that nobody would ever know he was wearing bronzer in the resulting photos.

Then again, he was making eight figures for a national Under Armour campaign for two days' work; maybe he shouldn't bitch. The worst injury he might sustain here would be a muscle pull running away from the multiple women hanging out at the photo shoot who had already made it clear they'd be interested in spending more time with him.

He was all dolled up in UA's latest. Of course, he typically didn't wear workout clothes that were tailored and/ or ironed before he pulled them on. The photo shoot was now in its second hour, and he was wondering how many damn pictures of him they actually needed. There were worse things than being a pro football player who looked like the cover model on a workout magazine, being followed around by large numbers of hot young women, and getting paid for it all.

"Gorgeous," the photographer shouted to him. "Okay, Zach. I need pensive. Thoughtful. Sensitive."

Zach shook his head briefly. "You're shitting me."

Zach's agent, Jason, shoved himself off the back wall of the room and moved into Zach's line of vision. Jason had been with him since Zach signed his first NFL contract. He was also a few years older than Zach, which came in handy. He took the long view in his professional and personal life and encouraged Zach to do so as well.

"Come on, man. Think about the poor polar bears starving to death because they can't find enough food at the North Pole. How about the NFL going to eighteen games in the regular season? If that's not enough, *Sports Illustrated* discontinuing the swimsuit issue could make a grown man cry." Even the photographer snorted at that last one. "You can do it."

Eighteen games a season would piss Zach off more than anything else, but he gazed in the direction the photographer's assistant indicated, thought about how long it would take him to get across town to his appointment when this was over, and listened to the camera's rapid clicking once more.

"Are you sure you want to keep playing football?" the photographer called out. "The camera loves you."

"Thanks," Zach muttered. Shit. How embarrassing. If any of his four younger sisters were here right now, they'd be in hysterics.

CAMERON SMILED INTO the camera for the last time today. "Thanks for watching. I'm Cameron Ondine, and I'll see you next week on *NFL Confidential*." She waited until the floor director gave her the signal the camera was off, and stood up to stretch. Today's guest had been a twenty-five year old quarterback who'd just signed a five-year contract with Baltimore for seventy-five million dollars. Fifty million of it was guaranteed. His agent hovered off-camera, but not close enough to prevent the guy in question from asking Cameron to accompany him to his hotel suite to "hook up."

Cameron wished she were surprised about such invitations, but they happened with depressing frequency. The network wanted her to play up what she had to offer—fresh-faced, wholesome beauty, a body she worked ninety minutes a day to maintain, and a personality that proved she wasn't just another dumb blonde. She loved her job, but she didn't love the fact some of these guys thought sleeping with her was part of the deal her employers offered when she interviewed them.

The sound techs unclipped her lavalier microphone and the power pack in the waistband of her skirt. She waited till they walked away and gave Jake Eisen a brisk pat on his upper arm.

"I'm really flattered, but I have several appointments later today. I'm not going to be able to make it." She didn't add that she was a few years older than he was, she'd been married before, and above all, she wasn't interested. "Thank you, though. I hope you're enjoying the visit to New York."

"I'd like it a lot more if we could get together, Cameron. How about tomorrow? I don't go back to Baltimore till Saturday morning." He gave her what she was sure he thought was a seductive grin. "I've had it bad for you since you signed with PSN. Make my dreams come true."

She resisted the impulse to barf all over his prototype Reebok shoes. "That's quite an offer, but no," she said.

She reached out, briefly clasped his hand, shook once, and walked away. She heard the name he called her under his breath. It wouldn't be the first time a guy called her that, and it sure wouldn't be the last.

Cameron rushed down the hallway to her dressing room, peeled off the loaner clothes she wore for a taping, and washed the TV makeup off in record time. She applied makeup with a much lighter hand, added swingy silver chandelier earrings, and bent from the waist to run her fingers through the long, blonde, highlighted hair that cost a fortune to maintain. She flipped it back into the just-out-of-bed tousle the show's hair person had spent forty-five minutes working on this morning. She stepped into black, strappy stilettos, a knee-length fuchsia floral sheath with a bow at the waist, and threw the items she needed into an evening bag: Cash, credit card, house keys, lip gloss, breath mints, and smart phone. She pulled a lightweight silk wrap around her shoulders.

A knock at the door announced her assistant, Kacee.

"Cameron, you need to be here at eight am tomorrow morning for hair and makeup. It's the Zach Anderson interview."

"Got it." *God give her strength.* She could think of a thousand things she'd rather be doing than spending an hour with Zach Anderson tomorrow, or any other day. She gave Kacee a quick nod. "Thanks for your help today."

"So, have you seen him yet? He's in the building this afternoon at a photo shoot."

"Seen whom?"

"Zach Anderson." Kacee gave her a look as if she'd grown another head.

"No." Cameron frowned at the noise and vibration coming from her bag. Her phone was going nuts. If she stopped to figure out what it was she'd be late, and she couldn't be late.

"Every woman in the building must have been in the studio during his photo shoot." Kacee let out a sigh. "He's beautiful. Have you met him before?"

"Yes." Oh, they'd met before. She'd spent the past ten years avoiding him. She had no interest in dating a professional athlete, especially in her line of work. Female sportscasters had a difficult time with some male colleagues in professional sports as it was; she wasn't going to add to the existing problem.

Cameron glanced up from her still-buzzing handbag to catch Kacee's eye as she hurried toward the door.

"If you're interested in talking with him, I'll make sure you get introduced tomorrow," she said.

"Oh, God. I'd *love* that. Thanks, Cameron!"

"You're welcome. Listen. I've got my phone if something happens, but it's Paige's rehearsal dinner—"

"And Paige will have a fit if you leave in the middle of it," Kacee finished. "Hopefully, nobody in the NFL gets arrested or traded over the next four hours or so."

ZACH SHOWERED OFF everything he'd been coated with over the past several hours, ran his fingers through the hair he kept short enough that it wouldn't curl, and pulled on jeans and a sports shirt. Jason made himself at home on the dressing room couch. Zach was used to having people in the locker room while he was showering and getting dressed, so it wasn't a shocking occurrence.

"You have an interview tomorrow with Cameron Ondine of PSN. The car's picking you up at nine am for makeup and prep. It should be fairly quick. We'll drop you back at the hotel, and you'll be picked up again to fly home at six pm," Jason said.

"The ice queen," Zach muttered. Some of the other guys on the team would give their left nut to spend time talking with her. He wasn't interested.

Jason glanced up from his smart phone with a grin. "It'll be an easy interview. Try not to stay out too late tonight, big guy."

He was going to have to learn to keep his voice down when other people were around, even somebody who was always on his side. "I'm going straight to bed. No clubbing for me," Zach said.

Sure he was. He was having dinner with a New York Mammoths cheerleader (and three of her best girlfriends). He would be in bed later, and he wouldn't be alone. The cheerleader had already made it clear she'd be accompanying him back to his hotel room later. He looked forward to it. If he didn't move his ass, though, he'd be late to the restaurant.

"You might try that one on someone who believes it," Jason said.

Zach just laughed. Being young, handsome, single and wealthy was a bitch, but someone had to live the life. It might as well be him.

Jason got up from the couch, shook Zach's hand, and walked out the door. "I'm out of here. See you tomorrow, old man."

Zach shoved his wallet into his back pocket, picked up his jacket, and jammed his feet into shoes. He yanked the dressing room door open and strode down a seemingly-endless hallway to the exit. Blowing through the front door, he ignored shouts of "Zach! Zach!" He saw people with Sharks paraphernalia out of the corner of his eye and felt vaguely guilty. Already late, he threw one of his arms into the air as he approached the curb and gave a piercing whistle. He needed a damn cab. The limo was nice, but he'd prefer to be somewhat anonymous.

The rush hour traffic of New York City didn't immediately yield a cab. He moved closer to the curb as a car stopped for him. A flash of hot pink and black appeared in his vision, just before a woman with luxuriant, long blonde hair, great legs, and a nice ass whipped the door open and hurled herself onto the seat inside.

She stole his damn cab!

"Hey," he shouted. "That's mine. Get out of my cab!" He reached out to grab the door.

"Too late." She didn't look up at him. "Gramercy Tavern, please."

"No. This is my cab!" He was now running alongside as the guy tried to pull into traffic. The woman in question glanced up, looked shocked for a split-second, and rearranged her features into a glare.

Jesus. It was Cameron Ondine. She'd been avoiding him for ten years now, but she was about to have another encounter with him if she didn't get the hell out of his cab. He knew he would see her tomorrow morning. He thought he'd have hours to pretend like she didn't matter. Her suddenly materializing in front of him felt like a punch to the heart.

She was trying to shut the car door. He pulled it open, shoved her over on the seat with his hipbone, and threw himself inside with one smooth motion. He slammed the door behind himself, and turned to look at her.

"What the hell are you doing? Get out!" she said. She clenched her hands together as she stared at him. He watched a flush spread on her chest, up her neck, and over her cheekbones. She tried to push herself further into the opposite corner of the cab seat.

"Scared?" he said.

"N-No!"

Her pupils expanded. Her dark-chocolate brown eyes were blazing. Their color didn't appear in nature. It must have been contacts. She was even more beautiful after losing the heavy TV makeup, too. It was ten years later, and she still made him wish he could pull her into his arms and kiss her.

"We can share the ride. Cabbie? Orsay, please."

"It's in the opposite direction from where I'm going. This will never work. I am already late," she said. Maybe he imagined the panic he saw on her face. She'd edged away from him, but she couldn't seem to take her eyes off of him, either.

"So am I. You stole my cab. You'll have to live with the consequences." He settled onto the seat, and slung one arm over the back. She shrank away. He pulled a money clip out of his front pocket and shoved a fifty into the little slot in the Plexiglas separator. "Orsay," he repeated for good measure.

She unzipped her purse, produced a few folded bills, and shoved them into the little slot as well. "Gramercy Tavern, please."

The cab driver finally spoke up, in heavily-accented English. "I cannot drive while people are fighting in my cab." He glanced over his shoulder at them. "Work it out between yourselves, or I will pull over and kick you both out."

They spoke in unison.

"He can wait."

"She stole my cab."

"Okay. That's it." The cab driver crossed three lanes of traffic, came to a screeching halt at the curb, and braked. "Get out. And don't think I'm giving your money back."

"You can't do this," Zach insisted.

"Yes. I can. Get out, or I'm calling the police," the cabbie said.

"I'm noting your cab number," Cameron said to the cabbie, and snapped a picture of it with her cell phone.

"I do not care," the cabbie snapped. "Get out."

Zach and Cameron scrambled out of the back seat. The cab screeched away the moment her feet hit the pavement. She gave Zach a look of barely contained disgust, but he noticed she didn't try to move away from him this time. She bit her lower lip and shuffled her feet a bit as she twisted her hands into the soft-looking wrap she held.

He remembered how it felt to rest his chin against the top of her head and how she felt in his arms. He moved a bit closer to her, just to see if she'd move away from him. She didn't.

"It's five-fifteen on a Friday night in New York City. What do you think the chances are of obtaining another cab?"

He raised one eyebrow. "Maybe you should show them some leg. I'm sure they'll pull right over, blondie."

Cameron whirled on him, and he saw a lightning-quick flash of hurt in her eyes. "You. You haven't changed at all. I thought I could be professional and give you the benefit of the doubt. Maybe the people I was hearing it from were wrong. But ohhh, noo." She stuck one arm in the air, shouted, "Taxi!" and scanned the traffic in front of her as she continued her tirade. Her voice shook. He wondered if she realized it. "You are the biggest ass I have ever met, and that's saying a lot."

"Is that so?" Zach said, giving her a completely insincere smile. People were stopping in the middle of the sidewalk by now to stare. Celebrities walked the streets of Manhattan every day, but to watch a prominent, nationally-known sportscaster and a pro football player engage in a loud public argument—if he wasn't careful, he'd wind up on TMZ.com. With his luck, cell phone video would be showing up on Twitter and elsewhere online in minutes, too, which he needed like a hole in the head. He wanted to stand and stare at her, but "You're the coldest, most unpleasant woman I've ever met" came out of his mouth instead. He took a breath. "You haven't changed at all, either."

She turned her back on him.

Cameron should call herself the Cab Whisperer; another car screeched to the curb. She opened the door, threw herself inside, called out, "Gramercy Tavern, please," and slammed the door in his face.

He'd rather miss his date entirely than spend one more minute with Cameron Ondine.

AN HOUR LATER Cameron sipped her second sidecar and pretended she was listening to her sister Paige's recitation of everything that had gone wrong that day. She was still trying to regroup from her unexpected encounter with

Zach, so she wasn't exactly giving her sister undivided attention.

Paige had a wedding coordinator, and their mother was taking an active role in making sure the wedding came off without a hitch. What on earth did Paige have to complain about, anyway? Cameron shoved down her impatience with brute force and acted like she was riveted.

Paige broke off mid-sentence and tapped her finger on the back of Cameron's hand. "Hey. Where are you, anyway?"

"What do you mean? I'm right here."

"You haven't heard a word I've said for the past twenty minutes. What's going on?"

"Nothing." Nothing but the fact she'd traded insults with a man who still made her heart pound. She hoped he didn't notice she'd been drinking in his closeness and his deep voice in her ear, or the fact she still felt protected standing next to him.

"Try that with someone who believes you. Maybe you should tell me what happened."

Cameron took another sip of her drink. "I just had to deal with a guy who makes Deion Sanders look reasonable."

Her sister's expression was blank. Of course Paige didn't know who Deion Sanders was. Cameron sometimes wished she didn't, either. "Football commentator," she explained.

"Cameron, why do you put up with these guys? Is the job really that good? Why don't you try to get on one of those entertainment magazine shows or maybe get a talk show? You wouldn't have to deal with them anymore."

Cameron almost rolled her eyes. "Oh, no. *Nobody* in the entertainment industry has an ego." She took a breath to calm herself. "Paige, I know you don't understand why I do this. I love sports. I love the job. I don't love some of the guys I have to deal with, but that comes with any job, and I'm fine. Let's talk about something else."

"Well, I don't understand. Mom would give you a job in the design firm any day if you asked for it. You can't love the traveling, either. Wait until I have kids. I don't want them watching Aunt Cameron on TV as they grow up instead of spending time with her. How do you expect to see them at all when you're constantly gone? I just think—"

Cameron smiled and nodded when Paige slowed down to take a breath, but she'd heard all of this before. Her job was an imposition on the family. After all, those from "old money" families were supposed to live quietly and get married after they graduated from college to someone who also wanted to live quietly. They certainly were not supposed to show up on nationally-televised broadcasts of sporting events. Cameron wanted something more from her life than appearing at whatever social or charitable function was the most pressing, according to her mom and dad. She loved Paige, but some days, she felt like they hardly knew each other. Her mother regarded Paige with an adoring smile from across the room. After all, Paige did everything her parents wanted.

"I need to excuse myself for a moment," she finally

said, breaking into her sister's tirade. "I'll be back." Cameron put her nearly-full glass down on a waiter's passing tray and hurried out into the hallway. Maybe a few minutes in the ladies' room would help her collect herself. She was so tired of being reminded that no matter what she achieved in her career, her parents still believed the best use of her time was settling down, marrying well, and giving them an acceptable number of grandchildren.

The bathroom proved to be a poor decision. Cameron ran cold water over her wrists after refreshing her lipstick. A rail-thin, dark-haired, early-twenties woman in a spray-paint-tight teal satin mini dress approached.

"Hi. Aren't you Cameron Ondine?"

Cameron forced a smile she didn't feel. "Yes, I am." She quickly dried her hands on a paper towel, and extended one to the woman. "Nice to meet you."

The woman took her hand. "My boyfriend would be pissing himself if he was here right now." She smacked her gum. "You're the wallpaper on his phone. He wore out the issue of *Maxim* you were in."

Cameron wasn't sure what to say to this, but there probably wasn't a great comeback. The other woman extended a dry paper towel in her direction. "Would you sign this for him? His name's Marty." She gave Cameron an ingratiating smile. "Write something dirty, okay? He'll get a big kick out of it."

"I don't have a pen right now. I'm sorry," Cameron told her. "If you'll visit the PSN website and send me an e-mail, though, I'll make sure he gets an autographed photo." Signed with just her name: She wasn't about to "write something dirty" that would end up on an online auction site or scanned and uploaded to a sports fan site in moments. She picked up her evening bag, and edged toward the bathroom door. "Thanks for your interest and tell him I said hi."

"Just sign it in lipstick!" the woman shouted after her, but Cameron darted into the hallway. The best thing would have been to walk out the front door of the restaurant, hail a cab, and go home, but dinner hadn't even been served yet. As the maid of honor, she was expected to make a toast. She was heading toward the private room once more, when a burst of loud feminine laughter brought her up short.

Zach Anderson was lounging against the Gramercy's bar, surrounded by four women who looked like they'd just crawled out of his bed. He must have decided he wasn't interested in Orsay after all. He caught Cameron's eye, winked, and turned back to his companions.

What an ass. He'd *followed* her here? She turned on her heel and walked away.

AT TEN O'CLOCK the next morning, Cameron clipped her microphone on, sat down in the plush on-set chair she used for interviews, and referred to the questions for Zach she'd printed onto index cards one last time. She was thankful to lose herself in work before Paige's wedding, which would be held over the coming weekend. She'd escaped the rehearsal dinner by sprinting out the back door of the restaurant ten minutes after the dessert course.

She glanced up at movement across the set. Zach strolled toward her as if he had all the time in the world. The hair and makeup people had worked their magic with him, too. One would think he spent last night reading a book and turning in early instead of tearing it up with four women at a New York City landmark. His buzz-cut dark honey blond hair was a testament to the artistic use of hair products, and he'd obviously been overdosing on the Visine. There wasn't a wrinkle or stray thread in sight. He treated her to a smile so dazzling it should come with eye protection.

Her palms were instantly sweaty. Her heart rate sped up. It didn't matter if they'd stood on the sidewalk squabbling with each other last night; she still wanted him, dammit. She did her best to freeze her features into a politely disinterested expression and told herself not to fidget.

"Good morning, Ms. Ondine." Zach lowered himself into the chair across from her, crossed his legs, and slung one arm around the back. He eyed her with a smirk. "Did you enjoy your evening?"

Cameron resisted the impulse to grind her teeth. Despite the fact she couldn't tear her eyes off of him, he was just plain annoying. She couldn't understand why women like her assistant, who was currently regarding Zach with an expression which should be reserved for infallible religious figures or Ryan Gosling, found him so alluring. He was one more entitled, egomaniacal pro athlete, and she wasn't buying into his crap ever again. She smiled innocently.

"Yes, I did. Would you like to get started?"

One side of his mouth twitched. "Let's do this."

Cameron heard the floor director counting, saw the cameraman move for a tighter close-up, and gazed into Zach's hazel eyes. Oh, they were definitely doing this. He lifted a brow. Of course he thought she was flirting with him. She recrossed her legs, shifting the four-by-six notecards in her lap.

"We're happy to have a few minutes with the Seattle Sharks' All-Pro defensive tackle Zach Anderson today. Welcome to *NFL Confidential*, Zach." She tossed her hair over one shoulder and leaned forward a bit. "You've been in the league ten years now. What are you looking forward to this season?"

"I'm looking forward to the same thing I do every season. Winning."

She saw something lurking behind the careless smile he gave her: smugness. He thought this was going to be just another softball interview, like so many others he'd had before. She ignored the carefully researched and previously agreed on questions on the cards in her lap. She had a few questions of her own.

Less than a minute later, she saw the happy-go-lucky smile melt off of Zach's lips.

"How do you respond to those who say you're 'slow,' 'too old,' and 'overpaid'? The Sharks retain your services to plug the center of their defensive line. You weren't able to do it last season. Do you think you can turn that around this year?"

Zach's mouth opened and shut repeatedly, like a salmon

that found itself impaled on the end of a long, shiny fisherman's hook. She swung one leg, just a little, and resisted the impulse to smile. "You've had injury problems. Why should the team believe that's going to improve? As an aging member of the Sharks' defensive line—"

Zach interrupted her. "I'm not 'aging.'"

"You're older than many of the players in the league, especially those who play your position—"

"They're full of shit." He took a rapid breath.

Cameron heard her producer through the earpiece she wore. "Careful," Ralph said. "Don't piss him off."

"The injury rate in the NFL is one hundred percent. I'm not any different than anyone else," Zach said.

"Wouldn't you agree that the Sharks should expect more?"

"What the hell?" Zach's eyes widened. He sat up in his chair. "Listen, you don't have the first idea what it's like to play in the NFL. I give everything I have, every play. It's obvious to anyone who's actually watching—"

"Are you suggesting that the Sharks and their fans don't deserve an answer?"

Zach ran a hand through his hair and let out a long breath in exasperation. "I'm bringing it this season."

"Maybe you should try something other than clichés, Zach."

His eyes narrowed, and he didn't respond. She saw the corner of his mouth move into a smirk. He didn't take her questions—or her—seriously, and she saw red. She took a deep breath, took another, and tried to calm herself. It didn't help.

She glanced down at the cards on her lap. She pretended to read for a moment. Seconds later, she brushed them off her lap. They hit the floor next to her chair with a soft *splat*. She knew she'd spent the past ten years concentrating on professionalism, but right now she was teaching him a lesson.

She lowered her voice and concentrated on appearing calm. "Do you think your well-publicized and turbulent love life is contributing to your woes on the field?"

The color drained out of his face, replaced by a flush that climbed up from his neck and over his cheekbones, and Cameron watched his fists clench on the chair's arm rests. Both of his feet hit the floor. He abandoned the relaxed pose he had when the interview started, leaning forward to shove his face inches from hers. His king-of-the-world, trouble-free demeanor had given way to obvious wrath. He shook his head, once, sharply.

"I'm not going to answer that. That question is beneath you, don't you think?"

Her voice dripped insincere concern. "Maybe I need to jog your memory."

They stared at each other. She leaned forward a bit more in her chair, too.

"I thought we were talking about football today, Ms. Ondine."

"Oh, we are, Mr. Anderson," she assured him. "Your personal life is affecting your on-field performance."

Her producer was talking through the earpiece. "Cameron, have you lost your mind? What the hell's going on here?"

She continued, ticking the bullet points off on her fingernails. "You've been linked with multiple actresses, models, and other high-profile women throughout your career. You went to Hawaii on the bye week last year with three of them instead of staying in Seattle with the team. The question is, Zach, why don't you take your career seriously?" She concentrated on forming the perfect concerned expression, despite the fact she knew the camera was on him. "How do you think that affects your teammates?"

His eyes flew wide open in shock. His lips were a solid, bloodless line. His voice was barely above a whisper as he bit out the words. "This interview is over." He jerked the microphone off, pulled the power pack out of the back of his pants, and got to his feet.

"You don't want to answer a few questions?"

He didn't speak. He was momentarily yanked backward by one wire; he ripped it out of the equipment, and walked away. She saw movement behind the camera. Several people followed Zach out of the studio. In the meantime, Cameron's producer was shouting into her earpiece.

"For God's sake, Cameron. What was that?"

Chapter Two

ZACH STORMED INTO the dressing room the show had
provided for him, picked up his jacket, and shoved both
arms into it. His agent Jason was talking. Zach heard the
words, but they weren't processing.

"Listen. We'll take a breath, get you some water and a
bite to eat, and we'll try this again with somebody else. I
don't know what happened out there, but this interview
has been teased all week. We don't want to be the ones
pulling out of it." Jason took a few steps toward Zach.
"Hey, buddy. You okay?"

No, he wasn't okay. He'd sent the cheerleader and her
three girlfriends he had drinks with last night home in
a cab after seeing Cameron in the restaurant he deliber-
ately followed her to. He didn't have the heart to close the
deal with anyone else, because he couldn't forget how he
felt when he saw her again. He was torn between frustration and fury. Lust played a part, too. Despite the fact

she jumped up and down on his last nerve a few minutes ago, he still wanted her more than he'd wanted any other woman he'd ever met.

"Everyone else on her damn show gets the softball interviews, the hair tossing, the endless leg crossing-and-recrossing, and the 'take me home tonight' lip licking." He was pacing by now. "She's attacking *me*? What did I ever do to her, anyway?" He knew damn well what he did to her, but he wasn't going to admit it, even to Jason. He was wearing a hole in the carpet. Right now, he was beyond caring. "She's never played the game. What could she possibly know about it?" Zach crossed the room to the window that looked out over Times Square, but he wasn't interested in the view. He jammed both hands into his pockets.

"For someone who never played the game, she had your number," Jason said.

"Whose side are you on?"

"Yours," Jason reassured him. "We need to figure out how to contain the damage, buddy."

"*Damage*? What are you talking about?"

"You need an interview. We promised Under Armour that their launch was going to get maximum publicity, and PSN is a major contributor toward that effort." He frowned at the screen on his phone. Not coincidentally, it rang. "Edwards," he told the person calling.

Zach continued to pretend he was staring out the window. His mind whirled. She couldn't still be mad over the cab thing. She wouldn't put him on blast for something that happened ten years ago, would she? Last season was tough for everyone in Seattle's locker room. It wasn't just him. A team that had expected to win the division handily had finished six and ten. If she still had a personal thing with him, it might have been nice if she'd mentioned it beforehand. One thing's for sure. He'd rather be dragged buck naked over broken glass than spend any more time with her at all at the moment.

Then again, who was he kidding? If she walked through the door right now, it would be all he could do to not pull her into his arms and kiss her breathless.

Jason's voice broke into his reverie. "They *what*? This happened half an hour ago. What the hell! Let me talk to him. I'll call you back." He pulled a bottle of water out of the stocked mini-fridge. "Zach, we've got a problem."

CAMERON'S PHONE HAD been ringing for the past fifteen minutes as she sat in her producer Ralph's office with the door shut. He'd spent the first ten minutes alternately shouting at and scolding her over the disastrous interview. He'd finally exhausted himself somewhat, and now he was perched on the corner of his desk with arms folded across his abdomen as she read off the identities of those texting or calling to inquire about what had just happened. She wasn't calling anyone back until she figured out what to do next.

Zach Anderson's agent had called. Her agent had called. Cameron's assistant texted one line: "Do I still have a job?"

She couldn't believe she'd lost it like she had. It was the smirk. He smirked at her, and she couldn't control what came out of her mouth. She should have ended the interview, gotten herself under control, and tried again. He was the only man she'd ever met that could get under her skin like he had.

Ralph heaved a long sigh. "Well, Cam, when you screw up, you really screw up. What was all that?"

She shook her head. Her phone rang again. It was one of the guys she regularly talked with at NFL Network. News traveled fast.

"Ralph, I wish I had a better explanation than the fact I let him get to me." She did. She was keeping the information to herself as long as she possibly could.

"What happened to the interview questions we discussed earlier in the week?"

"They didn't work." She took another breath. "He stole my cab yesterday. Did I mention that?"

Ralph raised an eyebrow and recrossed his arms. "So, you two have met before."

"I wouldn't call it a meeting."

He moved to the chair next to hers, sat down, and stared into her eyes. "Listen, Cameron. You're a professional. We need to fix this. What do you suggest?"

"Maybe Mark should interview him."

"Mark's on paternity leave."

She might have remembered that on her own, if she'd thought about it. Mostly, she wished she were anywhere else in the world but right here, right now. Today's festivities exhibited the most unprofessional behavior in her ten-year career. She'd love to blame it on the stress of Paige's wedding, PMS, the fact that Chanel was discontinuing her favorite shade of lip gloss ... No. Truthfully, she'd love to blame it on his behavior in the cab, or the way he showed up at a restaurant with four women in tow and taunted her as a result.

To say she disliked Zach Anderson would be an understatement. She loathed him. But she still desired him, and that fact horrified her. There wasn't a woman on the planet who would blame her, either. She guarded the secret of why she detested Zach like her own personal Fort Knox, a fortress she would protect with all weapons at her disposal. A breach would be catastrophic.

She rubbed her forehead to banish the beginnings of what she imagined would be a major-league headache.

"Fine. I'll handle it." Her phone rang once more. It was her agent. She'd better pick up. "Laurie."

"Cameron, we have a huge problem. Are you in your office? I'll be over there in ten minutes."

She felt an icy fist grip her stomach. "I understand I lost my temper, but we can fix—"

"The video of your interview with Zach Anderson is already up on YouTube," Laurie interrupted.

"It can't be."

"Oh, it is. You're nationwide. It's on YouTube, it's on TMZ.com, and it's trending on Twitter. There's a banner headline on Deadspin.com. ESPN just called to verify the story. I'm in a cab. I'll be there as quickly as I can." Laurie disconnected.

Cameron closed her eyes and tried to breathe. She

was going to have a full-scale panic attack, right here, right now.

She took a chunk out of the man—she'd been dying to for the past ten years—but it was at a horrific personal price. If things weren't bad enough already, her career was over.

THE STORY OF Cameron Ondine's going after a NFL player during an interview spread faster than anyone involved could have imagined, especially Zach. He was a bit dumbfounded by it all, too. Twenty-four hours and one million YouTube views later, it was all anyone could talk to him about. After all, men (and more than a few women) spent their spare time online looking for photos of Cameron. She was nicknamed "Cameron Online" for a reason. This was something else they couldn't stop looking at.

Public reaction was fueled by the fact that Zach was known to be a bit full of himself at times, and probably needed to be taken down a peg or two. Who the hell knew, he mused. The sports world was split between admiring Cameron's guts, and wondering if she should be allowed within a city block of a football broadcasting facility. He'd talked with more than a few guys over the past few days who asked him what he did to piss her off so much. Cameron brought to mind the icily perfect, blonde movie stars of days gone by, and obviously he'd failed to score.

Zach's representation sent flowers and an apology to Cameron. He couldn't figure out why he was apologizing—

he hadn't gone after *her* like a starving dog would pursue a big, juicy steak, had he?—but a large delivery was dispatched to the PSN studios the next morning. The text of the card was composed by a public relations consultant Jason commissioned to do so. The same PR consultant authored an apologetic statement from Zach that was released to the media. The phone was still ringing. At least Zach could sit on the couch in his house while he did the fifteenth interview this afternoon on whatever sports radio station wanted to talk to him now.

He was so tired of talking about this. He was angry. He was embarrassed. He couldn't stop remembering what it was like to be so close to her again, and he still remembered her perfume. He wanted it all to go away, but it wasn't going away until someone else in the league had a catastrophic screw-up. He didn't like to wish ill on others, but hopefully he'd get wiped off the front page sooner than later.

"Hey, now, Miami. We're here with Zach Anderson of the Seattle Sharks, otherwise known as the guy that won't be having dinner anytime soon with the lovely and talented Cameron Ondine of PSN. Zach, what do you have to say for yourself?"

"Damned if I know." Zach smiled into the phone receiver. "I'm just looking forward to training camp."

"Sure, you are," the interviewer laughed.

"Zach, we got some news this morning we'd like to ask you about. Is it true that the night before your ill-fated adventure with Ms. Ondine, you two fought over a cab in New York City?"

Nice to know the cabbie must have sold his story to a tabloid or something. "I don't know where you got that from, but it's not true," Zach said.

"The cabbie had a video camera in his dash, guy."

"I'll comment after I've seen his tape."

"Gotcha. Let's talk about something else. Cameron Online—oops, Ms. Ondine—accused you of being 'old, slow and overpaid.'" How about setting the record straight? You're still in the Sharks' plans this season, aren't you?"

"Of course I'm in their plans. We're looking forward to retaking the division crown on the way to the Super Bowl. If Ms. Ondine thinks I'm 'old and slow,' she's welcome to strap some pads on and meet me on the practice field."

This brought a cacophony of laughter from the other end of the phone, and one of the guys said, "Got it. Well, Zach, best of luck, and we'll look forward to seeing you during our 'Thirty-two Days at Training Camp' programming." There was a moment of silence, and then the main program host came back on the line. "So, Zach, how many hundreds of dollars of flowers went to the PSN studio this morning?"

"Hey, Mike, I'm laughing my ass off over here."

"She's on the show tomorrow. Want us to patch you in? You could apologize in person."

Zach rubbed his face with one hand. "Thanks for the offer, but I'll pass. I'll see you next week at training camp."

"Yeah, you will. Bye, guy."

Zach heard the call disconnect, and he shut off his cell phone. Everyone wanted to get into the act. His grandma had scolded him a bit over the breakfast table this morning, too.

"Zachary Anderson, you're a better person than that. Why did you take her bait, honey?"

"She pissed me off, Grandma. I don't have a better reason."

She shook her head. "You know you're going to have to apologize in person for your behavior. Flowers and a note from your agent aren't good enough."

He rose from the table. "I have to go." Ten minutes later he was in his SUV, speeding away from his house and the disappointed look in his grandmother's pale blue eyes.

He let out a long sigh. He hated training camp, but he was going to have to make an extra-special effort to kick ass this year. He'd make Cameron eat her words, too.

WHILE ZACH PUZZLED over his current problems, Cameron was in Hell: population one. She was at her parents' house in the Hamptons, getting ready for Paige's wedding. The wedding coordinator was nowhere to be found. Now that she was finished listening to Paige's hysterics and her mom's nagging about when Cameron was going to give up her career and settle down, she'd found a pinprick sized ink spot on the front of her matron of honor gown.

Paige's wedding was in less than two hours. The church was only ten minutes from the family's summer home, but Cameron knew the family was in an uproar.

Even her normally unruffled father was in the section of the backyard that wasn't taken over by the massive reception tent with a driver, a bucket of golf balls, and the portable net he used when he couldn't get to the driving range. The high-pitched feminine cries Cameron could still hear in the hallway outside her bedroom were punctuated by the rhythmic *thwack* of a golf club hitting a ball at full speed.

Cameron's mother flew into her room in a swirl of pale gold taffeta.

"Why aren't you dressed?" she demanded.

"The zipper's stuck. I'm afraid I'll break it. Dad's trying to put a hole through some golf balls out there," Cameron said.

Olivia Ondine studied the zipper for a moment, hesitantly tried to move the pull and attempted to frown at it. Her forehead did not move.

"The wedding planner will know what to do. I'm not breaking a nail on this." She glanced out of the bedroom window. "Your father will be fine. I'll get him a scotch." She walked toward the door, only to turn back to Cameron. "Pictures are in less than an hour, and you'll need to fix this." The door shut with a *click* behind her, and Cameron resisted the impulse to scream.

The zipper and the spot on the dress were the tip of the iceberg as far as she was concerned. It wasn't even the wedding. It was dealing with her family. Her mother and sister made a career out of being helpless. Her father catered to them. She was the weirdo here, the one who insisted on making a living, especially while doing something that horrified her parents and their old-money, country-clubbing friends.

There wasn't as much old money anymore, she mused. The financial crash of 2008 had left a few of her parents' friends "rich" instead of "wealthy." There was less conspicuous consumption, and more "evenings in," at least among those who weren't willing to gamble again on the quirks of the stock market. Her parents were affected by the initial destruction of her father's portfolio, too, but their fortune had rebounded. They spent lavishly on Paige's wedding. After all, standards must be upheld. Today was an embarrassment of riches.

Paige's wedding was nothing like Cameron's wedding. Cameron was twenty-two and less than a month from getting her degree. She was facing a lifetime of correct social behavior and scheduling her life around designer trunk shows and opening nights at museum exhibits. She loved her parents, but she wasn't interested in living their lives. She'd wanted something more.

So she had walked out of her Upper West Side apartment one afternoon during spring break with an overnight bag, hopped a jet to Vegas, and danced till the wee hours of the next morning in the hotel's night club. Shortly afterward, she found herself walking up the aisle of a seedy Las Vegas chapel. She was blissfully buzzed. The groom she'd met six hours ago and danced and drank all night with was drunk too.

She wore a limp bridal veil that must have been worn by a thousand other brides before and carried a bouquet of silk flowers, also previously used. The groom put a simple gold band on her finger and gave her a kiss that tasted like whiskey and lust. An Elvis impersonator pronounced them husband and wife, and launched into an off-key rendition of *Can't Help Falling In Love With You*, a song that still made her flinch.

She and Zach Anderson were married for seventy-two hours ten years ago, and she still wasn't over it.

Chapter Three

CAMERON'S SMART PHONE vibrated as she hurried toward Pro Sports Network's studios in Manhattan three days after her sister's wedding. She asked the cab driver to drop her a few blocks away so she could walk. The weekend had been full of rich food and too much alcohol, she would be hitting the gym later as a result. She pulled the phone out of her pocket, took a look, and groaned aloud.

It was never good news when Kacee called before eight AM. Cameron hit the "talk" button.

"Hi, Kacee. What's up?"

"Where are you right now?"

"About a block away."

"Ben wants to see you the minute you arrive in his office."

Cameron's heart rate picked up. Ben was the executive program director of PSN. "Did he say anything about what he wants to discuss?"

"He just told me to tell you to see him immediately when you get here." Kacee's voice dropped. "There's several people in the meeting. They ordered food and coffee, so they've already been there a while."

Cameron swallowed hard with whatever moisture was still left in her mouth. "I'll get there as fast as I can. Thanks, Kacee."

"You're welcome." Kacee took a breath. "Good luck, Cameron."

"Is everything still in my office?"

"Yeah. Hurry."

Cameron disconnected and forced herself to put one foot in front of the other as a sick feeling of dread skittered over her skin.

Ten minutes later Cameron knocked at Ben Levine's office door. "Come on in," she heard him call out.

She glanced around the room. The ten upper-level executives in the organization she'd met when she was hired were sitting at the conference table in Ben's office, and the HR director was there, too. People appeared to be taking notes on paper or via electronic tablet. This could not be good.

"Good to see you, Cameron," Ben said. "How about some coffee? Bagels and schmears are over there." He inclined his head toward the breakfast spread on the credenza behind the head of the table.

"Thanks. Maybe in a few minutes. Good morning, everyone," Cameron called out. She heard various responses. More importantly, though, everyone looked her in the eye. Maybe she wasn't fired. She sat down in the only empty chair in the room, which was next to Ben's.

"So, Ms. Ondine, you're probably wondering why we've invited you here." Ben got up from the table, and crossed to the floor-to-ceiling windows that looked over Manhattan behind them.

Cameron took a breath and resisted the impulse to either cry or throw up.

"It's a good chance to clear the air. I'd also like to apologize for the incident with Zach Anderson the other day. It was unprofessional, and I'm sorry. It won't happen again," she said.

"Your apology is nice, but it isn't necessary." Ben turned his back on the view. "Part of the reason why we asked you here this morning is to talk a little about what we expect of PSN's on-air personalities." He poured himself a cup of coffee and took a sip. "One of the objectives we had when the network was started was to offer professional athletes a forum that they'd look forward to visiting. We compete with many other entities for interviews and in-depth stories, and part of the reason we keep getting those stories is because players know they're not getting sandbagged when they give us their time." He put his coffee cup down on the table.

"Yes, Ben, and again, I'm so—"

He cut her off. "We sank significant resources into acquiring you from ESPN. We made that decision because of the demographics of your viewers, a high degree of professionalism and the fact that you brought value to our organization. Having said all that, we're thrilled with the ratings spike in your on-air appearances over the past few days. They're through the roof. *NFL Confidential* is now must-see TV! We're wondering how we can make that magic happen every time you step in front of the camera for PSN."

There was scattered applause around the room. "Congratulations, Cameron. It was spectacular," he said.

Was she hearing things? He wasn't mad at her, and they thought what she'd done was a *good* thing? She'd walked into his office convinced she was about to be fired, and now they were congratulating her.

Cameron clenched her hands in her lap. She took the deepest breath she could, tightening the invisible steel bands around her chest. "I'm a little confused," she said. "The ratings are *up*? I . . . I don't understand."

Ben smiled a bit. "You will in a moment." He crossed the room to the table where the breakfast items were spread out, poured another cup of coffee, and returned to press it into her hand. "We've been talking about this for a couple of hours now. Obviously, the network is pretty invested in turning your, shall we say, 'disagreement' with Zach Anderson into positive publicity for us." He leaned against his desk. "We think we have a solution, but we'd like your buy-in."

"Of—of course, Ben," she stammered. "I'm happy to help."

"You may not be so happy when you learn what we'd like you to do."

An on-air apology to Zach Anderson would be humiliating, but it was the least of what she expected Ben to tell her.

"We'd like you to go home and pack your bags. We're sending you to the Sharks' training camp for the next four weeks. You'll be leaving tomorrow morning."

Cameron's mouth dropped open in amazement. "But . . . isn't Kevin going to training camp?"

The network was rolling out their version of HBO's popular *Hard Knocks* program. This year, they'd focus on the Sharks. The Sharks were rumored to have fireworks in their locker room as aging vets retired and new guys took their jobs. It was considered one of the better assignments at the network. Kevin Adkins, a former NFL player and one of Cameron's colleagues, had appeared in teaser ads for over a month now.

"Oh, he'll be there, but you'll be spending most of your time with the players, looking for human-interest stories. He'll be doing the in-depth stuff." Ben took another sip of his coffee. "We think it'll be a great fish-out-of-water story, especially since you'll be spending an entire month with Zach Anderson and his teammates."

CATCHING CAMERON

Chapter Four

THE CORPORATE JET carrying Cameron and four of her co-workers touched down at Seattle's Boeing Field late on a Thursday night. The crew and their equipment would be following via charter flight tomorrow morning. Despite PSN's best effort to keep a lid on Cameron's involvement in the new show, sports media almost imploded when the information leaked on Twitter shortly after her meeting with Ben. "Coffee won't be the only thing keeping Zach Anderson 'sleepless in Seattle,'" one of the nicer sports website headlines read.

Cameron was starting to wonder where these leaks were coming from, especially since Ben had been emphatic with everyone in the meeting that her involvement was to be kept confidential until the network began filming in Seattle. Someone had leaked her disastrous interview with Zach as well. Of course, Kacee and the entire production group insisted they'd had nothing to do with it.

Kevin barely glanced in Cameron's direction during a five-hour flight.

"He's really pissed," she whispered to Kacee. She'd replaced numbness with feeling nauseated at what she was being asked to do by the network. She wanted to report the story, not be part of it.

"Ignore him. He's mad because he won't get as much air time."

"He can have it all as far as I'm concerned," Cameron said.

Kacee shoved her electronic tablet and a bottle of water into an oversized tote. "We'll be at the hotel in half an hour, and you won't have to see him until tomorrow," she comforted.

Kacee was right. She could soak in a hot tub, have a glass of wine, and contemplate her stupidity for the hundredth time since this all happened. It would be great.

The plane stopped in front of a smallish terminal, and she saw a long black limousine waiting on the tarmac through the window. The flight attendant popped the plane's door open, unfolding the short stairway. Kevin was first off the jet. He had a welcoming committee, which were probably guys from PSN. She grabbed her handbag from under the seat, stretched, and stalled for a few moments before walking to the plane's doorway.

Multiple PSN executives, Ben included, stood at the end of the staircase. Kevin was already gone, and Kacee wasn't waiting for her, either, which was very odd. The black limo waited, though. Maybe they were already in the car.

Cameron managed to make it down the staircase. Ben gave her a quick, impersonal hug.

"Cameron. How was your flight?"

"Very nice, Ben. It's good to see you."

"Good to see you, too." He took her elbow. "We'll drop you off on our way to the hotel." Her luggage was being loaded into the limo's trunk.

She shook her head. "I must not have gotten the memo." She tried to keep her voice light. "Are you all staying somewhere else?"

"You might say that." He held the car door open for her. "Get in, and we'll talk about it."

Twenty minutes later, Cameron was being escorted through the lobby of the Sharks' training camp facility, which was a dorm a short distance from the team's headquarters. There would be no luxurious, comfortable room for her. No glass of wine. Not even a hot bath. She'd be lucky if she got a sleeping bag, according to Ben.

"We talked to the Sharks about this yesterday, and they agreed. They've never had an 'embedded' reporter at training camp, let alone a female reporter. We think you'll have access to stories other sports reporters would kill to get," he said. She gave an extra tug on her suitcase, which seemed to be stuck on the indoor/outdoor carpeting. "You'll get to know the guys as people, not as pro athletes."

"Ben, this isn't a great idea. Where's Kevin going to be during all this? Wouldn't he be more suited to staying in the dorms with the players?"

"Again, we're going for that extra element. After all, a woman spending a month with a team will generate a huge amount of interest in the series. Women don't play football, but they'll tune in to watch another woman deal with eighty guys in a dorm for a month."

She barely stifled the impulse to groan aloud. She'd lived in the dorm her freshman year at Princeton, and then lived off-campus during college. She'd never shared a living space since.

Eighty guys. For a month. In a *dorm*.

Where the hell was she supposed to take a shower, for instance? Plus, what if she wasn't safe? Had anyone thought about *that*? She swallowed hard.

A few minutes later, the Sharks team representative that shook her hand while Ben was going on about how "unprecedented" and "groundbreaking" her month with eighty guys she didn't know would be unlocked a door at the end of a long hallway.

"Okay, Ms. Ondine. Here you are. It isn't luxurious, but it's not bad," he reassured. "Your door locks. Everyone staying on this floor is a veteran, so they know what's expected as far as their behavior and your privacy. You probably won't have to deal with many of the pranksters." He motioned Cameron inside. "There are a few creature comforts in here the guys aren't getting." She tugged her suitcase in behind her. He handed her a key on a Sharks key ring, waited until she walked inside, and turned to go.

"I don't have to share a bathroom, do I?"

"Oh, no. You have your own. It's to your left." He gave a short wave. "Let us know if you need anything."

He shut the door behind him. Cameron listened to his footsteps vanish in a roar of male laughter and a cacophony of conversation. Every guy on this floor must have been out in the hallway watching the whole thing.

The room was a bit more upscale than the dorm she lived in her freshman year. The walls were painted a pale shade of café latte. A double bed was neatly made with a fluffy comforter and crisp white sheets, and a nightstand with a multi-line phone sat next to it. A built-in desk across the room held a smallish flat-screen television and outlets for laptops or other electronic gadgetry. A dorm-sized refrigerator sat next to the desk. She crossed the room to pick up some paperwork left atop it.

She glanced around. "It's not so bad," she reassured herself.

Like most other teams in the NFL, the Sharks' marketing department had a packet for free agents. She wondered who had stayed in the room before, and why he'd left the paperwork behind. She thumbed through a few of the printed sheets. The Sharks' mission statement, and guiding principles of the franchise. A team schedule for training camp. Rules for training camp. Hopefully, she wouldn't be subjected to the nightly bed check. A printout of suggestions on how to deal with the fans that attended the Sharks' public practices.

She scanned a notice on hot-pink paper of a Sharks all-hands team meeting tomorrow morning. Attendance was mandatory. Those who were late would be fined fifty thousand dollars. A media consultant would be working with the entire team to prepare for their appearance on

PSN's *Third and Long*. The following team rules were in effect immediately.

Cameron Ondine would have a team representative with her at all times outside of her dorm room. Even better, players were not allowed to talk with her unless the questions were preapproved by coaches and the team's PR department.

"So much for those warm and fuzzy human-interest stories," she muttered to herself. She wondered what would be most appropriate: screaming or crying.

She smacked herself in the face with the sheaf of papers in frustration. Why invite an "embedded" reporter when they wouldn't let her do her job?

THE TELEPHONE ON Cameron's bedside table rang at six am the next morning. She snaked one arm out from under the covers to grab the receiver.

"Whuuuu?"

"Good morning. This is Coach Phillips. Get your ass out of bed and get down to the field. NOW."

"Excuse me?"

The line clicked dead, and Cameron sat up. He had to be joking. She could hear running feet in the hallway, so she wasn't the only one to get a phone call. She rubbed her eyes, swung her legs over the side of the bed, and hurried into the bathroom.

Half an hour later, Cameron made her way through dewy grass to the practice field. She would have happily handed over the deed to her apartment in New York City for a cup of coffee. It might be a while before she could get a cup; the entire team was already out there. Coaches patrolled the sidelines. Players were in shorts and jerseys. They obviously meant business.

Cameron fumbled through her bag for a notepad and her smart phone. She could take a couple of still photos while she waited for the crew to show up with their video cameras. She didn't see any other media people out here; maybe this was a good thing. She stifled a yawn.

ZACH ANDERSON GLANCED over at the sidelines, did a double-take, and stopped in the middle of a blocking drill.

"Anderson! What the fuck?" one of his teammates yelled.

Zach was still staring.

"Hey, asswipe," Derrick Collins gave him a playful shove. "You're acting like you've never seen a female before. We've only been here a day. Get your shit together."

She was *here*. Zach had known she was coming. He couldn't understand why he felt so shocked and surprised to see her again.

He gave himself a shake. Maybe he was calorie-deprived. After all, nobody ate breakfast until early morning practice was over, unless they wanted to barf it right back up. The whistle blew, and he glanced up to see what the coach had in mind now.

The coach was advancing on Cameron with all speed. If she failed to notice this, he was yelling at her as well.

All that exertion and stress couldn't be good for an out-of-shape older guy.

"What the fuck are you doing? Get out of here!" Coach pointed toward the practice facility, jabbing his finger toward the open doors. "You're not supposed to be out here without your team babysitter, either. Go back to your room!"

Most women would cry. Zach's most recent ex-girlfriend cried over a lot less on a regular basis. Cameron's blonde ponytail fell over one shoulder as she glanced up from whatever it was she was writing on the pad she held. She seemed to stand up a bit straighter. It probably pissed the coach off even more; Zach knew he liked it when others cowered.

"You called my room and told me to get down here," she responded, loudly enough that the now-silent players could hear it.

"I didn't mean you. I didn't want press here at all. Plus, you're not even supposed to be out here." He continued to point and yell despite being within her three-foot comfort zone, and Cameron continued to stand right where she was, looking him in the eye. "I don't need to spend the next month dealing with a female who shouldn't be allowed on a football field in the first place."

Cameron wasn't backing down. "That's too bad. Your organization seems to disagree with you."

One of the assistant coaches approached them on the run. "Hey, Coach. Why don't you let me deal with this, and we can get back to the drills?" He gave the coach a slap on the back. "Maybe she got lost on her way to the mall. I'll take care of it."

She'd have liked to say something about the fact she hadn't been inside a mall in quite some time. She had a stylist who shopped for her, on and off the air. She'd also have liked to say something about the fact that the assistant coach wouldn't dream of insulting a male sports reporter with anything like what he'd said to her.

The coach's finger was inches from Cameron's nose. He jabbed the air for emphasis.

"You and your network are a boil on the ass of the NFL. Women have no business in a locker room or interviewing male athletes. I'm not cooperating with you. I'll do my best to make sure my players don't cooperate, either," he spat. "I want you gone today." He pivoted toward his team and stalked away from her.

Cameron would die before she showed any reaction to the coach's tirade. She knew there were other female sports reporters who crumpled under the withering verbal attacks of some NFL coaches and owners, but she wasn't going to be one of them.

"Well, that was pleasant," she muttered. She'd faced worse while attempting to do her job, but not recently. She stowed her smart phone and notebook back into her bag.

"Ms. Ondine, you're going to have to leave the field," the assistant coach said.

"Actually, I won't." She took a deep breath, and forced a polite smile onto her face. "My network was invited here by the Sharks' front office. I'm not disrupting practice or doing anything else but my job."

All teams claimed they wanted press coverage, but when it came right down to it, they wanted a pre-negotiated "chat" with a coach or puff piece interviews with players: "What's your favorite TV show?" or "What's your favorite book?" or "Are you one of the best running backs the team has ever had, or are you THE best?" Pro football fans wanted to hear something interesting or different from their favorite players, which could go well, but mostly blew up in spectacular fashion. Web sites like deadspin.com and kissingsuzycolber.com were only too happy to capitalize on some of the ridiculous, embarrassing, or bigoted things a professional athlete might Tweet after one too many beers. Cameron wasn't rooting for anyone's career-ending statement or photo, but she was looking for something interesting and unique to report on.

The assistant coach was shorter than she was. His team logo polo shirt stretched across the expanse of his belly. She could tell it was all he could do to maintain his composure. He'd dropped the pleasant but firm tone of voice and facial expression. She watched the dull red flush spread up his neck, over his face, and tint the tops of his ears. His hands formed into fists.

"We're trying to cooperate with you, Ms. Ondine, but you present a distraction to our players. You'll need to leave."

"Don't you think standing here arguing with me is a bigger 'distraction' than anything I could possibly do or say right now?" She reached into her bag again, pulling out the notepad and a pen. "Maybe you'd like to talk with me a bit about some of the things the Sharks' coaching staff will be focusing on to improve the offensive line during training camp and the pre-season."

She saw a bit of movement out of the corner of her eye. It seemed the crew was in town after all. One of her cameramen, Logan, was advancing on them and filming, if the small red light over his lens was any indicator.

"How long has that thing been on?" the assistant coach called out to Logan.

"Long enough," Logan said with a snarky grin. "Thanks for the footage, Skip."

Skip's mouth snapped open and shut while he struggled to come up with something to say that wouldn't get him half a million hits on YouTube. He turned an even more alarming shade of red. Finally he pivoted and stalked away from them.

"Coffee's on its way," Logan said. "We're going to have some fun here, aren't we?"

THE SHARKS' PRACTICE continued without further incident, besides the coaching staff's lethal glares at Cameron and Logan from across the field. She breathed in fresh, pine-scented air, enjoyed the sunny morning, and took notes of what she observed. The first training camp practice wasn't rigorous. She got the general impression the coaches were more interested in subdued, compliant listeners for the subsequent all hands meeting than they were in which rookies committed the playbook to memory after the draft. The team was told to form a semicircle and take a knee after the whistle blew twice, signaling the end of practice.

"I want to see you showered, dressed and in the cafeteria in twenty minutes. We'll have a bite. Our mandatory meeting will start afterward," the head coach shouted. "I'd advise all of you to listen carefully to our media training expert. If you fuck up on camera, there will be consequences." He rubbed his thumb against his fingers in the universal signal for "cash." In other words, there would be fines. "Huddle up."

The men made a circle, put their hands inside, and shouted, "Go Sharks!" before running off the field. The head coach gave Cameron one last glare and made an obscene hand gesture on his way off the field. She had been lucky enough to avoid encounters with the Sharks' head coach previously—the guy made Neanderthals look enlightened—but it looked like her luck had just run out.

"Did he flip me off?" she asked Logan in disbelief.

"Why, yes, he did," Logan said.

"This is going to be a long month."

ZACH GLANCED UP from a tray of food that could feed three normal-sized adults, or one defensive tackle. Cameron and the camera guy were staking out a table in the corner. He recognized one of the guys from the front office at their table, too; he must have been the team babysitter. Zach didn't see a lot on her tray. She was probably eating some salad without dressing or some other damn thing. Maybe she was one of those women who thought not eating made them more attractive. He stared at his plate again. He'd rather go three hours on the field with the All-Pro starting offensive tackle than let her catch him looking at her.

He still couldn't figure out why she went after him like he was made out of meat on her damn TV show. They hadn't seen each other in ten years. It wasn't like that was entirely his fault, either. She couldn't still be that pissed about the cab, could she? He shook his head. He heard laughter across the table as he winced.

"What's a matter, cupcake? Got a chill?" his teammate, Derrick, asked Zach. Derrick played the same position on the other side of the defensive line. They typically got along, but today he was on Zach's shit list.

Derrick looked like the side of a mountain, if a mountain sported dreadlocks and attitude. His diamond grill sparkled in the sunlight from the windows that formed one wall of the team's cafeteria.

"Go to hell," Zach told him. Derrick just laughed.

"Maybe it's his time of the month," another teammate chimed in.

The rookie defensive end sitting next to Derrick—Zach didn't even know the kid's name yet—looked a little scared, especially when Zach leaned forward and hissed at Derrick, "How the fuck do you eat with that thing in your mouth?"

"How do you eat with your head up your ass?"

The two men shoved their chairs back from the table and stood up simultaneously. The team's punter, a much smaller guy with red curls, jumped to his feet with arms outstretched. He put one hand in the middle of each of their chests to shove them back.

"Guys. Guys. We're on the same team. Let's eat some food."

The table watched silently to see what was going to happen next. It wouldn't be the first physical altercation in the Sharks cafeteria, but most of them tended to happen out on the field toward the end of training camp.

Derrick's grill sparkled as he gave Zach a smile. "Shit, yeah. It's barbecue day."

"Can't miss that," Zach said. He sat back down. Derrick dragged his chair back to the table, dropped his grill next to his lunch plate, and took a massive bite of his pulled pork sandwich.

The punter made the "stay" motion with both hands, and sat down again.

Zach risked a glance to the other side of the room. Cameron locked eyes with him. *Fuck.* She'd caught him looking like some middle-school kid mooning over one of the cheerleaders or something. This day was getting worse and worse.

"So, what's Cameron Online doing here?" The rookie sitting next to Derrick must have decided he felt braver than a few minutes ago. Rookies didn't usually speak until spoken to.

Zach bit his tongue before a comment about a certain sexual practice that would get him a significant fine and a suspension from the league tumbled out. The coaching staff was still in the room. He took a deep breath.

"Why do you care?" he said to the kid.

"I—one of my boys sent me a text this morning. He said she's here for the entire month." The kid took a sip of orange juice. "He wants pictures."

"Maybe you can ask her out for a milkshake," the punter said.

Derrick was polishing off his pulled pork sandwich and eyeing the second one. "She's a little old for you, rook. Maybe we can take you by the high school later or something."

The kid didn't seem to notice that the vets were shoveling in the food as fast as they could get it down. He was staring across the room at Cameron, who didn't acknowledge his interest at all. He didn't realize that lunch at the Sharks' training facility was never a leisurely affair. He didn't have time to finish his lunch, let alone pick up a woman.

Zach wasn't the kid's dad, but Derrick wasn't cluing the kid in. He reached out and tapped the kid's tray.

"Maybe you should worry about getting laid later and eat up. There are meetings after lunch, and you'll be starving by three if you don't get some calories now."

The kid was stupid enough to look annoyed.

Zach picked up his fork again. To hell with him. He took a bite of coleslaw. He tried not to look in Cameron's direction again. His eyeballs were on an invisible string, and she was pulling on the other end. Damn it. He bent over his plate once more.

He kept telling himself that he could handle having her here for a month. She meant nothing to him. It didn't matter that she'd ripped his heart out of his chest once upon a time and all but showed it to him while he died. He couldn't believe he'd been so hung up on her in the first place. They were drunk off their asses, they got married, and it was over three days later. She wasn't important. It meant nothing that he hadn't been able to sustain a relationship with any other woman for longer than a few months since they'd broken up, either.

If he was really honest with himself, he'd admit the truth: He compared every woman he met to Cameron. None of them quite measured up. Yes, she was beautiful, but he'd spent three days with a funny, intelligent, and passionate woman, and he wanted more. He was attracted to her zest for life, to the inner fire and determination that matched what drove him, too. If he wasn't in a crowded cafeteria with his teammates and the coaching staff, he'd bang his head on the table until he forgot what she looked like, even for a moment.

He was still young. He had plenty of time to find someone else and settle down. Getting serious with anyone while he was still playing football was idiotic anyway. Cameron was the last person on his list, so he couldn't figure out why he was even thinking about her right now. Maybe he needed to spend some time thinking about the new defensive sets the coach put into the playbook this morning instead.

He was reaching out to snatch the extra brownie off Derrick's tray when he heard a commotion from Cameron's table.

Two of the coaches were over there, pointing toward the exit and ordering her and her cameraman out in loud, don't-screw-with-us tones. He couldn't hear what she said, but he noted the look on her face: She wasn't backing down. The camera guy hovered protectively over her shoulder as she stood up from the table. Seconds later, she grabbed her bag and her tray, sashaying past them like it was her idea to leave all along. She didn't glance back as he saw her drop the tray in the bus tub by the door and walk out of the room.

The camera guy said something to one of the coaches that made the coach turn brick red. He followed Cameron out of the cafeteria.

The head coach got to his feet, clapped his hands, and said, "Lunch is over in five minutes. You might want to get a beverage and clear off the table. You'll be expected to take notes during the media presentation." He'd had media training before. There would be an emphasis on interview techniques, brainstorming possible answers for loaded or leading questions from the press, and the usual warnings about mouthing off on social media. He glanced around at the tables full of players. The only people who really needed the instruction were most likely rookies. "I've already contacted PSN and demanded that Kevin Adkins be the only network personality allowed in camp. Miss Tits and Hair can find something else to do with her time. We're here to work."

The female media trainer who'd walked in a few minutes ago and had been hooking up a laptop for her PowerPoint presentation's mouth dropped open. Zach recognized her as one of the sideline reporters for Seattle's pro baseball team. This must have been a side business for her. She laid the laptop back down on the table in front of her and bent to unplug the power cord from the outlet. The only sound in the room was her heels clicking on the vinyl floor while she moved into the coach's line of vision.

"Excuse me? I must have misheard. What did you just call Cameron Ondine?"

The coach turned to her. "You heard what I said. Got a problem with it?"

The pleasant expression she wore faded from the woman's face as she regarded him for a moment. Zach saw her square her shoulders. She must have made a decision. "Yes, I do. It's inappropriate."

She turned on one heel, picked up the laptop, and began disassembling cords and the power source, stowing them in her bag as she went.

"What the hell are you doing?" the coach said.

She was close enough for Zach to see her swallow hard before she said, "I won't be able to offer your team any media training today. I'll return your deposit when I arrive back at my office." She clicked her laptop shut and slid it inside a computer bag.

"You can't just leave."

"I own the business. I set my own schedule. And yes, I can leave."

"I'll make sure you don't work anywhere else in the NFL," the coach taunted.

"Go ahead." She stared into the coach's eyes. "I'll make sure you won't be able to get a media consultant anywhere within a fifty-mile radius of your team." She picked up her handbag and nodded at the team members. "Gentlemen."

She strode out of the room.

"Oh, that went well," Derrick muttered to nobody in particular.

MINUTES LATER IT was announced that the media training would be "rescheduled" sometime in the next couple of days. The team was sent off to meetings with their position coaches instead. Zach resigned himself to an afternoon of brain-numbing lectures. He could feel his phone vibrating repeatedly against his thigh, but he knew he'd be fined if he pulled it out for any reason. He'd just flipped open his playbook and sharpened a couple of pencils when the door to the meeting room opened. The Sharks' general manager walked in, accompanied by the team owner and a couple of other front office types. The GM's administrative assistant hurried in behind him; she was the only female in the room.

"Hey, Steve," the GM said to Zach's coach. "How about you take a load off, and I'll talk to your men for a few minutes." He nodded to an empty seat in the front row.

Steve the defensive line coach picked up his iPad off the table and said, "There's coffee, water and some snacks in the back, if you all are hungry."

"Thanks," the team owner said. "Maybe I'll grab some trail mix or something."

Zach didn't typically spend a lot of time talking with the front office people. The team owner occasionally traveled to away games with them, but mostly he kept to himself. Maybe he was too busy catering to his much-younger third wife.

The other guys with the GM took up the rest of the seats in the front row of the meeting room. The GM pulled a barstool over and sat down on it.

"How many of you heard what was said to both Cameron Ondine and Alicia Larsen by Coach Phillips this morning?"

Every player in the room held up one hand.

"Would you be able to recount what happened for us if you were asked to do so?"

Derrick held up his hand. "Do I need to write this down?"

The GM grinned a little. "No. We'll handle it." He shifted a little on his barstool. "Are you familiar with the fact the team has a no-discrimination policy?"

Every male in the room nodded. The GM's administrative assistant was writing furiously on a note pad in one corner. "I'm glad to hear it. The Sharks take our corporate image and our mission statement seriously. We welcome diversity. We won't tolerate discrimination, and we'll take steps to remedy the situation as quickly as possible if there is a problem." He let out a sigh. "I have to ask all of you for a favor."

Zach was all ears. This would probably involve a visit to an elementary school or playing with a bunch of kids in one of Seattle's less-affluent suburbs. He could handle it. He actually enjoyed that part of his job. The kids loved spending time with him and his teammates, and it was a relief from the adult fans, who believed they knew better than he did how to play football.

"After Coach Phillips's comments this morning, the team has suspended him until further notice. Coach Stewart will be acting head coach. I understand this is a surprise, but we can't allow the rest of the league and our community to believe we condone or encourage Coach Phillips' attitudes toward the women who may work with our team, now or in the future. I realize this might come as a shock, but we didn't feel like we had a choice. Plus, we really don't need to get sued." He gave the room a wry smile and rubbed one hand over his face. A couple of people let out a laugh. "That's not the favor, though."

The buzz of whispers and "holy shit" that went up over his initial comments faded to silence. He looked directly at Zach. Zach felt the hair stand up on the back of his neck. The best way to distract the media from the shit storm the suspended head coach might start was to give the sports media something they would eat up, and he had a very bad feeling he knew what it might be. He took a deep breath and braced himself.

"I've offered PSN an exclusive interview with a Sharks player to discuss the changes. We contacted the media trainer before she left the building, and she has graciously consented to work with our choice for the rest of the day on answers to Ms. Ondine's pre-submitted questions."

Zach saw him smile.

"I'd ask for a volunteer, but I think the choice is already made. Anderson, will you help us out? I'd really appreciate it."

Chapter Six

THE SHARKS' GM was smiling and nodding at Zach as if this was already a done deal. Zach had a no-win choice: Tell him no, and find his ass benched or traded before the end of the day; probably somewhere he wouldn't want to go. Tell him yes, and have to deal with another on-camera incident with Cameron. He knew she considered herself a professional, but this would be too good to resist. She'd carve him up like a Thanksgiving turkey, and there was nothing to do but smile and take it.

Derrick reached over and slapped him on the back. "You're my boy, Anderson."

Applause broke out around the room. Nobody seemed to care he hadn't agreed to the idea. Somehow, he had a feeling it wouldn't matter. Maybe he should call his agent and ask for some advice, or maybe he should man up and stop acting like such a candy ass. She was one-third his size. Why the hell was he letting her in his head?

He could only imagine what questions she would dream up for him. Mostly, he wanted to go somewhere quiet and regroup before he saw her again.

It wasn't going to happen.

"It's important that we get out front of the news cycle with a positive story about the Sharks to minimize any damage to our brand from this morning. Even more, we'd like to announce our changes on *our* timetable, not FOX Sports's or ESPN's." He clasped his hands. "Zach, if you'll come with us, we'll get things rolling. Steve, the floor is yours."

The guys in the front row got to their feet. Zach followed them out of the room.

He expected bone-jarring hits and injuries from his career. Nobody ever told him dodging beautiful blondes with their own camera crews would be a bigger hazard than facing a ferocious offensive line sixteen Sundays a year.

AFTER A SHORT meeting with the PSN production staff and taking the fastest route possible back to her dorm room, Cameron locked the door behind her and leaned against it. The floor was silent. All the players were still at the media training. The room was just as she left it—rumpled bed, half-unpacked suitcase waiting for her to do something about it, and the message light on the multi-line bedside phone blinking frantically. It was a little past noon Pacific Time, and she felt like she'd already put in a twelve-hour day. She resisted the impulse to crawl back into bed and have a good cry.

This wasn't the first time in her life she'd faced opposition to what she did for a living; she went through this with her own family on an almost-weekly basis, for God's sake. Today, though, it struck at something inside that left her shaken. She knew most people made a snap judgment about her because a young, attractive blonde supposedly knew nothing about sports. It was still surprising to her that she would face the same attitudes after working her way up from a minimum-wage runner for on-air talent to a successful ten-year broadcasting career, but she'd probably still be facing those questions until she retired and went on to do something more "appropriate" for a living.

Her phone buzzed in her pocket. She fished it out, took one look at the screen, and let out a groan. She needed five minutes to pull herself together, and then she could answer her producer's questions. She sent the call to voicemail. Her phone rang again about a minute later. Same guy. She stabbed the button that answered the call with one finger.

"Hi, Ralph. How are you?"

"I'm fine. I heard you're having a great time." She stifled another groan. "Hey, I have good news, though. The Sharks would like to give you an exclusive, and they've asked for you specifically."

"That's great." She picked a piece of lint off her jacket. "When would they like to do this?" She tried to inject some excitement into her voice. "I'll need to come up with some interview questions. Do you know whom I'll be talking with?"

Ralph sounded positively gleeful. "We're on our way

over to pick you up for some lunch and a chit-chat. Why don't you meet us at the front door in ten minutes?"

Her stomach twisted itself into a knot. She'd already had something to eat. They wouldn't be meeting her face to face unless it was something she wasn't going to like, and she had a really bad feeling she knew what that might be. PSN's owner and management wouldn't rest until they forced another confrontation with Zach.

"I'll grab my purse and meet you downstairs, Ralph."

"I'm looking forward to it. See you in a few." He hung up.

Her parents would be happy. After all, she'd realized in the past fifteen seconds she needed a serious dialogue with herself over her career choice. She hurried into the bathroom, applied a swipe of neutral lip gloss, grabbed her handbag and room key, and hurried out the door.

She was relieved to see Logan waiting downstairs, too.

"Did they tell you who we're interviewing?"

"Oh, hell, no." He grinned over at her. "Shall we make it interesting?" He pulled a twenty dollar bill out of his wallet. "My money's on either their starting QB or Zach Anderson."

"Maybe it's both."

"Well, Cam, pick one." He nudged her with an elbow. "I'll make it easy on you. I'm going with Tom Reed. They'll leave Zach for an hour-long, endlessly teased special."

Cameron glanced up at him. She knew he was right, but she wasn't going to tell him that. "Okay. You're on. Forget the twenty bucks. I want a cronut when we go back to New York instead, you dork."

It was a challenge for the driver of the stretch limo

carrying Cameron, Logan, and the rest of the PSN production team to pull the car into the parking lot of a somewhat deserted-looking pub with no street appeal five minutes from the practice facility. He managed, though, and the group piled out of the car.

"It's a good thing we didn't dress up," Ralph joked.

"I thought Seattle was known for its seafood," Kacee said. It was nice to see that they remembered to pick up Cameron's assistant from wherever it was she was staying at. "Maybe we should have gone to a seafood place instead."

"I'll bet they have some fried shrimp here," Logan told her.

Kacee rolled her eyes and walked away from him. Logan had been flirting with Cameron's assistant for months now. Kacee wanted someone with a lot more money, for starters. Logan found her obsession with Wall Street frat rats in suits hilarious. Cameron needed to spend some time impressing on Kacee that money wasn't everything, but she knew she didn't have a lot of credibility in that area. Her co-workers all knew where she spent her summers, for instance, and it wasn't in stifling hot New York City.

A woman with two-tone hair, wearing a polo shirt with the pub's logo and an inadvisable number of colorful tattoos on both arms waved one arm toward the seating area. "Sit anywhere," she told them. She did a double-take when she saw Kevin. "Hey, I know you," she said. "You're on PSN."

He gave her a nod.

There weren't a lot of other customers. The lunch crowd had gone back to work, and it was too early for happy hour. Cameron grabbed one of the slightly sticky laminated menus from the center of the long table and pretended to study it. She wasn't hungry, but not ordering really wasn't an option. She didn't want to be accused of "not being a team player" on top of whatever else it was she was going to be upbraided for after this morning's confrontation with the coach.

"What are you getting?" Kacee whispered to her.

"Chef's salad with chopped egg and dressing on the side," Cameron whispered back.

"Want to split some fries?"

"Sure." She wouldn't eat them, but it would make Kacee feel better. If Cameron didn't stay ten pounds underweight at all times, she got nasty e-mails from viewers. As a result, French fries weren't something she indulged in typically.

While the server took their drink and food orders, Ben, executive program director of PSN, took a sip of the iced tea the server ran to get for him. Her speed probably had something to do with the twenty he'd handed her before he even arrived at their table. He got up from his chair and addressed the group.

"I thought it might be nice to take a few minutes to talk about what's going to be happening over the next few days. First of all, we're already seeing a ratings spike with the advertising we've done on Cameron's coverage of training camp. The most surprising contacts we've had were from women's magazines, female-oriented cable channels, and female bloggers who'd like to interview Cameron about what it's like to room with eighty guys for a month." He beamed like he'd thought it up all by himself, and glanced over at her. "We'll set up a conference call with the media who'd like to interview you later this week."

She smiled and toyed with the straw in her glass of iced tea. Kevin glared at her from across the table.

"As far as the training camp coverage, I got a phone call from the Sharks' GM an hour ago." He stopped talking while the server delivered plates and silverware to the table. She put a huge cheeseburger and fries down in front of Cameron.

"Excuse me. I didn't order this," Cameron said. "I asked for a chef's salad with chopped egg and dressing on the side."

"We're out of salad," the woman told her. "Plus, your collar bone is going to injure somebody. Eat up." She put a large container of ketchup down in front of Kacee along with another cheeseburger and fries. "You, too. You can diet when you go back to New York City."

Her comments were met with uproarious laughter from every male at the table, and a look of horror from Kacee.

"I don't eat red meat," Kacee told her.

"You do now. Take a bite. Maybe you'll get through the afternoon without passing out." She swished further down the table, and put a grilled chicken breast and steamed vegetables down in front of Ralph. "I am *not* giving you a bacon cheeseburger, so you can get that thought out of your head right now. Does your wife know you eat this badly?"

"I don't have a wife."

"Well, then, it's my job, isn't it? Does anyone need anything else—napkins, a refill? Okay then." She walked away without waiting to see if anyone at the table made a further request.

"I thought they were more polite in Seattle," Ralph said.

Ben was still laughing. "Maybe not." The two customers at the bar had left, but Ben glanced around before leaning toward the others at his table. "Okay. PSN has been given an exclusive, and Cameron will conduct the interview. We'd hoped to save any contact with this player until later in the season, but we believe her interview with Zach Anderson will break ratings records."

Cameron hadn't been able to resist the siren song of golden brown, perfectly done fries after all. She choked on a French fry. Logan slapped her on the back until she stopped coughing.

"Easy," Logan told her. Ben waited until Cameron seemed like she'd live.

"We'll tape the interview as quickly as possible, either late tonight or tomorrow morning. The Sharks have breaking news, and we'd like to scoop everyone else as a result."

"So, what's the breaking news?" someone else asked.

"The Sharks' head coach is suspended indefinitely as of about an hour ago. The assistant coach is now the acting head coach. I was also told that the suspension is a formality. Unless he agrees to diversity training and formally apologizes to Cameron and Ms. Larsen, he's fired. The Sharks are trying to distract from the upheaval by offering the interview. They asked for pre-submitted questions, and I told them that would not be a problem. We'll formulate those this afternoon."

Cameron stopped in the midst of cutting the cheeseburger in half so she could eat a few bites. It actually smelled pretty good. Flinging the uneaten half at Ben wouldn't be a great idea, but it would be nice if she could actually do the job she was hired for. When she wasn't pissed off about that, she was breathing deeply to stave off a full-scale panic attack. She was going to have to face Zach again on her own. She didn't want to. Her colleague Kevin was smirking at her from across the table. He'd take the interview in a heartbeat. If only that was an option.

"Were there guidelines for those pre-submitted questions?"

"No. There were no guidelines." Ben took another bite of his chicken breast and chewed for a few minutes. "Maybe we shouldn't ask Zach Anderson about his sex life this time, hmm?"

A few hours later, Cameron was back in her dorm room with carefully formulated and pre-negotiated notecards full of questions. According to the phone call she'd just gotten, Zach was making rapid enough progress with the media trainer that the team felt comfortable taping the interview this evening. Cameron had an hour to figure out what to wear, get makeup and hair done, and go over the questions one more time. She laid the note-cards down on the computer desk in her dorm room and rifled through her suitcase to find something suitable for a formal on-air interview.

"Too pink. Too red. Too low-cut. Too high-necked. Too last season," she muttered to herself. She yanked a slightly wrinkled, above-knee length, cobalt blue sleeveless sheath dress out of her suitcase, and pulled out the portable steamer she always traveled with. She rifled through her jewelry roll for the dangly bronze-pearl-and-brown-gold earrings she'd bought last week. She tossed a pair of nude pumps with slender heels on the bed. Truthfully, how she looked on-air was the least of her problems at the moment. Her stomach was churning. She could feel cold sweat trickling down her back. She was shaking.

She could hear the guys shouting at each other and laughing out in the hallway. If she got her ass in gear, she could step out there, spend a few minutes observing, and maybe write a little later about what happens when grown men are forced to live like college students for a month. The network would post whatever she came up with on their NFL blog. Her bosses would be happy about coverage that would thrill the average football fan.

She couldn't figure out why she was so freaked out about seeing Zach again. They had been married for three days, ten years ago. Her father and his attorneys told her Zach was more interested in her money than he was in her. They offered him a financial settlement for his agreeing to an annulment, and according to them Zach didn't need five minutes to think about it. He'd signed where they told him to, her father handed him a check, and he'd walked away. He'd never tried to contact her again.

She sank down on the dorm room bed. Her chin was shaking. She wrapped her arms around herself. Why was she still so hurt over something that meant nothing?

ZACH WALKED INTO a quiet, dimly lit room inside the Sharks headquarters. One of the laundry guys had been tasked with ironing the long-sleeved team polo and warm-up pants he was now wearing. The makeup artist and hair person for PSN had spent the past twenty minutes brushing, spraying, and spackling him to a high sheen.

He stepped over the power cords on the floor and into the false daylight afforded by the multiple TV lights illuminating two chairs that sat face-to-face and less than three feet away from each other.

The speakers over his head crackled. "Want some water before we start, Zach? Cameron's a bit delayed."

He nodded. Of course she wasn't on time. A production assistant hurried out from behind the stationary camera and extended an ice-cold bottle of water to him. He took a swig and put the half-empty bottle on the table next to his chair.

"I'm sure you've glanced over the questions by now. Is there anything else you'd like to discuss prior to the interview?"

"I'm good," he assured them. He really wasn't. He wanted to jump out of his skin. He walked out of the circle of light, took a deep breath, and heard the door open. The light from the hallway backlit Cameron's hair as she darted into the room.

"I'm so sorry I'm—Oh!" In the split second before she landed against his chest, he realized she must have tripped on the power cords. His arms shot out to wrap around her before she hit the floor. She felt so small against him. His fingertips moved over the soft fabric of her dress, while the top of her head brushed his chin. She must have been as shocked as he was. She rested against his chest for a few seconds. He smelled the same subtle, exotic perfume she'd been wearing ten years ago. He'd smelled a lot of perfumes since then, but he'd never forgotten hers—the clean scent of lilies and musk. He'd never forgotten what it was like to hold her in his arms, either.

He felt her fingers wrap around his biceps as she tried to right herself. His arms slid away from her, and he braced her forearms with both hands.

"That's quite an entrance, Cameron," he said. He took another deep breath. "Are you okay?"

She sounded flustered. "I'm fine. I think I just fell over the cord." She hauled in some breath. "It was dark." She took a cautious step back from him. He saw her swallow hard in the dimness. "Are you okay?"

Actually, he wasn't. The memories were flooding his brain now. He'd smelled her before he saw her that morning in the Vegas hotel room; her perfume mixed with the scent of brain-melting sex. He had the worst hangover of his life, but he forced his eyes open. It was worth the effort. Her hair was rumpled. Her skin was flushed. She beamed at him as she clutched the sheet closer. She was nude and still felt shy about it, evidently. His modest darling.

He'd reached out and pulled the sheet away from her. "Don't ever cover them up again," he'd said to her that morning.

Right now, though, he said, "I'm fine."

"Thanks for catching me."

She stood still. He didn't move, either. He knew there were other people in the room that might want to get this show on the road. He didn't want to let go of her soft skin. He forced himself to drop her arms, and held out his hand. "Come on."

CAMERON SETTLED INTO the chair opposite Zach and tried to concentrate on the notecards in her lap. The production group was waiting for her cue. They would start counting when she indicated she was ready to start. She took another sip of water and tried to compose herself. She'd memorized the questions. She had cue cards for the introduction. This was no different than a thousand other interviews she'd ever done in her life, but she couldn't seem to signal the production group. She licked her lips again.

Zach locked eyes with her. She saw his Adam's apple bob as he swallowed hard. He leaned forward in his chair, reached across, and took her hands in his much bigger ones. The notecards she'd been holding dropped into her lap. He stroked his thumbs across her skin.

"What happened to us, Cameron?" His voice was raspy. He held her hands in his, scooting onto the edge of his chair, surrounding her.

"I—I," she stammered. He waited. The laughing, carefree Zach wasn't there anymore. His typical smile faded as pain etched his face. The makeshift TV studio was silent as they fought for words.

Cameron hauled breath into her lungs. Her lips quivered as tears rose in her eyes. The words tumbled out before she could stop them.

"Why did you leave me?" she said.

Chapter Seven

A FEW SECONDS later, Zach heard some shuffling and gasps from the group standing behind the camera and TV lights. He knew the production staff had skin in the game on the successful taping of this interview, too. Their bosses would expect something worth a ratings bonanza. He also noticed the red light over the lens was on. He realized that maybe he should ask how long they'd been filming, but right now, he was too busy getting frozen out by his ex-wife. He'd spent every day of the past ten years trying to forget her.

She'd dropped her guard for approximately five seconds, and he watched the wall of ice in her eyes re-form in milliseconds. She let go of his hands. She didn't answer his question, but he didn't answer hers, either.

"I might need a touch-up," she called out to the group behind the camera. Sure enough, a slender brunette attired in black and sporting an eyebrow piercing advanced on Cameron with brushes, makeup, and a clear tube that looked like Visine. She hip-checked Zach back into his chair.

"What the hell was that?" he snapped. Cameron didn't even glance at him. "Talk to me, Cameron."

The makeup person ignored him and bent over Cameron. "We can fix this," she soothed. She bent to administer eye drops, dabbed carefully around Cameron's eyes with a tissue, and repaired her makeup. "Okay. You're all set. Do you need more water?"

"No, I'm fine, thank you. Are you all ready?" Cameron said. She wouldn't meet his eyes. She straightened the cards in her lap, sat up in her chair, and turned toward the camera. "Let's do this." She nodded at the production group.

"Starting in five, four," and the woman holding the cue cards counted off "three, two, one" with fingers instead of aloud.

"I'm Cameron Ondine, and this is a special edition of *NFL Confidential*. My guest this evening is defensive tackle Zach Anderson of the Seattle Sharks. Zach was drafted in the first round by the Sharks in 2002 and has played his entire career with them. He was selected to the Pro Bowl five times. He is a three-time All-Pro. He is considered one of the preeminent DT's in the league. We're happy to have him with us today. Welcome, Zach."

She turned toward him. Her smile was completely insincere.

"Well, thanks, Ms. Ondine." He gave her a grin to equal hers. "It's an honor."

He saw her nostrils flare a little. He caught a lightning-fast glimpse of hurt and anger lurking in her dark-chocolate eyes.

"Zach, let's talk a little about this season's training camp. How do you feel about the changes the Sharks defensive line coach made through the draft and free agency over the offseason?"

It was all Zach could do not to roll his eyes. So, she wanted to be all professional and shit? He'd see about that.

"There are a few new guys, but we're mostly sticking with the same guys that brought us to the championships we've enjoyed. It's important to reward loyalty, Cameron." He paused for a moment and gave her an especially toothy smile. "I hope you don't mind my calling you by your first name, by the way." She gave him a stiff nod. "I feel confident when I'm playing next to guys who would walk through fire for the team. These guys don't cut and run when there's a problem. They work together toward a common goal." He paused again. "I'm sure you know what that's like."

He watched her expectantly. She'd narrowed those gorgeous eyes at him. If looks could kill he'd be dead, and she swallowed hard. She glanced down at the notes in her lap again. It was so quiet in the studio he could hear someone talking through her earpiece. She gave whoever was talking a slight nod.

"The Sharks had some struggles last season. Did you make any personal adjustments on the offseason to prepare for a different outcome?"

"I spend the offseason preparing as a rule, but I'm also a firm believer in adjusting to the situation I might find myself in. I'll do whatever I have to do to win, Cameron."

"That's great to hear, Zach. You signed a huge contract extension in the offseason as well. Talk to me about the fact you'll spend the rest of your NFL career in a Sharks jersey."

"Funny you should mention that. I'm a pretty big believer in dancing with the one that brung you, Cameron. The Sharks have treated me well over the years. It's an honor to stay with those that do." He leaned forward. His words were weapons, and she was about to find out how sharp his weapons were. "Plus, the money's great, but it really doesn't mean that much to me. It's all about the people I love. My needs are taken care of, and I have a few of the things I want, too. Ultimately, it's about what's important in life." He gave her another big, smarmy grin. Her face flooded with color. She looked like she was about to erupt off her chair. "Money's not a lot when you don't have someone to go home to at night."

She gave him an equally forced smile. "That's an interesting perspective, Zach."

"Oh, it is," he said. "I knew you'd agree with me."

CAMERON HAD AN entire notecard of questions left to ask, but she was tired of playing cat-and-mouse with Zach. She also wondered if the fact she was afraid he was going to bust out on-camera with additional information about their history together showed on her face. She'd had to cover or conceal her true feelings many times on the air before, but thank God she'd insisted this be taped, not live. Maybe they could piece together enough of an interview that she wouldn't have to re-tape before broadcast. Right now, she was torn between running away from him, or taking off her shoe and smacking him with it.

"Money means little to me"? This was the same guy who took a five million dollar check from her dad to annul a seventy-two-hour marriage. He was lying through his teeth, and another wave of hurt and embarrassment engulfed her. She took a deep, centering breath and faced the camera again.

"It looks like Zach might be on the hunt for a special lady. We wish him luck with that—"

"*One* special lady, Cameron. Let's make sure those watching don't forget that." He lifted one eyebrow. "I'm a one-woman man."

She ignored the comment; it made her want to scream. He might want to inform the four women he'd been at the Gramercy Tavern's bar with a few days ago, too. "In the meantime, there's breaking news from the Sharks. Maybe you'd like to share that with our viewers."

"Absolutely." He had a notecard of his own in his lap, she noticed. A prepared statement: lovely.

"It's only the first day of training camp, ladies and gentlemen, and it's already quite a ride." He gave the camera a you-can't-resist-me grin. "The Sharks' head coach allegedly made some objectionable comments to Ms. Ondine and a local female sports reporter, Ms. Larsen, this morning. Coach Phillips has been suspended indefinitely by the team as a result. The Sharks organization apologizes to Ms. Ondine and Ms. Larsen for the alleged comments, and promises it won't happen again. As a result of this morning's incident, Sharks assistant coach Ryan Stewart has been named the team's interim head coach." He gave the camera another nod. "I'm sure I speak for everyone on the team when I say we're looking forward to working with him."

"We'll also look forward to an interview with the Sharks' new head coach at his earliest convenience, then. And I'd like to thank my guest, Zach Anderson, for visiting with us tonight. I'll see you next week. As always, keep it on PSN for breaking news from the NFL. From this special edition of *NFL Confidential*, good night." She waited for the usual signal from the production staff that they'd gotten it all on tape, and glanced through her mostly unused notecard questions.

Zach's voice was quiet. "So, that's it?"

Her head jerked up. "Yes. That's it. Thanks for the interview."

"You didn't ask me very many questions, Cameron." They were sitting close enough to each other that a whisper would suffice. Even more interesting, the production staff had gone silent, too. Of course they were eavesdropping.

She closed her eyes briefly, and fought to control the tone and volume of her voice. "No, I didn't. I didn't want another sermonette about how money is just not that important to you, and how much you prize loyalty." She looked into his eyes. "You didn't seem to care about "loyalty" or sticking by me ten years ago in Vegas. The only thing you cared about was seeing how quickly you could get away."

"That's not true. I meant what I said when I married you. I would have stayed with you until the end of time. You can't tell me you had nothing to do with what happened."

She could hear the gasping and "Oh my Gods" through her earpiece from the production booth.

"What happened? You walked out, you never came back, and I had to deal with my family," she said.

He leaned toward her again. "You didn't want me back." He got to his feet, pulled the microphone off the neck of his polo shirt, grabbed the battery pack out of his waistband, yanked it all loose, and dropped it onto the chair across from him. She heard the door open seconds later.

CAMERON HEARD THE producer's voice in her ear as she jumped out of her chair. "It might have been nice to know that you had prior history with Anderson."

She heard another voice responding to him. "We'll cut the personal stuff and figure out how long we still have to fill." She didn't need her earpiece to hear multiple people arguing over what to do now, and *oh-em-gee*, how did no one in the world not know that Zach and Cameron were married before?

If the previous interview was a disaster, this was the complete and total collapse of her career and her privacy.

It reminded her of the Vegas hotel implosions she'd seen on videotape. A few seconds later, all that was left was rubble. She resisted the impulse to blurt out a word that was definitely not permissible by FCC standards.

"I'll be right back," she said. Nobody seemed to care.

Despite the fact her eyes were re-adjusting to the dimness of the surrounding room as she negotiated the electrical cords on the floor, she managed to make it into the hallway. Zach was lounging against the wall, which was a surprise.

"I can't believe you're still here."

His mouth curved into a slight smile. "Hey, darlin'."

"Don't call me that. What the hell? All we had to come up with was a twenty-minute interview, I ask you about your new head coach, and everyone is happy with both of us." She was just getting warmed up, and he was looking at her like the whole thing was hilarious. "Does it occur to you that I don't want everyone in the world to know we were married? I don't talk about my personal life on the air or in the media. That's private. I—"

She could feel emotion surging through her, wild and uncontrolled. She didn't like lack of control, and she really didn't like messy and ridiculous displays of feelings—hers or anyone else's. The accompanying adrenaline swamped any remaining restraint. The tears she'd held in by sheer will earlier were threatening another appearance. She shoved them down one more time. She still had things to say to him, and she'd be damned if she'd act like one of those women who cry over stuff at the drop of a hat.

His voice was quiet and annoyingly calm.

"You don't want anyone to know we were married, huh? Too late for that." He tried to look regretful, she thought. "I'm in a truth-telling mood, too. Confession's good for the soul."

"No, it's not." The tears were rising again, threatening to wipe out everything in their path with sheer force. "If you'll come back in there and sit down—" She blinked as hard as she could, raised her face to the ceiling, and fought for control. "We can start over. We'll get something on tape, and I'll spend the next month pretending like you're not even here. I promise."

He shoved himself off the wall, and reached out for her hand. It felt so small in his. She couldn't quite make herself yank it away, either. She was flooded with the knowledge of how it felt to be close to him. She breathed in the scent of his recently-showered skin, his freshly washed and ironed clothes, and a faint smell of liniment. He was twice her size. She concentrated on staring at the middle of his chest. If she looked up, he'd be giving her the half-indulgent smile she'd seen on his face a hundred times in seventy-two hours ten years ago.

"Is that so?" He bent over her. His voice was soft and sensual in her ear. "That's not going to work for me." She felt the warmth of his breath brush her skin. "You'll pretend like I'm not here. Well, I'm going to make sure you can't forget me, or the fact I'm here, twenty-four hours a day. I want you to remember me the way I've remembered you." He let that sink in for a minute. "Your daddy's not here to rescue you this time around."

She squeezed her eyes shut. "He didn't 'rescue me' the first time around! I—" It was hard to make air quotes with only one hand. "That's not what happened."

He slid his fingertips over her mouth. "I have twenty-nine days to make sure you'll never forget me again. It starts now, Cameron."

Chapter Eight

CAMERON COULDN'T SPEAK. Even worse, she couldn't think. He was too close. The memories of him were too intense. Mostly, she needed to get away and pull herself together before she did something really stupid, like tell him she'd never forgotten what it was like to kiss him. She pulled her hand out of his, turned on one heel, and hurried down the hallway away from him.

He didn't call out to her or try to stop her. She didn't hear anyone following her, but she'd forgotten about the portable mic and battery pack.

"Cameron, where the hell are you? Get back in here," her producer said into her ear.

She smacked the bar that opened the facility door leading to the practice field with one hand. Maybe a few breaths of fresh air would help. She could walk around outside for a few minutes and calm down a little.

"Cam," the producer said. "What is going on?"

"Nothing. I'll be there in a minute."

Dusk was falling, and the practice field was deserted. A slight breeze ruffled her hair. She glanced across the empty expanse of grass that looked out over the lake, which beckoned to anyone who wanted quiet and solitude. She noted there weren't even boaters on the lake tonight. She wrapped both arms around herself, and resisted the impulse to keep walking until she found a way out of here.

"Cameron." She didn't miss the warning note in his voice. "We still need some voiceovers, and we'll have to piece this together. We're not done yet."

"Fine. I'll be right there." She turned to go back into the building, and reached out for the doorknob. She pulled hard. It didn't open. She pulled again, rattling the door in its frame. It still didn't budge. "I'm locked out," she said into the mic still pinned to her dress.

The producer swore extravagantly into her earpiece. A few minutes later, Kacee appeared in the hallway and held the door open for her. She didn't look happy, either. Cameron reached up, yanked off the portable microphone and earpiece, and faced her assistant.

Kacee didn't even wait until the door slammed shut behind Cameron.

"I can't believe you didn't tell me you guys were married. Married! Are you kidding? You were going to introduce me to him! Why? I saw the way he looked at you. Are you crazy?" Kacee was waving her arms around. "When did you get married? Why didn't you give him a chance?"

The sheer number of Kacee's questions made her head pound. Cameron started walking away from her, wrapping her arms around her midsection. Her stomach was churning. Maybe she should have eaten more at dinner, but she wasn't all that hungry these days. Kacee tried to grab her elbow. Cameron pulled away from her.

"I'm not discussing this right now. I have to get back to work."

"I can't believe you've kept this a secret for *how* long now? Why? He's really cute, and I—what's wrong with him? Was he bad in bed? *What*?"

Kacee was still following her, still chattering, and Cameron wanted to put both hands over her ears. "I can't believe you won't talk to me about this. I thought you trusted me. Why won't you discuss it?"

Cameron let out a groan. She didn't want to consider what would happen when this all got out.

ZACH VAULTED OFF the bench in the Sharks' weight room and mopped his dripping face with a towel. Maybe he should go for a run next. He needed to work off the adrenaline and nerves still surging through his body. One thing was for sure: He was an idiot. He'd just told Cameron he would do whatever he had to do over the next twenty-nine days to get her back. He'd meant every word, but he'd lost the element of surprise. Talk about showing one's hand in a high-stakes poker game. He was stuck in a dorm with seventy-nine other guys who wouldn't object to a date with her.

It wasn't as if the usual items for wooing a female were at his fingertips. Champagne and candlelight dinners for two were pretty thin on the ground at an NFL training camp facility. He should be concentrating on keeping his damn job instead of chasing a woman who'd made it clear she didn't love him, didn't want him, and had other things and people occupying her time. Then again, he loved a challenge.

He couldn't get her off his mind before, and now it was worse than ever. She'd grown even more beautiful in the past ten years. He remembered how she'd felt when she'd fallen into his arms earlier, the unguarded, slightly embarrassed smile on her lips when she looked up at him. The fifteen seconds or so before she'd glanced away from him with remembered pain and pulled herself free.

He wanted her back. He wasn't sure how he was going to accomplish this, or what he could say to make her understand how much he regretted that he hadn't fought harder for her.

There had to be something that would turn her to putty in his hands. He wasn't unimaginative in the romance department, but he hadn't had to chase a woman for a long time now. They chased him. To admit that to another person would make him sound like an egomaniac, but it was true. He sat down on the bench again and mentally sifted through the crap he remembered other guys had done to try to get one of his sisters to go out with him over the years. He wasn't as whipped as those guys were. He'd like to keep a shred of his dignity. Then again, he was whipped enough to be pursuing a woman millions of other guys wanted, too. He'd bet she'd seen it all over the years, so he'd have to come up with something she found irresistible. He'd also better keep things on the down-low. He was surrounded by other guys who really didn't have to chase to get a woman's attention, either, and he didn't care to be the laughing stock of the locker room.

Most of the other guys were too busy Skyping with their wives and kids or screwing around in the game room upstairs tonight to care what he was doing, which was always a bonus when one was formulating a plan.

Flowers weren't his best bet. He knew she probably got flowers on a daily basis from other guys who were trying to make an impression. He'd have to find out what her favorite flower was; if he sent those it might score him some points. She probably liked candy, but the only type he had at his disposal right now were the Skittles in the vending machine. It was a little early for jewelry.

He had to woo her. The only way he could earn her love was to show her that he'd never forgotten her. He never would, and this time he was all in.

An idea popped into his head: Maybe the simplest way to his destination was a straight line. He dropped his face into his hands in response. Taking her for a walk in the moonlight on the practice field was really ridiculous, but they'd have a chance to be alone.

"Fuck, no. Too corny," he said to himself.

The more he considered it, though, the more he liked it. Plus, if he was going to catch Cameron, he'd better go big or go home. Climbing a mountain started with a single step. He could chant clichés all he wanted, but they all led to the same thing: Get off his ass, and go get her.

ONE HOUR LATER, Zach stood in front of Cameron's dorm room door. He'd showered, dressed, and styled his hair. He wore a clean pair of warm-ups, a hoodie, and running shoes. In other words, he'd made an effort, but he didn't try too hard. He'd spent the entire time in the shower planning out what he had to say, too. It was good to be prepared.

Who was he kidding?

His hands were shaking. He forced himself to take a deep breath because his heart was pounding. She wasn't the first woman he'd ever asked out, but he was sure feeling like it. He reached out to tap one knuckle on the door. Seconds later, he heard Cameron's light footsteps approaching and her soft voice. "Kacee, can we do this tomorrow? I'm really tired—"

"It's not Kacee," he said through the door.

The doorknob turned, and the door opened about an inch. Judging by the view, she'd ditched the pretty dress and heels she wore for her interview with him. She wore glasses, some type of knit outfit with little cupcakes all over it, and—to his amazement—bunny slippers. Her eyes were red-rimmed. She was still sniffling. The skin on her cheeks was blotchy and the tip of her nose was a bit red.

He'd wanted to jerk her chain a little during that interview, but he'd laid it on pretty thick. Instead of offering answers that would let her use the pre-negotiated questions, he'd made his points, and now he was the last guy she wanted to see, if the expression on her face was any indicator. He'd screwed up again.

"Have you been crying? What's wrong?" he said.

"What are you doing here?" she blurted. "How did you know where my room is?"

"Mine's at the other end of the hall," he said. He jammed his foot in the door before she had a chance to slam it shut. "Talk to me. Maybe I can help."

She ignored that. "Please go away."

"I'd like to go for a walk with you, Cameron."

She was shaking her head before the words emerged, and she didn't meet his eyes. "I can't. Kacee is on her way up here to go over some stuff for tomorrow. Plus, I'm not dressed."

"So, go put some clothes on. I'll wait."

"Kacee—"

"You were in the midst of blowing Kacee off when I knocked at your door. You don't want to see her, either," he said.

He pushed a little on the door. She moved in front of the gap his foot made in the doorway to push the door closed. He had a few seconds to take a better look at her. Her face was scrubbed clean. Her hair was in a ponytail. She looked like she was about to make popcorn in the microwave, cuddle with a stuffed animal on her bed, and go over her notes for tomorrow's Psych exam. She looked at him like he'd kicked her puppy, though.

"That's not true. I'm busy right now. Thanks, but

no thanks." She gave the door another shove. He didn't move.

"You'll sleep better if you walk a little before you go to bed. Plus, we have things to talk about," he said.

She shook her head again. "This isn't a good idea. Let's just go with the original plan. You do your thing, I'll do mine, and I'll stay out of your way." She closed her eyes for a couple of seconds, and let out a long sigh. "We managed to piece together an interview. It will air in about twenty minutes, and that should be the end of it."

He heard the cell phone in her pocket ring. She ignored it, but it started ringing again.

"Please go," she said. "I have to take this." He moved his foot out of the doorway.

She pulled her phone out of her pocket, turned her back to him, and said, "This is Cameron," as she elbowed the door shut in his face.

CAMERON'S HEART WAS pounding. Her palms were damp. Her knees were knocking, and the reason for her accelerated heart rate and general unease vanished behind a closed door while she listened to Kacee. She knew her behavior was rude, but she really wasn't in the mood to listen to Zach after his earlier comments. Plus, he now knew she'd been crying, which was even more embarrassing.

She would know Zach's voice anywhere. She couldn't imagine why she'd been stupid enough to open the door to him in the first place. She'd like to spend the evening dwelling on her stupidity (again) and having a glass of wine or two, but the only alcohol currently available to her was a beer vending machine at the end of the hall. She didn't need the calories or the bloat. Then again, if the Junk Food Fairy dropped off a shopping cart full of chips, cookies, and ice cream, she'd eat her way through it right now.

There had to be another guy on the face of the earth she wanted more than she still wanted Zach. She hadn't met him. She'd tried. He was still the only one who cared enough to listen to her when she'd confided her dreams for the future during their three-day marriage, the only one who made her feel like the things she wanted to do in life were important and would make her happy. Maybe she should get over her hopes of a man who found her ambitions and goals in life were as important as his own.

Maybe he wasn't what he'd seemed after all. Maybe she was wrong, and she'd made another colossal mistake.

"Kacee? Kacee, is that you?" She could hear a tremendous amount of racket in the background. The guys in the production room must be arguing about something.

"Yeah. Cam, the production group wants to talk to you. Will you come down here?" Kacee shouted into the phone.

"The interview's done."

"Uh, they don't think so," she said. "They want a meeting. Right now."

"Can't it wait till tomorrow? I'd like to get some sleep."

"If you don't get down here, they'll come up there after you," Kacee said. "We're in the studio. Ben is flipping out."

Cameron could hear him in the background, too. She stifled what she'd like to say and grabbed a pair of jeans and a shirt out of her suitcase. "I'll be there in ten minutes."

She hit the button to end the call, pulled her clothes on, and jammed her feet into running shoes. She stuck her phone and room key into a side pocket. She swiped at her face with her fingertips one more time, but it wasn't going to do any good. She wished she had time to scrub her face with the washcloth again. Maybe her glasses would hide the tell-tale redness of recent tears in her eyes and on her cheeks.

She pulled the dorm room open, walked through it, and came to a dead stop. Zach was leaning against the wall a few feet from her doorway. The nervous, jittery feelings she had whenever he was nearby returned with a vengeance.

"I heard there's a meeting," he said. "Why don't we walk downstairs together?"

"I'll be fine."

She wasn't going to wait for him or ask how he knew she was wanted downstairs. He was still trying to talk with her as she hurried down the stairs to the first floor of the facility.

"So, the big boss is unhappy about something."

"I don't know what's going on. He doesn't usually call a meeting at ten pm, especially when it's been a long day already." She faced a hallway full of even more doors, and she had no idea which was the correct door to the PSN temporary studio. She was upset, frustrated, lost, and wished she didn't have to ask for his help again. Unfortunately, there didn't seem to be any way around it at the moment. "I also don't know where I'm going," she said.

"Good thing I'm here," he said. She saw a grin spread over his face. "Follow me." He managed to find the correct door and get them through it. She broke into a sprint as she saw the studio door open.

Ben walked into the hallway and folded his arms over his chest.

"When were you planning on telling me that we're missing the whole story here?"

ZACH WATCHED THE color drain out of Cameron's face. "I don't know what you're talking about," she said. She folded her arms across her chest, too. Ben nodded at Zach. Zach didn't nod in return.

"You were married to each other. You have kept this a secret for how many years? You didn't tell us before the initial interview, and you didn't tell us before you got here. Why not? Didn't you think we might want to know and explore this as part of *Third and Long*?"

"Ben, my private life won't be used as the plot of a TV program. I'm not interested in having people I've never met speculate on things that aren't their business in the first place. I don't give my consent to have any details about our former marriage aired, either." Zach saw color surging into Cameron's face as she spoke. "Please expect a call from my agent on this subject."

Ben interrupted her. "Come on now. Everyone's doing it. Plus, it will generate huge ratings. Do you know how many women from eighteen to forty-eight will tune in to see another female dealing with her ex-husband in close quarters for a month?" He rubbed his hands together. "This is a prime viewer demographic, too. We'll get huge ratings and a ton of advertising dollars. It's genius, and I can't wait." His excitement was tangible. He practically bounced up and down as he spoke. "I'll get the writers to work on this right now."

"Writers?" Cameron said.

"Oh, *hell* no," Zach said. "I'm not interested."

"You wouldn't ask Kevin to expose his private life on-camera," Cameron said. "Why are you asking me?"

"Zach, you'll cooperate with us," Ben said. "It would be great for the team, too. I know they'll be impressed with your initiative."

"Cooperate with what? I'm not really into this either—" Zach said.

Ben cut him off. "I think the Sharks will feel differently. It's a great human-interest story." Ben was rubbing his hands together again. "Maybe you should go get some sleep. We're going to have quite a day tomorrow."

Chapter Nine

CAMERON WATCHED BEN pull the studio door open and vanish through it seconds later.

"Where are you going, Ben?" Zach asked.

The door clicked closed. Zach reached out for the doorknob and tugged. It was locked. He pounded on the door with one fist. Nobody answered it.

"Open the damn door!" he shouted.

Cameron pounded on the door a few times, too. "Why are they ignoring us?"

"I don't know, but I'm getting to the bottom of this." He pounded on the door one last time, called out, "This isn't over!" and reached out to take Cameron's elbow in his fingertips. "We need to strategize."

He'd moved closer. She backed up instinctively. He followed her, one step at a time. She stopped. He did, too.

"I can't believe he just walked away from us. Why is he locking me out of the studio? I *work* for him. Plus, Kacee's in there. I need to find out what's going on." She pulled her smart phone out of the pocket of her jeans and hit Kacee's cell number.

The call went to voicemail. Cameron tried calling again, and got the same result. "Hey, Kacee, I need to talk with you," Cameron said. "Call me back ASAP." She ended the call. Zach still held onto her elbow, which was a little weird, but nice. She thought about yanking her arm out of his grasp, but he was already tugging her away from the studio door.

"Come on," he said.

"I need to call my agent. Maybe I should go back to my room. I—"

He pulled her through another doorway, cut through the silent weight room, and pushed open a glass door leading onto the practice field.

A sliver of moon illuminated a thousand stars above them. Wispy clouds marked an otherwise clear sky. A slight breeze mussed his hair. He still held her elbow.

"Walk with me," he said.

"We shouldn't be doing this," Cameron told him. "I need to go upstairs and make a few calls. I'm pretty sure my contract forbids my private life being used as a plot point for a reality program. Plus, I think I should get some sleep."

He ignored the fact she was still telling him why this was the worst idea ever, and dropped her elbow long enough to hold out his arm for her to take.

"You'll sleep a little better if we take a walk."

"I'm not sure you get why this is such a disaster." She

ignored his arm and took a few steps away from him. He caught up with her.

"Of course I do. I don't need the few things I can still keep private splashed all over PSN for everyone's entertainment." He let out a sigh. "I really don't care to enthrall sports fans everywhere with the story of our marriage." His fingertips brushed the small of her back as he guided her onto the grassy practice field. It felt like an electrical charge.

"You'd wonder to yourself why anyone else would care."

The dew hadn't fallen yet. Their feet made *swish-swish* sounds as they walked in the carefully manicured grass. She breathed in clean, rain-washed air and the warm smell of recent sunshine.

She heard a snort, and the smile in his voice. "Oh, they'll care. Imagine what would happen if Erin Andrews announced she was secretly married to JJ Watt."

"The Internet would explode."

"There would be a one-hour ESPN special on the subject."

"He'd be the envy of every guy in America," Cameron mused.

Zach stopped. She wondered what was wrong, so she stopped, too.

His hand brushed hers. "Kind of like I'll be when this gets out," he said.

His eyes were hidden in shadow. She couldn't see their expression unless she got closer, and right now, getting closer was asking for it. She stifled a sigh of her own.

There were a few topics that needed discussing between them, but right now she was too freaking tired—and, too attracted to him, if she was truthful—to even have the conversation.

He was even more gorgeous than he'd been ten years ago. He'd added muscle. She could see the laugh lines bracketing his full lips and the crinkles at either side of his eyes. Maybe he'd been with someone that made him happy; he'd learned to laugh since she last saw him up-close.

Maybe she should find someone that made her happy, too.

"So," he said, "Let's start with the easy stuff." His fingertips brushed her lower back again, and she fell into step next to him. "You asked me why I left you."

Her head shot up. She opened her mouth to speak, and the phone in her pocket rang. His phone rang, too. She looked at her agent's smiling face on her phone's screen.

"Excuse me for a moment," he said. He stabbed at the button to answer his call. "Hey there," he told his caller.

He listened for a few moments. Her phone was still going off, but she sent the call to voicemail. "Well, thanks for the update. I'm in the middle of something," he said. "I'll call you back in a few minutes." He ended his call.

"What happened?" she said.

"My agent would like us to know that not only is our little secret out, they're still talking about the story on *SportsCenter*. NFL Network has it on a perma-crawl. We're also trending nationally on Twitter."

"What do we do now?"

"Hang on and enjoy the ride," he said.

ZACH'S GRAND PLAN of an evening walk and a conversation with Cameron was spoiled by two perma-ringing cell phones and her agent's hysterics. Cameron was currently trying to soothe the agent, who was screeching over speaker phone.

"Did you think this *might* be something you should have told me awhile ago? What exactly is it you're expecting me to do now?" her agent screeched.

Zach reached out to take the phone out of Cameron's hand. "Hello, this is Zach Anderson." Cameron tried to reclaim her phone. He turned away from her while he spoke. "She's much too polite to tell you what you're supposed to be doing right now, so I'll do it for her. You need to do your job. She didn't keep this to herself to inconvenience you." He let out a breath. "Call PSN's ownership and management and tell them Cameron's personal life isn't for sale. Tonight."

"You have no right to tell me what to do," the agent sputtered.

"No, I don't, but I will, and I'll keep doing it until I see some action," Zach said.

Cameron was still trying to grab the phone out of his hand. "Just a moment, Laurie," she called out.

"Let's put it this way," Zach continued. "If you'd pulled anything like this with me, I would have fired you a long time ago. You work for her, not the other way around."

Cameron had now resorted to running in little half-circles around him and trying to grab the hand holding her phone. It would be funny if he didn't see the infuriated look in her eyes.

"You have no idea what I went through to get this job for Cameron, and the clean-up I've had to do over the past week after her little outburst. Instead of handling her business off-camera, she brought everyone into it. She—"

Zach hit the button on her phone to disconnect the call. Cameron grabbed the phone out of his hand at last.

"What the hell do you think you're doing? You just hung up on my agent!"

"She'll call back," he told her.

"It doesn't matter! Why are you screwing around with my career? You can't do this. Now I'm going to have to call her back and apologize, and I'd rather avoid that." Cameron's phone was ringing again. She poked at the screen, and he heard the phone vibrating with calls as she slid it back into her pocket.

His phone was vibrating, too. He knew he was going to have to answer it at some point, but he also knew they probably had only a few minutes before all hell broke loose for both of them. He took a couple of deep breaths and glanced up at the starry sky.

"You're right. I shouldn't have gone after her, but she's not doing you a favor, Cameron. She shouldn't be treating you badly because you didn't tell her something that isn't any of her business in the first place." Cameron looked at the grass under their feet and wrapped her arms around her midsection again. "If you want me to call her back and apologize, I'll do it."

"It's nice of you to offer." Her voice was scratchy. She cleared her throat. She glanced up at him again.

"My agent wants to talk to me, too."

"Maybe they'll keep us after class and make us clean the erasers," she said.

"I always hated that when I was a kid." He let out a sigh. She shuffled her feet, and clasped her hands in front of her. The silence was broken by a male voice shouting from one of the facility's windows.

"Hey, dickweed. NFL Network just called McCoy looking for a quote. McCoy told them Cameron Online left you because you couldn't get it up. You might want to get your ass back in here."

Another voice rang out. "You're all-ESPN, all the time, dawg."

Cameron turned to look at the building. Every window on the third floor was open with at least two guys hanging out of it, and they were all laughing while heaping abuse on Zach. They must have searched every part of the building until they found him.

"You know she found out his grandma lives with him."

"She left him for Tom Brady, I heard."

"She wanted someone who could actually play, didn't she?"

He could almost see the wheels turning in her head. He knew she interviewed guys in the locker room as part of his job, but she didn't get to see what happened up close and personal when team reps and other reporters weren't around to encourage even somewhat adult behavior. If she was anything like his sisters, she was probably a little scared right now, too. He knew the guys were harmless. She didn't.

He'd walk her back to her room, and then he would deal with men who made frat boys look responsible.

A few minutes later, Zach saw Cameron to her door. The welcoming committee—otherwise known as his teammates—must have tired of their fun and gone upstairs to the game room again. She tried to yank her elbow out of his fingers a couple of times, but he resisted her efforts.

"I'll put my number in your phone. If anyone tries to mess with you, call me. I'll take care of it," he said.

"I can handle it. If I can deal with New York's locker room, this is a piece of cake," she said.

He remembered hearing that a female reporter had been harassed by a player and the coach of the team in that locker room the season before. He wondered if it had happened to her, too. He shook his head and held out his hand.

"Give me your phone."

"I don't need your number—"

"Come on, Cameron."

She shook her head and let out an irritated huff. "Fine." She dug the phone out of her pocket with her other hand. Her phone case was pink. He was a bit surprised at the yellow Lab puppy wallpaper on the smart phone's screen. He didn't know she liked dogs.

He programmed his phone number into her contacts and handed the phone back to her. "We have bed check in half an hour. I'd like to talk with you tomorrow morning if you have some time."

She fit the key into the lock and didn't answer right away.

"Cameron. You can't fight Ben and PSN alone. I'll be fighting them, too. Let's work together."

SHE TURNED TO face him. He leaned one hand on the doorjamb over her head. She watched the muscles in his forearm and his biceps bunch and flex. She wondered how many women would give almost anything to stand so close to him right now.

"It didn't go so well the last time," she said.

"There's strength in numbers, isn't there?"

She couldn't answer him. She walked inside her room and shut the door. Less than thirty seconds later, she heard the stampeding feet of grown men who were told when to go to bed by another group of grown men. She sank down on the side of her bed and pulled out her phone to take a look at the missed calls. She closed her eyes and let out a groan as she saw her father's cell phone number in the group.

This day just kept getting better and better.

ZACH PULLED THE blankets up around himself and waited for his defensive line coach to poke his head through the door and verify that yes, he was in bed for the night. He'd spent the past five minutes pounding a beer he got from the vending machine a few feet from his dorm room door and talking with his agent on the phone. His agent promised a vigorous discussion with Ben Levine of PSN about the legalities involved in broadcasting the details of someone's private life they didn't want broadcast. He also spent a few minutes trying to persuade Zach that being featured on *Third and Long* wasn't the worst thing that could possibly happen to him or his career.

"Maybe you could tell me exactly how you managed to marry Ms. Ondine in the first place. You know, when you have a few spare minutes.".

"Jason, it's not open for discussion right now."

"CBS Sports already managed to get a copy of the marriage certificate and your annulment decree." Zach stifled another groan. He'd spent the evening doing it already. "You were married for three days?"

"Yes, we were, and now, we're not."

"You're the envy of every red-blooded male in America, guy. Do you know what her family's worth?"

"Nope, and I don't care."

He should have gone to the grocery store before he moved into the dorm. There was an empty bar-sized refrigerator in his room, but it was empty. He twirled the can of a brand of light beer he wouldn't drink any other time between his fingers as he propped himself up against the headboard of the bed. They had to be kidding. He was essentially trapped here for at least another two weeks before players were allowed to leave the premises. A good microbrew—or a shot of JD—would have gone a long way toward easing his current distress.

Cameron was at the other end of the hallway. He wondered if she slept in that pink cupcake number she'd answered the door in earlier. When they'd slept together, she'd worn toenail polish, a thin gold wedding band, and that perfume she liked that drove him crazy. Then again, he would have torn whatever she wore to bed right off her. He remembered how she'd wound the sheet around herself each morning when she'd padded into the bathroom.

"We're married now," he'd called after her. "You don't need to cover up, you know."

He'd heard the soft sound of her laughter. He still remembered how it felt to watch her walk. She'd managed to be graceful even while tripping over a king-sized bed sheet. The early-morning sunshine streaming through the hotel room windows made her skin glow.

He heard a key being inserted into the lock on his dorm room door, and the door swung open. "Anderson," his coach said. "Lights out."

"Got it. Good night."

The coach pulled the door shut and moved down the hall to check on the other guys. Zach took the last swallow out of the can and dropped it into the wastepaper basket under the nightstand next to him. He could drink until he blacked out, and he'd never get the memories out of his head. He'd also never be able to forget how she looked earlier standing in the moonlight, or how it felt to hold her hand again.

She'd called her dad ten years ago to get out of what he was fairly sure she viewed as a colossal mistake, but he was stupid enough to still care for her. She wanted to know why he "left" her. In other words, she wanted to twist the knife. A little voice in the back of his head told him that the hurt on her face might not be a game, but maybe she was a really good actress.

She sure had no problem telling Ben how mad she was about the fact her private life was now up for discussion and he wanted the network to mine it for ratings, too. Things didn't quite measure up here. He wondered if she was lying awake, too, trying to figure out what happened. Maybe she thought this whole thing would enhance her career, making her even more valuable to PSN.

He hadn't actively avoided her over the years, but he didn't go out of his way to encounter her, either. Other than the typical PR stuff from the network, he really hadn't heard much about what she'd been doing with herself for the past ten years. He had heard that she went out of her way to stay single, though, and would not date a professional athlete of any sport. He played with guys he knew had tried to get to know her outside the job or had asked her out. The results were the same: She'd turned them down, politely yet firmly. She didn't involve herself in situations that could be misread, such as spending the evening before a game drinking and dancing with players. She seemed intent on being recognized as a professional.

He wondered if she ever felt the same way he did: lonely. Empty. Longing for more, even though he had more of pretty much everything than any guy his age had a right to have.

He went from hearing a stadium full of people clapping and cheering everything he did to a quiet, dark house. His sisters weren't going to sit up and rehash things with him; they had school in the morning. Things were a little better for him since he had gotten Butter the puppy, and since he'd installed his grandma in his house, but he wished he had someone who loved him waiting at home after a big game. He'd like to spend his nights holding a woman wrapped in sleep, instead of lying awake, reliving every snap of the game he'd just played. He'd think about how to improve his game on those long nights. The next morning, he'd get up and get her some coffee or something.

He wanted something more from his life and his future. All he had to do was get her.

Chapter Ten

CAMERON'S ALARM WENT off the next morning before the team's wake-up call. Her phone was already ringing, too. She wondered how she could possibly convey to the entire East Coast that they might want to check what time it was in Seattle before business calls. She picked her phone up off the nightstand and hauled herself to a sitting position, stabbing the speaker function button on the keypad a second or two after she answered.

"Good morning, Dad. How are you?"

"I'm fine. How are you doing, Cameron?"

"Things are great." She heard running feet in the hallway. There must have been a few more guys that set an alarm, too. "I'm getting ready to start my day," she said.

"About that. Would you mind telling me why I found out you are on the other side of the country for a month from my caddy?"

"Dad, I got less than twenty-four hours' notice myself—"

"Your mother is very upset. She can't believe that you wouldn't let us know you weren't here, and she was hoping you'd be joining us for a couple of weeks at the Hamptons house. She also invited a young man you'll be interested in spending more time with."

"Dad, it's nice of her to think of me, but I can't make it. I have to work."

"I know you get vacation days. Maybe you should take some time off. Your mother wants you here."

"I'm working on a big project right now."

"You're living in a dorm with eighty football players." He let out an exasperated sigh. "That's not a 'project.' I really don't like hearing all about your exploits at our club, or when I'm out on the golf course. What's it going to take to get you to quit that job and do something a bit more appropriate?"

"I'm sorry that you don't approve of my job, but I'm not quitting, Dad." She wasn't sorry at all, but telling him she wasn't would bring on an argument she didn't have time for right now.

"I've golfed with Ben Levine, you know."

He let that one hang in the air for a minute or so. In other words, he'd take matters into his own hands, and do his best to make sure Ben would either fire her outright or force her out of her job. Cameron said nothing in response. She'd had this argument with him before. It didn't help to argue in return, and logic didn't sway him. Maybe she needed to use the nuclear option: Hang up on him and send her parents a letter telling them that if they continued meddling in her personal life and her career, she would stop seeing them. Ending the call right now meant she'd have some time to think of what to do next to impress on her family that she was an adult who could make her own decisions and she did not appreciate their interference.

It was amazing that her parents were now so hyper-concerned with where she was and what she was doing. She and her sister Paige spent their childhood and teen years answering to a succession of nannies or their teachers at boarding school. People in their parents' tax bracket didn't raise their own children, and they saw their children infrequently. As a result, her parents were the last people she turned to when she needed help or encouragement of any kind.

She was also a bit amazed that her father didn't mention last night's "Zach Anderson and Cameron Ondine were married" media bonanza. Maybe every source of media at her parents' command was temporarily broken.

Maybe she should be thankful for small favors.

"Dad, I have to go. I'll talk with you later. Give my love to Mom."

"Cameron Bennett Ondine—"

She hit the button to end the call before he could sputter out anything else, and shoved herself out of bed. She'd better get dressed.

ZACH'S PHONE RANG at 5:44 AM. He grabbed it off the nightstand. After checking the caller ID, it seemed that Zach's agent Jason must have been up early with his kids this morning.

"'Zup?"

"You called me, guy," Jason said. Zach could hear the kids in the background saying something about Cheerios and cupcakes. "No, Blair, you're not having a cupcake for breakfast. Get over here and sit at the table. So, Zach, I heard Ben Levine wants to turn *Third and Long* into *The Bachelor*, starring you."

Zach resisted the impulse to use a four-letter word Jason probably didn't want his kids to use at day care later. "That's funny. I was wondering if you could possibly give him a call and let him know I don't appreciate my private life being aired on national TV."

"You've talked about your past before."

"I haven't said a word about Cameron Ondine. She's not interested in being Ben's guinea pig, either. I'm looking for contract language or some other reason why I can tell Ben I won't be participating."

"Maybe I should talk to Ms. Ondine's agent. I'm curious to know what she's telling her client. I can't think of anything in your contract that might get you out of the filming, especially since you've already agreed to participate in the show. Ms. Ondine is an employee and a public figure. In other words, she most likely has no way out of this, either."

Zach could hear Jason's German shepherd barking like someone was breaking into the house. The kids were screaming about how they *wanted a cupcake, Mama wouldn't let them have a cupcake, and they wanted a CUPCAKE!* He heard a "thump," and then Jason's wife called out, "I left you in here with the kids for five minutes, and they just dumped the gallon of milk onto the floor. What the hell?"

Jason said, "I'll call you back."

Zach dropped the phone into the blankets of his bed. Some of his teammates were married with kids. It was pretty tough to resist a two-year-old trying on Daddy's football helmet, for instance. He felt a little left out when a pint-sized version of somebody he knew would zoom out onto the practice field during Family Day to dispense some of those slurpy little kisses or call out, "Da Da." He hadn't spent a lot of time musing over whether or not he wanted a few rugrats of his own. He was too busy making sure his four sisters were happy and pursuing their own dreams. He wondered, though, what it might be like to be the opposite of his own father: There for the duration. A loving and permanent presence in the life of a child. He could be more to his own children than a collision of DNA and bad judgment.

Cameron seemed like she'd be a good mom. She was calm, patient, and fairly unflappable, unless she couldn't get a cab at 5:15 pm on a Friday night in Manhattan. He wondered if she'd encourage her daughters to be girly-girls, or play sports and never be afraid to compete in whatever they chose to do with their lives. Maybe she didn't want any kids; she seemed pretty into her career. It was tough to deal with the day-to-day at home when she traveled at least four days a week, six months a year.

He needed to get up, take care of the morning business, and get down to the practice field, but he wanted his agent to handle this crap first. He knew the smartest thing was to hold up his end of the agreement he'd struck with Cameron last night, but somehow the cold light of day made him wonder if that wasn't the best plan. Maybe he should cover his own ass first and worry about hers later.

He picked up his phone and texted Jason:

MAYBE YOU SHOULD GET ON A PLANE AND GET OUT HERE.

If it was a choice between breakfast duty for three-year-old triplets and butting heads with Sharks coaches, management, and the owner of PSN, he was fairly sure Jason would choose him.

TWO HOURS LATER, Zach was sweating from every pore during morning practice and doing whatever he had to do to stop looking at Cameron. She stood across the field from him. She wasn't sweating. She was holding a digital recorder while she talked with Damian Drake, former Sharks cornerback and now one of the Sharks' broadcast team. The sunlight bounced off her hair as she tossed it behind one shoulder. He couldn't see what she was looking at behind the large sunglasses she wore. Drake said something to Cameron that made her laugh, and Zach wanted to go over and clothesline the guy. He'd played the first couple of years with Damian. He enjoyed chatting with him, but Drake needed to find another woman to chat up in a hurry.

Cameron should laugh at stuff *he* said, dammit. Zach was so absorbed in imagining what he'd like to say to Broadcast Boy he wasn't paying attention to the QB's signals.

Clay Morrison, rookie left tackle, burst across the line two seconds after the snap and knocked him on his ass. "Rough night last night, huh?" he said.

"Fuck off," Zach said.

"Want to go again?"

Zach responded with a laugh. He was going to make Morrison wish he had never been born, at least for the next two or three minutes. Tackling during a practice was somewhat frowned upon these days, but so was blasting across the line and knocking your teammate on his ass. The QB had all Zach's attention for the next minute, and when the ball was snapped, he threw himself on Morrison.

The assistant coaches broke up the fracas that resulted. The rookie LT forgot the first rule of professional football: No matter what, rookies were always wrong. Coach Stewart made the "huddle up" motion to the team, and everyone gathered around him in a half-circle.

Zach actually liked Coach Stewart. He couldn't say that about many of the coaches he'd had since he was drafted by the Sharks. Coach was fair. He made sure he kept his constructive criticism of different players and their skill sets inside the locker or meeting rooms, and he was young and fit enough to be able to run drills with them. The vets respected him for actually asking what they thought about the Sharks' upcoming opponents.

Most of all, he didn't treat his players like something he'd scraped off the bottom of his shoe, which meant they would play hard for him. Zach was also fairly sure that the former head coach's days were numbered even before yesterday's ill-advised comments. In other words, he'd given the Sharks' ownership and front office administration a convenient excuse.

"Men, I'm planning on meeting with your position coaches this afternoon, but first of all, I'd like to spend some time talking with all of you. I'd like to know what you think is working on this team, what isn't, and why." He held up a hand, palm out. "Of course, our meeting is private. Our guests from the media will be taken to an alternate activity they will enjoy this afternoon. I would appreciate honesty from all of you, and I will offer it as well." He looked into the eyes of the men surrounding him. "From now on, the finger-pointing and BS is over. We've lost as a team, but we will win as a team. I love winning. I'll bet you do, too, and we're going to do a hell of a lot more of it from now on." He took a look at his iPad. "We'll finish up here after a few more drills, and then we'll go into meetings." He reached out a hand. Eighty other guys reached out their hands, too, shouting "Sharks!"

It was, officially, the first team meeting that didn't put anyone to sleep. It was also the first team meeting in which Zach could remember a head coach telling the group that as of today, nobody's job was safe, including his own. The former head coach would have stirred anger and resistance with anything similar. So far, all Zach heard was occasional rustling when a large body shifted position in the chair, or the sound of a plastic water bottle being set back down on a tabletop after someone took a sip.

Everyone on the team would be competing for his position, starting right now. There was no time to coast or dog it during practice, even for the All-Pros. Zach glanced around at the shocked faces of his teammates. Maybe they thought the new head coach would go easy on them because he was a fill-in, or because he believed the Sharks would soon bring in someone more experienced. Even more surprising, the new head coach watched and listened as, one by one, his teammates spoke up about the fact they wanted change, too. They were embarrassed by last season's ten losses. They were tired of being confronted by Sharks fans when they went to the grocery store or out to dinner over the fact they didn't try harder or seem to care what those fans thought.

"My girlfriend said someone let her have it at the doctor's office the other day," Derrick said. "They were bitching to her about how they didn't spend five thousand dollars for Sharks season tickets to watch a six-and-ten team. I don't like coming home to a woman who's grilling me, too."

"I had a couple of fans follow me home from OTAs last month," Drew McCoy said. The big blond linebacker passed one hand over his face in frustration. "They came up to the door and wanted to know why I thought I was worth ten million dollars last season when we're playing like shit."

"You answered the door? What the hell? Call the cops," Tom Reed, the Sharks' All-Pro QB, advised.

"I called them. I called NFL security, too. I'm thinking I might have to move. My parents were visiting. It scared the hell out of my mom."

The room fell silent again for a few minutes. Zach had had a few encounters with drunken or belligerent fans over the years, but he'd installed the best security system money could buy when he bought the house he and his family lived in. It kept out anyone who wasn't invited.

One by one, team leaders stood up from their chairs and spoke: They wanted more than a taste of the postseason, and they really wanted another Super Bowl ring. The suspicion and defensiveness on the faces of guys he'd played with for years morphed into excitement.

Zach was quiet until Clay Morrison turned to look at him. "So, Anderson, that includes you, too. If you're not in, you're out, and you'd better spend a lot more time busting ass on the field than looking at hers." He continued to be pretty mouthy for a rookie.

"What the hell are you talking about?"

"You know what I'm talking about. You were staring at her yesterday, too." The entire room erupted into gales of laughter at his words. Zach glared at him.

The whistles and stamping feet of grown men taunting Zach echoed off the walls.

"Did she turn you down, brah?" A running back who'd just announced to the entire team he was in pursuit of Adrian Peterson's league-best rushing title grinned at Zach. The gold tooth in the front of his mouth sparkled.

"She wants me. Did you know that?" the kicker joked.

"Cameron Online isn't dating anyone as big and ugly as you, dawg." Derrick said.

The new coach held up his hands to quiet the players. "Guys. Settle down." He glanced over at Zach. "I understand Ms. Ondine is quite a distraction, Anderson, but you're going to have to keep your head in the game while we're here." He gave Zach a nod. "Speaking of Ms. Ondine, she's a member of the media, and an influential one. I'm sure you'll agree it's important she has a good impression of the Sharks organization. She will be treated with respect. If she asks to interview one or more of you, you will cooperate, and you will behave as you would with any other media professional toward her at all times. Is that clear?" Eighty guys nodded. "Okay. We'll meet again later, but right now let's grab some lunch. Anderson, please see me before you leave."

"You've been with this team eleven years," the coach said when everyone but Zach had filed out of the room. "I need to know that you are stepping it up this season. You didn't bring your best last year."

Zach was nodding before he even stopped speaking. "I am giving it a hundred percent every day. I plan on staying with the Sharks for the rest of my career."

"Great. We'd like to have you here. Don't slack off. If I see you ignoring what's going on in front of you again because you're staring at Ms. Ondine, I'll bench you." The coach got to his feet. Zach rose from his seat, too. "I understand the two of you have previous history, but we are here to work. I also heard about PSN's turning *Third and*

Long into a romantic comedy. Mr. Levine has been told as of this morning there will not be significant disruptions or distractions to the team, or he'll be dealing with me." The coach extended his hand to Zach. "You're a leader, Anderson. I'm counting on you to be an example for the other knuckleheads."

Zach shook his hand. "I'll do my best."

CAMERON WAS WHISKED away from the Sharks' training camp on a tour bus with the fifty other media members in attendance that afternoon. There was more than a little grumbling when the press was told training camp was closed to them until further notice, but the fact it was sunny and eighty-five degrees in Seattle went a long way toward smoothing things over. Kacee sat across the aisle from her, playing a game on her phone. Logan was responding to e-mail on his iPad and attempting to talk with Kacee, who ignored him.

"So, where are we off to?" the guy from CBS Sports called out.

"The Sharks would like to treat our media partners to lunch and a sail around Puget Sound. We'll be back in plenty of time for bed check, Ms. Ondine," the tour guide joked. Cameron resisted the impulse to grind her teeth. The guys thought it was hilarious she was stuck in a dorm, while they enjoyed the hospitality (and much better amenities) of a local hotel.

She'd heard the team was having a meeting all afternoon and the press was not invited, but taking them off campus while the meeting happened was a little extreme. Her colleague, Kevin, tried to wheedle his way into the meeting room and had been escorted onto the bus by two of the Sharks' coaching staff. In other words, whoever found out what was said in their absence was going to have one hell of a scoop. She was on a dorm floor with twenty Sharks veterans. If there was one thing she'd learned from being in this business for the past ten years, it was the fact there was always one guy who couldn't wait to be an uncredited "source" for stories about any team in the league. She had to find him before Kevin or her other colleagues did, and she'd better come up with a strategy to do so before she arrived back at the dorm.

She pulled out her iPad. Maybe she could review production notes for the next episode of *NFL Confidential* for a little while as the bus traveled to wherever it was they were having lunch. She saw new e-mails, so she clicked over there.

The first e-mail was from Zach: I HAVE NEWS FOR YOU. PLEASE SEE ME ASAP.

She shook her head, and realized that Kacee was staring at her.

"What's wrong, Cameron?"

"Nothing. Everything is fine."

She clicked onto the next e-mail, which was from her father. YOUR MOTHER AND I ARE SENDING THE JET FOR YOU THIS WEEKEND. YOU NEED SOME TIME OFF. THE PILOT WILL BE AT BOEING FIELD IN SEATTLE AT 8 AM ON SATURDAY MORN-

ING TO FLY YOU HOME. DON'T DISAPPOINT US, CAMERON.

She resisted the impulse to groan aloud. If she wasn't on the plane and wheels-up by 8:15, her father would most likely either show up himself sometime next week or send one of his Pacific Northwest-based golf buddies over to make sure she was "okay." She realized there were many people whose parents didn't care what they did, and they would welcome having parents who interfered in their lives to this degree, but she was tired of it.

Her phone chirped with an incoming text. She pulled it out of her pocket. Of course it was Ben. WHERE THE HELL ARE YOU, KACEE, AND LOGAN? WE HAVE FILMING TO DO. He must have somehow escaped the all-media dragnet at the Sharks' headquarters, and now he was pissed because he had nothing else to do besides go to the pub and let that waitress harass him some more.

She resisted the impulse to bang her head on the nearest hard surface until she lost consciousness. She heard Kacee and Logan's phones going off, too. She glanced over at them. "Ben, right?"

"Of course," Logan said. "How did he get away from the Sharks PR folks?"

Kacee's fingers flew across the keys as she responded. A few seconds later, she got up and headed toward the bus' bathroom.

"He's probably still at the hotel," Cameron said. "What's with Kacee?"

"She told me earlier it's not going well between her and the latest Wall Street frat boy she's been seeing. She's probably texting with him. He's mad because she's not back in New York yet."

Everyone else on the bus was too busy talking to each other or using the free Wi-Fi to be listening to them. Cameron leaned across the aisle.

"When are you going to ask her out, you big dork?"

He raised an eyebrow and leaned across Kacee's seat to hiss, "I'll be happy to do that, right after you have a dinner date with Zach Anderson."

"Excuse me?"

"I'm really not into having her crush me like a bug, Cam. She's made it clear I'm not her type." The typically easygoing Logan folded his lips and shook his head. "She goes for guys who couldn't care less about her, and I seem to gravitate toward women who have no interest in me whatsoever." He rolled his eyes and tried a grin. "Imagine how it feels to know I'm not irresistible."

She had to laugh a little, and she heard Logan snort-laugh, too. He was as lonely as she was, but he was a lot more willing to joke around about it. He also was doing his best to find someone and fall in love. She loved spending time with Logan, but he was a friend and always would be. There wasn't a spark between them. There never would be. Logan was the kind of guy who showed up at your apartment after your latest break-up toting Ben & Jerry's and a couple of six-packs. She'd showed up at his place before, too. She was fairly sure his single male neighbors were still talking about it, because Logan told her that maybe next time, he should stop by her place instead for her safety.

He lived in a city with millions of single women. It was only a matter of time until he met the right one, but she wondered for the hundredth time now if he'd be interested in her sorority sister, Angela. Cameron was gone four days a week for six months out of the year, and Angela apartment-sat for her on those days. Maybe she should introduce them.

She leaned closer to Logan. Kacee was still gone; she must be having a confidential phone conversation in the bathroom. "I pick the wrong ones, too."

"He wasn't the wrong one," Logan said.

Cameron glanced down the bus aisle. Kacee had taken a seat in the back of the bus, and looked like she was still texting. She got up and plunked herself down next to Logan.

Her voice dropped to a little over a whisper. She didn't need the entire sports media group to overhear what she had to say. "You don't know him. He left me, Logan. He walked out of the hotel room, and he didn't even say goodbye. Do you know how that felt? We were married a grand total of three days. Plus, he took five million dollars from my dad to sign the annulment paperwork." She wondered if Zach would have taken less money to get away from her after all, and how long he had bargained with her dad. Four million? One million and tech stocks? How about a hundred bucks and a case of beer? She felt the stab of anger and hurt in her chest again.

Logan looked a little shocked. "That can't be true."

"Oh, it is."

"So, why's he trying to talk to you again?"

"Maybe he wants more money."

"He's got plenty of his own," Logan said.

Zach evidently needed more. She still remembered how mad her dad was, talking about that five million dollar cashier's check. Her dad didn't seem to care how much it hurt her every time he brought it up, either.

"Why are you sticking up for him?"

Logan thought for a few seconds. "I saw the look on his face when you asked him why he left you. That wasn't 'Wow, I'll get my hands on more money.' That was 'I'm still in love with her and I don't care who sees it.'"

Cameron shook her head. She didn't remember that look on Zach's face at all. She remembered how sick she felt when she realized she'd blurted out a secret she'd kept for ten years in front of a group of colleagues, however.

"Let's talk about something else, Logan. We had the interview with Zach, now we need to catch up with the head coach. Maybe we can brainstorm some questions for him, huh?" She positioned her iPad to take a few notes but Logan's comments were still ringing in her ears. If anyone would know if another guy was lovelorn, it was Logan.

Maybe it was time to lay all the cards on the table with a certain Seattle Shark.

ZACH HAD SOME lunch with his teammates, did some lifting, and went to a defensive line meeting. He had a couple of hours before dinner. Cameron and the rest of the press still weren't back. After a lot of thought and after talking one of his non-football-playing buddies into running an errand for him, he had a plan for later, as long as she arrived back at least an hour before bed check.

He'd told her over text message he had things to discuss with her. He did, but they weren't what she thought. He'd talk to her a little about the taping. Jason was still fairly convinced that there was no way either of them could avoid the broadcast of their personal struggles, but they had one ace in the hole: They could talk all they wanted when everyone else was absorbed in other things.

The Sharks' chef showed him how to use one of the ovens in the kitchen. His buddy picked him up a couple of add-water-only brownie mixes, some chocolate sauce, a candle in a jar, and some whipped cream in the can from the grocery store and dropped it off at the dorm. Zach could create a candlelight dessert for two and get a few minutes alone with her.

He'd also checked out his plan with his youngest sister, who didn't laugh. She said, "Please tell me this isn't for Cameron."

"I can't tell you that, Whitney."

"She broke your heart, Zach. She hurt you so much, and you know what her dad did to all of us. Why are you talking to her at all? I don't understand."

His sisters were staying at his house this summer with their grandma and his dog. He heard his puppy, Butter, barking in the background. Someone must have passed within a one-mile radius of his front door. What Butter lacked in menace, he made up for with gusto. He'd probably lick the potential axe murderer walking through Zach's neighborhood to death before he actually tried to bite him.

"It's not what you think. I won't let her hurt me this time." It was a good thing his nose didn't grow like Pinocchio's when he told a lie. It would stretch across the football field right now. "We're just talking about the reality show and her coverage of training camp."

"I really wish you wouldn't talk to her at all."

"I know you do. What else is happening there?"

"We're cleaning up after dinner. Grandma is watching *Jeopardy!*" He could hear her smiling on the other end of the phone. "Remember when I got put on the waitlist at the University of Washington? They sent me an admissions packet yesterday." She sucked in some air. "I'm in."

"Congratulations! Are you excited?"

"Yeah," she said. She let out a breath. "Zach, I applied for a couple of on-campus jobs today. I have to live in the dorm for my freshman year."

There was an instant lump in his throat. "You don't have to get a job if you're taking a heavy class load. There's plenty of money to pay for your tuition."

"But Shelby, Ashley, and Courtney are all in school, and you don't have unlimited money . . ."

"I'll be fine. There's more than enough for you, too. You fill out that paperwork and send it back right away. When do you need to be on campus?"

"The end of September. Zach, maybe I should work for a year and then go to—"

"No," he said. "Money's not an object, sweetie. How do you feel about living on campus?"

"I'd rather live with all of you. I don't want to leave home."

"You'll have so much fun you won't even miss us," he assured her. "The school year will go fast, and you'll meet lots of great people. We can talk more about this when I'm off for a day or so, but I want you to start filling out that packet tonight."

"Got it," she said.

He could hear the excitement in her voice, tinged with the fear they all still carried around. She didn't want to end up in that trailer park again, either, even if she didn't remember it well. He couldn't believe she wasn't off at the mall already figuring out what she needed to buy to go to school or calling some of her friends to trumpet her good news. She wouldn't, though. She'd be asking his sisters and his grandma questions about what she should expect. Mostly, she'd be freaking out about money. He had plenty now, but his sisters still worried about it.

The best part of playing in the NFL was the fact he could single-handedly make sure his sisters didn't end up broke, drug addicted, and staying with a deadbeat because they didn't have any other options in life. It wasn't a question as to whether or not they'd graduate from college: They were going if he had to drive them over and sign the paperwork himself. He'd make sure they finished school, too, if it was the last thing he did in life.

His eldest sister, Shelby, was in grad school. She was working toward becoming a psychologist. It was her way of helping others with the same trauma they had dealt with growing up. His middle sisters, Ashley and Courtney, had chosen the medical field—Ashley was in school to be a nurse, and Courtney was studying to be an emergency room doctor. They hoped to work with children, so he was guessing their majors might change before they were done with school. His youngest sister, Whitney, was sensitive and artistic. He had a feeling she wanted a Master of Fine Arts degree but she was talking about majoring in computer science, of all things.

"I'm so proud of you, Whitney."

"I'm proud of you, too, Zach."

She might tease him a little, but when he got home for a day off, he knew she'd be the first one at the door to wrap her arms around his waist and tell him she missed him while he was gone.

He knew if he played hard for the Sharks and stayed out of trouble off the field, his family's lives would all be better. It was the thing that drove him. His little sis would never know how much it meant for him that they were all okay.

"Tell everyone I love them. I'll call you tomorrow. But you text me if you need help with the paperwork," he said.

They hung up, and he dropped his phone into the blankets on his bed. He picked it up again, and hit "redial" on Jason's number. It was almost ten on the East Coast. He knew Jason was probably catching up on work he didn't get done while he was chasing his three-year-olds.

Zach's call went to voicemail.

"Hey, Jason, Whitney's starting at the UW in a month.

Didn't you tell me there was another endorsement you were going after? Call me."

CAMERON DRAGGED HERSELF up three flights of stairs to her dorm room after eating a shocking amount of seafood and drinking a few mojitos, thanks to the Sharks PR department. She couldn't believe the ship they saw the sights of Puget Sound from didn't capsize from all the food and alcohol, either. She wasn't hungry for dinner at all. Maybe that was a good thing.

She could take a shower, answer some more e-mail, and go to bed. She still hadn't figured out what she was going to say to her father besides "Please don't fly anyone out here to get me." She yanked open the heavy fire door that opened onto the third floor, and stopped in the doorway.

Zach's room was twenty feet ahead, and his door was open. There was no way she could walk by his room without him seeing her. She wasn't exactly in the mood for a heart-to-heart at the moment. Maybe she could tiptoe past.

She turned to let the door close slowly against her back. If she could keep the door from latching—

CLICK.

Zach poked his head out of his room. "There you are."

Damn. She resisted the impulse to run to her room and slam the door.

"How was your afternoon on the high seas?" he asked.

She wondered if he'd asked someone where she was, or figured it out on his own. This, of course, made her remember Logan's comments, too. Why would Zach care where she was at all?

"It was fine. I'm pretty tired. I think I'll go to bed." She pivoted on one foot and tried to move past him. He reached out and caught her elbow in his fingertips. His grip was gentle, but it was there.

"I have a surprise for you."

"Maybe tomorrow," she said. "I really need to get some sleep."

"If we go now, you won't have to share with the rest of the guys. C'mon."

"Share what?"

He patted his warm-ups pocket with his other hand, most likely checking to see that he had his room key. He closed the door to his room as well. He moved her back toward the door to the stairs, pushed it open for them, and walked her down the stairs.

"I think you'll like this," he said.

"Where are you taking me? Don't you have bed check pretty soon?"

"Not for another couple of hours."

He opened the door on the second floor for her, and they moved down the dim hallway toward the open cafeteria. The Sharks front office staff was gone for the evening. The players didn't spend a lot of time in this part of the building, but Zach seemed to know how to use it for a shortcut to wherever it was he was taking her. The only noise they heard was some distant laughter and talking from the game room upstairs.

Zach's fingertips brushed the small of her back. "Let's

go in here for a minute." He gestured toward the commercial kitchen. She angled her body so he couldn't touch her again, but she felt it all the same. *Zzzap.* It had nothing to do with static electricity, and everything to do with the fact they were alone in a darkened building.

"What are you doing?"

"Making a little dessert. Want to help?" he said.

She shook her head. "I ate so much food on that cruise . . ."

He broke out in a grin. "I've been told there isn't a woman on the planet that can resist freshly baked brownies with chocolate sauce and whipped cream." He pulled a couple of add-water-and-bake brownie mixes, a jar of chocolate sauce, and a candle out of a grocery bag. He must have refrigerated the whipped cream—at least, she hoped he did.

"You're going to make me some brownies?"

"I'm making myself some brownies. I'm asking you to share them with me."

"I shouldn't be eating them," she said. "I thought you had something you wanted to talk with me about."

"I do," he said. "How about helping me mix these up while I make sure nobody made off with my can of whipped cream?"

She was a little surprised to see he knew how to preheat an oven. He moved around the kitchen like he knew what he was doing, too. She watched him measure some water, pull a wooden spoon and a metal spatula out of the drawer by the stove, and retrieve a couple of hot mats.

He pushed the measuring cup of water and the paper "pan" of brownie mix toward her.

"Okay, but I'm not eating any."

"We'll see about that." A few minutes later, the brownies were in the oven. He'd located his untouched can of whipped cream, let the jar of chocolate heat to room temperature, and showed her to one of the tables in the cafeteria. "I'll be right back," he said.

He dashed into the kitchen and reemerged a minute or so later with the lit jar candle, which he placed in the middle of their table.

"*Now* we can have a chat." He dropped into the chair across from her and pulled out his smart phone. "I have a timer on here, so we won't burn the dessert." He put the phone on the table face-up. "I thought this might give us a little privacy for a conversation."

"We could have talked in the lobby!"

"And anyone could have walked in on us, too," he said. "The guys don't usually hang around in here at night because there's food available upstairs." She shook her head, but she knew he was right. Dammit. "I had a long talk with my agent today, and he had a chat with yours before he called me."

"Your agent talked to my—why?"

"We're trying to present a united front here. Jason told me we're pretty much screwed. You work for them. I agreed to participate in the program. The production group can make up almost any story line they want, and there's not a lot we can do about it. There is one thing we can control, though."

"What's that?"

"Access and content. If we're not giving them anything juicy to tape, they're not going to have much to work with. It's up to you, but I think we tell them they can have all the access they want. We'll tell them we're cooperating. At the same time, we'll need to make an arrangement while we're here."

She didn't like how that sounded at all. He leaned over the table toward her. Their candlelit table for two was an oasis in the dimness of the huge cafeteria, and her heart rate picked up a little. She could see the twinkling lights of boats bobbing around on the lake outside of the facility. It was surprisingly romantic for the most inexpensive date she'd been on in her life.

Date? Oh, no. Not a date. What was she thinking? He was still the guy who'd left her, and he didn't even have the courtesy to tell her why.

He reached out and patted her hand with his much bigger and warmer one. "You and I seem to rub each other the wrong way."

She was shaking her head before he even finished his sentence. "No, we don't. That's not true. I stopped thinking about you a long time ago—"

"That's why you went after me like a pit bull on a porterhouse the last time we saw each other, huh?"

"You took my cab."

"You took *my* cab." The timer on his phone went off, and he let out a long sigh. "Let me go get the stuff, and I'll be right back."

A few minutes later, he returned to the table with two

bowls full of freshly-baked brownies, laced with chocolate sauce, and the can of whipped cream tucked under one arm.

"I told you I shouldn't be eating this," Cameron said.

"Just a few bites." He held the can of whipped cream over his forearm like a waiter displaying a rare bottle of wine. "Want some?"

She was going to have to invade the team's weight room tomorrow or go for a long run, but the warm brownie and chocolate sauce smelled like the best thing ever. She gave him a nod.

He squirted some whipped cream on her dessert, and a little on the back of her hand, too.

"What was *that*?"

"A little extra."

She reached out and took the can away from him. "I'll give you some extra," she told him.

"Ooh. I'm scared."

She reached out and squirted some whipped cream on his bowlful of brownies, and squirted a little on the end of his nose. He wiped it off with one finger, sticking his finger into his mouth. He also reached out to grab the can again. She put it behind her back.

"Oh, I see. Playing hard to get."

"No. I just want to make sure there's some left in case I want some—Zach!" He dodged around the table and disarmed her with shocking speed.

"Game's over. Eat up, Cameron."

She took a bite of the dessert, and almost moaned out loud. She hadn't eaten junk food in a long time, so fresh-out-of-the-oven boxed brownies were heaven in a bowl to her. She closed her eyes as the chocolate melted on her tongue. Nobody knew she was hungry all the time now—even a weight gain of a pound or so showed up on camera, and she'd hear about it from those who watched PSN. It really wasn't their business. She worked in a profession that demanded female perfection, though, and she'd learned it was easier to avoid foods that caused her to gain weight.

Tonight, though, she wanted to dive face-first into the bowl.

Zach took a couple of bites, too, and rested his spoon inside the bowl. "As I was saying before we got into our latest spat, we're going to have to figure out how to at least be friendly toward each other. If we don't give them anything to blow out of proportion, they'll get bored and go tape some of the other guys, or concern themselves with our new coach or something."

"You were just as responsible as I was for the *latest spat*—"

He glanced at his phone. "We have an hour before I have to be in my room for the night. Maybe we should spend the time trying to figure out how we're going to spend the next twenty-eight days together, instead of sniping at each other. What do you think about that?"

Chapter Eleven

CAMERON SHOVED THE half-eaten bowl of brownies, chocolate sauce, and whipped cream away from her before she ate every last bit, and whatever was left over in Zach's bowl, too. The dessert was delicious, but she was looking for any distraction from her current circumstance: She was alone in a dimly-lit cafeteria with Zach, the man she could never seem to forget, and he was on a mission. She felt a little jittery, and it had nothing to do with the sugar and caffeine content of the dessert.

She was getting the truth, and there was no time like the present to start asking questions. She hauled breath into her lungs.

"I asked you a question the other day. You still haven't answered it."

He forked up another bite of dessert. His words were a bit muffled. "What are you talking about?"

She clasped both hands together in her lap. "Why did

you leave me, Zach? You walked out of our hotel room that day, and I never heard from you again until I ran into you on the street in New York. I called your cell phone. I left messages at Sharks headquarters for you. You ignored all of it. Why do you think I should just forget about that and pretend like everything between us is great?"

"I didn't leave you."

"You were on your way to the hotel gift shop, you said, but you never came back. I was so freaked out I called my parents and asked if I should file a missing persons report. Imagine how shocked I was to learn that you'd already signed the annulment paperwork, you'd taken five million dollars from my dad, and you were on your way back to Virginia." She'd thought she'd cried her last tears over Zach Anderson, but maybe not. She blinked them back. Again. "You couldn't even call me and say, 'Hey, Cameron, it's not working for me. I gotta go'?"

He leaned over the table. "I didn't leave you. I was ambushed in the hallway outside of our room by your dad, his attorney, and four guys from hotel security, who forced me into another room."

Her mouth dropped open in shock. "That can't be true—"

"It is. Your dad told me you'd called him and said you'd married me against your will. He'd obtained a restraining order against me before he left for Las Vegas. He told me that if I left quietly and agreed not to contact you again, he wouldn't have me arrested. He told me that his attorney had already talked to the five teams most likely to draft me. They told him they weren't interested in any player that had a criminal record, which is exactly what I would have ended up with if I tried to contact you again."

Cameron was shaking her head. "I called to tell him we were married and I wasn't coming back to New York. I said nothing about 'against my will.' I told him I was happy, and I wanted to stay with you."

His eyebrows shot up. "When did this happen?"

"You were in the shower the morning after we got married. I knew I didn't want to go back. I wanted to stay with you."

Zach's eyes flashed with anger. "Well, then, it was one hell of a misunderstanding. I might also mention that your dad told me the other thing he was planning on doing was having my younger sisters removed from my care and sent to foster homes. He said a twenty-two year old college student wasn't a fit parent for four young girls."

She closed her eyes. She wanted to tell Zach he was a liar and she wouldn't sit here and listen to him malign her dad, but she knew better. Her dad mowed down anything in his way. He always had. She should have known that the concern her dad exhibited when he arrived to fly her back to New York was an act. Zach was just one more impediment in his plans for Cameron's future.

Her father would die before he'd let his daughter stay with a guy who grew up in a trailer park. Zach had graduated from a very good college, but it wasn't Ivy League. She couldn't imagine him at her parents' country club, or attending the Metropolitan Opera's opening night. It was a large part of the reason why she'd married him less than eight hours after they met: For once in her life, she could forget excruciatingly correct etiquette and attire at the boring social functions her parents insisted she attend and spend her time with a man who found joy in things like eating pancakes in the wee hours of the morning at a diner.

"My dad is not the nicest guy, but his story doesn't mesh with yours," she said. "He told me you demanded five million dollars to sign the annulment paperwork."

Zach pursed his lips. "That's interesting, Cameron. He offered me a cashier's check, which I tore up in front of him." She regarded him in shock. "I signed his annulment paperwork. He told me that he wanted me to sign a non-disclosure, and I tore that up in front of him, too." He leaned over the table a bit. "I flew home, got my sisters and our grandma, packed what little we could, and drove to Seattle." He stared into her eyes. "I wasn't sure I could outrun your dad's goon squad, but I was sure as hell going to try. My sisters didn't need any more upheaval and trauma." He shoved away his empty bowl. "My littlest sister finally stopped having nightmares about being taken away from us a couple of years ago. She's been accepted to the University of Washington, but she told me last night on the phone she doesn't want to leave us. Gosh, I wonder why."

"My dad wouldn't have gone through with it . . ." she sputtered.

"Maybe you should ask the Sharks about it, Cameron. The general manager told me shortly after I signed with the team I had a very powerful enemy, and they almost didn't draft me over the existing restraining order your dad had filed."

She felt sick to her stomach. "You're joking."

"The team's attorney found another attorney who managed to have the restraining order lifted, but it took a couple of years. I had to have permission from the court to enter New York to play games while it was in force since you were living there, too. Did you think it was a coincidence that I didn't play the days you were doing sideline reporting with PSN at a Sharks game for a couple of years?"

"I—I just thought you didn't want to run into me—"

"It's a good thing the team could handle the problem quietly and internally. Most teams get rid of guys with any hint of problems with the law. Guys who have restraining orders don't get endorsements, either. I didn't do anything wrong, but I wonder to this day how the hell your dad got a judge to sign off on that. The team also had an investigator who verified that there was no criminal wrongdoing in the first place." He let out a long breath. "Imagine what would have happened to my family if I wasn't able to make a living."

The impulse to defend a family member was swept away in the uncomfortable, hot flood of guilt and embarrassment that washed over her. If Zach was telling the truth, there was no defense for her father's actions toward him and his family.

"Where are your parents?"

"We never got to that while we talked the night away before our wedding, did we?" He clasped his hands on the tabletop. "My parents were out of the picture. I never met my dad. My mother died of a drug overdose when I was sixteen. My four younger sisters have three different fathers who signed over their parental rights so they wouldn't have to pay child support. The girls were too little to know the difference." He leaned back in his chair.

She couldn't believe how calm and unemotional he was about a situation that would bring most sixteen-year-olds to their knees.

"We'd be a big hit on Maury Povich, wouldn't we?" he said.

Cameron gaped at him as everything he'd told her sank in. Her father had made Zach's life a living hell when he'd done nothing to deserve it. She knew many NFL stars came out of significantly underprivileged backgrounds, but this was insane. She couldn't imagine how he'd managed to keep his family together on his own, either. He couldn't work while he was playing college football, so he and his sisters must have lived on almost nothing for years.

"How did you all survive?"

"Our grandma lived with us after Mom died. The girls got Social Security benefits because our mom had passed away, and Grandma had a little bit of a pension. Keeping up with my sisters was tough for her, but she managed to do it until I could take over." She saw his mouth twitch. "It sure wasn't filet mignon and *pommes frites* at our house for dinner. There was lots of Top Ramen, peanut butter sandwiches, and macaroni and cheese from a box, but it kept them fed, and I was grateful. A couple of the alumni pointed us toward some help with clothes, shoes, utility bills, stuff like that. It was a good feeling to make enough money so I could handle it myself."

She still wavered between a kernel of disbelief that her father would go to the extent Zach claimed he had, and feeling the most intense humiliation she could remember. Her father had attempted to destroy Zach's life and his immediate family because Cameron married him on a whim. Her attempt to gain some freedom from her meddling, overbearing parents had almost ended in tragedy for six people who had nothing to do with her family problems.

She reached out to lay one hand over his. He covered her small hand with his bigger, rougher one. She bowed her head. For someone who made a living by talking, she was fresh out of anything besides an abject apology. She also resisted the impulse to pick up her phone and call her father on the spot. There would be time for that after Zach went to bed. She had a feeling it was going to be a long and very unpleasant conversation, and she would prefer to have it behind a locked door.

"So, Cameron, to make a long story short, I didn't leave you. I'm sorry I could never tell you why I didn't come back to our room. I wasn't sure if your family ever told you what happened."

"Oh, they told me something, but evidently it wasn't the truth." She looked up into his eyes. "I'm the one who owes you and your family an apology, not the other way around."

"I thought you called your dad to rescue you, and I was pretty upset at the time. It took a while, but I finally realized I wasn't quite what they had in mind for you." The candle in front of them flickered as he spoke. "I thought you'd marry someone else and I'd never see you again."

She could tell him she'd never forgotten him, no matter who she went out with or how attracted she might be to another guy. She could tell him that she'd let her job take over instead of dating the guys her parents threw in her path, too. She didn't want any of the men her parents approved of because their lives were dominated by social climbing or the fact they wanted her family's fortune, not her. She'd spent the past ten years wondering if the little glimpse of Zach she'd had during their three days together was everything she believed him to be. They'd spent most of those seventy-two hours in bed. Maybe the cold light of day, and living together for a longer period of time, would bring the same shock and dismay a bucket of ice water might provide.

Maybe the cold light of day would have shown she'd made the right decision, and she could be happy for a lifetime with a man who'd already proven he wasn't afraid to take a risk.

When training camp was over, he'd walk out of her life again without a second thought. She had twenty-eight days to get to know him, and to show him she was her own woman now. She had those same twenty-eight days to try to make amends to him and his family for what her father had allegedly—and she was fairly sure he wouldn't admit to it anyway—done to them.

She also had twenty-eight days to see if her feelings were more than a whim.

"I didn't marry anyone else," she said. His hand tightened slightly over hers. "I was afraid he might leave me, too." She heaved a sigh. "Maybe I wasn't enough."

"Not true," Zach said as he shook his head vigorously. Heavy footsteps sounded behind him.

"I've been looking everywhere for you, honey," Drew McCoy called out to Zach. He walked up to the table, grabbed the can of whipped cream, and shot some into his mouth. "It's bedtime."

DREW HELPED ZACH and Cameron load the few utensils and bowls Zach had used for their dessert into the dishwasher. Drew and Zach had fifteen minutes to make it back to their rooms before they would be fined one hundred dollars a minute. The trip through the Sharks' administrative floor to the stairway was accomplished at a sprint. Cameron wasn't out of shape, but she couldn't hope to keep up with a couple of pro athletes. Drew stopped at the doorway to the stairs and motioned for her to hop onto his back.

"Piggy back ride up the stairs," he said. "More cardio for me."

Zach turned halfway up the first flight of stairs to glare at him. Drew didn't seem to care. He squatted a little until Cameron threw her arms around him from behind, and he hoisted her up onto his back. She tried to avoid pulling on his long blond ponytail as they went.

She hadn't had a piggy back ride since she was a kid, but she was a little surprised at how fast he climbed the stairs while carrying someone else. He threw open the fire door, swung her onto her feet, and said, "We'll make it if we run."

She glanced over at Zach. "Good night," she said. "Thank you for the dessert."

He gave her a nod. "Good night," he said.

Drew grabbed her arm. "You can visit with each other tomorrow. Come on."

A minute or so later, she was in her room again, and she heard Drew's voice through the door. "Good night, Cameron."

"Thanks for the ride," she called out. She heard him laugh, and the hallway was quiet again. Two minutes later, she heard the *slam* of the fire door, followed by male voices, as the coaching staff went from room to room.

It was two am in New York City. No matter how angry and embarrassed she was at what Zach had told her, she wasn't going to be able to talk with her father until tomorrow morning. She threw herself down on the bed with a groan and willed her heart rate to slow a little. She didn't think she was going to be able to sleep at all, and she didn't have time for insomnia.

She shoved herself off the bed, washed her face, brushed her teeth, and scrambled into a pair of pajamas. She knew she needed to tape the latest episode of *NFL Confidential* tomorrow, and she and Zach weren't done with their conversation. He'd done a remarkable job of shielding his family from the press. Most NFL teams' PR departments would kill to highlight such a tragic but triumphant story on their broadcasts, but he evidently valued his sisters' and grandmother's privacy enough not to subject them to it. She certainly wouldn't report the story, even though doing so would give her a huge boost with PSN. It would make things worse for Zach. He'd suffered enough.

She grabbed her iPad off its charger and made a quick check of some of the more prominent sports-related websites. She saw reports of the Sharks' "players only" meeting this afternoon, but nobody seemed to have any quotes on what was discussed. Maybe she should try asking Drew McCoy, otherwise known as her closest dorm neighbor, what happened. He'd either blow her off, or point her toward whoever on the team was known to be a Chatty Cathy.

Cameron texted her dad's smart phone: I HAVE TO WORK THIS WEEKEND. DON'T SEND THE PLANE. I'LL SEE YOU AND MOM SOON. She sat down in the desk chair and tapped on the screen of her iPad, preparing to do a little research, but she couldn't concentrate on work. She kept seeing the look on Zach's face as he told her what had really happened ten years ago, which was not what she'd been led to believe. The brownies she'd eaten sat in her stomach like a lump, too.

She dropped her head into her hands. It was going to be a long, sleepless night.

Chapter Twelve

THE SUN WAS punching Zach in the face. He opened his eyes long enough to focus on the bedside clock: 5:45 AM. He needed to grab a bite and do some lifting before practice. He wondered if Cameron had gotten any sleep at all; he hadn't gotten much himself. He stretched and threw one forearm over his eyes. That would teach him to leave the freaking blinds open overnight.

He kept seeing the look on Cameron's face when he told her the truth about his life. He'd told interviewers for years that any questions about his living situation or his family were off-limits. The Sharks' PR department gave out a fictional bio someone with an extremely good imagination had thought up. He'd answer questions about football, he'd entertain a little probing about his love life—or lack of it—and he'd throw out a tidbit every once in a while about his likes or dislikes. He'd made an appearance to sign autographs at some black-tie fundraising dinner put on by the Seattle Humane Society last summer—he didn't mind people knowing he liked dogs. He met a Labrador retriever breeder at the event who helped him adopt Butter a couple of months ago. His grandma was still getting used to the pup, but his sisters adored the cuddly yellow chewing machine. Hopefully, the obedience instructor Ashley and Courtney were taking him to was weaning Butter from his favorite snack: shoes.

He'd also like to believe Cameron would not use the things he'd told her last night against him.

Mostly, he wanted his family to have the freedom of relative anonymity. His family shouldn't have to deal with fame and its downside, even though he did. He still remembered one of Whitney's teachers freaking out when he walked in to one of her parent-teacher conferences a few years back. His grandma wasn't feeling well that day, and the teacher sent home notes requesting another "conference"—otherwise known as a date, he discovered—throughout the rest of the school year.

It might be interesting to ask Cameron how she dealt with people who approached her in public and printed stuff about her he couldn't imagine she was happy about. Journalists were not supposed to be the story, but he'd read a lot about her over the years. It would be fascinating to find out how much of it was true.

"Probably as much as the crap they write about me," he muttered to himself. He shoved himself off his bed and padded into the bathroom. It was time to get this day started.

Half an hour later, he'd pulled on Under Armour from head to toe, and he was banging on Derrick's door with a closed fist.

"Hey, cupcake, get your ass out of bed. Rise and shine," he called out.

He heard the rumble of a just-awakened male voice. "Fuck off and die, Anderson."

"Not today. Get out here before I call your ex and tell her you're reconsidering."

He heard the thump of a very large man's feet hitting the floor. "I'm kicking your ass," Derrick shouted back. "I'll be out there in ten minutes."

"Oooh. I'm scared."

He spotted Drew out of the corner of his eye. "Just because you couldn't sleep doesn't mean the rest of us have to be up at the asscrack of dawn," Drew said.

"Does dawn have an asscrack?"

"It did today. My next-door-neighbor was taking a shower at 5:30. I'm going to have to talk with her about that." Drew shook his head. "Major party foul."

The door at the end of the hall opened, and both men turned to see Cameron let herself out of her room. She looked like she'd just stepped out of the pages of a magazine. She wore jeans, a jacket, some kind of silky-looking red top, and flats. She had a tote bag, too. In other words, she thought she was going to practice.

"Ms. Ondine," Drew said. "Where are you off to this morning?" He held out one arm.

She gave Drew a sweet smile as she slipped her fingers through his elbow. Zach wanted to punch him. She didn't even glance at Zach, and he wondered what the hell was going on now. She'd liked him just fine last night. He wanted some attention, too.

"I have to do some work before I tape my show later," she said. "I'm wondering if I could ask you for a pretty big favor."

"Anything," Drew assured her.

Zach was now counting to ten in his head.

"I'd like to interview you for my show. Do you have a little time after practice today?"

"I have all the time you need," Drew said. "Let's grab some breakfast and talk about it." Drew tugged her away from Zach, still talking.

"Just a second," she said to Drew, and she turned to smile at Zach. "Good morning. Would you like to join us?"

CAMERON SAW THE poleaxed look on Zach's face as she walked away from him. He didn't like the fact she was talking to any of his teammates, and she wondered if he had an even bigger problem with the fact that she'd made a beeline for Drew. Drew was one of the better linebackers in the league, but he was also a big female fan favorite. With his high cheekbones, square jaw, piercing blue eyes, and long blond hair, he had that whole "ladies love outlaws" thing going. He looked like a modern-day Viking. If all that wasn't enough, he was single. "Very single," he'd said in more than one interview.

They were currently sitting at a table in the team's cafeteria. She knew the players had been told when she first got there they needed a team babysitter to talk with her, but whoever it was that had Cameron Patrol this morning evidently had other things to do right now. The Sharks' chef fed over three hundred people a day during training camp—players, team employees, the media covering training camp, and whoever else wandered in looking for something to eat. The sheer volume of breakfast selections was a bit overwhelming. The other Sharks in the room were covertly staring at their table in the corner between shoveling their food.

Cameron had some oatmeal garnished with fresh fruit and a latte. Drew piled his plate high with complex carbohydrates and protein. And a peanut butter cookie.

She gestured to Drew's cookie. "Do you often eat cookies for breakfast?"

"Hell, yes. The chef makes them for us. They're vegan and protein-packed. Want one?"

If his rippling muscles, glowing skin, and thick, luxuriant hair was any indicator, maybe she should start eating cookies for breakfast, too. "Sure," she said.

He shoved his chair back, strode into the kitchen, and returned moments later with a cookie wrapped in a paper napkin. "You'll be hooked on them, too." He sat back down at the table and took a large bite of his scrambled egg whites with vegetables. "Everyone wants something different for breakfast around here, and the chef does a good job of offering variety. The best part of training camp for the vets is either heckling the rookies or getting something you like to eat at least three times a day."

She nibbled at the cookie. He was right: It was delicious.

"You seem like you enjoy being interviewed," she said.

"It's not too bad. I don't like being misquoted."

"I'll do my best to make sure that doesn't happen," she said. "Would you like to do a little 'welcome to training camp' feature for me? If you could talk about what you do at training camp, maybe my cameraman can follow you around and get some footage. I think it would be a great addition to *NFL Confidential*. Plus, the fans would think it was fun."

Drew's smile turned a touch calculating. He put down his fork for a moment. "So, Ms. Ondine, out with it. I'm all about being cooperative with you and your network, but you must want something in return. Am I right?"

She nodded a little and tried to look penitent. "Okay, you've got me. Would you like to be an unnamed, occasional 'source'?"

He took a swig of orange juice. "One condition. Actually, two."

"What are they?"

"If I tell you no, you have to accept that. In other words, if I know something that would put me in some hot water with my teammates, my first loyalty is to them." His eyes bored into hers, cornflower blue and intent. He didn't look away or avoid her gaze. "My second condition: Don't wake me up at 5:30 AM with your shower running."

"I'm guessing I messed up this morning."

He pointed his fork at her. "If I didn't have a little time this afternoon already scheduled for a nap, Cameron, I'd be pretty pissed at you." She thought he was mad, but his smile was playful.

"Got it. I will stop with the crack of dawn shower taking. What time do you guys get up, anyway?"

"It depends on when practice is, or whether there's something special going on, like picture day or a pre-season game. Derrick gets up at the last minute every day. He's going to kill Anderson for waking his ass up."

Zach sauntered into the cafeteria with an enraged-looking Derrick on his heels. Drew watched them vanish around the corner into the kitchen area. "This ought to be fun," he said. "Hopefully, we won't have to clean up any blood. When did you want to start the filming?"

"After practice. Maybe you could talk a little about your daily schedule and how you all feel when fans come to watch your practices."

"May I invite special guests?"

"Guests?"

"My teammates." He took another bite of cookie. "I'll make sure you'll get some good footage."

She was a little concerned about what he might think "good footage" was, but Logan would be there. Hopefully, it wouldn't be *nude* footage.

"That would be great, Drew." She tried to appear casual as she geared up to ask the big one. "So, what was the meeting about yesterday?"

"Which one?"

"Your teammates and the new coach."

His mouth quirked into a grin. "You're going for the gusto, aren't you, Cam? May I call you Cam?"

She wasn't especially enamored of the nickname, but every time one of these guys gave her a nickname, it meant they accepted her. She'd work on their trust, but right now, she'd take his acceptance.

He leaned forward in his chair, and lowered his voice. "Here's the deal. The new coach wanted to make sure we were on the same page going forward. There was a lot of stuff said, but mostly the Sharks are letting the past be the past and moving on. We want to win. We think Coach Stewart can get us there." He reached over, broke her cookie in half, and jammed the other half into his mouth. He chewed, swallowed, and said, "There isn't a guy on this team that's busted up about the fact that the former head coach probably won't be back. Again: You never heard this from me. We never even discussed it."

She made the zipping motion across her mouth and nodded. "Got it. By the way, that's the last time you're stealing most of my cookie."

Drew laughed and got to his feet as he scooped his tray and empty orange juice glass off the table. He loped away.

ZACH HEADED STRAIGHT for the table Cameron sat alone at. Derrick was still on his heels, and still fuming. Maybe some food would calm him down. Zach had encountered people who were grouchy when awakened suddenly before, but this was a whole new level of pissed off. He'd played with Derrick since they were rookies, but he hadn't seen this before.

"Maybe you should just calm down, guy. You had to get up anyway."

"Not for another hour."

With no warning at all, Derrick slammed his tray down on the table, sending a small river of apple juice over the table top and spraying droplets on everyone sitting there. Cameron threw her hands up in self-protection, but she was seconds too late.

"Excuse me?" Cameron said. She grabbed the napkin dispenser in the middle of the table and pulled a few out, dabbing at her face and her hair with them. Zach knew from the look on her face—a little panicked and definitely angry—she was going to have to change before she went outside for her first stand-up interview this morning.

Derrick reached out one big paw toward her. "Give me that goddamn thing."

He could see her knuckles show white as she gripped the edges of her tray. She stood up from her seat, assembled her empty juice glass and apple juice-soaked napkins on her tray, and said, "It's all yours."

She put the dispenser down and walked away without saying another word. Great. There went his best chance to have a little more conversation with her. She didn't seem like herself this morning, in his opinion. Women could cover up the dark circles and bloodshot eyes of a sleepless night a lot better than men could, and she looked like she'd slept like a baby as a result. When he wasn't a bit uncomfortable over the fact he'd spilled his guts to her last night, he wondered how he could talk to her again without seventy-nine teammates listening to every word.

He was also pretty irritated over the fact she'd had a cozy little conversation with McCoy. That guy would make any woman run for the hills. All he wanted to talk about was some freaking 750-page biography of Lincoln he was reading right now. Or some documentary he'd just seen. The guy was boring.

Zach slapped his palms down on the damp and sticky table. "What the fuck is your problem?"

"I got NO sleep."

"Maybe you should stop watching so much porn, then—"

Derrick's eyes practically bulged out of his head.

"The fuck? I was dealing with my now ex-girlfriend for most of the night. She's pissed off that I don't spend more time with her. How the hell did she think I was going to fix anything when I'm not going to be home for at least another two weeks?" Derrick's big hands formed into fists. "THEN she's all over me about why I haven't asked her to marry me yet. Marry her? Sweet baby Jesus. She bitches at me because she doesn't see me, I'm not making her happy, but she thinks I'm going to marry her?" He took a bite of his food and made a face. "This has apple juice all over it. Goddammit."

It was one of those times when silence was better. Zach handed his relatively-unscathed plate across the table. Hopefully the angry and frustrated Derrick liked a freshly-made Denver omelet and some fresh fruit. He'd go get some more for himself.

Derrick waved a big paw in the air. "Thanks, A, but you eat it. It's my fault the table's a mess." He took another bite of his scrambled eggs. "Actually, this isn't terrible. Apple juice is probably good on the bacon." He consumed the contents of his plate in less than five minutes and looked up from the rest of the food on his tray. He let out a sigh.

"I shouldn't have dragged your ass out of bed," Zach said. "I thought we could get an early start on the lifting today."

Derrick crammed half a banana into his mouth. "I acted like a little bitch."

Zach bumped his fist with Derrick's. "Friends?"

"If you start talking about your feelings, I'll throw up," Derrick said.

Chapter Thirteen

AFTER HER SECOND shower and wardrobe change of the morning, Cameron strolled along the sideline of the Sharks practice field in bright sunshine. She was still annoyed with Derrick's behavior at the breakfast table, but she knew she'd laugh about it later. She'd be quiet while she passed his room tomorrow morning on her way to the stairs for sure.

Practice was forty-five minutes away, and she wanted to take a few still photos and make some notes on her iPad beforehand. Sharks fans were already staking out seats on the grassy hillside overlooking the field to watch the first public practice of the season. Logan wasn't out here yet, either. Maybe she could use her tablet to record a few comments from the fans.

Speaking of people who hadn't made an appearance, she'd also texted Kacee three times this morning, and Kacee hadn't acknowledged any of them. Cameron hadn't seen her in over twenty-four hours, either. Mostly, she wanted to know Kacee was safe. Cameron would rather handle the absence privately than drag their boss into it, too. She clicked on her text app once more and tapped in PLEASE LET ME KNOW YOU ARE SAFE AND FINE, ASAP.

If Cameron didn't hear from her by the time practice was over, she'd see if Logan had any ideas on how to track down her assistant.

When she wasn't fretting over Kacee and her unexplained absence, she was still musing on last night's conversation with Zach. Getting sprayed with apple juice was a great excuse to leave the breakfast table, but it wasn't the real reason she beat feet out of there.

After a mostly sleepless night, she wasn't sure what to say to him. She used to think he was the one who owed her an apology. She couldn't have been more wrong. She needed to apologize to him, but she couldn't imagine what she might say that would have any impact at all after what he and his family went through as a result of their brush with her father.

Last night she'd opened the blinds in her dorm room and gazed out into the darkness. The field was silent and partially lit. Lake Washington looked like an ink stain at three AM—dark and impenetrable. She saw a few boats moving out there; maybe there were other people who couldn't sleep, either. She wondered what they might be thinking about as they bobbed around in an endless night. She'd climbed back into her bed as the first rays of dawn streaked over a purplish-pink sky.

Cameron would have to deal with her personal problems later; work came first. She approached a couple of female fans leaning against the three-foot-high movable steel fence that gave the illusion of separating Sharks fans from their idols. It wouldn't be hard to hurdle the thing and run out onto the field, but nobody did. The Sharks organization provided security during these practices, but most fans would be more afraid of inviting the wrath of a six-foot-six, three-hundred pound tackle. She smiled at the two women, who appeared to be in their late twenties, and extended her hand.

"Hi. I'm Cameron Ondine from PSN. How's your day going?"

"Oh, wow! I watch *NFL Confidential* every week. I can't believe you're here," the shorter, petite brunette told her.

"Are you really living in the dorms with the guys?" her bleached-blonde friend asked. "Have you met Drew McCoy yet? Is he still single?"

Cameron resisted the impulse to laugh at the question about Drew. The guys in the league were used to women making their interest clear, but she'd never get used to being asked about specific players and their love lives.

She side-stepped the question about Drew.

"Yes, I'm living in the dorm, and I'll be there until training camp is over. I was wondering if you would let me video a short interview with you. I'd like to put it up on the PSN blog, or we might use it on *Third and Long*."

"We'd be on TV?" The blonde let out a squeal. "*Oh, my God!*"

"I should have worn more makeup today." The brunette whipped a mirror out of her handbag and inspected her lipstick. "Do you have someone that does your hair every day? It's always perfect."

"Thank you so much. The hair person slept in this morning, so I was on my own." Both women laughed as Cameron indicated her high ponytail. "So, what are your names, and how long have you been Sharks fans?"

"I'm Serena," the blonde said, "and this is Marcella." Her voice dropped. "We like football, but we like the single guys more. Maybe you could hook us up."

Marcella leaned closer to Cameron. Her voice dropped to a murmur. "Were you really married to Zach Anderson for three days? He's gorgeous."

One of her colleagues from another sports network was close enough to hear the conversation. "Of course it's true," she sang out. "Cameron won't discuss it with any of us, though. I wonder why."

The sick feeling in Cameron's stomach was immediate. She wasn't going to turn to acknowledge the comment. Even more, she wasn't giving the reporter in question the satisfaction of reacting to it.

She knew she was going to be asked questions about her life, but her job was to get the story. She also realized she'd been living in a bubble for the past three days. She'd seen some of the reporting on her and Zach's short-lived marriage on sports websites and Twitter, but this was the first time she'd faced questions or comments from anyone outside of her insular little world. She forced herself to smile. Other fans had noticed the commotion, and were advancing on them. She'd better make this quick.

"Serena and Marcella, I'm going to ask you a few questions and video your responses. Just be yourselves. Don't worry, there are no wrong answers." She held the iPad screen up in front of the women, making sure she had them centered in frame, and said, "It's the first public practice of training camp for the Seattle Sharks this morning. Let's welcome Serena and Marcella to our show." Some of the fans that had clustered around the two women broke into applause, and there were a few more chants of "Go Sharks!"

She held up one hand for silence and said, "How long have you been Sharks fans, ladies?"

Serena moved closer to Cameron's iPad camera and struck a pose. "I've been watching the team since I was little. My mom told me my dad put my bouncy chair in front of the TV every Sunday—"

Marcella interrupted her. "My dad has been bringing me to the games since I was a month old."

"How do you feel about their chances this year? Do you think the coaching staff can fix some of the problems they had last season with the offensive line?"

Serena half-turned toward Marcella. "I remember my dad talking about the fact the OL needs some serious help, but I haven't been focusing much on it." Cameron heard some groans behind the two women. Serena gave the camera a dazzling smile. "Of course we're going to the Super Bowl again."

Cameron had better ask another general question.

"Who's your favorite Shark?"

"Drew McCoy," both women said in unison.

"He's gorgeous," Serena said.

"I love his hair," Marcella said. "I want to run my fingers through it."

"I heard he's single," Serena told the camera.

"I'll make sure to ask him about that later. Thanks, Serena and Marcella. It looks like practice is about to get underway, so we'll bring you some more Sharks fan interviews later. This is Cameron Ondine for PSN."

She shut off the video on her iPad, and reached out to shake hands with the two women again. "Thank you so much for the interview."

"That was *it*? Aren't you going to ask us a few more questions?" Marcella demanded.

"I may come back to you later. Thanks again, ladies."

She walked away as quickly as her legs could carry her. She'd spied three little boys in Sharks jerseys pressed up against the fence on the far end of the field. She wanted to talk with them before any other media member got to them first.

ZACH RAN OUT onto the field with a few of his teammates. Practice didn't officially start for another twenty minutes or so, but a little extra time to stretch beforehand wouldn't hurt anyone. He could hear Sharks fans yelling his name and cheering, but he couldn't take his eyes off the slight figure in red with the blonde ponytail on the sidelines, crouched down in front of three little boys. Zach noted with a smile that one of them was wearing a replica of his jersey, which meant the kid was getting an autograph, and maybe a hug, or perhaps he would even be boosted up onto Zach's shoulders for a photo later. He *loved* seeing people in his jersey, which meant those fans always got a little extra attention from him. He saw Cameron producing paper-work out of her tote bag, which she handed to what must have been their proud fathers. It was most likely some kind of release; the kids were underage, and her network prob-ably required it. Her cameraman was standing next to her, filming her interaction with the kids. He'd seen the guy sprinting through the practice facility five minutes before.

The three little boys tugged on her pants leg and pointed at the field as they talked to her. He wished he could hear what they were telling her. There would be an autograph session for the younger fans after practice. He and his teammates knew they'd have to keep an eye on the smaller kids in line; adults would cut right in front of them or shove them aside in their zeal to get autographs that often went for sale on eBay within minutes of those same fans leaving the practice facility.

He lowered himself to the turf a few feet away from Cameron, eavesdropping shamelessly. He began the gentle stretches he'd learned in the yoga class the Sharks partici-pated in once a week. He heard the high-pitched voices of young boys.

"Dad! Dad! There's Reed! He's my favorite."

"Maybe he'll throw the ball over here, son."

"Cameron, do you know him?"

"Sure," he heard Cameron say. "He looks forward to

meeting his fans. Maybe he'll sign your football later. What do you think of that?"

"I brought it with me. See?"

"That's great," she told him. He could hear the smile in her voice.

Zach saw the camera guy get on one knee. He couldn't hear Cameron's questions any more over the din of the rest of his teammates running out onto the field, and the cheers and clapping of the fans who now packed the hillside overlooking the field. No matter how long he lasted in the league, he'd never get used to the fact that several thousand people showed up to watch training camp practices.

He heard feminine voices shouting, "Zach. Zach! Over here!" He glanced up to see his four sisters beaming at him.

His sisters were ensconced on a blanket a few yards behind the portable fence, all wearing his jersey, and all waving at him. To see them together at any event was a big deal now. No matter how busy they were with school and their own lives, though, at least one of them was at every home game for him. He waved back, grinned at them, and Shelby blew him a kiss.

"We love you," Courtney shouted. "Go Sharks!"

"I love you, too. Talk to you later," he called out to them. His defensive line coach blew the whistle, and he ran over to his teammates.

CAMERON FINISHED WHAT she knew was an adorable interview with the three first-grade Sharks fans and their dads, and glanced over at the four college-age women wearing what she knew were probably game-worn Anderson jerseys from UVA and Zach's pro career. The jerseys were knee-length on the women. They must be his sisters, whom she'd never met.

Zach had fiercely guarded their privacy over the years. She'd seen a few candid photos on sports websites and Twitter, but she'd never seen them interviewed before. They were old enough by now to consent to be filmed. She wondered which of her colleagues was reckless or crazy enough to try to ask them some questions.

Logan stepped closer to her as he moved his camera back and forth, panning the crowd.

"Have you seen Kacee?" Cameron asked. "I've been calling her for two days now. Where is she?"

Logan shuffled his feet and didn't meet Cameron's eyes. "I haven't seen her, either."

"Did she go back to New York?"

Logan finally met her gaze. "Nope." His lips formed a bloodless line. "She's doing a 'special project' for Ben."

"What kind of special project might that be? She's supposed to be helping out with my stuff. Come on. I have the right to know what's going on."

From the way Logan was acting, he knew more than he was telling her. He wasn't sharing. She considered him a friend. When did they start keeping secrets from each other?

He spread his hands wide. "That's all the info I have right now. Whatever it is, she can't hide from us forever."

Cameron felt the hair on the back of her neck rising. Something was wrong. Ben had his own assistant— actually, several assistants. She couldn't imagine what Kacee could be doing for him, unless it was personal. Ben wasn't immune to the charms of a younger woman, but he'd sat through the same sexual harassment seminars she had, and he'd never done or said anything inappropriate to her while she'd been with PSN.

Cameron's phone vibrated, and she pulled it out of her pocket. It wasn't Kacee.

"Come on," Logan said to her. "Zach Anderson's sisters are over there. Maybe we should introduce ourselves to them."

She reached out to pull him back.

"Are you sure? He'll freak out. The guys from CBS Sports tried to talk to his grandma on-camera last year and Zach wouldn't talk to them for the rest of the season. We need to leave them alone," she said. "Tom Reed's wife will talk with us. Let's ask her how she feels about getting asked for her autograph at football practice."

The quarterback's tall, stunning blonde wife was standing several feet from the Anderson family. Sure enough, she was signing autographs and posing for photos with thrilled Sharks fans. A younger woman, probably their nanny, was wrangling three boys who looked to be kindergarten age.

"That's nuts. Why are they asking for her autograph?" Logan said.

"Her lasagna recipe got over a million hits on the Sharks' website. Everyone here loves her."

Cameron started toward Megan Reed. She'd have to pass Zach's sisters to get there. She felt someone reach out to grab her sleeve.

"Logan, what was that?" she said.

It wasn't Logan. A young woman with Zach's eyes, full lips and dark-blonde hair held onto her jacket. She was strong. Cameron almost crashed into the portable fence as a result.

"Whitney, don't," one of Zach's sisters called out. "Get back over here and sit down."

"Do you have a minute?" Whitney said to Cameron. Her eyes narrowed to slits. There were two spots of color high on her cheeks. She continued to clutch Cameron's sleeve.

"I'm working right now," Cameron said. She told herself to smile despite the fact Whitney was glaring at her. "What can I do for you?"

"I'm Whitney Anderson," the young woman said. "Zach's little sister. I know what you did to him. My sisters won't say anything to you, but I will." She stared into Cameron's eyes. "Leave him alone."

"I'm not bothering him."

"You're here, which is bothering him. You should go somewhere else." She gave her head a quick shake. "I don't like you. You hurt him, and you never apologized."

Cameron felt like Whitney had slapped her. She had no idea how to respond. She thought the incident with the NFL Network colleague sneering over her and Zach's marriage would be the most embarrassing thing to happen to her this morning. No such luck. She was reeling, and she needed to hold it together long enough to get somewhere she could regroup for a minute or two.

All three sisters were up off the blanket by now and at the fence. One of them wrapped her arm around Whitney's shoulders and said, "Come on, Whit. Let's go sit down. This isn't our business."

"Move it. Now," the only sister with dark hair said to Whitney.

"Let's go, or we're going to have to leave. Zach will be pissed because you're talking to a reporter."

Some of the other fans were loudly complaining because Zach's sisters were blocking their view of the field. Cameron pivoted away from the sisters, walking as fast as she could to the area behind a small set of bleachers. She'd be concealed from prying eyes for a few minutes until she could get herself together. Logan trailed her.

"Are you okay, Cam?" he asked.

"I'll be right with you," she said. "Please, give me a minute."

She closed her eyes, took several deep breaths, and tried to force herself to stop shaking. The look in Whitney Anderson's eyes was chilling. She hated Cameron, and they'd never met before. Cameron had had to grow a thick skin since she worked in the media; there were people who would say nasty things to her while she did her job just to get a reaction. But this was personal.

Logan swung the camera off his shoulder and patted Cameron on the back. "Shake it off," he said. "She's a kid. She's just trying to stick up for her brother."

"She doesn't know what happened."

"She heard Zach's version." He rested a hand on the edge of the bleachers and bent over her. "Why do you care what she thinks?"

It would be difficult at best to explain her tangled, confused feelings about Zach. It upset her that someone who knew nothing about her couldn't stand her; she'd only heard one side of the story. Ultimately, she needed to get back to work. Practice wasn't going to wait until she managed to regroup.

She'd go talk to Megan Reed, and she'd locate more Sharks fans who wanted to be interviewed. She could stew over the incident with Zach's sisters later.

ZACH GLANCED AT the sidelines to find Cameron talking with not one but all four of his sisters, and his sisters didn't look happy about it. It was all Zach could do to resist the impulse to storm across the field and break Cameron's co-worker's camera. She knew his sisters were off-limits to the media at all times. So what did she do? She sashayed right over to them.

Trying to explain why he didn't talk to her for ten years was a huge mistake, he realized with a shock. He might still be interested in her—God knew why; maybe he was a glutton for punishment—but she would exploit him and his family for PSN if he gave her the chance. He'd wanted to believe she wouldn't do this to him. When would he learn? Plus, he saw the look on his little sister's face when Cameron was talking to her. Whitney looked angry. He could only imagine what Cameron had said to her.

If that guy had his camera on, Zach would sue.

He'd done everything in his power to protect his family from the press. He couldn't believe Cameron thought he'd backed off that stance one iota since their chit-chat last night. He didn't have time right now, though, to set her straight. He was too busy blocking the shit out of whoever on the Sharks' offensive line was stupid enough to appear in his line of vision. Fear and hurt weren't options for him when he wore a Sharks uniform; there was only aggression.

He broke through the line with a spin move, darted through a hole the size of Renton, WA, and grabbed Tom Reed. Tom wasn't able to throw the ball away before being dropped to the turf. The Sharks fans responded with a wall of shouts, clapping, and whistles.

Tom rolled over and looked up at the heavily breathing Zach, tapping himself on the chest.

"RED. I'm wearing red. That means you do not tackle me. Got it?"

Zach rubbed his hands over his face. "Yeah. Sorry. I got a little carried away there."

"Sure." Tom didn't look happy. Zach was going to catch it for the mistake later. Right now, though, he extended a hand toward Tom and helped him to his feet.

"I'll give you a piece of advice," Tom told him. "You need to spend more time focusing on us and less time staring at her."

Zach walked away from him without another word.

CAMERON TAPED A short interview with Megan Reed and asked Logan to get a little footage of the Reeds' angelic-looking blond kids after securing their mother's permission. Tom's sons wore cut-down football jerseys and gap-toothed smiles. One clutched a mini-football with his dad's autograph on it. Megan laid one hand over her barely-there baby bump. Cameron knew Tom Reed was thrilled with their three healthy sons from previous interviews with him, but he longed for a baby girl that looked just like his wife.

"How are you feeling?" she asked Megan Reed when Logan shut off his camera.

"Better than I was last month," Megan said. "The first three months of my pregnancies are not especially fun, but the last six months are wonderful. Tom talked me into hiring a nanny this time around, though. My mom isn't coming out from Oklahoma until the baby's almost here. I just don't have as much energy as I did before I had Connor." The youngest Reed hid behind his mother, peering up at Cameron as he did. "Three boys are a challenge, even if I adore them." She ruffled her son's hair. He let out a laugh.

An hour and a half later, practice was over. The players were besieged by hundreds of fans looking for autographs and pictures. Logan filmed Cameron giving a short recap they could use later, and she stowed her iPad in her bag as she approached Coach Stewart. A couple of Sharks employees were setting up a team logo and sponsors-covered backdrop closer to the building for the press conference he gave after each practice. She waited until he finished talking with one of the assistant coaches and turned to her.

"Coach, I'd really like to interview you in the next couple of days for *NFL Confidential*. Do you have a little time in your schedule?"

"There's a press conference in ten minutes. Would it be possible to ask your questions there?"

"I'd really like some one-on-one time. Is there a way to make this happen?"

He rubbed one hand over his face. "I'll give you fifteen minutes late this afternoon. I'm thinking closer to dinnertime."

"Perfect. I'll make the arrangements." The Sharks PR department probably knew more about his schedule than he did, so she'd be talking with them about an exact time. She stuck out her hand to shake his. "Thank you so much. Also, congratulations."

His voice dropped. "I probably don't need to tell you I wish this had happened another way."

"Of course not."

Coaches in the NFL got a promotion because someone else got fired. It was a rough and difficult business. She was a bit surprised he'd mention his misgivings, but she could ask him about it later.

They shook hands again, and Cameron moved off toward the knot of media shouting questions at Tom Reed. She saw Zach approaching her out of the corner of her eye.

"Hey," he called out. "I need to talk to you." He wasn't smiling. Unless she was wrong, he was really mad, and he blocked her from moving any further by standing in front of her.

"Good job on the sack."

"I don't care about that. Why the hell were you talking to my sisters? If that guy was filming them, there's going to be a problem."

Livid color bloomed on Zach's face. He folded his arms over his chest. Even more than his obvious anger, she saw hurt in his eyes.

"You *know* I don't allow media to interview my sisters, let alone film them. I thought you'd respect that. They came here to see *me*, not answer a bunch of questions. They deserve their privacy. Of course, you don't know what that means, do you?" He stared at her. "It's all about what you want, or what's going to help your career."

Her mouth dropped open.

"I might have to put up with this BS, but they don't. Leave them alone. Got it?" He turned and walked away from her. She ran after him.

"I did not ask for an interview. Your youngest sister grabbed my sleeve as I walked past."

"Bullshit."

"Ask Logan. He'll tell you what happened."

"The guy who's filming us right now?" He pointed toward Logan, who stood only feet from them. Even worse, Cameron saw the red light on his camera. It was on.

"Logan, shut it off, please." Logan shook his head no.

"I'm done talking to you," Zach said. He increased his pace, and she couldn't keep up with him.

She whirled on Logan. "What the hell was that? Why were you filming?"

"Ben wants footage."

"That was personal. Ben doesn't need it," she said.

"He told me he wants footage of everything that happens here."

"He might want footage, but he's not getting personal conversations. Those are off-limits."

Logan's expression didn't change. "They're open season now. He's looking for tape, the more inflammatory the better." He lowered the camera from his shoulder. "This isn't your first time at the rodeo, Cam. If you don't give me anything, then we'll have nothing to use."

Logan gave her a nod, and walked away.

ZACH SPENT THE rest of the day avoiding Cameron. He was still angry. Even more, he was hurt. He couldn't believe he'd opened up to her, and this was how she'd rewarded his confidence. He didn't feel like hanging out with the guys after dinner, either. If he got a little extra shut-eye tonight, he might feel better tomorrow.

He sat down at the computer desk in his dorm room and opened his laptop to read his e-mail. He was a bit surprised to see an e-mail from his sister Shelby, who typically texted or called him. He clicked on it.

Zach,
*Cameron Ondine passed the fence in front
of us today while she was working. Whitney*

*jumped up and grabbed her arm before we
could stop her. Whitney also said some pretty
nasty things to her. Just a heads-up in case
she mentions it to you, okay?
We love you and miss you. Grandma sends
her love. Butter's trainer thinks he might need
another obedience class after this one.
Love, Shelby*

Zach stared at the screen. Finally he dropped his head into his hands. He'd jumped to conclusions. Cameron hadn't approached them after all. That didn't mean her co-worker didn't film them.

He searched every major sports website he could think of, starting with the Sharks' website. No film or photos of his sisters there. PSN's site and their NFL blog had nothing as well. There were photos and video of a few of the other people Cameron had met earlier, but nothing about his sisters. He did a Google search. The only photos of his sisters were school or yearbook photos.

Cameron hadn't lied to him.

He owed her an apology this time around.

Chapter Fourteen

It was day four of training camp, and Cameron was already behind. She needed interviews. She'd had her fifteen minutes with the new head coach yesterday, but his comments weren't going to fill an hour-long program. She needed to tape her own show tonight, and the only footage she had were the interviews with the two women interested in Drew McCoy and the three little boys. Logan had tipped her off for her own good yesterday. That didn't mean she wasn't still angry with him for what she saw as his betrayal of their friendship. Kacee still hadn't texted her. Maybe she'd been eaten by bears or something. According to Logan, Kacee was fine, so Cameron could stop worrying about her safety. Her anxiety was replaced by irritation. She pulled out her cell phone and texted Ben: DO I NEED TO HIRE A NEW ASSISTANT?

Zach wasn't speaking to her. She'd tried talking to

him at dinnertime yesterday, and he'd walked away from her again. She was back to square one.

Practice wasn't for another three hours. She had a million and one things to do before taping later, but maybe she needed to go for a run to clear her head. She pulled on yoga pants, a sports bra, t-shirt and cross trainers, stuck her phone and dorm room key in her pocket, and walked into the still-silent hallway. Unfortunately, Zach was leaving his room, too. There was no way to get by him without his seeing her.

He glanced toward her and gave her a nod.

She didn't smile back, and she sped up in an attempt to pass him through the fire door to the stairway. It didn't work. He made it to the door before she did, smacked the bar to open it, and took the stairs at a high rate of speed.

They passed through the door on the way to the cafeteria. "Actually, there is something we need to talk about." He turned to face her. "I was wrong about your approaching my sisters yesterday. I'm sorry."

"What?"

"I didn't realize you weren't approaching them to interview or film. I thought you did. I was mad because I thought I made myself clear—"

"Why would you think I would do that? You told me not to." She stared up at him in disbelief. "What kind of person do you think I am, anyway? You *said* you didn't want your sisters dealing with the press. Did you think I wanted to piss you off?" She let out a huff of breath. "Oh, forget it. Thanks for the apology."

She took a few steps away from him. He reached out, snagged her elbow, and walked her through the still-silent administrative area. "Come on. Let's get this over with."

"Get *what* over with? You're the one who freaked out at me. I appreciate the apology, but I have things I need to do right now."

His voice dropped. He spoke slowly, like he was addressing a recalcitrant preschooler.

"Your buddy Logan talked to me last night before I went to bed. He says your boss needs footage. We're going to have breakfast together, we'll let him film us, and then you can spend the rest of the day dealing with the things you have to do. How about it?"

She opened her mouth to tell him she wasn't interested, but "I'm going for a run," came out instead.

"You can run after breakfast."

Running on a full stomach was never a great thing to do. He should know this.

Zach pulled her into the cafeteria. Logan was sitting at a sun-drenched table in the corner with his camera, sipping a cup of coffee. He raised one hand in a half-wave. Zach gave him a nod as he tugged Cameron into the food line.

A younger woman in a hair net grinned at them. "You're early this morning, Zach."

"It's good to be first. How's my favorite Sharks fan?" He handed Cameron a tray, a plate, and utensils wrapped in a paper napkin, and grabbed his own breakfast supplies.

The woman in the hair net regarded him like he'd just cured cancer. "I'm fine. I hope you're having a good day so far, too."

"Things are great for me. I get to see your smiling face," Zach said.

The young woman's eyes sparkled. Of course she was half in love with him, Cameron thought waspishly.

"I'd like another one of those excellent Denver omelets, if it's not too much trouble. I'm not sure what Cameron would like this morning," he continued.

Cameron was still staring at the sheer amount of freshly prepared breakfast items on offer to whoever was eating breakfast in the cafeteria this morning. She made a concerted effort to shut her mouth. Again. She hadn't seen this much food in the college cafeteria, or anywhere since. She managed to recover her voice. "I'd like some scrambled eggs and fresh fruit, please."

"How about a croissant?" Zach said, and set one on Cameron's tray.

"I can't eat that."

"Croissant or doughnut. Your choice." He gave the server another nod. "I'm hoping there's more of those great seasoned potatoes you make, too."

"I don't need a croissant or a doughnut—"

Zach was ignoring her while focusing all of his attention on the young woman. She wasn't sure if she should be jealous or infuriated.

Cameron saw the server blush and smile. "Of course there are," she said. "Let me get your order started and I'll be right back." She sped away from them. Zach grabbed a few pieces of bacon out of the steam table with a pair of tongs and dropped them on his plate.

"I think you need some of this, too." He reached in for another slice of bacon and laid it onto her plate.

"I don't—Zach, you can eat as much as you want, but the rest of us can't. Stop trying to feed me."

"You'll burn it off by lunchtime. You need the calories."

Cameron did not, but she realized that arguing with him about it was useless.

"Do you know that woman?" she asked.

"I saw her every morning last training camp. I'll see her every morning during this one." He darted around Cameron with his plate and loaded up on the seasoned potatoes. "The employees are local college students. She knows my sisters, for instance. They make enough in thirty days to put a nice dent in their fall tuition bill." The server returned with their freshly-made entrees. Zach gave the server a fist bump after he put the second plate onto his tray. "Thanks, Holly."

He took Cameron's elbow and steered her into the seating area. "Want some coffee?"

"I'd really like a non-fat latte, if that's possible," Cameron said. Whoever made her plate of scrambled eggs must have used the whole carton. There was an entire day's calorie count on her tray. Maybe Zach would eat most of it.

"Why don't you sit down, and I'll do battle with the coffee machine for you," he offered. He set his tray down at Logan's table. "Where's your breakfast?" he asked Logan.

"I already ate."

"When was that? Get up there and help yourself."

"I'm supposed to be working," Logan told him.

"Go talk to Holly, and she'll hook you up. Everyone around here eats breakfast. Get in there before the other guys clean her out."

Zach loped away to get coffee, and Logan glanced over at Cameron's tray. "Did they give you all the eggs in the kitchen?"

"It's a little out of control, isn't it?" She draped the paper napkin over her lap. "If you'll get a plate and a fork, you can have some of mine." She reached out to grab his forearm. "Zach told me you're planning on filming our breakfast."

"I'd like to."

"What if I don't want you to?"

"Well, then, you're going to have to give me another suggestion. Ben made it clear I'd better deliver."

Cameron's cell phone chirped with an incoming text. She pulled it out of her pocket.

I'M FINE. I WILL SEE YOU IN AN HOUR OR SO.
KACEE

LOGAN MOVED AROUND their table, filming all the while. Zach patted his belly after feeding himself and making sure Cameron ate more than three or four bites of scrambled eggs and fresh fruit. He'd noticed she picked at any food set in front of her, and he knew she needed more calories. He refused to dwell on why he was concerned about her eating habits. After a few minutes of silence between them, he discovered what got Cameron talking.

"Come on, Cameron." He picked up the saucer holding a fresh croissant off her tray. "Eat half of this."

"No. No. I'm not eating it. Maybe you should eat it." He almost laughed out loud at the obstinate expression on her face. Any second now she'd stick her tongue out at him. Maybe she was so used to having cameras around she'd forgotten Logan, still a short distance from their table and still filming. "You made me eat that entire plate full of food. I'm going to explode."

"No, you're not. I haven't seen you finish anything put in front of you in the past four days." He picked up his knife and cut the croissant in half. "Eat at least half of this, and I'll eat the other half."

She stared at him. "Excuse me. How do you know how much I eat?" Her ponytail swished as she shook her head in outrage. "That's a little creepy."

He ignored that. "If you finish this, I'll go for a run with you before I have to lift."

"I'm not sure I can stand up right now, let alone run," she grumbled. She took a sip of her coffee.

Logan displayed a real talent for blending into the woodwork with his camera running while Zach and Cameron bickered over her nutritional needs. Zach could only imagine what the footage would look like. He had to admit her reaction to his goading her into eating was fairly comical. He now knew she quivered a little when she was frustrated with him. At least it was playful bickering, not angry or resentful words. There were other things for them to discuss, but that would need to happen privately.

It would be quite a feat to discover anywhere in the facility besides her room that they could talk privately, but he was going to make the effort.

Logan had moved away from them and turned his camera onto a table full of defensive linemen consuming enough food to sustain a small nation and discussing the best place in Seattle to get Caribbean food. Kacee skidded into the cafeteria. She hurried over to plunk herself down at Zach and Cameron's table. She seized Cameron's half-empty coffee cup, peered inside, and took a long, appreciative sniff of the contents.

"Where's the coffee?" Kacee said.

"Where have you been?" Cameron countered. "I've been worried. You didn't call me back and you vanished for three days. What the hell's going on?"

Kacee didn't look her in the eye, Zach noticed. He wondered if Cameron did.

"Ben had some stuff for me to do."

"Like what? You're my assistant, not his. I needed your help."

"We both work for him," Kacee said. "I finished the project, it's over now, so let's talk about what's going on today with you."

"Maybe you should tell me about this mysterious 'project'—"

Kacee got up from the table. "I need some coffee. I'll be right back." She reached out, scooped up Cameron's empty tray and dishes, and hurried away.

"She's hiding something from you," Zach said in a low voice.

"Yes, she is." Cameron let out a sigh. "At first I was freaked out that something might have happened to her, and now I'm mad. I can't do my job if she's going to vanish on me whenever she feels like it. She's convinced I'm not going to get angry enough at her to fire her, either. She let me have it over you the other night, which was inappropriate." She shook her head.

"She did, huh?" Zach got up from the table, grabbed his own tray of dirty dishes, and gestured to Cameron. "I have to hit the weight room in half an hour. Let's talk about this outside."

He wanted a few minutes of whatever privacy they could manage to snatch from PSN and their cameras.

THE MIDSUMMER EARLY morning sun filtered through the maple trees that lined both sides of the dead-end street in front of the Sharks headquarters. The temperature rose as the sun continued its path through the sky, but the grass was still covered with dew. Cameron's shoes got a bit wet as they crossed the grassy strip in front of the sidewalk, and she was surprised at the stillness. She heard birds singing, the leaves rustled in a gentle breeze, but all was quiet—at least temporarily. She leaned against a tree trunk to stretch before she took off at a slow jog on the deserted street.

She couldn't keep up with Zach, who ran in place when he noticed he was alone a hundred feet or so up the street. Her food was still settling, and he wanted to sprint? *Uh, no.* Despite his apology, she was still irritated over his behavior the day before. She'd like to find out what his problem was. Of course, there was no time like the present. She stopped next to him.

"So, would you mind telling me why you were acting like I had some kind of communicable disease yesterday?"

His eyes blazed. "My sisters aren't fair game for PSN. I saw you talking to them, and I assumed the worst."

"Your sister grabbed me as I walked past."

He was already shaking his head. "I know that. I didn't know at the time. I was wrong, and I am sorry." It wasn't the most eloquent apology, but he'd given her one, and she needed to accept it.

"Logan saw the whole thing."

"I thought Logan was *filming* the whole thing. How would I know?" He blew out a breath and started off on a slow jog again. Maybe she could keep up with him without needing oxygen. "How about that?"

"If it happens again, and I hope it won't, talk to Logan. He might accidentally 'lose' the tape," she said, making air quotes with her hands. "He's a lot more reasonable than Ben." Plus, Logan wouldn't be interested in getting into it with a guy who outweighed him by at least fifty pounds.

"I'll bear that in mind," Zach said.

An older car with patches of primer approached in the opposite lane, slowing to stare at them both. The driver screeched to a halt and must have set the brake, because seconds later, he was out of the vehicle and advancing on them. His dark, shoulder-length matted hair was unwashed, he had a straggly beard and wore dirty clothing, and he made a beeline for Cameron. He didn't look friendly, and the hair went up on the back of her neck.

"Cameron! Cameron! I've been looking for you. You need to come back home with me."

Zach pushed Cameron behind his back and straightened to his full height. "Can I help you?" he asked the guy.

"Do you know if there are any available tickets for today's practice?"

"No, I don't," Zach said. "You're blocking a public street."

"I'd like to talk to my wife," the guy said. He was within three feet of Zach, and he continued toward them. "She never answered my letters, and I'd like to know why."

His wife? Oh, God.

Cameron had never seen the guy before in her life, but his rambling sounded familiar. She broke out into a cold sweat. She scrabbled around for her phone, but her hands were already shaking so hard she couldn't seem to jam her fingers into the small pocket in her yoga pants. She cowered behind Zach. What if the guy had a weapon?

"Back off." Zach's arm shot out. "Don't get any closer."

"I just want to talk with her. We have a few things to straighten out."

"I don't think so." Zach used his body to walk the guy backward, blocking him into the hood of his vehicle. "Cameron, call 911, will you?" His voice was as calm as if he'd asked her to get him a cup of coffee.

Cameron scrabbled again for the cell phone in her pocket. Her trembling had increased, but she finally succeeded in gripping the phone enough to hit the dialer. She also hit the speaker function so Zach could hear.

"911 operator. May I help you?" the woman who answered said. Zach had the guy by one upper arm while he gestured for Cameron to get away from them with his other hand.

"We're outside of the Seattle Sharks' headquarters. We need help."

"What is the problem?"

"My name is Cameron Ondine. I have a stalker," Cameron said. Her voice shook. "He's here, and we have him. Please help us."

Zach grabbed the guy by one arm, bent it around behind his back, and threw him over the hood of his car. The guy smelled like he hadn't had a bath in a couple of weeks. He also was skeletal, but had superhuman strength. He tried to shove Zach in return.

"Let me go!" the guy shouted.

"Fuck, no. The cops are coming." He twisted the guy's arm a little more for emphasis, and laid into his back.

"You're breaking my arm."

"Good." Zach turned his head to glimpse Cameron, who was white as a sheet and visibly shaking. *God, don't let her pass out before the cops come.* He couldn't grab her before she hit the pavement, and this guy was trying to get one hand free. "Cameron, stay with me," Zach commanded. He could feel the cold outline of a pistol stuffed in the guy's rear waistband and digging into his abdomen. He hoped like hell it didn't go off.

Zach grabbed his other wrist, twisting it behind the guy's back. "Keep it up, and I'll break your wrists."

"Fuck you," the guy gritted out. "You can't keep her away from me."

"Call the front desk, Cameron," Zach shouted. "They'll send security out here, too."

He could hear her still talking to the 911 operator, the terror in her voice. She told the 911 operator she needed to call the Sharks front office for help. The operator must have dialed the number for her.

"They'll get here quicker than the cops," he told her. Even if she screamed, they weren't close enough to the building right now for anyone to hear. The place was secure, but the guards who were usually at the entrance must have had a shift change or something. He didn't see any of them as he whipped his head around.

He shoved himself into the guy again with all his weight, and heard him grunt in pain.

If Zach didn't care about his future he would pound the guy to a pulp, but the best thing to do was make sure the guy couldn't grab his gun and wait for law enforcement. A few seconds later, he heard sirens in the distance. He also heard running feet heading in their direction. The guy was trying to fight him off, but he couldn't get a solid punch in bent over like he was. Let the son of a bitch try to sue him later, too.

He saw the team's security guards running toward them out of the corner of his eye. Two of the guys made a beeline for him and the guy he was holding down. "He's got a gun," Zach shouted to them.

The security guards had the guy unarmed and on the ground with twist-tie handcuffs in seconds. The guy kept screaming, "She's my wife! Let me talk to my wife! You can't keep her away from me!"

Zach whirled to check on Cameron. One of the other guards was leading her away while the fourth guy held a Taser on the guy on the ground. He heard multiple police cars, sirens going, heading toward them at what must have been maximum speed.

CAMERON DIDN'T REMEMBER the walk back into the Sharks' headquarters. She didn't remember a thing the security guard said to her. She knew she'd talked to him, but everything was fuzzy and indistinct. Her legs felt like rubber. She also had an overpowering urge to throw up. An older woman with a soothing voice guided her into the ladies' room.

"I feel like I'm going to be sick," Cameron said. Her voice sounded like it was coming from a hundred miles away.

"Let's go in here," the woman said as she helped Cameron into a larger stall. To Cameron's embarrassment, nature took over. She was alert enough to realize she'd just thrown up in front of another person. At least she managed to not make a mess, but the woman didn't seem alarmed by this. She rubbed Cameron's back and made comforting sounds. "You had quite a scare, didn't you?

You're safe now. Everything is going to be okay." She dashed out of the stall long enough to grab a paper towel for Cameron to wipe her mouth with. Cameron saw the view of the bathroom stall turn a bit watery as tears spilled over.

"Do you need to sit down for a few minutes, Cameron?"

"I—I don't know. I—"

The woman folded her into a hug. "You cry all you want, honey. I would cry, too. Shh." She rocked Cameron back and forth, still making those comforting noises. "Take some deep breaths, and relax. You're going to be fine."

It was like focusing a camera. The indistinct things around her slowly became clear. She heard running steps outside the bathroom, a few male voices calling out her name, and a loud knock at the bathroom door.

"Joanna, are you in there?" a deeper male voice said.

"Yes, I am."

"Is Cameron with you?"

"Yes, she is."

"The cops want to talk to her. May I come in?"

The woman Cameron now knew as Joanna spoke softly. "You don't have to let them in right now if you don't want to." Cameron straightened up. Joanna patted her cheek. "I have a new toothbrush and some mouthwash at my desk. Would you like me to get them for you?"

She nodded. "Yes. Thank you so much." She moved to the sink, rinsing her mouth as she heard knocking again.

"I'll be right with you," Joanna called out. She patted Cameron on the back again. "I'll just be a minute or so."

Joanna crossed to the bathroom door, shutting it behind her as she left. Cameron heard low voices outside, and what sounded like a herd of footsteps moving away from the bathroom door. The news from the mirror over the sink wasn't encouraging. Her eyes were bloodshot and swollen from crying. Everywhere that wasn't pasty white was tear-streaked. Makeup would cover most of it, but her nerves were shredded, to put it mildly. She wished she could curl up on the clean tile floor and rest for a while.

She remembered enough of what had happened outside to realize that Zach had put himself in danger to make sure she would be safe, and she needed to talk with him about this. If she started thinking about what could have happened if he hadn't been there, she'd throw up again. Her legs seemed a bit less rubbery than they were a few minutes ago, so she headed toward the bathroom door. It opened, and she halted mid-step as she grabbed for the counter to support her.

Joanna slipped inside the room. "You look better already," she reassured.

"I feel awful."

"I'm not surprised." She put a small white plastic bag onto the counter. "My son's a dentist. He's made sure I have a lifetime supply of oral hygiene products. These are for you."

"Thank you so much for helping me," Cameron said. The tears rose in her eyes again.

"Shhhh. You're going to be fine. The guy is on his way to jail, Zach has a great story to tell his teammates, and now we know we need a little extra security at the entrance to the facility."

There was another knock at the bathroom door, and a female police officer poked her head inside. "May I come in?"

Chapter Fifteen

AFTER SEVERAL MEETINGS with police detectives, the team psychologist, and Sharks security, Cameron was back in her dorm room. Any plan she'd had to get additional interviews with Sharks fans or players was not going to happen, at least in the short term. Practice had been cancelled for the day. She hadn't seen Zach since this morning. She knew he was safe because the police assured her he was, but she needed to see for herself. She couldn't imagine how to thank him for putting himself in danger for her safety. The guy he'd tackled was out of his mind on substances and had a gun; the police officers even had a tough time dealing with him. She was supposed to be changing her clothes before the most stressful meeting yet with the production staff from PSN.

It was no secret that Cameron had stalkers. It was, unfortunately, an occupational hazard for anyone in the public eye. The PSN studios were well-fortified. She had personal security whenever she did sideline reporting for a game, too. She didn't see her own mail until Kacee and PSN security verified it was safe. She was escorted home from work, and she knew there was at least one guy with an earpiece and extensive martial arts and firearms training in her vicinity at all times in New York City. The last place she expected to be confronted was a quiet street in Seattle's suburbs.

Her attacker had been so high on meth he'd told the police his name was Moonfire Starshine; he'd been packing a gun and several hundred rounds of ammunition in his car. Mr. Starshine had driven to the Sharks headquarters from somewhere in Idaho. He'd told the police that he was her husband, and he was sent from God to start a family with her. He'd also told the police that she was disobedient and she needed to be punished. That's what the gun was for.

Cameron threw herself down on the bed, covering her face with her hands. She wasn't sure she could face what she imagined would be Ben's less-than-sympathetic grilling and, most likely, Kevin's smirking. Kevin was about to get his fondest wish: more airtime at PSN. Sharks security and the local police department told her it would be safer for everyone concerned if she did interviews in a more controlled area, and they sent Logan to the practices to do the filming. In other words, she couldn't do the job she'd been sent here to do, and there would be consequences for her—and additional air time for him—as a result.

She'd brushed her teeth three times already. She felt like her stomach was tied in a series of knots. She knew she'd feel better if she ate something, but she was afraid it would come right back up. She wanted a few more minutes to get it together, but she let out a groan as she glanced at the clock on her cell phone. She was going to be late.

Someone tapped at the door as she pulled herself into a sitting position. "Who's there?" she called out.

"Cameron, it's me. May I come in?"

Letting Zach into her dorm room wasn't the smartest idea ever. She was going to do it anyway. She crossed the room and pulled the door open.

"Hi," he said. The look on his face was inscrutable. He had a paper lunch sack in one hand.

"Hi," she said.

They stared at each other for a moment. Cameron resisted the impulse to run her hands over him, checking for injuries. He wasn't fragile. He spent Sundays from September until February each year doing battle with guys as big as he was. They weren't carrying a loaded weapon onto the football field, though.

Tears swam in her eyes again. She battled them back. *He wasn't hurt*, she told herself. *He walked away*. She did, too. Why did she feel so guilty, then?

How would she have ever explained to his family if it hadn't turned out so well?

He crossed the threshold and let the door shut behind him. He set the bag down on the computer desk in her room.

"The chef said you needed some soup to settle your stomach." He nodded at the bag. "There's a roll in there, too. If you're still hungry, we can get you something else to eat."

"That's really nice of him. Thank you for bringing it."

It was always good to thank someone else for doing something kind for you, but it wasn't the thanks she should be offering right now. She rubbed her hands over her face again.

"Zach, I don't know what to say right now." She felt herself shaking again. Her stomach was churning, and her voice quavered. "You saved my life this morning."

"I did not. I threw some guy who wanted to hurt you over the hood of a car until the cops got there."

"No. You—I don't even want to think of what would have happened if you weren't there, or you hadn't figured out so fast that there was something wrong with that guy. I . . ." She shook her head. "It sounds so inadequate to just say 'Thank you,' but I don't know what else there is to say."

His big hands closed over her upper arms as he pulled her into him. His arms slid around her. She wrapped her arms around his waist and leaned her head on his shoulder. She listened to his heartbeat and the rhythm of his breathing. The cotton of his t-shirt was soft against her cheek, and she felt the scratch of the stubble on his chin against the top of her head. He always smelled like he just got out of the shower.

She couldn't stop thinking about it since she saw the security guards disarm her stalker: She could lose Zach. It had nothing to do with a breakup or a divorce. It had everything to do with the strong, vital man in her arms, and the thought that a bullet, a speeding car, or a plane crash could take him away from her permanently. He would be gone, and there would be nothing she could do to bring him back again.

She'd thought she could live without him. She'd spent ten years telling herself that he didn't matter, that the spark she felt when he was anywhere near wasn't real. She would have laughed outright at any other woman who insisted that somehow she knew she'd met her twin soul after he spilled a beer on her in a crowded night club. Her spirit responded to what was inside him, too.

His voice dropped. "He wasn't getting past me."

"He had a *gun*."

She heard the emphasis in his voice. "He wasn't getting past me. Does this happen a lot, Cameron?"

"The network has security. Have I received mail and threats from stalkers? Yeah. Do I think about it every day? No. I wouldn't leave the house if I did, let alone be able to do my job." She let out a sigh. "I have to go downstairs and meet with Ben and the PSN group. I don't want to."

She saw his lips purse in concern. "That's convenient," he said. His arms tightened around her. "The meeting was called off about fifteen minutes ago."

"I don't understand. How do you know this?"

"Here's the quote. 'The Sharks and PSN have suspended the filming of *Third and Long* until further notice. Both organizations are strategizing security upgrades for players and coaches after this morning's incident at Sharks headquarters.' I was standing there when our GM read the statement on-camera. Plus, I told Ben you weren't meeting with anyone but me for the rest of the day." He snorted a little. "I think he wanted to ask if he could film us."

"I'm afraid PSN will fire me for being a security risk. This was a really close call," she said. *Film them doing what*?

"Nope," he said. "Not gonna happen."

He hadn't let go of her, and she made no move to step away from him. He was supposed to be mad at her. She was supposed to pretend like being so close to him didn't make her heart pound, her palms sweaty, and bring back every memory she had of feeling safe and protected in his arms.

"Do you boss everyone in your life around?"

"Nobody but you, Cameron."

She felt the warmth of his breath on her cheek as he nuzzled her hair. His hand slid to the side of her neck. He tipped her chin up with his thumb, and his lips brushed hers seconds later—the barest, most tender touch. Their breath mingled.

Her eyelids fluttered shut, and she whispered, "You taste exactly the same." She slid her arms around his neck and laid her cheek against his much scratchier one.

"You smell the same." He didn't seem to mind that she'd flattened herself against him. Certain parts of him seemed to really like it. "You feel the same, too."

She worked her fingers into his hair and let out a contented sigh.

"Darlin'?"

"Mmhmm?"

Seconds later, she heard the heavy footsteps of an unknown number of men outside of her door, and raised voices.

"Where the hell is Anderson?"

"Damned if I know."

"He's going to be late to the meeting."

"Like he's getting a fine for anything he screws up on for a while. The PR department practically has an orgasm every time his name is mentioned."

"I saw him heading up here a few minutes ago."

"He's probably in his room." The herd moved away from Cameron's door and back toward Zach's. Zach and Cameron heard pounding on a door and shouts of, "Anderson! Answer the door!"

"Maybe he's outside getting interviewed again. Isn't it enough that he had Cameron Online? I'd like to talk to that babe from NFL Network, too."

Cameron could identify Drew's voice from behind the shut door. "All you'll have to do to get her attention is save her from a crazy stalker with a gun. Piece of cake."

She heard the rumble of Derrick's voice. "Shit, yeah. No problemo."

"It doesn't look like he's home right now. Maybe he's being interviewed by CNN or something."

"Do you *know* how much ass he's going to get because of this? The women out there have totally forgotten about you, McCoy. They're on his trail now."

Gales of masculine laughter and name-calling greeted that statement.

Zach stepped away from her, but he still held her

hand. He spoke softly enough that the guys weren't going to hear him.

"I gotta get out of here before the coach kicks my ass for being late. Take it easy. Eat the soup, will ya?" Zach said.

"You can't leave right now," she said. "They'll see you walking out of my room, and it will be on Twitter five minutes later."

"Uh, yeah." He glanced around. "It's too far up to climb out the window. Maybe they'll give up and go elsewhere."

Of course, seconds later she heard Derrick's voice again. "Let's check in on Cameron. Maybe she needs some company."

ZACH DIDN'T WANT to leave Cameron's room at all, or even spend five minutes away from her right now. The incident this morning had been a little too close for comfort. He had a few hurdles to jump before he got to the finish line with her, though, and he needed to talk with her about one of them as soon as possible.

She felt the same, she smelled the same, she kissed the same, and goddammit, his feelings for her were the same. He wasn't afraid of what her dad could do to him and his career anymore, either. He wasn't sure how he was going to explain to his little sisters. He wanted another chance with her, and they weren't going to approve. Even worse, they wouldn't accept her. He loved his sisters, but they could really kick up a fuss when they weren't happy about something.

He was resisting throwing her on the bed in her room and tearing her clothes off with everything he had. If they were anywhere else, he would have done it. He wasn't so sure being caught in her room right now was such a great idea, though, and he'd like to rekindle their relationship with as much privacy as possible.

He heard a number of his teammates' footfalls moving closer toward her room. He glanced around for somewhere to hide. Hiding places were thin on the ground at an NFL training camp. He'd be seen immediately if he got under her desk. There wasn't a big enough gap between her bed and the floor to roll under there. It was the closet or her bathroom, and he made a split-second decision. He threw himself in her closet, pulling the door shut behind him.

He heard several knocks at Cameron's door, and she called out, "Who is it?"

Like she didn't know, but he had to smile. She wasn't making it easy for them.

"We have a meeting in a little while, but we've got some time to kill. Want to play *Just Dance* with us for a few minutes?"

He'd bet five hundred bucks that game had never darkened the doors of the Sharks training facility, but it wasn't like they were inviting her to play *Madden* with them. They probably thought a dancing game would appeal more to a female. He was willing to bet she didn't play a lot of video games, but would choose something more challenging and action-packed like *Halo* or *Grand Theft Auto* if she did.

"I'm a little tired."

"Come on, Cameron. We'll have a good time," Drew coaxed. "Open the door."

Through a crack in the closet door, he could see her turning the knob.

"There she is," Derrick said. "How are you, gorgeous?"

Six guys invited themselves into her room. She looked a little embarrassed, but she smiled at them as they filed in.

"I thought you guys were outside or something."

"We did some stretching. Practice was cancelled today. It isn't the same when you're not out there." Zach was going to kick the ass of that rookie who kept flirting with her.

"Awww. You're sweet. Did you all have lunch?"

"Yes. Are you hungry at all? We'll get you something."

"Thank you, but I'm fine."

Drew nodded at the paper sack sitting on her desk. "It looks like someone dropped food off for you already."

"It's some soup. I'll eat it in a few minutes," she said.

Drew raised an eyebrow and looked toward the closet. "Have you seen Zach? We're looking for him."

Zach could see the slight flush moving over her cheekbones. She didn't look into Drew's eyes, either. He'd better tell Cameron she might want to forget about playing poker—her "tells" when she was lying were pretty obvious. "I think he went downstairs to the meeting room."

Drew's voice was silky. "Is that so? We'd better go track him down, then. Come on, ladies. Good to see you, Cam."

"It's nice to see you all, too." She watched the other guys file into the hallway. Drew seemed to be hesitating. Zach tried to move further into the closet, and ended up smacking into some shelves. It friggin' hurt, and he couldn't stifle the "Shit" he let out.

Drew strode to the opposite side of the room, pulled the closet door open, and stared at him.

"You suck at hiding, Anderson. I could see your ugly mug through the crack in the door. Get your ass out here. You'll have to try to pick up on Cam later."

Zach was going to kill him. Slowly. Maybe he'd pull all that pretty blond hair out by the roots. McCoy wouldn't get so many dates if he were bald.

"C'mon, brother. Let's go," Drew said.

Cameron patted Zach's arm. "Thanks for the soup."

"Yeah. We'll talk again later," he said as he was being hustled out into the hallway.

The rest of Zach's day passed in a blur. He wanted some time with Cameron, but he knew she wasn't going to be alone for the foreseeable future, and he had things to discuss with her he didn't want to talk about in front of others. There were typically several meetings a day with the position coaches. He knew football fans would be amazed to learn that it wasn't the on-field action that wore their asses out. He drank black coffee and ate handfuls of sunflower seeds to stay awake during mind-numbing discussions about the playbook and the endless hours of watching game film.

He strolled out of the last meeting of the day to en-counter Cameron's co-worker, Kevin Adkins, leaning against the hallway wall. Kevin straightened up and stuck out his hand.

"Good to see you, Anderson. How are you doing after this morning's adventure?"

Kevin had retired from San Francisco's team four years ago after a ten-year career as a wide receiver. Zach imagined that most people would think they'd have something to talk about as a result, which would be wrong. He'd never been much of a fan. Kevin was a loudmouth and a show-off. Most of the guys who played with or against him wanted nothing to do with him. Zach wasn't interested, either.

Zach shrugged a massive shoulder. "Fine. Maybe you should ask Cameron Ondine how she's doing instead."

Kevin tried to look concerned. "I haven't seen her all day. Plus, PSN thinks that this all might be too much strain for her. They've asked me to take on some of her interviews. I'd love to sit down with you and get a few comments on tape."

Zach edged away from him. "Maybe later." He didn't want to give the guy an interview, especially since he knew Cameron was perfectly capable of handling her job. He also had a voicemail full of other sportscasters that had already asked. He knew if Kevin scooped her, he would be hammering on Cameron's dorm door as quickly as he could to crow about it, too. What an ass.

"We're going live in an hour or so. I'd love to get an exclusive."

"No, thanks, Kevin."

He started to walk away, and Kevin stopped him in his tracks.

"I have three separate reports that you were seen in Cameron's dorm room this afternoon. Care to comment?"

Zach stopped mid-step, and pivoted to face the smirking Kevin. He pulled breath into his lungs. He realized his hands were forming into fists.

"I can see you're a little upset about this," Kevin said.

Zach stared him down. "Oh, not at all, Adkins. I'd have to actually care what you think to get upset, and truthfully, I don't." He let out another long breath. "I realize you believe that knifing your co-worker in the back will help you get ahead, but you seem to forget that everyone here likes her a hell of a lot more than they like you."

"Doesn't matter. I'll get her airtime anyway."

Zach and Kevin stared at each other as Zach moved closer to him. Zach noticed the sheen of perspiration on Kevin's upper lip. He almost laughed aloud as Kevin took a step back.

Zach shook his head. "You're not worth it."

He spun on his heel and walked away.

Chapter Sixteen

ONE WEEK LATER Zach hit the remote for the security gate and turned into the driveway of his house. The sprawling ranch painted in neutral colors was bathed in late-afternoon sunlight. He smiled at the Elmo sprinkler on the front lawn. His sisters must have taken Butter out for some playtime in the water earlier. His grandma and sisters had no idea he was a few minutes away from the front door. He craved a little bit of home and his family's routines the way some guys wanted an overnight at the Playboy Mansion.

To everyone's surprise, the Sharks head coach had given the players the evening off. He'd sleep in his own bed tonight. The first cuts were coming up next week, co-inciding with the first preseason game. Even a few hours at home with his grandma, sisters, and Butter would do him a world of good.

The first episode of *Third and Long* was broadcasting

tonight. After investing in the best security-consulting money could buy, the Sharks' training camp now resembled a high-security compound with better food and the latest video games. Cameron's stalker was still in jail, unable to raise the half a million dollars in bail the judge asked for during his arraignment. The Sharks front office knew there most likely would not be a repeat of last week's incident, but they didn't want to risk it.

Cameron was still on the job. She was interviewing fans and players in an off-field location. She was trailed by personal security everywhere she went, though. He knew she was spending the evening answering carefully-screened viewer questions on PSN's Facebook page.

He stuck the key in the front lock, only to hear the frantic barking of a twenty-pound puppy. "Butter. Buddy, it's me. I'm home."

The puppy's tail wagged so hard his entire body moved. He barked again.

"Sit, Butter."

Butter looked up at him as if to say, *Are you kidding? Play with me!*

"Butter. Sit."

The puppy sat. Zach gave him a pat on the head, which earned him more tail wags. He walked inside, tossing his keys on a small table inside the front door as he shut it behind him.

"I'm home," he called out.

Seconds later, five women advanced on him at a run. Actually, his grandma couldn't run any more, but he could see the glowing smile on her face as she moved toward him. Five women tried to talk to him at once, too.

"Zach! What are you doing here?"

"We made baked spaghetti for dinner. There should be plenty."

"Butter learned to roll over at obedience class."

"That show's on tonight. Are you watching it with us?"

Whitney threw her arms around his midsection. "I missed you."

He ruffled her hair. "I missed you, too. Did you get that paperwork in?"

"Yeah." She nodded vigorously. "It wasn't as hard to fill out as I thought it was going to be." He knew that wasn't the whole story, but he'd be talking with her about that later.

He wanted his kid sister to have the time of her life in college. Maybe she could pledge a sorority or go to some of the sporting events. Mostly, he hoped she could overcome the fear of being on her own for the first time. He would work to impress on her that even though she might be on her own, they weren't far away.

His sisters were tugging him toward the kitchen, and he let them. It smelled great in there. He felt a breeze from the open kitchen windows. The sun was still high in the sky, but late afternoon tinted everything in gold. Their kitchen décor was simple: He'd bought a hardwood expandable rectangular table and chairs from Ikea a few years ago. His sisters usually had a plant or flowers as a centerpiece in one of his grandma's old glass vases. Whitney had painted a huge, colorful flower arrangement on a canvas which hung on one wall.

Butter the puppy ran circles around them, barking excitedly and trying to jump on Zach. He reached down to scoop up the wriggling puppy, and Butter licked his chin.

"How many times a day are you walking him now?"

Shelby grinned up at him. "He goes out twice, but we're wondering if he needs a walk at lunchtime. He's crazed."

"The breeder warned me about that. I know it's rough on all of you while I'm gone. How's the chewing?"

"We haven't lost any shoes lately. He tried to snack on one of your game helmets, though." Courtney scratched under Butter's chin, which sent him into a wriggling, licking frenzy. "He didn't like the taste. Even with the chewing, the trainer says he's making great progress. She wondered if he'd like to take a few more classes so he could get a certification to be a therapy dog. He could visit kids in the hospital. He has the temperament for it, she said."

Zach held the little dog up to his face. "No eating the football helmets. Bad puppy."

Butter licked his nose and gave him a puppy grin. So much for the scolding. He cuddled the little dog against him. He knew he'd have to be firm with the dog, but it was hard to resist anyone who was so excited to see him. He also liked the idea of Butter's getting additional training so he could come along when Zach went to visit sick kids at Children's Hospital, for instance.

"Do you want me to help you all with dinner?" Zach said. His grandma sat down at the kitchen table and nodded toward another chair. He lowered himself and Butter into it.

"It's all under control," Shelby assured him. "We'll eat in twenty minutes or so." She sat down in the other chair. "How's training camp going?"

"So far, so good." He leaned back in his chair and reached out for his grandma's hand. "How's my favorite girl?"

"I'm fine." She squeezed his hand with her much frailer, thinner one. He gave her hand a gentle squeeze in return; he knew her joints hurt. Her arthritis was getting worse. The girls would all go to school or work during football season. It was time he started thinking about a companion or nurse for her during the day and for when the team was on the road. She had so much trouble getting around, and she still tried to cook and clean for all of them. He'd told her he'd take care of it, but she resisted every time.

"Grandma, what did the doctor say about those anti-inflammatories he had you on? Did he give you some that worked a little better?"

"He says I would feel much better if I took up swimming or maybe a yoga class for older people." She made a face. "I don't know, honey. I'll miss my shows if I'm gone all day." His grandma was a daytime-TV junkie. She was always after him about what Dr. Oz had to say on any subject, which he found comical. She didn't seem to understand that pro football teams had the best medical advice money could buy, but that was okay. He knew she loved him and was only trying to help.

"Maybe I could find a yoga instructor who would come to our house. Would you like that?"

"Just as long as he or she doesn't expect me to get on the floor."

He had to laugh. "I promise he or she won't. Let me look into it." He set the puppy down on the floor by their feet and said, "Grandma, I have something to talk with you and the girls about."

ZACH PATTED HIS belly after a second helping of baked spaghetti, garlic bread, and salad. "That was delicious."

Ashley grinned at him from the other end of the table. "We're glad you liked it. There's freshly-baked chocolate chip cookies for dessert."

"I'll try not to eat them all." He glanced around at his sisters and his grandma. "Maybe we can have dessert in a few minutes. We need to have a conversation about something."

Whitney pushed her plate away and folded her arms. Ashley exchanged glances with Courtney and Shelby.

His grandma started to stack the empty plates and got out of her chair to carry them to the sink. "No, Grandma," he said. "Let me do that. You relax. Does anyone want some coffee or something else to drink?"

"No."

"We're fine."

"Don't worry about it."

He had a bad feeling all four of his sisters knew what the topic of discussion was. Sure enough, when he returned to the table with a glass of his grandma's sweet tea for himself, Whitney spoke up.

"Is this about Cameron Ondine?"

He tried to look casual. "That's not a problem, is it?"

"I don't like her. She broke your heart. She's not a nice person," Whitney burst out.

Of course, the other three chimed in.

"Why are you talking to her?"

"Her dad spread rumors about all of us—"

"Please tell me you're not going out with her again."

They'd evidently discussed the matter before he got there and agreed to present a united front as a result. He loved his sisters, but it would be great when they had other things to focus on besides his love life.

"Girls," his grandma said. "Let him talk."

All four had now folded their arms over their chests and regarded him with varying degrees of anger and disappointment reflected in their faces. He let out a sigh.

"Whitney, I was pretty mad at her when I thought she was trying to talk to you on-camera. You grabbed her as she went by, didn't you?"

His sister slouched in her chair. In seconds, she was the eight-year-old he remembered that got in trouble for throwing peas at her older sisters during dinner. "Yes," she mumbled.

"I heard you weren't very polite to her."

Whitney's head snapped up. "I don't like her! Why can't you date someone like Holly? She's nice. She likes us."

He hauled breath into his lungs, and sat up a little

straighter in his chair. "I enjoy talking with Holly, but she's eleven years younger than I am. Even if I was interested, that's a pretty big age gap." He looked around the table at his sisters. "I understand that you are worried about my talking to Cameron or spending time with her again. The reason why I wanted to talk with you about what's going on is that I'm sure you're not going to be happy with some of the things you'll see on the TV show tonight, and I thought you might want a little warning ahead of time."

"What things?" Shelby demanded from the other end of the table.

"Are you dating her?"

"Zach, why?"

His grandma reached out to put her hand over his again.

"People have made snap judgments about all of us since we were little. What did we learn from that?" he asked them.

"It's not the same thing," Ashley burst out. "She's going to hurt you again."

"Yes, it is the same thing. You've never actually talked to her. You don't know anything about her besides what's been on TV or in magazines. Maybe you should give her a chance before you make up your minds." He pulled in another huge lungful of air. "I want to bring her home for dinner with all of you next week."

"Do you get why we're worried about this?" Courtney asked.

Tears stood in Whitney's eyes.

"Whitney, honey," his grandmother said. "Why don't you help me get the plate of cookies."

His littlest sister got up from the table without another word and walked away from him. His grandma patted his shoulder as she moved away from him. The other three stared at him.

"So, there's nothing we can say to talk you out of this?" Shelby said.

"I'll bring her home. Just give her a chance. Listen to what she has to say. What happened to me with her dad— it wasn't her idea. She had nothing to do with it."

"*Sure* she didn't—" Ashley burst out. Courtney grabbed her hand.

Shelby stared at him and said, "I hope you're going to remember this when we bring home a guy you might not like."

THE ANDERSON FAMILY gathered in the family room to watch the premiere of *Third and Long* with chocolate chip cookies and tall glasses of cold milk. Zach was fairly positive that most of his teammates were out on the town, not sprawled on a huge sectional couch with four sisters, their grandma, and a puppy rapidly falling asleep in his lap.

"Grandma, there might be a lot of cursing in this," he warned as the opening credits scrolled across the screen.

"I'll plug my ears," she replied. He had to smile. He heard Cameron's voice over a montage of Sharks players.

"Welcome to the Seattle Sharks training camp. I'm Cameron Ondine. I'll be spending the next month living in a dorm with eighty men who want to be able to run out on the field for the first game of the NFL season in a Sharks uniform. The Sharks can sign only fifty-three of them. We'll be following them and their stories over the next month."

He bit into a cookie and watched as his teammates ran onto the practice field the first day of camp. The camera-person zeroed in on Drew McCoy and Derrick Collins. Their comments on audio were crystal-clear.

"Did you see the rookie LB yet? Mr. Butkus Award winner?"

"That kid is huge. We'd better watch our asses."

Derrick snorted. "He's not so tough. He probably still sleeps with a teddy bear and calls his mama each night before he's tucked in."

The next piece of film featured the defense lining up against the offense. The rookie linebacker burst through the line and gave the Sharks' QB a shove before he could get a pass off.

"Nice," Derrick yelled at him. "Now that's what I'm talkin' about."

"Hey, old man," the kid yelled back at him.

Derrick looked momentarily pissed, and then started to laugh. "You're all right, rook. You're all right."

To Zach's surprise, the show didn't gloss over what happened with the former head coach. They let video tell the story, including the incident between the head coach and Cameron, which he was amused to note Logan had caught in its entirety. He wondered how she felt about being part of the story.

The rest of the hour program, to his chagrin, was a re-telling of his and Cameron's attempts to spend some time alone. He had to laugh at the shaky, hand-held camera attempts to film their stroll on a darkened practice field while his teammates heckled him over the fact the media had discovered he and Cameron were previously married. He was surprised to see a few minutes of video of their late-night brownie feast in the cafeteria one night. He laughed again at the video of his having breakfast with Cameron, and badgering her to eat more than a few bites.

He wondered who had edited the video. They'd managed to catch Cameron at her most likeable and sympathetic. It also wasn't lost on him that his sisters smiled at the footage, and laughed when she interviewed the three little boys watching practice that first day.

The last ten minutes of the episode made his stomach clench. Security cameras must have picked up Cameron's being led away from being confronted by her stalker outside of the facility. The security guard was telling her, "Officers are here. Let's get you inside the building."

He could hear her frightened voice. "We can't leave. He's still there with Zach. We have to help Zach. Please."

"Zach's right behind us, Ms. Ondine. The other officers have the suspect in custody."

She tried to break away from the guard. "I don't see Zach. Where is he? Please tell me he's not hurt!"

The screen faded to black, and the credits rolled. The room was silent.

Chapter Seventeen

CAMERON AWOKE THE morning after the *Third and Long* premiere to a madly vibrating cell phone and insistent knocking on her dorm room door. She wasn't surprised about the phone. She was so tired last night she fell asleep despite the noise. Right now, it scooted across the nightstand of its own accord. If that wasn't enough, one glance at the clock radio on her bedside table told her she'd overslept.

She heard more knocking at her door.

"Who's there?" she called out.

She recognized Drew's voice. "There's two guys in the lobby looking for you," he said. "And good morning."

"Good morning," she said. She crept closer to the door in the soft gray light of an overcast morning in the Seattle area. "Did you recognize them?" She grabbed for the Princeton logo hoodie at the foot of her bed and pulled it on, jamming her glasses on seconds later.

"I think you're going to recognize them," he said.

She opened the door a crack. She was willing to bet it wasn't the first time Drew saw a woman with no makeup, glasses, and bedhead. Over the past few days, he and most of his teammates seemed to forget that she was the enemy—a working member of the media—and started treating her like a pesky kid sister. She couldn't decide whether she was insulted or complimented by the fact he'd seen her multiple times now when she was less than camera-ready, and it didn't seem to matter to him.

He grinned at her. "I'm pretty sure it's your dad. He's with a guy who looks like he has a stick crammed up his ass."

Her stomach dropped out. She really wasn't in the mood for a confrontation with her father today. She'd avoided his phone calls since the night Zach told her what really happened in Las Vegas ten years ago, too. She'd realized any discussion with him was going to have to happen in person to have any impact at all. He'd just hang up on her and do what he wanted if it didn't.

"Thank you for letting me know," she said.

"He tried the 'Don't you know who I am?' line with Joanna the receptionist. She wasn't having any of his shit." Drew's laughter echoed in the hallway. "She told him she didn't care if he was the President of the United States. He wasn't getting into the players' dorm, and that was final."

Cameron owed her. She wondered if Joanna would prefer a spa weekend or a piece of fine jewelry more. She didn't have time to think about it right now, though. She made a mental note for later.

"I appreciate the warning, Drew. I'll get myself down there."

"Want us to duct-tape him to the goalpost?" he asked. She must have looked surprised. "Zach mentioned he can be a bit of a handful."

"No, thank you. I'll take care of it. Thanks again." She shut the door and hurried to the bathroom.

One hour later, Cameron was showered, dressed, and ready for her day. She called downstairs to discover that her father and his unidentified guest had taken themselves off to the nearest Starbucks. She'd also had a tense conversation with Kacee via cell phone. Kacee was unavailable. Again.

"I'm working on something for Ben," Kacee insisted. "I can be there in a couple of hours."

"That's not good enough, Kacee." Cameron let out a long breath. "I've been really patient with you and all of your 'extra duties for Ben,' and it's not helping. If you don't want the job, tell me and I'll find someone else."

Cameron glanced down at the huge list of "to-do's" on her iPad. She needed a new assistant as soon as possible. Interviewing candidates in the middle of her existing responsibilities would be all kinds of fun, but she couldn't put it off any longer.

"Ben won't let you fire me," Kacee shot back.

"Really? The last time I checked, you work for me, and you haven't been working for me for several days now. Again, Kacee: If you don't want the job, quit. If you're not here in an hour, consider yourself fired."

Cameron stalked downstairs. Her day hadn't even started yet, and she wondered if it was too late to crawl back into bed. She knew Zach had spent the night at his house. He was probably in the weight room by now. She wondered what he'd thought of last night's show. She wasn't especially happy with some of the footage PSN featured. She hated having her private life exploited for ratings, and according to some of the texts she'd seen on her phone before she fell asleep, ratings were through the roof. In other words, it was about to get worse.

Ben was probably delirious with happiness over the sky-high ratings and resulting advertising sales. She'd be a lot happier if he'd stop stealing her assistant.

Speaking of ratings, she was going to have to get some additional interviews and some film for tonight's taping of *NFL Confidential*. Logan covered Drew and Derrick's pre-practice workout yesterday, and they talked some of the other guys on their floor into taping a funny segment showing off their dorm rooms. She could hear the guys cleaning yesterday before Logan arrived with his camera.

A couple of dark-haired, tall guys in suits with earpieces met her as she stepped off the elevator. They did their best to blend into the woodwork but never took their eyes off her. She beckoned them over.

"I need to go outside to do some work."

"We'll follow you, then." The guy she thought of as Earphone One nodded at his colleague.

"Do I need to tell you where I'm going?" She wasn't even sure what to say. She didn't want anyone to think she was ungrateful, but she wished—again—she didn't have to be trailed by security everywhere she went.

"Go about your business," Earphone One said. "Don't worry about us." His partner nodded.

Cameron walked out to the practice field. The Sharks had resumed their public practices a couple of days ago, but the team had instituted the same rules the NFL put in place for game day—no handbags, no backpacks, nothing brought onto the grounds that wouldn't fit in a gallon-sized clear plastic bag. The fans wouldn't arrive for another hour or so.

She introduced herself to a couple of the rookies doing a little stretching out on the field after their lifting. The two guys stopped what they were doing and got to their feet.

"How's your day?" she asked, trying to get the conversation going.

An offensive guard several inches taller and at least a hundred pounds heavier than she was gave her a nod. "Happy to be here, Ms. Ondine," he said with the thickest Southern accent she'd ever heard. His teammate seemed to be struck dumb by her presence; he stared and said nothing.

"Please, call me Cameron," she said.

"Mah mama would smack my hide," he said. "She told me to treat you like I treat her." He stuck out his hand. "I'm Caleb, ma'am. Nice to meet you."

She knew he'd attended a tiny school in Louisiana that wasn't known for offensive linemen. He was so talented scouts were beating a path to his door by the time he was a junior in high school. He didn't take the four-year scholarship at a bigger school because he didn't want to leave his mother after Caleb's younger brother died at seventeen in a drive-by shooting. When he was asked at the Combine what he wanted most in life, he said he wanted to buy his mother a house so she'd never worry about being homeless again.

Caleb was every bit as humble and polite as she'd been told by more than one of her colleagues. She was really looking forward to featuring him during her training camp coverage. It was a pleasure to talk with someone who deserved every bit of success that came his way.

"What do you think of training camp so far?" She grabbed the stylus for her iPad and pulled up the note-taking app. "What has surprised you most?"

She saw his shy smile. "The weather. It's the beginning of August, and this would be cold back home."

She glanced up to see the sun peeking through the formerly leaden skies. This was a well-known phenomenon in Seattle called a "sunbreak." For anyone used to summertime in the South, though, they'd be looking for a sweater in the mid-sixty degree day.

She spotted movement out of the corner of her eye. Her father and a guy she'd met once before were striding across the field. Her dad didn't look happy, to put it mildly. To her amazement, Caleb stepped between her and her obviously irritated parent.

She tugged on the sleeve of his jersey. "Caleb. That's my dad. It's okay."

"I don't recognize him. You stay behind me, ma'am." She saw Caleb square his shoulders, fold his arms across his chest, and spread his legs slightly in a power stance.

"May I help you?" Caleb called out.

"You can get away from my daughter," her father demanded.

The guys with the earpieces were quick to surround her, too. "Freeze," one of them called out to him.

"Guys. Guys. It's my dad."

"He was told nobody but team personnel, media, and security are allowed on the field without an escort during non-practice hours," Earphone One told her. He addressed her father. "I don't appreciate this. Who's your guest?"

"Do you know who I am?" her father said. Cameron stifled a groan. Her dad's life motto seemed to be "when in doubt, threaten people and act like a jerk." Sure enough, he narrowed his eyes and glared at Caleb. "I could end your NFL career on the spot." He curled his lip at Earphones One and Two. "I could also have you fired immediately."

The guy standing next to her dad might be handsome if he wiped the superior smirk off his face.

Cameron couldn't see the expression on Caleb's face, but she could see Earphones One and Two. They didn't look happy.

"You can threaten us all you'd like, sir, but the front office put these rules into place for a reason. Ms. Ondine will meet with you inside the building at her convenience."

Another security guard stepped into Cameron's line of vision. "Let's go," the guy said to her dad.

Her father glared at her. "We'll be talking about this shortly."

"I'm sure we will," she said. She resisted the impulse to roll her eyes.

Her father and his guest walked away, accompanied by the security guard. She patted Caleb's arm when they were out of earshot.

"Thanks for protecting me."

"Any time, ma'am. You let me know if you need any more help."

"Would you like to do a little interview today when you're finished with practice and meetings? I'll ask you a few questions about training camp. It'll be fun." She scribbled "Ask Caleb about his roommate" on her iPad. All rookies had a training camp roommate. She already knew Caleb's roommate was a bit of a handful.

She saw him smile again. "I'd love to. Thank you for asking."

Cameron walked inside the practice facility to write up a few more notes and organize the rest of her to-do list for the day. She had to go talk to her father, which she wasn't looking forward to. The longer she put it off, however, the worse it would be for Joanna. She was more worried about inconveniencing Joanna than making her father angrier.

Cameron and her father weren't close. He was incensed about her career choice, and he'd made that plain on a number of occasions. She'd noted his increasingly irritated phone calls about last week's confrontation outside the facility, but she hadn't called him back. She knew it would be nothing but another long argument, and she was tired of dealing with it. It was time to pay the piper, however. She shoved the door open to walk into the lobby and came to a halt, partially hidden behind a large trophy case full of Sharks memorabilia.

Zach and her father were glaring at each other about twenty feet away. The guy standing with her father was regarding Zach like something he'd scraped off his dress shoes.

"I'd say it's good to see you, Anderson, but that would be a lie," her father said.

"I'd have to say the same." Zach didn't smile. He gave her father a nod. He glanced at the guy with him. "Who's this?"

The guy didn't extend his hand, and neither did Zach.

"I'm Eugene Redmond," the guy said. "And you are?"

Eugene worked at her dad's hedge fund. He was introduced to her at the company holiday party last December. Her parents had been badgering her to go out with him ever since. She was fairly sure other women would enjoy his company, but she'd rather jam her hand into a blender and hit "frappe."

He was tall, handsome, and had plenty of money. He was also shallow, a social climber, and really impressed with himself. In other words, she'd rather stay home alone with Netflix and the only snack she allowed herself these days—a big bowl of steamed edamame.

Truthfully, she'd rather stay home with Zach. He looked like a guy who would appreciate a big bowl of popcorn and a movie. They could think of many other things to do at home alone as well. Cameron snapped out of her memories of what an evening alone with Zach had meant a few years ago and realized Zach had taken a step toward Eugene. Eugene stepped back in response.

"I'm Zach Anderson. You and your friend should go back where you came from."

"My daughter has been avoiding her family responsibilities long enough. We expect her to do something more important in life, something that utilizes her education. She's quitting her job today and coming home with us," her father snapped.

Zach looked incredulous. "I used to think guys like you only existed in bad action-adventure movies." He glanced over at Eugene. "What's in this for you?"

Cameron's father stared at him. Eugene's mouth opened and shut. He must have thought better of saying anything at all to a guy big enough to break him in half.

She'd heard enough. She stepped out from behind the trophy case and walked toward her father.

"Maybe we should find somewhere more private to have this conversation," Cameron said.

"There won't be a conversation. Go pack your things. You're quitting your job today. We'll be on our way home as quickly as we can get to the airport."

Joanna was trying to pretend like she wasn't observing all of it. Zach's fingertips brushed the small of Cameron's back. It was comforting that Zach was sticking around for her right now, but she couldn't rely on him to deal with the situation. She wasn't a little girl anymore. She could take care of herself. At the same time, the fact he stayed was very sweet.

"I'm not leaving, Dad. I love my job, and I'm keeping it."

Her father's eyes narrowed even further. "Your mother is terrified. Your sister is embarrassed. Haven't you taken this far enough?"

"I'm sorry they're not happy, but I'm not changing my mind." She gave the same nod to Eugene he'd given to Zach. "Flying to the West Coast? You must have missed your tee time."

"If you're choosing him over me, I'm not sure I'd want to date you in the first place," Eugene said.

She almost laughed out loud. What an ass.

"I'm fairly sure she didn't want to date you at all, Redmond," Zach said. "That hedge fund VP job must not be pulling the ladies like it used to."

Cameron wasn't even going to ask how he knew what Eugene's job title was. In the meantime, her father was flushed, his lips were pressed together so hard they were white, and his eyes were barely slits. "You should have learned last time, Anderson. I protect what's mine."

"Are you threatening me in front of witnesses?" Zach looked like he was discussing the weather. "I'm not the same naïve college kid you went after then. I protect what's mine, too."

"I should have finished you and your family before. It'll be much more enjoyable now."

"Leave Zach and his family out of this," she snapped.

Neither man moved. Cameron still felt Zach's fingers on her lower back. She let out a sigh.

"What a treat that you stopped by, Dad." She couldn't keep the fury out of her voice. "I'm fine. I don't need your help, and you need to go back to New York. Goodbye."

Her father wasn't there to protect her. He was all about appearances—the perfect, socially prominent family. He wanted her to marry someone he could control, too, which was the reason for Eugene's trip to Seattle. Her father's concern didn't extend to Cameron's happiness, and it never would. Her mother bought into her father's manipulations, too. She was done appeasing him, because it would never end.

She turned away from him and took a few steps. She heard her father's voice again.

"This discussion isn't over."

She whirled to face him. "Yes, it is. I'm over twenty-one. I have a job, and I have my own money. Go back home."

ZACH WATCHED CAMERON'S father and his guest stalk out of the building to their waiting limo without another word. Preston Ondine must have been late for his next dastardly act. All he needed was a mustache to twirl, and some helpless woman to tie to the railroad tracks. Cameron must have retreated to her room for a little while to regroup.

He'd had no idea that Cameron's relationship with her family was so strained. He knew there was trouble. She'd mentioned that her parents were mad at her for not wanting to be involved in their various pursuits ten years ago, and he was fairly sure he was the only person in her life that encouraged her to follow her dreams of being a sports reporter. She'd also told him the other night that her father had been after her to quit her job since she got it.

Most parents would be proud of a daughter who worked her way up from a minimum-wage runner to a prominent on-air job in ten years at a hugely popular cable sports network. He realized she'd never had the money challenges he did, but she worked every bit as hard. She had fire in her belly. There was no amount of money that could purchase ambition and determination.

He gave Joanna a wave. She grinned back at him. "You're a good man, Zach Anderson," she called out.

"Thanks. You're pretty great yourself," he responded.

He exited the lobby and paused in the hallway outside of the weight room. He pulled his phone out of his warmups pocket, and dialed a number.

"Shelby Anderson, please," he said to the person answering the phone.

CAMERON'S PHONE RANG less than five minutes later. She glanced at the screen, saw it was her mother, and hit the button to send the call to voicemail. The phone rang again a few minutes later. Her sister. She sent her to voicemail, too.

She had to focus on work right now, but she wanted to talk to Zach. She glanced out a window that faced the practice field. She could hear the sounds of Sharks fans filing in to sit on the grassy hill overlooking the field, and the DJ the Sharks used to pump up the crowd. She grabbed her phone again, hit the text app and his number, and typed in THANK YOU. I OWE YOU. It wasn't the most romantic thing she'd ever said, but it was true.

She'd taped the latest episode of *NFL Confidential* last night. She needed to do a couple of voice-overs before the episode was complete, and she should interview a few more players today. She hit the button to read the texts that had come in over the past hour. Ben wanted her to know that the Sharks' head coach gave the okay to start filming *Third and Long* again. She was a bit surprised Kacee hadn't enlisted him to demand Cameron not fire her, but maybe that was coming later.

She knew next week's filming would be dominated by the cuts that would be happening shortly after the Sharks' first pre-season game, and teasing additional cuts after the second game. Hopefully the interest in her and Zach's "storyline" would wane as a result. In the meantime, she had a list of players she was already building stories around.

The kicker and the punter were practicing at the far end of the field with a portable upright, one of the long-snapper candidates, and an assistant coach. Most football fans didn't give a lot of thought to kickers and punters unless a game was won or lost because of them. She made another mental note: *Talk to those guys about an interview.*

She heard her phone chirp with an incoming text. She grabbed it out of her pocket.

MEET ME IN THE LOBBY AT 7 TONIGHT. ALSO,
   YOU'RE WELCOME. ZACH

She resisted the impulse to twirl around with sheer happiness. She couldn't wait to spend some time with him again.

Chapter Eighteen

ZACH HEARD THE final double-blast whistle as he watched Derrick knock the rookie tackle on his ass again. Practice was over for the day. Derrick offered his hand to the kid to help him up.

"C'mon. Let's go get some water."

"I'll be knocking you on your ass soon," the kid told him.

Derrick let out a laugh and slapped the kid on the back. "No, you won't."

The kid nodded to the fans crowding the fence. "I'm at the autograph table today." The autograph table was typically populated with rookies that spent an hour signing pint-sized footballs for the kids attending training camp practices.

"Have fun with that," Zach told him.

Zach was going to spend the next hour or so signing his name hundreds of times, too. The fans that lined up at the fence that ringed the practice field were thrilled and sometimes a bit nervous to spend even thirty seconds conversing with a Shark. He got a kick out of most of them. He made a special point of signing for the kids that snuck away from the table to talk with a vet. He'd encourage conversation with the adults, if they were courteous and friendly.

Most football fans would be amazed to know how many people would sit through a practice and wait in line for half an hour to tell you they were still pissed off over a play that went wrong last season, or that you'd screwed something up in a game in college. He kept thinking he'd get used to it eventually, but it was always a shock to have some sweet-looking little old lady demanding to know why he failed to knock Adrian Peterson into the middle of next year.

He trotted over to the huge box of Sharpies that the PR department put out each afternoon after practice and grabbed a couple of them. He caught a glimpse of Cameron inside the facility. She appeared to be scribbling on her iPad, while Earphones One and Two tried to blend into the woodwork again. He stared at her until she glanced up, grinned at him, and went back to what she was doing.

He had a surprise for her. It took an outrageous number of phone calls, making a side arrangement with Earphones One and Two, and promising Cameron's boss he'd play in the network's charity pro-am golf tournament next year during the offseason, but he hoped things would go off without a hitch. He wondered if she'd read his text yet.

CAMERON HEARD A tremendous cheer from the practice field. She had been told the coach was giving the team twenty-four hours off to rest and relax before the final preparations for their second pre-season game in Oakland. She sent Logan out to Autograph Alley to film a few of the rookies signing this morning, with a special emphasis on Grant Parker, the Sharks' latest QB prospect. She would have to reschedule tomorrow's interview with him for later in the day, which might be a challenge. Everyone else wanted an interview with him, too. He was a first round draft pick that the organization hoped would be the heir to their All-Pro gunslinger Tom Reed in a few years. Most Sharks fans greeted Grant's arrival in Seattle with cautious optimism. He was the Sharks' third try to bring in a kid smart enough to listen and learn from someone who was winning high school and college championships while Grant was still in Pull Ups.

Grant seemed to have it all: articulate, friendly, and handsome, he had a blemish-free personal life, a rocket for an arm, and he was smart and fast enough to scramble out of the pocket at will. It was Cameron's job to find out if the too good to be true twenty-two year old was really all that.

Her phone chirped with an incoming text, but this one vibrated as well: Urgent. She pulled it out of her pocket to check.

I'LL PICK YOU UP IN AN HOUR AND A HALF.
BRING A TOOTHBRUSH. ZACH

She clicked on the attached photo. She saw a covered wooden porch-style balcony with comfortable-looking wooden chairs weathered to light gray and an equally-weathered table for two. The balcony's view was of serene water and blue skies. She had a million and one things to do today between another taping of her show and dealing with the continuing filming of *Third and Long*, but she wondered where Zach's balcony was and how long it would take them to get there.

She was still scribbling notes on her iPad when she heard the click-clack of football cleats on flooring. She heard Zach's voice: low, sensual, and for her ears alone.

"I'll be out of the shower and dressed in half an hour."

The mental images that phrase produced made her blush. She'd been in the shower with Zach before, but it had been a while. Maybe he'd learned a few more moves. She wasn't going to think about where—and with whom—he'd learned whatever he had in the past ten years, but she was fairly sure she'd enjoy them.

"That's nice to know," she said.

His lips moved into a confident grin. His eyes twinkled. "Why don't you go grab your toothbrush and a change of clothes? I'll pick you up at your door."

"Where are we going?"

"You'll see." He sauntered away before she could tell him that she had a ton of work, that it wasn't like she could just leave, that she had to reschedule her interview with Grant, that she . . .

She needed to get a life.

The Sharks' training camp facility wasn't unpleasant. The food was good, the room was comfortable, and she wasn't unhappy. The shows being filmed here were setting ratings records, despite her colleagues' continual mocking of the Zach and Cameron content. At the same time, she longed for a few hours of relaxation. She hadn't had a day off since she got here. She'd ended up having to fire Kacee for absenteeism a week ago, so she was handling all the details herself, like scheduling interviews and dealing with the production staff. She'd also like some time alone with Zach.

Ambition warred with sheer exhaustion. She set her own schedule, so it wasn't like she couldn't get any time off if she needed a day. If that balcony in the picture was anywhere near, she wanted to go there, even if she knew she had to be back first thing in the morning.

She grabbed her phone one more time, pulled up the contact information for PSN's production staff, and tapped in I'M ON ASSIGNMENT. I'LL SEE YOU ALL TOMORROW MORNING.

Her phone rang less than five minutes later. She hit the answer button and held it up to her ear. "This is Cameron," she said.

"Have a great time," her producer Ralph said. "We'll see you tomorrow, *chica*."

Cameron raced to her room and threw a change of clothes, underwear, and some toiletries into the Birkin bag her mother insisted she couldn't live without. She upended the contents of the bag she typically carried inside the Birkin, too. Maybe her mother thought that carrying a twenty thousand dollar handbag big enough to function as an overnight bag was a good thing. One of the additional benefits of carrying a big-ass bag: She wasn't advertising to everyone in the dorm and team facilities that she was planning on an overnight stay elsewhere.

She stepped out of her high heels and into a pair of flats. She locked her iPad in the room safe. She was fairly sure nobody would steal it, but after the unpleasantness with Kacee, it was always good to be careful.

Speaking of "safe," Cameron dug through her suitcase for the box of condoms buried under the still-rumpled clothes she'd never quite unpacked. As always, it was the single—in her case, divorced—woman's conundrum: Bring them, and let Zach know she was a sure thing, or forget them and end up either declining or on a frantic hunt for a drugstore at some ungodly hour. She hadn't slept with every guy that offered over the past ten years, but she'd slept with enough to know that Zach was the best she'd ever had. She'd like more.

She stuffed them into the bottom of the Birkin.

A minute or so later she heard a knock on the door and Zach's voice: "You ready?"

"Not quite yet."

"Open the door, will you?" She could hear many heavy, running footsteps in the hallway, and she heard Drew's voice, too.

"Cam, you'd better get your pretty little ass out here, or I'm going with him."

Zach had devised a method of getting out of the building that bypassed the media still hanging around, his teammates, coaches, and everyone else that might find it interesting that he and Cameron were obviously leaving together. It was really nobody's business where they were off to, but she knew Ben would think differently.

Fifteen minutes later she and Zach were in the back seat of a black SUV with tinted windows, and Earphone One was driving.

"Where are we going?" she asked for the fifth time.

"You'll find out." Zach leaned forward and patted Earphone Two on the shoulder. "We have a reservation at the ferry dock both ways, so we just get in line."

"Got it," Earphone Two said.

"The ferry dock?"

Zach reached out for her hand. "The ferry dock." He looked amused. "You seem a little stressed, Cameron. Let's try something I learned from yoga class. Take a deep breath, hold it until the count of eight, and release that breath."

She concentrated on lowering her voice. Earphone One and Earphone Two did not need to hear everything she had to say. "We only have twenty-four hours. I blew off everything I had to do today, but I can't do that tomorrow. I have to—"

He captured her chin in his fingertips. He brushed his lips over her mouth. The temperature in the car shot up twenty degrees in ten seconds or so. He stroked a gentle fingertip down her nose.

"I have things I have to do tomorrow, too, like make the football team. We'll be back in plenty of time. Right now, though, I have you all to myself for a few hours, and I'd like to enjoy them."

ZACH'S PREPARATIONS HAD paid off in a big way. They arrived at the dock in record time. Late morning and mid-week turned out to be the ideal time to take a ferry to Whidbey Island.

"Have you been on a ferry before?" he asked her.

"In New York." Cameron grinned at him. "It probably isn't any different."

"Sure, it is. You're with me. Let's get out and go stand at the bow," he said. He took her hand as they wove amongst the parked cars together. He took deep breaths of the fresh air and salt water spray as they advanced on Whidbey. It was a perfect, gorgeous sunny day in the Seattle area, and he was with a woman that made the day pale in comparison. He knew one of the earphones was close by, but nobody else approached them as they stood wrapped in each other's arms.

Earphones One and Two also proved to be adept with programming an address into the car's GPS. Zach and Cameron arrived at the Inn at Langley a short time after the ferry docked on Whidbey Island.

The Inn at Langley was secluded, private, and offered a 180-degree view of Saratoga Passage, a peaceful waterway. There was a beach steps from the building. Zach couldn't wait to get out there with a blanket, a bottle of wine, and Cameron.

"Zach, this is gorgeous," she breathed. She glanced around eagerly as she grabbed her huge handbag off the floor of the car. The bag was big and sturdy enough to double as a weapon.

"I hoped you'd like it," he said. "Let's go get checked in." He opened the door for her to precede him into the lobby. Earphones One and Two would be enjoying a day on Whidbey Island as well. Zach was fairly certain they wouldn't have a lot to do. Maybe they could practice incapacitating someone with a paper clip or something.

MINUTES LATER, ZACH and Cameron were shown to a luxurious guest suite with an unobstructed view of sky and water through panoramic windows that took her breath away. The sitting area featured a cozy-looking couch, a wood-burning fireplace, a flat-screen TV and a table perfect for two. Cameron saw a window seat on one side of the doors opening out onto the balcony that would be great to snuggle into on a stormy day.

The bedroom was dominated by a queen-sized bed made with sumptuous white linens, a down comforter, and fluffy pillows. The bathroom had a soaking tub built for two. The porch-style balcony was the thing that drew her, however. She dropped her bag on the floor next to the couch and walked out to take a look.

"Zach, you have to see this," she called out to him. She turned to see him grabbing the bottle of Chateau Ste. Michelle Eroica Riesling out of an ice bucket, along with two glasses and a corkscrew, and heading out to her.

Cameron's parents could afford the finest of everything in life. She made a great living, too. She didn't want for much, and if she saw something she needed, she bought it without a second thought. She'd been some pretty wonderful places in her life, too, and stayed in some of the greatest hotels in the world. This was better than anyplace else she'd ever been before. The combination of rustic, cozy charm, the quiet, and the beautiful view was irresistible. She'd just gotten here, and she knew she was coming back again as soon as possible.

Maybe it was the company.

She glanced around at 180 degrees of blue skies and water. Zach gestured to the weather-beaten pair of lounge chairs on the balcony. "Sit with me?"

"Absolutely."

The wine was cool, crisp, and refreshing on a summer's day. She leaned back in her chair, propping her feet up on the conveniently placed footstool. Zach moved his chair closer to hers, and reached out for her hand. He sprawled back in his chair, too, crossing his feet at the ankles.

They absorbed the view for a few minutes. He took another sip of wine and put his glass down on the small, low table between them. She glanced over at him.

"The hotel's chef made a picnic for us. Want to go to the beach with me?" His smile melted her heart.

She took another sip of wine as she nodded. The stuff was great. She tasted peaches, a hint of lime, and a burst of subtle sweetness. She tried to remember when wine had tasted so wonderful, when the air had smelled so fresh, and when holding any man's hand had made her heart beat *rat-a-tat-tat*.

She'd felt the same way ten years ago in the desert outside of Las Vegas. This time, she wanted it to last. She couldn't bear to let him go again.

"Let's have some more wine first," she said.

"We don't have to leave, you know. We can have our picnic right here."

"It's good to have an option."

He picked up his glass again and touched it to hers. "To options," he said. He held her eyes, and he didn't look away as he sipped. She sipped, too.

Putting her glass down, she got to her feet and moved to stand between Zach's spread knees. Holding his gaze, she perched on his thighs. He scooped her legs up and settled her against his chest. She rested her head on his shoulder and sighed, "Do we ever have to leave?"

"Not tonight, darlin'. Not tonight."

CAMERON'S HALF-LYING AGAINST him was worth every bit of effort it took to get them out here for twenty-four hours.

"This is perfect," she said.

"It could be this perfect all the time, Cameron," he said. He rested his cheek against the top of her head. It was go big or go home, and he had no intention of going home without her again. "Stay with me."

He felt her let out another long breath. Her arms tightened around him.

"What happens when we go back?" she said. "Your sisters don't like me. My dad's going to ratchet things up.

I still have to work with people who are mad at me for firing Kacee and think I shouldn't be involved with you, and I need another assistant."

"My sisters will come around. Do you care that your colleagues mouth off to you about being involved with me?"

She peered up at him, and he saw her mouth curve into a smile.

"Truthfully?" He felt her exhale. He also felt the tension draining slowly from her. "Nope." He'd like to ask her about it. He'd like to ask her about a lot of things. Right now, though, he had another agenda.

"We'll talk about how we'll make it work. I promise." She gave him a squeeze in response.

"It's a miracle anyone gets together, isn't it? Don't all these people focusing on us have something else to do?"

"That's their problem," he said. "I'd rather concentrate on you." He nuzzled her temple, which won him a breathy little laugh. She kissed the side of his neck. He had to kiss her again.

Her mouth was soft, cool, and tasted like the wine they'd been drinking. He felt her tongue slide against his, and she moaned a little. The party in his pants was definitely on.

"Let's make out," she whispered, and he had to laugh.

He held her against him with one arm while he slid his other hand over her belly, under her top, and cupped her breast. He felt her nipple harden against his hand. The breeze blew strands of her hair over his face. He could smell the shampoo she used, the clean scent of cotton clothes, and the lilies and musk scent she had been wearing since the first time he held her. It still drove him crazy.

They didn't have to worry about anything at all for the next twenty hours or so. Nobody was asking for an autograph. They were safe from crazed stalkers, his teammates and coaches, her co-workers at PSN, and both of their families. They had food, wine, a cozy bed behind a locked door, and each other.

The sun bathed them in light and warmth. The scent of salt water mixed pleasantly with the wine in their glasses. Things were amazing.

She pulled her mouth off his and straddled him, scooting up to rock against him. Her soft palms flattened against his abs, sliding her hands up and taking the polo shirt he wore with them.

"You don't need this right now," she said.

She pulled it over his head, dropped it onto the floor beneath them, and bent her head to swirl her tongue around one of his nipples, pulling it into her mouth. She suckled him. He almost came in his pants.

"Cameron," he rasped.

"Mmm?"

He saw a flush rise over her cheekbones, but he loved her sweet boldness with him.

She teased his now-hard nipples with gentle fingers as she leaned forward to kiss him again. He didn't think it was possible, but he felt himself get even harder.

He brushed the hair out of her eyes, and drank in the half-lidded look of desire on her face. She wanted him.

He wanted her, too. He shoved himself off the chair, wrapping his arms around her bottom and carrying her inside to the neatly-made bed.

He gave the glass door leading out to the balcony a nudge with one foot as they passed. They were three floors up, still kissing. Their clothing flew as they undressed each other.

The mid-afternoon sun spilled onto Cameron's nakedness. She speared her fingers into his hair, twining her arms around his neck. His fingers were a little busy, too, as they roamed over the body he was getting reacquainted with. She was thinner than ten years ago. He felt muscle built by workouts, but her skin was sun-kissed and even softer than he remembered. He pulled her into him with both hands.

"Cameron," he said. He was already breathing hard. She was, too. He tossed her on the bed and followed her down. She let out a sexy little laugh as she bounced a bit on the mattress beneath them. She wound her legs around his hips as she took his face into her hands. Their tongues slipped, stroked, and twined around each other.

She pulled her legs higher around his hips. She slipped her arms around his neck again and ground her pelvis against his. It was his turn to groan.

She yanked her lips off of his long enough to say, "Will you think I'm a really huge slut if I tell you there's a new box of condoms in my bag?"

He suckled one of her nipples and she arched against him. He slipped his fingers through the moisture between her legs and slid one finger inside of her. She gasped. He had to smile.

"Will you think I'm a big man-whore if I tell you I bought the twelve-pack at the drugstore yesterday?"

"I want you so badly," she said.

"I want you, too, darlin'." He reached over her head and yanked the bedding down with one big paw so she could scramble under the sheet. The party hats were in his overnight bag. "Hang on. I'll be right back." He crossed the room on a run, banged his shin on the coffee table, and let out a "Shit!" But he managed to grab his bag.

She sat up, the sheet falling away from the perfect breasts he remembered. He couldn't wait to get his hands—and his mouth—on them again.

"What's wrong? Are you okay?"

He grabbed the box of condoms. "I'm fine." His shin hurt like a mother, but what was a bruise when he was about to make love to a woman he hadn't been able to forget for the past ten years?

While he was at it, he grabbed the still-chilled bottle of Riesling from the coffee table he'd just crashed into. He could think of some interesting uses for the wine, but they would happen a little later. Right now, he was going to get back in that bed, suit up, and make sure she enjoyed herself.

Cameron pulled him back into the nest of pillows and blankets with her, shoving the sheet off so she could see his leg. "Let me see." She bent closer to get a better look. "It's all red. Are you sure you didn't hurt yourself? It might be a little swollen—"

"It's fine," he told her. "Don't worry about it."

"Doesn't it hurt?"

"Hell, no."

He ripped the pull tab right off the box, grabbed a foil-covered condom, and tossed the rest of the mangled box onto the nightstand next to the bed, tearing open the foil packet with his teeth. Attempting to roll the slippery latex disc onto himself and kissing her at the same time took more dexterity than he possessed at the moment.

"Shit," he muttered. "They're tricky."

SHE HAD TO grin. Seeing someone typically so in-charge fumble with a condom was adorable. "I've got it." She took it out of his fingers.

She held it up, noted which way she needed to roll, and pulled it over the head of his penis. She knelt in the bed next to him. Instead of rolling the condom on with her fingertips, though, she pushed him onto his back and used her mouth to make sure it was on correctly. He groaned. He moaned. He begged.

"Jesus. Where did you learn—oh, hell, I don't give a shit. God, that feels good," he said through slitted eyes and clenched teeth. He speared his hands into her hair, but he let her decide where she was going next instead of pushing her head down. She took the head of his penis into her mouth, swallowed, and heard him gasp.

"Want more?"

"Fuck, yeah. Your mouth—" He groaned again. "That feels—Jesus!"

It took a few more minutes to make sure the condom was secure, and she swirled her tongue over his thick, long penis as she slowly inched the latex to the root. She cupped his balls in her hand, too, gently manipulating them as her mouth moved over him.

An already excited and aroused man grew even more so, and she heard him say, "Jesus, Cam, I can't hold it, I—*Fuck*!"

HE'D TRIED EVERYTHING. Multiplication tables, thinking about Sharks defensive sets, remembering the last meeting he'd had with his financial advisor. Nothing helped. Her mouth was warm, wet and soft, and she seemed to know exactly where he wanted it and what he wanted her to do with it. Then again, anywhere on his penis worked for him. The oral stimulation combined with the visual of a naked, gorgeous Cameron in daylight was more than any guy could withstand.

At least he hadn't made a mess.

She sprawled across him. He cupped her ass in one palm.

"How's your shin?" she asked.

"Darlin', my shin's the last thing on my mind right now." He let out a breath. "I—I—God. I came so hard."

He saw the flush creeping over her cheekbones again. She was an intriguing mix of siren and sinner, but he remembered *that*, too. "I'm glad you liked it."

"There isn't a guy in the world that wouldn't like it."

She propped herself up on one elbow and didn't meet

his eyes. "I read about putting a condom on a guy with my mouth. I wondered if it really worked."

He let out a chuckle. "Uh, yeah." Knowing she'd tried something new with him sent a thrill through his entire body. He felt a little embarrassment that he couldn't last under her onslaught, but there wasn't a guy on the planet that wasn't going to make sure she had even more fun than he had. First, though, he needed to make a pit stop. He reached out to kiss her again.

"I'll be right back," he said.

He got rid of the used condom, wiped himself off a little so putting the next one on wouldn't be such a pain in the ass, and hurried back into the bedroom. She was resting against the pillows. She'd pulled the sheet up and over herself. He got back into the bed and wrapped his arms around her again. Their mouths fused. He thrust his tongue into her mouth the way he wanted to bury himself inside of her, and he felt her tongue slipping against his.

Before they got into the car this morning, he thought about slow caresses and teasing her until neither one of them could stand it anymore. He'd enter her slowly. He'd move languidly. He'd take his time, and he'd let things build. Maybe he could try that next time, because right now, his penis had other plans. He pulled one of her nipples into his mouth while his hand strayed over her torso, moved over her belly, and traced through a small patch of pubic hair.

"Oh," she said. He felt the little pearl between her legs. It was already slick. He rubbed one finger around it. "Oh. Oh, that feels good."

He was about to make it feel even better. He sucked

harder on her nipple. She arched against him, and he saw her reaching up to rub the other nipple he didn't have in his mouth with her free hand. She still loved nipple stimulation, and he was going to make sure she got as much as she liked.

He stroked two of his fingers through the wetness between her legs, rubbed a little more on her clit, and she let out a long moan. Her head tossed on the pillows.

His greatest fantasy was still watching Cameron touch herself. His dick seemed to love it, too.

She was still rolling her other nipple through her fingers, pinching and manipulating it. He stroked his tongue over the hard nipple still in his mouth, and he reached a little lower. He slid two fingers into her, found her clitoris with his thumb, and stroked in and out as he rubbed her. Her legs fell open.

Her moans gave way to "Oh, God, don't stop. Please don't stop."

He pulled his mouth off her nipple. "Tell me what you want," he whispered.

"I want you to fuck me. Hard," she said. "I want to come."

"Just once?" he enticed.

"No. Over and over. God. Please!" she cried out.

Her hips were moving, slamming against the mattress. He teased her clit with the heel of his hand, stroked his fingers faster and faster inside of her, and grabbed her nipple in his mouth again. She bit her lower lip, and he felt her tensing.

"I know you're there. Come for me, Cameron."

He was still pounding into her with two fingers. Watching her touch herself and listening to her beg him to fuck her was the hottest thing he'd ever experienced.

He felt her clenching around his fingers, and she let out a shriek. He saw the tell-tale flush of orgasm spreading across her face and upper chest, the smile that turned up the corners of her lips. He felt her body relax against him. She looked dazed. Even more, she looked sated. For the moment. He wasn't done yet, though.

She stretched, clasped her hands behind her head, and let out a satisfied sigh. "Amazing," she said.

He gently extracted his hand. He reached back, grabbed another condom, and managed to put it on without help this time. "You're about to feel even better." He pulled her legs open again. He was inside her with one long slide, and she wrapped her legs around his hips. She reached out to grab his ass.

"I remember this," she said. "I remember you."

Oh, hell, yeah. It was even better than it was before, if that was possible.

"Faster," she said. "Oh, God, faster."

"You want more?"

"Yes. I—I want you. More. Harder!" she cried out. She half-sat and wrapped her arms around him again. He leaned down to kiss her and moved faster. She raked her nails down his back and cried out, "More!"

He was only too happy to accommodate.

He flipped her onto her belly, pulled her up onto her knees, entered her from behind, and kept thrusting. The best part of this position was the fact he could play with her breasts and her clit. He lightly bit the side of her neck.

"Do you know how many times I've dreamt about fucking you? I'd wake up hard as hell," he said into her ear. "I'd dream about how you feel, how you smell, the noises that you make when I'm deep inside you. I dreamt about how you tasted."

His fingers rubbed her clit. He thrust into her again and again. He was pretty sure she was so far gone she couldn't say anything in response, so he kept talking. "I wonder how many times I can make you come in a day. Let's find out."

"Oh. Oh! Don't stop," she cried out.

He was still pounding into her, still playing with her clit with one hand, and he felt the contractions of her orgasm gripping him. She let out another loud cry. This was so much more than two bodies doing what bodies were designed to do. He could have sex with anyone, but he was making love with his sweet Cameron.

She brought him off, too. He came so hard he saw stars. He felt her slump into the bedding, and he wrapped his arms around her waist. He was still inside her. He wanted to stay.

Zach snuggled closer to Cameron as he tried to catch his breath. He nudged the hair off the side of her neck and kissed the exposed skin as he spooned around her. She slid her fingers through his. He reached out, grabbed the balled-up sheet from the foot of the bed, and tossed it over them.

"That air conditioning is frosty, isn't it?" he blurted

out and immediately wanted to hit himself with something. That was all he could come up with at a time like this? She probably expected something tender and meaningful, and he had a whole bunch of nothing right now.

Actually he did have a few things, but now he was the one who felt a little shy. He knew he didn't have the words to tell her how thrilled he was she took the lead, or how he could encourage her to do it again. Making love with her again was even better than every erotic dream about her he'd had over the years. There was no greater aphrodisiac than being with a woman who let you know how much she wanted you, except for a woman who let you know she wanted you again.

He felt himself slip out, despite his best efforts to stay.

Cameron rolled over in his arms and traced his lower lip with one finger. "I had fun."

"I did, too."

He watched her bite her lower lip. She was a little tongue-tied, too. She glanced up at him through her lashes. He pulled her closer with one arm and freed the other to cup her cheek in his hand.

"You know I have to kiss you now," he whispered.

TWO HOURS LATER, hunger and thirst drove Zach and Cameron to temporarily abandon the bed. They'd have to clean up the foil wrappers on the rug next to Zach's side of the bed. It was a good thing she'd bought the big box, too. She couldn't stop the grin that spread over her face again.

They pulled on hotel-provided white terry robes and padded into the living room in search of the picnic basket. Zach pulled perishables out of the mini-refrigerator. Cameron popped a few grapes into her mouth as she spread the bounty across the coffee table.

"No PB and J?" Zach joked.

"Not unless it's organic." She pulled out a sliced loaf of crusty bread and nodded at a selection of toppings. There was more sliced fresh fruit, a bag of sweet potato chips, a green salad with dried cranberries, walnuts and feta cheese, dressing, olives, and a package of grilled chicken. There was a package of salted caramels, and another container of some type of cookie bar she'd never had before. She popped the lid on them and held it out for Zach.

"Dessert first?" he said.

"Always."

He pulled a bar out of the container and held it up to her lips. "Take a bite."

Normally she would refuse what looked like a calorie-laden treat, but she had to try it. She almost moaned aloud as chocolate ganache, coconut, and buttercream frosting exploded on her tongue. She held the bar up for him to take a bite, too.

"We're going to have to talk the chef out of a few more of those before we leave," he said. "They taste almost as good as you do."

They made a respectable dent in the food. Zach poured them each another glass of wine. Cameron tucked her legs beneath her and put her almost-empty plate on a side table. Zach shook the container of cookie bars at her again. "There's two left."

"Let's leave them for a midnight snack," she said.

"Perfect." He cleared off a place on the coffee table and put his feet up. "So, darlin', I believe I promised you we'd have a conversation about a couple of things."

Chapter Nineteen

THE SUN WAS still high overhead and streaming through
the windows of Zach and Cameron's suite. It was a perfect day on Whidbey Island, but they wouldn't be going
outside right now. It was time for what Zach knew might
be a pretty uncomfortable conversation.

He and Cameron were still perfect for each other in
his opinion, but there were a lot of problems to work
out before they could ride off into the sunset together.
She was worried about whether or not his sisters would
accept her if their relationship continued to develop. He
wasn't especially happy to have to deal with her dad again
in any capacity. Her job and her family kept her on the
other side of the country. Even if the Sharks were willing
to trade him, he was not going to uproot his family to
play on the East Coast. When the family and geographical issues got sorted out, they could discuss the ongoing
problems with the programming director of PSN being

a greedy, uncaring ass who exploited them both for his own ends.

She got off the couch, opened the mini refrigerator door, and pulled out a bottle of sparkling water. She waved it in his direction. "Would you like some, too?"

"That sounds great."

She grabbed another bottle, returned to the couch, and handed it to him. They were both stalling, but he knew the longer they put it off, the worse it would be.

"Let's start with the easy stuff," he said as he reached out for her hand. "I want you. I want to stay with you." He hauled in a breath. Suddenly, he felt like a teenager asking the prettiest girl in his class on a date, with all the accompanying nerves and adrenaline rush. Maybe he should try to keep this light. "Would you like to go steady, as my grandma would say?"

She burst out laughing, but her eyes softened. "I want you, too. I missed you and I—" She scooted closer to him on the couch, pulling her legs up beneath her and leaning into his side. "Then let's go steady." She reached out to kiss his cheek. "Does this mean we'll be together on national holidays?"

"Absolutely."

"So, what does this—a relationship—look like for us?" she asked.

"We'll hang out. We'll date. We'll have fun together. What do you think?"

He saw her lips curve into a wistful smile. "I'm pretty sure I'd like that. So, we'll hang out together and see what happens?"

His voice was soft. "I'm in it for a lot more than 'seeing what happens' between us, Cameron. Are you, too?" He caught her hand in his much bigger one and brought it up to his lips to kiss her knuckles.

"Yes," she whispered.

He had to kiss her again. Truthfully, he never wanted to stop kissing her. Her mouth was so soft against his, and he felt her arms slide around his neck. She even managed to not club him with the sparkling water bottle she still held, which was nice. Mostly, he couldn't get enough of how she felt, how she tasted and how he wanted to take her right back to bed. If he did, though, they'd never get any of the stuff between them out on the table, and it needed to happen.

"Speaking of hanging out, I would really like it if you would come over to my house and have dinner with my sisters and my grandma after my game this weekend," he said. "I'll get a day off, and I'd like to spend it with you."

"Zach, your sister Whitney can't stand me." She tucked her legs beneath her again and took a sip of water. She didn't meet his eyes.

"That's not true. My sisters are angry about what happened before. I told them they need to give you a chance, and the only way that's going to happen is if you all spend some time together."

She finally looked at him, but the smile slid off of her face.

"I'm not sure having dinner with them is going to work. At all."

"Just once. Will you have dinner with them once? If it doesn't work, I'll accept the blame."

"Maybe we should let them get used to the idea first," she said.

He cleared a spot on the table and propped his legs on it. His shin still ached a little. It was nothing compared to how he felt at the look on Cameron's face. She wasn't happy. She set her bottle of water on the end table next to her and folded her arms across her chest.

She heaved a sigh. "I don't understand. Why is this so important to you?"

"I realize it's rude to answer a question with a question, but when was the last time you spent any time at all with your family? How did that go?"

She tightened both arms around herself and looked at the floor. "I saw them at my sister's wedding. It was fine."

"That was several weeks ago. Do you visit often? Do you spend time together, or do you only see them once or twice a year, or whenever your dad decides to fly in somewhere?"

"We're all pretty busy—"

"Not too busy to spend time with the people who are always in your corner," he said.

The typical warmth in her brown eyes had faded. She stared at him for a moment, and shook her head, sharply.

"Why is that, Cameron? Do you avoid seeing them?"

She glanced away from him again. She seemed to shrink into herself, too. "Maybe we should talk about something else for a while."

He felt an icy fist squeezing his gut. She was willing to share her body with him, but she wasn't letting him inside her head. Most guys might be relieved to have a woman who wouldn't talk, talk, talk about the things she thought about. Not him. They'd spent three days together ten years ago, but the best part of Cameron's enforced presence in his world the last couple of weeks was the fact he was getting to know her. He'd like to know more.

Their lives were as different as they could possibly be, and it was more than financial worth. He had money, too, but his resources were nowhere near her family's. She didn't think about how much things cost, because she never had to. The money was always there. It wasn't even a consideration for her. He and his family knew what it was like to wonder where their next meal was coming from or whether they'd have to choose to pay the light bill or the water bill, so it never quite went away.

Even more than the money, Cameron was the poorest rich girl he'd ever met. No matter what happened with his career, there were five people waiting at home who loved him for himself, not because he had elite athletic ability. If he got cut from the Sharks tomorrow, he had sufficient money now to take a job coaching high school football and live a relatively normal life. He also knew his sisters and grandma would be happy with the simple life he could provide. His sisters would find husbands and settle down, but their adult lives would be vastly different from their beginnings.

He couldn't imagine an evening spent with Cameron's family. She'd told him before that she grew up with nannies and that she and Paige went to boarding school. Did the Ondine family ever make popcorn and watch TV together? Did they do yard work or have any hobbies in common? Did they have pets? Did they share themselves with each other at all?

"Well, then, how about this: Have you ever lived anywhere else but New York City?" he said.

"Besides living in Connecticut while I was in prep school, not really. We spend the summers at the Hamptons, but that's a short trip. PSN's studios are in New York, so moving anywhere else might be a challenge."

He felt that. Her words stung like a lash. They were done before they even started, and she wasn't willing to negotiate.

"In other words, if things worked out between us, we'll have a pretty big geographical problem."

She thought about that for a few seconds. "Not really. That's what planes are for."

"How many days a week would we be able to spend together, then? We both work every weekend six months a year. You're probably working on pre-production a couple more days a week, too. I'm here at practice, and Tuesday is typically my only day off during the season. Would we meet halfway, then? How do you see this moving forward?"

She got to her feet.

"I'm sure we could work something out." She went into the bathroom and shut the door. Seconds later, he heard the shower come on.

This was even worse than he'd envisioned. He'd thought the conversation about the problems that they faced would be uncomfortable and might cause an argument. He never imagined she'd refuse to talk with him at all. He wondered if it was worth trying to restart the conversation elsewhere.

He glanced over at the rumpled bed. Their first mistake had been getting out of it. They seemed to communicate just fine when they were both nude. He got to his feet and strode over to the bathroom. She hadn't locked the bathroom door. He swung it open, dropped his robe on the floor, and reached out for the shower door.

She let out a shriek. "What are you doing?"

"We can't fight when we're naked." He stepped inside the shower stall, pulling the door shut behind him. He picked up the small bottle of organic shampoo. "Let me wash your hair."

"I can do it." She wrapped her arms around herself again.

He reached out to stroke her cheek. "I'd like to. Please?"

He saw her mouth curve into a smile, and she nodded. She ducked beneath the spray, turning her back to provide better access. He massaged shampoo through Cameron's long hair, talking all the while.

"So. We have a geographical problem. We have a family problem on both sides. I want my sisters and grandma to get to know you, and your dad detests me. We work on opposite sides of the country, and neither of us can move. How are we going to resolve some of these things?"

She tipped her head back as he massaged her scalp

with gentle fingers. "Maybe we should discuss this later. I'd like to enjoy what you're doing right now instead."

"I'd like you to enjoy what I'm doing right now, too, but I want to make this work." He resisted the impulse to back her up to the shower wall, pick her up so she could wrap her legs around his waist, and plunge into her again. *Later.* They'd already had a lot of sex. They needed to start talking with each other.

"That feels great," she sighed. The warmth was back in her voice. Of course, parts of him were responding to the wet, naked parts of her.

It was too bad he couldn't train his dick to obey on command. *Down, boy.*

All this coaxing Cameron to talk about her feelings meant that he'd most likely given up his man card for life, but he knew from living with five women that females fell in love through their ears long before their hearts were involved. He'd learned to listen first. If she knew that he cared about the things she found important and tried to understand why she made the decisions she did, they might be able to find common ground on the bigger things, like how the hell they were going to see each other six months a year.

Maybe he should start small.

He rinsed the shampoo out of her hair with the hand-held shower attachment and picked up a washcloth. He grabbed the small bottle of shower gel. "So, question. Do you want to be a sidelines reporter and have your show for the rest of your career? What's your ultimate goal?" He was smoothing the washcloth over her, leaving a trail of suds. He saw her shoulders move up and down more rapidly. She turned to face him and wrapped her arms around his neck. She backed him up against the shower wall. The hot water cascaded over them, and he pulled her closer.

"Do you want to talk, or do you want to do the wild thing?" she said.

She reached up and bit his lower lip. Of course, he felt the tug in his groin, too. She fit against him like they'd been made for each other. One great advantage to making love in the shower: The clean-up was a lot easier.

"Actually, I had another idea." He sank to his knees. "It seems I forgot to return the favor earlier, darlin'."

Twenty minutes or so later, Zach wrapped her in towels and his discarded robe, and half-carried her to the bed. She was pretty boneless after two huge orgasms. He resisted the impulse to pat himself on the back when he looked down at a satisfied, drowsy Cameron, who beamed up at him.

"Where'd you learn that, hot stuff?"

"I may have read it in a book or something," he teased.

"Remind me to send the author some flowers."

She rolled over a bit in the bed so he could join her. A discarded condom wrapper stuck to the bottom of his foot. He rubbed the sole of his foot against the other to get rid of it, and pulled the sheet over them as he wrapped his arms around her again.

"That won't be necessary."

They'd both had partners before and after each other, but he didn't want to be reminded of them right now. He pulled them into the cocoon of pillows. Most of the day had passed without venturing out of the suite. They could have spent the time anywhere, but the salt-tinged breeze still wafting through their room relaxed and soothed him. "How about that question I asked you a little while ago? I'm curious."

She rested her head on his shoulder as her fingertips traced the outline of his six-pack. "About my job?"

"Exactly."

"I enjoy reporting from the sidelines, but after this latest incident, I'm wondering if that part of my career is over." She let out a long breath, and he resisted the impulse to punch the air in victory. His efforts to listen and ask questions were earning her trust. "There's security at NFL stadiums, but I can't imagine Earphones One and Two wanting to deal with a stadium full of potential threats. I enjoy doing my show, but I have to find interviews. The contacts I made at games came in pretty handy there. It's either keep doing what I'm doing, or push myself to the next level." She was silent for a minute or so. "My dream is to be the first female NFL game analyst."

He couldn't have been more shocked if she'd hit him with something. He never considered most of them someone to emulate, and Cameron wanted one of their jobs. He knew she'd run rings around those guys. But in order to understand the nuances of the game she'd have to work twice as hard as the guys who'd played it.

"Those guys sit behind a desk for an hour a week during the season and mouth off about stuff they don't understand," he blurted out.

"That's not true. Most of them are former players. There are some that are better-spoken than others, I'll give you that, but they're not inexperienced."

"Why do you want to join them? You're a journalist, darlin'. Won't you miss that?"

She rolled onto her side and brushed her lips over his. If he found her ultimate goal shocking, he was even more surprised at the gratefulness he saw in her eyes. "You called me a journalist. That's one of the sweetest things you've ever said to me."

"It's true."

"There are lots of people who would argue with that, especially some of the guys I work with. They think women can't really understand or effectively report on the game because they never played it on a professional level."

"Then they are dumb shits, and you shouldn't listen to them. I know you understand the game. I've seen your sideline reports."

He saw the corners of her mouth turn up. "You're such a sweet talker." He couldn't prevent the laugh that rolled out of him, and she looked pleased. She rested against him for a minute or two. "Do you think I've lost my mind to go after this?"

"It's no different than wanting to be drafted in the first round or chosen an All-Pro. It's work and determination and extra effort. I heard another player say once that the separation is in the preparation. It's true. If you are better equipped than the guys, they'll have a hard time over-looking you."

She propped herself up on one elbow. "So, I told you my ultimate goal. What's yours?"

"Personally or professionally?"

"Whichever you'd like to tell me. Or both."

He propped himself up on an elbow, too. Their sweet intimacy struck him anew: He longed for a lover and a friend. A woman he could confide his hopes and dreams to. Someone he could laugh with. He wanted that woman to be Cameron so badly it took his breath away.

He pretend-coughed a little to disguise the wave of emotion he felt.

"Do you need some water? I'll go get it," she said.

"I'm fine. Don't worry about it." He gazed into her eyes, which were a hundred shades of brown. "My professional goal is to make it to the Pro Bowl at least one more time, and I am already preparing for my retirement from the NFL. Every game you get after thirty years old is a bonus." He hauled in a breath. "After retirement, I'd like to be a coach."

A huge smile spread over her face. "Really?"

"Absolutely. I'd like to start at the high school level. Coach the kids up, and teach them the fundamentals. I'd have a blast. There's not a lot of money in it, but that's okay. I'll be fine with what I have now."

"What about your personal life?"

"That's easy. All I have to do is make sure my sisters get through college and find guys to marry who deserve them, which might be a tall order. Right after that, Grandma might want a place of her own, so I'll work on that, too."

"So your grandma really does live with you." She looked interested and curious. "Tell me about her."

"She's my mom's mom. She helped raise my sisters after my mom died." He stroked the hair off Cameron's forehead. "She's—she still cooks and cleans for us. I told her she doesn't have to do that shit anymore, I can hire someone else to handle it, but she says she wants to pull her weight. That's nuts. She's done so much for me and for my sisters. She let me hire a dog walker and she's okay with my making sure she has transportation when she has errands or needs to get out of the house for a while, but that's it. She loves Judge Judy and all those crap daytime TV shows. If they make her happy, though, I'm glad she likes watching them. She's kind and funny and accepts people as they are. I think you'll like her. We love her."

"Does she hate me, too?"

"Not at all. She's not like that. She'll want to feed you, though." He kissed the middle of her forehead.

Cameron let out a soft laugh. He laced his fingers through hers.

"You have a dog?" she said.

"His name is Butter, and he's a yellow Lab. He's a four-month-old chewing machine. He also likes to lick."

"You must miss him right now."

"I do, but I'll see him again soon. Do you have a pet?"

She looked regretful. "No. I'd like one, though. I wish I could have a dog, but I live alone and I travel. It wouldn't be fair. My family didn't have pets at all, and I've always wanted one."

He loved the mental picture of Cameron and Butter playing in the back yard of his house, hanging out with him and his family, and long nights spent holding each other and talking before they fell asleep. Even the smallest things would be special if she was with him.

"Maybe we could make some kind of deal about honorary dog ownership. One thing's for sure—if Butter chews up one more pair of Shelby's shoes, she might want him to move in with someone else."

The sun sank lower in the sky as they talked and laughed about the minutiae of their lives. She told him about her adventures on the subway. He told her about what it was like to deal with teenage sisters. He'd tried to eat his weight with the picnic basket earlier, but he was hungry again. He'd like to broach the subject of her family, and maybe he should do so when they both had a full stomach.

He scrambled out of the bed, grabbed the one-size-fits-all hotel robe that Cameron could wrap double around herself, and padded into the living room.

"Don't eat those cookie bars," she teased him.

"That's right. I was going to call and see if we could get more before we have to leave." There weren't a lot of leftovers from their feast earlier. He knew there was a prix-fixe eight course dinner in the inn's restaurant each night, but he didn't want to spend the entire evening with anyone else but her.

"Are you hungry again?" He could hear laughter in her voice.

"Always."

CAMERON SPEARED ANOTHER bite of her salad with a fork as she swirled the wine in her glass. She'd worked up more of an appetite than she thought. They ate a Mediterranean take-out dinner at the weather-beaten wooden table on the little balcony overlooking the water, and drank some more excellent wine as the sun set.

"I wish we didn't have to leave," she said.

"I wish we could stay, too." Zach touched the rim of his glass to hers. "Maybe we should come back soon."

"Maybe," she said.

She took another bite of food and managed not to choke, which was always a good thing. It wasn't that she didn't want to spend more time with Zach. She never wanted to let him go. She had had a taste of what the last ten years of her life could have been like, and she wished this peaceful enjoyment could be their reality. She didn't see how it could realistically happen. She took another sip of wine.

He was right. They would be apart at least six months a year, unless she quit her job and followed him to Seattle. One didn't take a job in the fourteenth-biggest TV market after earning and holding a national job in the number one market in the United States, if not the world. She maintained editorial control over her work and scheduled her own interviews. She knew she would never get the kind of independence she craved in a smaller market, nor would she be able to have a career that would continue to grow commensurate with her ambition and willingness to work hard.

Zach wasn't going to play football forever, but he also

was not going to want to retire a five-hour plane ride away from his family. She loved her family and she knew they loved her, too, but they weren't as close as Zach's. He'd told her he talked and texted with at least one of his sisters and his grandma every day, and most of the time, it was all of them. He'd described the simple things that most families shared—cooking together, playing games or watching TV in the evenings, taking Butter to the dog park on weekends he didn't have a game and was in town. He made sure his sisters brought the guys they dated home to meet him first. His focus was completely different than any other thirty-two-year-old she'd ever met.

"We're not perfect," he'd said about his family, "but we love each other, and we're happy together."

Her musing was interrupted when Zach passed a hand in front of her eyes. "Hey. I lost you for a few minutes, didn't I? Tell me what's on your mind."

She put her fork down on the plate and reached across the table to lay her hand over his.

"I've been thinking, and I'm not sure how this is going to work."

He looked startled for a few seconds, but covered his confusion with a big grin. He knew exactly what she was talking about. He wasn't giving up on their future quite so easily.

"What do you mean? I have plenty of those cookie bar things now. We can split them. We'll eat our dinner, and we don't have to finish the bottle of wine if you don't want to. Things are great."

"No, Zach, that's not what I'm talking about." She

forced herself to look into his eyes. "I'm not sure we should take this any further. You don't want to move, I don't want to move, our families won't get along, I have to deal with my job, and—"

"If we handle this stuff one obstacle at a time, we'll be fine." He squeezed her hand. "It's not like we have to get married tonight or anything."

Just that fast, she remembered standing at the altar in the tiny wedding chapel in Las Vegas. They were a bit buzzed from the evening before. She could still see the shabby decorations and hear the couple in the back pew, who spent the entire time Zach and Cameron were repeating their vows trying to shove their tongues down each other's throats.

She also remembered the joy in Zach's eyes, the way his big hand trembled when he slid the plain gold band onto her finger. He needed a custom-made ring due to the size of his fingers, so they'd decided to buy him a ring later on. She remembered the gentleness of his kiss, and his whispered, "I'm crazy about you, Mrs. Anderson."

They weren't even married long enough to get him that ring. She still had hers. The gold band lying in the bottom of her jewelry box at home was a daily reminder that there was no such thing as a happily ever after.

"That's the point. I'm not sure we could get married at all." She picked up her wine glass and drained the contents. There wasn't much left in the glass, but she hadn't chugged alcohol since she was a freshman in college. "Everything is great as long as we're in bed, but when we get out of it, there's all this stuff waiting for us."

He picked up the wine bottle and poured a serving into her glass.

"So you think that's all we have together?"

"No," she said. She picked up her glass again and took a swallow. Maybe she should lay off the wine, but she was in pain thinking about what had to be said, and maybe it would be easier if she were drunk while she did it. "It's even worse that I know what I missed out on before. I also know that I can't do this again."

"What do you mean?"

"My heart will break in a million pieces if we try and it doesn't work, and I don't think I can survive it. I lost you before, and the only way I got through it was to tell myself that it was like a dream, and I woke up." She made herself look into his concerned eyes. "I have a good life now. I work. I travel on the weekends six months a year. I go to the gym, I get take-out, and I go over my interview questions. Sometimes I do some more research or sit on the couch and watch something on TV. I don't miss what I never had, so maybe I shouldn't try for it at all."

She picked up her glass again. He took it out of her hand, and set it down next to him. She was a little surprised at his actions, but she didn't reach out to yank it back.

"So you're just going to keep running away from anything in your personal life that's a challenge?" he asked. "How's that working for you?"

"You don't understand—"

"Try me, Cameron." He tipped her chin up with gentle fingertips to look into her eyes. "I've loved and lost too. I've lost dearly. Your dad made my life a living hell because I dared to get involved with you. But I'm still here." His eyes entreated and seduced. "I tried to forget you for ten years. It didn't work. I'd rather see how far we could take this instead of settling for someone else who's a pale imitation of you."

He got up from the table and walked into the bedroom. She heard the sounds of his hunting around for his clothes, water running in the bathroom, and a couple of muttered obscenities when he must have banged into a piece of furniture again.

She got to her feet and started clearing away empty to-go containers. She left her glass of wine, but dropped the empty bottle into the wastepaper basket. Zach reappeared in the living room.

"I'm going for a walk on the beach. Want to come along?"

She nodded. He held out his hand to her.

THERE WASN'T A lot of conversation during their stroll. Zach was encouraged by the fact she didn't let go of his hand, though. Earphones One and Two did a great job of giving them some privacy while they watched the sun set over Saratoga Passage. He knew the guys were there, but they must have had invisibility cloaks or something.

He found a long piece of driftwood that made a great place to sit and admire the pinks, oranges, and purples that washed over the sky as the sun slid behind the horizon. He took a couple of pictures with his smart phone. They saw the first few stars twinkling overhead.

"So, darlin', I take it you're all talked out about our situation right now." He rubbed her much smaller hand between both of his. "What else would you like to talk about?"

"Are you going to be able to sleep in a queen-sized bed tonight? Your feet are going to hang off the end."

He couldn't help it. He laughed. She was right: He was squirming around earlier, trying to get comfortable while she took a little nap. Maybe he should bunk on the couch. Then again, he wanted to hold her all night, and he couldn't do that from the next room.

"I'll make it work," he said.

She half-turned to look into his face. To his shock, her eyes were filled with tears. He wrapped his arm around her shoulders and pulled her into him.

"What's the matter?"

"I don't know what we're going to do, but I know I don't want to lose you again."

She laid her head on his shoulder. He felt her tears against the side of his neck, but she didn't make a sound.

"Shhh," he comforted. "Everything will work out. I promise it will."

He expected her to argue and tell him he was wrong. He waited for her to speak. She brushed the tears off her face with one hand.

"I'll have dinner with your family," she said.

Chapter Twenty

ZACH HOPPED OUT of the black SUV about a block away from the Sharks' practice facility the next morning. A slight breeze brushed his skin. He knew it would be a great day for football practice already. A short walk along the peaceful street outside of the facility was a good thing, especially when he knew Cameron was a bit nervous about their arrival together at Sharks headquarters. A cell phone photo of the two of them on the beach in Whidbey Island had shown up on several online gossip sites and trended on Twitter last night. He also had multiple texts from sports media on the subject this morning already. He would do the Walk of Shame, and be a better man for it.

He'd gotten a one-word text from his sister Courtney already, too: NICE.

The skies were overcast. He knew this weather phenomenon was called the "marine layer" in Seattle. It wasn't going to rain, and the clouds would burn off by early afternoon. He wondered what kind of torture Coach Stewart had dreamed up for all of them today at practice. More cuts were coming in a few days. He wasn't especially worried, but there were a few other vets who were. The average NFL career was three and a half seasons, so guys who stuck around for any length of time made the extra effort.

His phone was vibrating in his pocket again. It was probably another text from one of those bullshit entertainment shows that wanted to ask questions about his and Cameron's relationship, but he pulled it out to take a look. If he was really lucky, it might be Cameron instead.

He saw an unfamiliar New York City number. His cell number was not exactly public knowledge, so it might be worth answering.

He stabbed at the button with one finger. "Anderson," he said.

"Good morning, Anderson. Preston Ondine. Do you have a minute?"

Zach pulled the phone away from his ear and stared at it. What the fuck? He resisted the impulse to hang up. He strolled over to a large, flat-topped rock engraved with the Sharks' logo and set into the landscaping at the entry of the facility. He sat down on it.

"Not especially, but what's on your mind?"

Mr. Ondine cleared his throat.

"My wife is unhappy about my behavior toward you the last time we saw each other, Anderson."

"Is that so?"

"Mrs. Ondine and I would like to thank you for what you did the other day for our daughter. You saved her life, and we are grateful. We'd also like to let you know that we are in your debt for your heroic actions on her behalf."

The guy sounded like a dictionary fell out of his mouth. Even more, it was somewhat comical that Mrs. Ondine had obviously told her husband off, or he wouldn't be making a phone call.

Zach was silent for a minute or so. There were so many things he wished he could say at this moment, but he seized on the most obvious one. "I appreciate it, Ondine. Please tell your wife I care about your daughter, and I would do whatever I needed to do to keep her safe." He let that one sink in for a moment. "In the meantime, since you're in my *debt*, there's something I'd like to talk with you about."

"Okay, then. Let's hear it." Cameron's dad sounded a little nervous.

"I think life's too short to hold a grudge, so we're not going to talk right now about your actions toward me and my family ten years ago. That's a discussion that needs to happen in person."

"You had a golden opportunity a couple of weeks ago, Anderson."

"I did, but I was at work. I'm sure you understand that." Zach attempted to rein in the sarcasm. He couldn't stand the guy, but he was still Cameron's father. In the meantime, he had a point to make. "What I *would* like to discuss, however, is the fact you don't support your daughter's career. Why is that? Do you have any idea how hard she's worked to get to where she is today?"

"Her mother and I would prefer she didn't work in the entertainment industry at all—"

Playtime was over, and practice was in an hour and a half. His teammates were driving by on their way into the facility parking lot. Of course, that didn't prevent Derrick from half-hanging out of his car window and yelling, "Hey, asswipe, get back to work."

Zach pulled the phone away from his ear and shouted back, "Kiss your mother with that mouth?"

Derrick's response was to flip him off. He burned rubber into the Sharks' parking lot.

"Excuse me?" Preston Ondine said. "Were you talking to me?"

Zach stifled a sigh. "No. It was one of my teammates." Hopefully, he could mute the background noise before another of his teammates decided to drive by. "Your daughter isn't in the 'entertainment industry.' She's a sports reporter. She works hard at what she does, and I know it hurts her that you don't seem to care about her achievements."

"That's not true—"

"She thinks so. Maybe you need to do something about this, Ondine. I'm feeling generous today, so I'll give you a hint. Your golf buddy Ben, program director of PSN, is making her life intolerable right now. Perhaps you could give him a call and tell him to treat your daughter like the other professionals he has working for him."

Zach heard some incoherent sputtering at the other end of the phone. Mr. Ondine had evidently forgotten those fancy Ivy League manners and was good and pissed off, like any other father would be if someone was mistreating his daughter. "Is he *sexually harassing* her? I'll sue."

"No, the scumbag is using her private life to increase ratings." Zach saw cars in the distance. He had about thirty seconds to get his ass back into the building before more of his teammates arrived. "I know you think I'm going to hurt Cameron, and I'm not good enough for her. While you're focused on me, though, you're missing the opportunity to protect her from someone who's doing real damage—her boss." Zach wasn't going to wait around for Cameron's dad to give him some bullshit answer. "I'm glad we had this talk. Please give my best to your family, and thanks for calling." He hit "end," and strolled toward the front doors of the facility.

Cameron was going to be pissed, but he'd just served notice on her dad.

LATER THAT AFTERNOON, Cameron packed up her mic and headphones and sagged in her chair. She was happy with the voiceovers she'd just recorded for the latest episode of *Third and Long*. It had been several hours of work without a break, but there were few things that made her happier than to know she'd done a great job. She felt her phone vibrating in her pocket. Those who had her cell phone number were on her VIP list, so she pulled the phone out of her pocket to answer.

She saw Zach's smiling face on the screen, and her heart soared. She hit "answer" and smiled. "Hi there," she said.

"Hi there, yourself. I'm going to need to reschedule dinner tonight. Coach is on the warpath. Let's get together later on, okay?"

"Let's do that," she agreed.

She'd spent the past couple of days freaking out about spending time with Zach's family, but now she felt oddly disappointed. She was nervous about meeting his sisters, but an evening with his family meant a little more time with him. Any time away from cameras and prying PSN production staff members and Sharks teammates was treasured.

"I'll meet you on the basketball court at ten p.m. Let's see what kind of game you've got, darlin'."

"You know I played intramural basketball in college, right?"

"Oooh. I think I'm scared now." She heard the bark of his laugh, and he said, "I'll look forward to that. See you later." He disconnected his call.

Cameron gathered up her things to leave. She grabbed her phone one more time and scrolled through "calls received." She found the number she was looking for and hit "dial."

"I must be out of my mind," she muttered to herself. She originally wanted Zach with her at dinner with his family so he could act as a buffer, but if it went any further between them, she was going to have to face his sisters on her own. Maybe it was time she did that.

She said, "Hello, Shelby, it's Cameron Ondine. Is this a good time to talk?"

Shelby's voice was brisk, but not unfriendly. "It's fine. How are you doing, Cameron? Zach just called a few minutes ago to cancel tonight's dinner."

"I'm fine. I hope things are going well for you, too." Cameron pulled in a breath to steady her nerves. "I was wondering if you all wouldn't mind if I came over tonight anyway. I'd be happy to order pizza or get some take-out so nobody has to cook."

Shelby let out a laugh. "My sisters would love that. We were planning on making something easy like spaghetti or stir-fry, but if you'd like to bring dinner, we won't say no. Thanks for the offer."

"If you have a favorite pizza place, I can go there. I also have a security guy that will be joining us. I hope this will not be a problem for all of you. He's friendly, but mostly stays out of the way," Cameron said.

"Zach told us about him, too. Of course he's welcome."

Cameron scribbled notes on her iPad of the sisters' favorite pizza place and toppings, which beverages they preferred, and how much pizza Shelby thought they might eat. By the end of the call, she was smiling.

Maybe this would go better than she thought.

A couple of hours later, Earphone One picked her up in the black SUV with tinted windows. She'd learned a couple of weeks ago his name was Chuck, and he had a wickedly dry sense of humor.

"Where are we going, Ms. Ondine?"

She'd spent almost three weeks being followed around by these guys now. They should be on a first-name basis.

"Please, call me Cameron."

She pulled the phone out of her bag and located both the pizza place and Zach's address. She glanced up to see a huge grin spread over his face.

"Will do, Cameron."

"Chuck, I have an address, but I'm also wondering if we could stop to pick up some pizza on the way."

"Absolutely." He cleared his throat. "They know to expect me, too, right?"

"Yes. They do."

She worked on show research while he drove. They managed to get three pizzas, a big garden salad and multiple beverages without too much trouble, and loaded them into the back of the SUV. Zach's house wasn't far from the pizza place. The car slowed, and Chuck turned onto a long driveway framed by a manicured, rolling lawn.

Zach's house was a huge, gorgeously maintained, window-filled one-story featuring a carriage house over the two-car garage. A winding path to the front door was framed by carefully-pruned shrubs. A small sign hung over the door: *Home is where the heart is*. She rang the doorbell once, and heard excited barking, hurrying footsteps, and "Butter, shhh!" from someone behind the door.

A tall, slender young woman with Zach's dark blonde hair and sparkling hazel eyes pulled the door open. She crouched down to pick up a barking, bright-eyed, wriggling bundle of yellow fur.

"You must be Cameron. Come in. I'm Shelby." She indicated the dog with her head. "This is Butter." The dog squirmed until he could lick her face. "Okay, Butter. I love you, too." Cameron had to smile at the irresistible puppy.

"I hope you like dogs," Shelby said. She shook her head at Butter.

"I love dogs. He must be so much fun to play with."

She saw Shelby smile. "He'll play with you as long as you want him to." She backed up so Cameron and Chuck could get inside the house and then put Butter down on the floor after the front door had closed behind Chuck.

She reached out for the salad and grocery bag of sodas Cameron carried. "I'll take that if you'd like."

"That would be great. Thanks." Cameron turned toward Chuck. "Shelby, this is Chuck. He—he provides security."

Even with the little dog trying to jump into her arms, juggling dinner for seven, and wanting to observe and mentally catalog every inch of Zach's house from sheer curiosity, she didn't miss the "Hi there. Who are you?" look that passed between Shelby and Chuck or the color rising in Shelby's face.

Chuck balanced the pizzas on one hand and stuck the other out to Shelby.

"It's nice to meet you, Ms. Anderson—is that right?"

"Call me Shelby," she said. "It's nice to meet you, too."

The two of them could stand in the front hallway of Zach's house for the rest of the night staring at each other. Zach's other sisters must have wondered what the holdup was. They streamed out of what must have been the kitchen.

Three of them looked a lot like Zach—dark blond hair, hazel or green eyes, big smiles, and somewhat tall. Whitney was dark haired, petite, and not smiling. She regarded Cameron warily.

Her two older sisters glanced between Chuck and Shelby and nudged each other. One stepped toward him and stretched out her hands. "I'm Ashley," she told him. "I'll take the pizza into the kitchen, if you'd like."

"I'm Chuck. Just point me there," he said. He managed to tear his eyes away from Shelby for a moment. She trailed behind him with the salad and the bag of drinks.

Ashley and Courtney nudged each other again.

"We never even got a chance," Courtney joked.

"He's gorgeous," Ashley agreed. She turned toward Cameron. "I bet it's awful having that guy following you around all day." The sisters grinned at her. The corners of Whitney's mouth even turned up a little.

"He typically keeps to himself, but there's usually two of them. They're both pretty nice to look at."

"Is the other one single?" Ashley asked.

"I think they both are," Cameron said. "I'll find out for you."

To her surprise, Courtney reached out for her hand. "Come on, Cameron. Let's go introduce you to our grandma."

A few minutes later, the group sat around a well-worn kitchen table that had been hastily set by Whitney. Butter was shown to his crate for a nap. Chuck made sure he was sitting next to Shelby. They tried to pretend like they were interested in the conversations swirling around them, but Cameron noticed they half-turned toward each other and the food really wasn't disappearing off of their plates.

Whitney chose the chair farthest away from Cameron's. Zach's grandma sat down next to her, though.

Zach's grandma was probably in her mid-seventies. Her gray hair was twisted into a loose bun on top of her head, and she wore reading glasses on a brightly-colored beaded chain around her neck. The joints of her hands were swollen and misshapen with what Cameron imagined was arthritis. She didn't move quickly, either. At the same time, her smile was bright. Cameron was willing to bet that Francesca made the pitcher full of iced sweet tea that graced the middle of the table.

"I'm Francesca. It's nice to meet you."

"I'm happy to meet you, too, Francesca. Would you like some pizza, or would you like me to get you some more sweet tea?"

"I think I'd like some more pizza, please. How about some of that vegetarian kind, unless the girls have eaten it all?" She leaned closer to Cameron. "Maybe we can have a talk later."

"I would like that."

Francesca's pale blue eyes locked onto Cameron's. "My grandson is still in love with you."

All she could do was nod.

"I think you're still in love with him, too, or you wouldn't have braved coming here by yourself. What's the holdup?" Francesca said.

Cameron could tell Francesca that it was none of her business, or she could make up something that would placate a nice older woman who wanted her grandson to be happy. She couldn't do it. She pushed the salad around on her plate with her fork.

"We have a geographical problem, among others," she said. "Also, my father owes Zach a huge and heartfelt apology. I'm not sure he'll ever give him one."

Francesca picked up her slice of pizza and nibbled on one end. She dabbed the napkin to her mouth. "Your dad will butt out when he sees you're happy."

"You've never met my father. He doesn't know the meaning of the words 'butt out.'"

"I've heard a lot about him." Francesca patted Cameron's hand with her frailer, wrinkled one. "He'll come around. Most parents do."

"I don't know, Francesca." She let out a sigh and leaned back in the chair. "Why do you think he would do that?"

"Old age is a good time to look back on your mistakes in life and do the best you can to make things right with the people that you've hurt. I know he wants you to be happy."

Cameron took a bite of her pizza instead of telling Francesca that her father thought regrets were for the weak. She also wondered how her life would have been different if she were part of this family instead of the one she was born into. She loved her parents and her sister. There just wasn't a lot of warmth or the informality of people who knew they were loved and accepted for who they were.

The sisters continued to talk and laugh with each other around the table, drawing Chuck and Cameron into their conversation.

Chuck got to his feet and glanced over at Francesca. "Does anyone here need anything else while you're visiting?" He was met with a chorus of "no, thank you."

"Well, then. I'll make myself scarce so you all can chat some more . . ."

"That won't be necessary," Shelby told him. "We'll get this cleaned up a little, and we can all go hang out in the family room. How about that?"

Cameron got to her feet and helped the sisters clear the table. There was an entire pizza left; she stashed the box in their refrigerator. The group made their way into the family room and sprawled out on a huge, overstuffed sectional couch and a couple of comfy-looking overstuffed chairs.

Ashley made sure Francesca was settled into one of the chairs close to the couch, then put her glass of sweet tea next to her on a low end table. She gave her grandma a pat on the shoulder, and glanced over at Cameron.

"So, Cameron, we've heard Zach's description of what happened ten years ago in Las Vegas. Maybe you could tell us why you married our brother and then wanted a divorce three days later."

Chapter Twenty-One

CAMERON GLANCED AROUND the room at the five women. Their facial expressions ranged from a bit skeptical (Shelby's) to angry (Whitney's). Chuck was pretending to read a sports magazine he'd grabbed off of the coffee table. Francesca reached out to pat Cameron's hand again. Cameron had been thinking about answers to the questions she'd imagined were coming since Zach had told her he wanted her to have dinner with his family. She still wasn't sure what to say, so maybe it was best to stick with the truth.

The best place to start any story was at the beginning. She pulled air into her lungs.

"I went to Las Vegas the weekend before I graduated from college. I wanted to go to a place where nobody knew me for a few days so I could think about what to do with my life."

"And?" Ashley said.

"The hotel I was staying at had a nightclub, so I thought I'd dance a little. After a while, I wanted a drink. I went up to the bar, and Zach was standing next to me. He offered to buy my drink. When he held out the money to the bartender, he accidentally tipped his beer over on both of us. He was so apologetic and funny, I couldn't be mad at him. He asked me to dance. We had so much fun."

"How did you go from 'Oops, sorry about that' to 'I do' in one evening?" Courtney asked.

"Zach and I danced together until the wee hours." There was a lot of drinking, too, but maybe she should leave that part out. "He asked me if I wanted to get some pancakes, so we went to a diner." She forced herself to stop fidgeting. "We couldn't stop talking to each other. I felt like I'd known him my entire life. After he ate a *lot* of pancakes"—she heard Ashley's laughter—"we walked outside and found a limo driver idling at the curb. Zach asked the guy if he could take us to Red Rocks."

"What's Red Rocks?" Whitney said.

"It's a huge rock formation in the desert outside of Las Vegas. It's very beautiful," Shelby said. Cameron noticed Whitney's sisters scooting closer to her. Ashley put an arm around Whitney's shoulders, which seemed to soothe Whitney.

"We went to Red Rocks to watch the sun rise." Cameron still remembered that morning—the chill of a desert waking up for the day, the sun sliding over the horizon, and Zach's arms around her. She'd never forget him saying "Marry me. Right now" into her ear, either.

"What happened then?" Courtney asked.

"Zach proposed to me, and I said yes."

"Even though you knew each other for less than ten hours?" Whitney said.

"By the time we walked into the wedding chapel, we'd known each other for ten hours."

"Why would you marry someone you didn't even know?" Whitney asked. "Is it because he's rich?"

Her three older sisters spoke at once.

"Whitney, that's rude."

"Shhh."

"Let her finish her story."

Whitney looked mutinous.

Cameron recrossed her legs. The three older sisters had unfolded their arms and were listening carefully. They weren't her BFFs yet, but they were at least letting her explain. Whitney wasn't giving her an inch.

"I understand why you probably think it's weird." Cameron stared at her hands clenched in her lap. "I wasn't especially sober at the time, but that wasn't the reason. I said yes to Zach's proposal because I wanted my life to be different, and I knew if I married him it would be." She made her living by knowing the right thing to say at all times, but right now, searching for words to explain the immediate attraction she'd had for their brother, the fact she knew she wanted the simple life he embraced and envied his enthusiasm for things and people sounded so incomplete, even to her.

She had to try. She watched as Shelby, Ashley, and Courtney's arms folded over their chests again. They thought she was insulting him, and that wasn't the case at all.

"Please tell me exactly what you mean by your life being different by marrying Zach," Courtney said. She didn't sound happy. Her sisters were nodding.

"Obviously he's handsome, and I was attracted. Even more, he's interesting to talk with. He loves the little things—going out for pancakes at three o' clock in the morning, watching the sun rise. He told me that he'd been drafted by the Sharks and he was due in training camp in a couple of months, but that wasn't all we talked about. He told me about all of you. He is so proud of each of you and your achievements. You were all in school at the time, he said. He talked about your good grades, which sports you went out for, and the fact that Whitney painted a huge canvas for the dining room of the house you all lived in. He told me that he wanted to do great things in life so you'd be proud of him, too," Cameron said.

Shelby leaned forward to hear Cameron's voice more clearly.

"He was so sweet and modest," Cameron said. "He asked me questions about myself. The guys I dated asked me about myself, but they didn't seem to care what I had to say. He asked me what I thought I might want to do next in life. He listened while I talked to him about wanting something different than what my parents wanted for me. He didn't laugh. He encouraged me to go after the things I wanted. He could have told me I was a spoiled little rich girl and I had no idea how bad things could get in life, but he didn't do that, either. I didn't have a clue how rough it was for your family when you were growing up. He never told me. When I look back on it, Zach must have thought I was shallow and superficial, but he—I think I fell in love with him then and there."

Cameron took a deep breath. Just thinking about the nights she'd spent with Zach ten years ago made her heart beat faster. She'd been so certain that he would change her life. But then it all fell apart. He'd never gotten that chance. After all, she had everything anyone else would want, or so she'd been told since she was old enough to receive yet another parental lecture about how she was disappointing them. Zach showed her things money couldn't buy—things she wanted desperately.

Franciñe leaned forward in her chair and patted Cameron's hand. She appreciated the quiet support from a woman she hoped had already forgiven her.

"So, we got married. I understand other people would think that was ridiculous. If we were so in love, maybe we should have waited to see if we were suited for each other. I know it sounds so stupid, but I knew he was the one." She picked up the glass of water she'd set on the little end table next to her and took a sip. His sisters were still silent.

"We went back to the hotel and didn't leave our room for three days. I called my parents the second day we were married and told them I was coming back to New York long enough to pack my things and get my college diploma, and then I was moving to Seattle to live with Zach. I told them I was happy, and that I hoped they would be happy for me. They weren't." She heaved a sigh. "I'm not sure why I thought they would accept our marriage, but they didn't. Zach needed to run an errand at the gift shop the third day we were at the hotel, and he didn't come back. It should have only taken him a few minutes to get back to the room. I called his phone, and he didn't answer. I called the front desk to ask if they had seen him. I got dressed and went downstairs to see if something was wrong or he'd gotten hurt somehow."

She took another sip of water. Her mouth was dry, and she wondered if they would think she was even weirder if she just chugged the contents of her glass. "He'd checked out of the hotel. He didn't call me back. He hadn't left any kind of message. I was so freaked out I called my parents to ask if I should file a missing person's report. My dad called me back."

She was shaking now. She couldn't seem to get enough breath into her lungs. She remembered how she felt when she listened to her father tell her Zach had demanded five million dollars to sign the annulment paperwork he'd had drawn up. "We told you he just wanted your money," her father spat out over the phone that day, "but you didn't listen. You don't listen to us at all. He never loved you. He knew he was walking away from this with millions."

The five women in the room didn't care about her family problems. They cared about Zach and they'd believed she'd married him, then told her dad to get her a divorce as soon as possible. Shelby got up from the couch and stooped down in front of Cameron.

"Are you okay?" she asked. "You're shaking and really pale. Take a deep breath, Cameron."

"I'm fine—" She closed her eyes and concentrated on her breathing until her racing heartbeat slowed and she was calm again. She'd had panic attacks before. This was random anxiety, which she knew how to deal with. She felt someone sit down next to her and take her hand.

"Things are fine. I'm just checking your pulse," Courtney said. "Take a few more deep breaths." She laid two fingers over Cameron's wrist. "Are you dizzy or faint?"

"No. I'll be okay." Just talking about what her dad had done in front of other people was humiliating. She knew other people had to deal with overbearing parents, but she knew her dad was over the top on all occasions. If she was freaking out over telling Zach's sisters what happened, she was going to need some type of sedative to get through the conversation she still had to have with him.

Courtney patted her hand. "Your pulse is normal. Would you like some more water or a little something to nibble on? You didn't eat a lot at dinner."

"No, thank you. I'll be fine. Back to the story." She glanced around the room. Francine had scooted to the edge of the chair next to her, and without a word she reached out for Cameron's other hand. Courtney didn't move from her seat next to Cameron. Shelby and Ashley still flanked Whitney, whose hands were now clasped loosely in her lap.

"My dad told me he was in Las Vegas and he and his attorney had signed and witnessed annulment paperwork from Zach. He also told me Zach had demanded five million dollars to sign them." She heard gasps from around the room.

"He did not!" Shelby said.

"Zach said he tore up the check in front of your dad," Courtney said.

"Why did your dad lie?" Whitney said.

"Did you try to contact Zach at all?" Francesca said.

"I called his cell phone so many times. I even called the Sharks headquarters when he went to training camp the first time. He never called me back or acknowledged my trying to contact him, either. I finally found out why."

Francesca squeezed her hand. Cameron knew she'd asked her question aloud for Whitney's benefit.

"My dad had filed a restraining order against Zach before he flew to Las Vegas with his lawyer and the paperwork they forced Zach to sign. If Zach called me or contacted me in any way, he'd go to jail. Zach finally told me three weeks ago, and I checked it out with Chuck's help." Five pairs of eyes swiveled to look at Chuck, who'd abandoned all pretense of reading.

"Why would your dad do such a thing?" Courtney demanded.

"He wanted me to marry someone else." Cameron knew explaining her dad to Zach's family would take all night. She still couldn't believe the lengths her father had gone to or that he still believed he'd done nothing to apologize for. She heaved a sigh. "I didn't want to marry the other guy. I didn't want my parents' life. I wanted Zach."

Francesca didn't have much of a grip on Cameron's hand, but her touch was comforting. At least one person in the room believed her.

"There's a couple more things I need to tell all of you. Zach and I are together. There's issues that still need to be worked out between us, but we want to stay with each other. I have already told my dad to butt out of our lives, but I am going to make sure he knows any more interference in my life, or your lives, is unacceptable. I'd like it if we could be friends someday. It would mean a lot to me. My family isn't especially close, and, well, I—I would like that."

She could hear the proverbial pin drop, but she saw Courtney, Ashley and Shelby smile. One of Whitney's eyebrows went up. She was silent.

The sisters glanced at each other, and Shelby said, "I'm glad you're here, Cameron."

"Want some more water?" Ashley asked her.

"I can get it," Cameron said.

"No. I'll get it." Ashley got up off the couch, grabbed the empty glass off the end table, and said to Francine, "Grandma, would you like some more tea as well?"

"No, honey. I'm fine."

Courtney and Whitney were having a whispered conference on their end of the couch.

"Shelby, would you please point me toward the men's room?" Chuck said, and gave Cameron a quick nod as well.

Shelby got to her feet to direct him toward the bathroom. Francesca got up from her chair and walked toward the kitchen. Courtney got up and followed her.

Whitney got up from her seat and plunked herself down next to Cameron. Dusk was falling. Cameron knew she needed to leave soon if she wanted to spend the night in her dorm room. Also, she had an appointment with Zach at the basketball court.

It would be interesting to see his reaction when she told him she'd gone to see his sisters on her own. Right now, though, she needed to see if Whitney would consider forgiving her for the mess involving her older brother.

"It was nice to have dinner with all of you," Cameron said to Whitney. "Zach talks about all of you so often. I know he misses you while he's at camp."

"We miss him, too," Whitney said. She was fidgeting a little. Cameron couldn't imagine what was going through her mind, but she was relieved that Whitney didn't look quite as antagonistic as she had when she confronted Cameron during practice a couple of weeks ago or earlier that evening at the dinner table. Whitney released a long breath, tucked one leg beneath her, and half-turned to face Cameron.

"How do I know you're telling us the truth about what happened?"

"Ask Zach," Cameron said. "Or Chuck. He knows the private investigator I worked with."

Ashley walked into the room again and set a glass of ice water down on the table next to Cameron.

"We're in the kitchen, if you'd like to join us. Grandma just got out the ice cream and chocolate sauce," Ashley said.

"I think I'm going to pass on the ice cream, but thank you for offering." Cameron would sip water and try to pretend like she didn't want the additional calories. "Want some ice cream, Whitney?"

"I have some work I have to finish before tomorrow," Whitney said. She still wasn't smiling. It looked like Cameron was going to have to accept the fact that Whitney wasn't ever going to like her, and hope that Zach would give her credit for trying to get along with his family. Ashley walked out of the room again, and Cameron got up from the couch. She extended her hand to Whitney. Whitney shook it.

"It was nice to meet you, Whitney. Good luck with your project."

Whitney stared up at her, opened her mouth to speak, and shut it again.

"Is there something else you wanted to ask me?" Cameron said.

"Do you love my brother?"

They stared at each other for a moment. The look in Whitney's eyes was wary, but she'd lost the attitude.

"Yes," Cameron said. "I love him very much."

She picked up her glass of ice water and turned to go to the kitchen. She didn't wait for a response.

Chapter Twenty-Two

CAMERON AWOKE THE next morning in her dorm room before the alarm went off. Rolling over to face the window, she rubbed her eyes at the pearly-gray, overcast sky she saw through her open blinds, wishing she'd closed them before she fell asleep last night. She'd left them open to see the half-moon and thousands of twinkling stars. She waited for her body to adjust to the idea of getting out of bed.

She wasn't BFFs with Zach's sisters quite yet, but they were at least talking with her and being civil. She'd made the point she hoped to make by showing up at his house for dinner on her own: She wanted to apologize to them herself for what had happened to their family ten years ago when she and Zach got married on a whim. She'd like to be friends, or at the very least friendly, with them. She was trying to come up with a solution for the problems she and Zach encountered in any attempt to renew their relationship. The tears and heartache she suffered when they split up before were minor compared to what would happen now—she knew what she'd be missing out on, and it wasn't just the sex.

She was also in love with Butter the puppy. Maybe Zach would let her walk him if she stuck around.

Speaking of Zach, she missed him like crazy. He'd texted her while she was on the way back to the facility last night and cancelled their late-night basketball date. There was yet another meeting he was expected at. I'LL SEE YOU TOMORROW AT BREAKFAST, he'd written. I HAVE SOMETHING TO TELL YOU.

She had a few things to tell him, too.

An hour later, she'd showered, dressed, texted her dad that she needed to talk with him at his earliest convenience, and let herself out of her room. Derrick darted out of his own room seconds later. It was almost like he'd been waiting for her, but that was a little out there.

"Ms. Ondine," he said. He caught up with her easily. She was always amazed when the big guys on both sides of the ball moved like cheetahs. She was one-third their size and couldn't outrun them. In her profession, this was a double-edged sword: If they were not interested in being interviewed, she'd need a car to catch up with them.

"I'm Cameron," she told him.

"Cameron, then." He heaved a long sigh. "I acted like a real ass the other day at the breakfast table. I'd like to apologize."

"You're not a morning person?"

"That would be a no. Anderson's been on my back about it for ten years now. He told me he was going to kick my ass if I ever did anything like that to you again. I told my mama what happened, and now she's pissed at me, too." He did his best to imitate a woman's voice while wagging his index finger in the air. "I taught you better than that, Derrick. I'm ashamed of you. She's a nice girl and shouldn't have to put up with your bad attitude."

Cameron resisted the impulse to laugh. "Was she here to visit?"

"Oh, HELL, no. My mama and my grandma ain't invited to training camp. They'd sit out there on the hill and tell the fans all the things I did as a child." He shook his head with ferocity. "They'd be hearing about how I drank all the grape juice for Communion at church when I was eight, how I tried to drive my grandpa's car when I was twelve, and how I got caught feeling up a girl at the school dance when I was thirteen. I wasn't that bad," he said, "but my mama is convinced I was some kind of juvenile delinquent."

Derrick opened the door to the stairwell for her and slipped one big hand through the crook of her arm as they descended.

"You be real careful now, Miss Cameron. Let me help you."

She had to admit his chivalry was kind of cute. He'd played for his home state's University of Alabama in college, so she could only imagine what a tongue-lashing he'd received from every woman in his family aware of the breakfast incident.

He was still chatting away as they reached the floor the cafeteria was on. The Sharks front office employees weren't in for the day yet. She glanced around at empty cubes and lots of Sharks promotional materials on display. The coaching staff usually arrived by six am, and they would be hard at work in another part of the building. She'd already started her workday, too. She knew other Sharks had friends and family attending their practices; maybe she could interview a few of them for her show. This week's *Third and Long* would be all cuts, all the time.

Holly, the server, greeted Cameron with a bright smile as she walked into the kitchen area of the cafeteria. "Scrambled eggs today? I have some fresh off the grill."

"Yes, please. May I also have a few of those roasted potatoes as well?"

"Of course." Holly spooned eggs and potatoes onto Cameron's plate. Holly also spooned sliced fresh fruit into a smaller bowl and held it out to her. "Zach told me you like this."

"I do. Thank you so much."

"Are you sure I can't talk you into some breakfast bread or maybe a croissant?"

Everyone wanted to feed her. She couldn't figure it out. Derrick was about to eat everything Cameron denied herself, as usual. He grabbed one of the croissants with a pair of tongs and dropped it onto Cameron's tray.

"I'll help you eat it," he said. He loaded bacon onto an already-heaping plate. "It's time to get some calories." She saw him wink at Holly, who turned bright red.

Cameron emerged from the kitchen to see Zach sitting at a table near the huge windows that looked out over the practice field. He waved her over, and her heart skipped a beat. The rest of the cafeteria was deserted. She didn't see any of the Sharks or the PSN production staff at any of the other tables, which was a bit shocking. They never turned down free—and excellent—food. She knew they were working today.

Earphones One and Two must have had an urgent errand elsewhere in the building, too, which was a bit odd. They hadn't told her they weren't going to accompany her today.

"Where is everyone?" she asked Zach as she set her tray down on the table. She wished she could kiss Zach hello, but PDA in front of his teammates and her colleagues was inappropriate. Derrick parked himself in a chair across from them.

"Cuts are happening this morning. Your friend Logan and a couple of other guys are following the assistant coach who is telling the guys."

She'd gotten no notice. She was willing to bet Kevin had, though. She remembered the NFL commissioner insisting in the press that roster cut-downs had to be done in a more "humane" manner. According to her colleagues, nothing had changed. Some of the guys that weren't on the team anymore might catch on with the Sharks' practice squad or with another team. Some would never play on a pro football team again.

"Maybe I should go find them." She started to rise from the table, and Zach put his hand over hers.

"Stay here," he said. "Logan will get the footage PSN needs. Let Kevin cover this one." He pulled in a breath. "It's not especially fun and some guys don't react well." He leaned a little closer to her, and his voice dropped. "Your security guys are trailing Logan right now. We're keeping an eye on things up here."

"Are we in danger?" She looked at him in horror. "What about Logan? Is he safe?"

"There's nothing to worry about. The guys getting cut will be upset, but they're not homicidal. Everything will be back to normal in an hour or so." He nodded at her plate. "Eat up. You got a croissant, huh?"

"I put it on her tray," Derrick said between mouthfuls of his breakfast. "I talked her into a splurge."

"I can feed myself—"

"My sisters said you ate about a cupful of salad and two bites of pizza last night. It's not enough, Cameron." He looked into her face. "We'll talk about your nutrition later. When were you going to tell me you went over to see them?"

"I thought you'd like my going to visit with them on my own." She put her fork back down on her plate. "Are you mad at me?"

Derrick's head was swiveling back and forth as he watched them and shoveled food in at the same time.

"Of course not. I'm surprised. And I'm proud of you. I thought you wanted me to go because you were worried about how they'd react to you."

She took another bite of eggs and potatoes while she thought of what to say. "There were things I needed to say to them. They deserved to hear it all, and I didn't see any point in putting it off."

"True," he said. "I heard it went well."

Derrick reached across the table, cut the croissant on Cameron's tray in half with surgical precision, and popped the other half in his mouth.

"I fixed it for you. Eat the rest," he said.

She stuck her tongue out at Derrick, who let out a huge bark of laughter.

Cameron watched Zach put his fork down and focus on her. He didn't want his family life exposed to the press, but it didn't seem to matter to him that Derrick was still at the table listening to every word. She took a sip of her latte.

"I enjoyed talking with your family. I really like your grandma. I think there's hope your sisters will accept me one day, or at least I'd like to think so. I did my best to explain what happened ten years ago, and I hope they know how badly I still feel about what happened." She took a breath. "Speaking of ten years ago, I called my father this morning and asked to talk with him. We're about to have it out."

Zach picked up his fork again and took a bite. "Your dad called me yesterday morning."

"He *what*? What happened?" Her hand stopped halfway to putting the coffee cup back down on the table. "Why didn't you tell me before now?"

"Oh, it's *on*, buddy," Derrick muttered.

Zach pointed a crispy strip of bacon at her and arched an eyebrow. "You have your secrets, and I have mine."

"It wasn't a secret! I just didn't tell you yet. You were in a meeting last night, and I—" She put her coffee cup back down on the table before it slipped out of her hand. "What did my father say? How did he get your number?"

Zach took his time polishing off the bacon on his plate. In the meantime an unwelcome thought popped into Cameron's head. "My father probably thinks we cooked this up between us," she said. "He's going to think we're manipulating him."

Derrick picked up his tray with his empty plate and juice glass and said, "That's it, I'm out. See you later." He loped off toward the kitchen, and Cameron stared after him.

Zach tapped her forearm with one finger. "You're not done yet. Eat some more food."

She didn't answer him and put her fork down on the plate. "What did my father say to you?"

It was impossible to explain to someone who could have a second career as a professional eater with no negative repercussions that she did her best to find foods that had as few calories as possible, and eat minimal amounts of those. Every calorie showed up on the TV screen, which prompted people she'd never met to write her horrible e-mails about getting fat. She stuck to a diet of lean meats and vegetables and did her best to resist the siren song of carbs. Holly's seasoned potatoes, though, were delicious. She'd had some at breakfast every day this week. Croissants and bacon weren't even in her vocabulary before she'd arrived at the Sharks training camp, but she picked up the half–croissant on her breakfast tray and savored a bite.

She'd "splurged" more in the Sharks' cafeteria than she had for the past year. Oddly enough, her clothes fit the same.

She was also wondering why her dad called Zach, and why Zach was being so secretive about it. If he and Zach got into it again . . .

Zach's voice broke into her troubled thoughts.

"I understand you think you're staying below a certain calorie count when you eat. It's not helping you, Cameron. You need to eat foods that will give you the energy to get through your day." He nodded at her plate. "Protein's good, but you need some balance here. Why are you doing this to yourself?"

She appreciated the fact he thought he was helping, but right now he was pissing her off. She stood up from her chair, yanked her tray off the table, and turned on her heel to walk away from him.

"Where in the hell are you going?" he called out.

"Downstairs. I need to get to work."

She heard him shove his chair back. She glanced behind her to see him grab another piece of bacon off his plate before putting his tray into the bus tub by the doorway. She reached out for the elevator's control panel, punching the "down" button multiple times.

"It's not getting here faster because you're irritated." He crammed the last piece of bacon into his mouth.

She ignored him. The elevator door opened. She stepped on. He got inside, too, before she could punch the "close doors" button.

She was silent during the thirty-second ride to the

ground floor of the facility. He reached out to hit the "stop" button on the panel before the doors could open.

She heaved a loud sigh and looked at the floor. She crossed her arms across her chest, too.

"Maybe you should tell me why you're flipping out over this," he said. "Is it the food? Your dad and I talked to each other? What is it that you're pissed off about? We're going to stay in here until you start talking. I'd recommend doing so now."

"I can handle my own life." She stared up at him. "I don't need you monitoring my food intake or telling me how to fix my family problems. Joanna will call the fire department if these doors don't open in a minute or so."

He leaned back against the elevator car's wall. "She's not in yet. She doesn't get here until after 8:30 AM." He reached out, grasping her shoulders and turning her to face him. She averted her eyes and stared up at the elevator car's ceiling. "So, why don't you talk to me, instead of freezing me out?"

"If you thought that was going to make me want to have a discussion with you on just about any topic right now, you're wrong."

He leaned forward and hit the 'stop' button once more for good measure.

"Listen," he said. "Let me talk to the team's nutritionist. I'm not doing this to be an ass. I want to help, and you'll feel better. Plus, I want to tell you about the stuff I talked with your dad about."

In the part of her brain that wasn't really irritated with him right now, she understood why he was trying to help. He needed to drop it right now, though. She also had a bad feeling she was about to walk into a buzzsaw as far as her father was concerned. She would appreciate some information about what was talked about during what must have been one hell of a phone call. If the two of them managed to be on the phone long enough to discuss her, it didn't bode well.

"We can be here all day. It's up to you," he said.

"You'll get a huge fine if you are late to practice. If you don't lift and warm up beforehand, you're risking injury." She stared into his eyes. She reached out and pushed the "doors open" button, stepping out of the elevator before he could grab her. She walked away without another word.

AFTER A LOT of trial and error over the past couple of weeks, Cameron could find the temporary production room assigned to the PSN production staff without a GPS. Logan was lounging against the hallway wall outside the room, which also helped.

"Hey, nice to see you. Where were you this morning?" he asked her.

"I had no idea you all were starting so early. Why didn't you tell me?"

He avoided her eyes, glancing at the floor. "I got the call at 5:30 am myself."

"Who was doing the on-air stuff, then?"

Logan had added foot-shuffling and lip-licking to his repertoire. He still wasn't looking directly at her. Something was wrong. "Ben said we'd fill that in later."

"*What?* Someone else was there with you. Who was it?"

"Kevin and a new on-air personality."

"Who might that be?" she blurted out. Ben chose that moment to walk into the hallway with them.

"Great job," he said over his shoulder into the room. "I can't wait to see the tape. I'll be right back." He shut the door behind him and gave Cameron a less-than-sincere smile. "Good to see you, Ms. Ondine."

"It's nice to see you as well, Ben. Why wasn't I aware of this morning's assignment?"

"We're trying out a new on-air person. She's already working on the voice overs. I wonder where she's been all my life. She's amazingly talented." Ben raised one eyebrow and strode away.

Cameron ran after him. "Excuse me?"

"Concentrate on your romance, Ms. Ondine. Leave the sports reporting to the rest of us."

"Really?" Her mouth dropped open in shock. "Are you firing me? I have a contract."

"You think you're going to manipulate me and PSN's owner by running to your daddy and complaining that I'm exploiting you and your private life? You've got another thing coming."

It was a good thing Cameron hadn't finished her plate of food that morning; it felt like it was ready to come right back up. Zach had talked to her father. Ben was trying to replace her, and he had also talked to her father. She really didn't like what this added up to.

"I haven't spoken to my father without several witnesses present for two weeks now. I have no idea what you're talking about. Plus, how are you going to explain to those currently happy with my ratings that you've replaced me for no apparent reason?"

"Maybe you texted him," Ben spat. "Why the hell should I care? My new sideline reporter is more than happy to handle whatever I throw at her."

The door behind them opened, and the television-ready Kacee stepped through it.

Chapter Twenty-Three

CAMERON HEARD THE door into the Sharks' lobby slam shut behind Ben.

Kacee pointedly ignored Cameron, strolled up to Logan and said, "Are you ready? We can get that interview before practice starts, if Drew's done with his lifting."

Logan's shoulders slumped. "Yeah." He picked up the camera resting on the floor at his feet and didn't meet Cameron's eyes.

"I fired you, Kacee. Why are you still here?" Cameron said.

Kacee spun on her heel to face Cameron. "Ben says you don't have the authority to fire me." Her expression turned calculating. "I'm going to love scooping up all of your player interviews, too." She gave Cameron a little wave as she flounced away. "Buh-bye now."

"I've already interviewed Drew this week," Cameron called out.

Kacee laughed. "You've never asked him these questions."

"I still have time later," Logan said to Cameron.

"How nice," she said. "See you then." She didn't know if she still had a job at PSN, so it really didn't matter if he was around to film with her or not.

"I don't think so," Kacee sang out as she hit the metal bar that opened the door onto the practice field. "He'll be busy with me."

Cameron let out a long sigh as she pulled her phone out of her pocket, sent three texts, and left the building through the door Kacee and Logan had just vanished through. She darted behind one of the wooden pillars that held up the front of the building. Logan had his camera up on his shoulder filming, and she wanted to see what was happening without being seen.

A few seconds later Drew emerged from the weight room's open garage-style door. He sauntered onto the cement walkway in front of the practice field and dumped a bottle of water over his head to cool off. He was probably getting ready to run a few laps or do some stretching in the grass.

He either didn't see or didn't care that Kacee and Logan were less than two feet away from him as he bent from the waist, flipping his long hair back and spraying water everywhere. Kacee's professional hair style, TV make-up, designer dress and heels got the brunt of the shower. Cameron resisted the impulse to laugh as her former assistant let out a screech. Kacee had abandoned any attempt at professionalism; she stamped her foot like a child as she shouted at Drew.

"Why did you do that? Now I'm a mess! Didn't you see me?"

Drew glanced over at a dripping and sputtering Kacee. "I didn't realize you were standing there. Sorry about that." His expression was less than penitent. "It's a warm one already, isn't it?"

Cameron could see Logan's shoulders shaking with laughter as he tried to steady his camera. Logan got a little water, too, but she knew that wouldn't scare him off. She wondered how long it would be before the footage of Kacee's meltdown was uploaded to YouTube. In the meantime, Kacee was still ranting at Drew.

"Now I'm going to have to change. It's all your fault," she wailed.

"Again, I'm sorry. I'll have to be a little more careful next time." He glanced over at Logan. "Where's Cameron? I need to talk to her about something."

"She's in the building," Logan said to him. "She should be out here pretty soon. If I see her first, I'll tell her you're looking for her."

"I'm right here. You can talk to me right now," Kacee insisted.

"Is that so? Well, then." Drew's voice was deceptively soft as he turned toward Kacee. He didn't smile. "Tell whoever it is that submitted those interview questions to me last night that there's no way in hell I'm discussing what I look for in a potential date, or my 'turn-ons' and 'turn-offs.' I'm not a *Playboy* centerfold. If you want to talk about football, I'm happy to do that, but my personal life's off-limits."

"What do you mean?" Kacee wailed. "They're just fun questions. What's the problem?"

"If you have to ask that question, you're already wasting my time," Drew said. He glanced over Kacee's shoulder and caught Cameron's eye. Cameron put a finger over her lips and hoped he wouldn't call attention to her temporary hiding place. "If that's what you consider an interview, you're going to have the same problem talking with every other guy in this facility," he said.

"Those are Cameron's questions," Kacee said. "She told me she wanted to try something different for her next show."

Drew laughed in her face. "I don't think so. Cameron wouldn't ask those questions. Thanks for trying, Kacee. I have to go." He turned and walked back toward the weight room, giving Cameron the barest wink as he passed.

"But I have questions for you! I really need an interview. What can we work out?" Seconds later, Cameron heard loud voices from the weight room.

"Get that camera out of here!"

"What the hell are you doing? Stop filming!"

"Media isn't allowed in here!"

The last voice she heard she'd recognize anywhere: Zach's. "What do you think you're doing, Kacee?"

Cameron hurried back into the building through another door. The items on her mental to-do list had just tripled.

JUST LIKE A lot of guys in the building, Cameron was hearing footsteps, too. If Zach's encounter with Kacee and Logan in the team's weight room was any indicator, Kacee was attempting to take Cameron's job.

After a rough few days when she first came to camp, the guys had decided they liked and trusted Cameron. She'd already passed up reporting on more than a few incidents that could have been pretty embarrassing to guys on the team or to the Sharks front office. She was professional. She was friendly, but not too friendly. He realized he was biased, but he liked the fact the guys had already closed ranks around Cameron.

Kacee had chased five different Sharks around the facility today. All five refused an interview with her, especially when McCoy filled them in on the list of questions he'd gotten via text from Kacee's phone last night. Kacee wasn't interested in actual sports content. There wasn't a guy in the league that would answer questions about his love life; they'd be laughed out of the locker room.

Drew also told him that Kacee had bragged to Drew about how both the owner of PSN and Cameron's boss were none too happy that Cameron's father called to let them have it right after Zach spoke to him. According to Kacee, this would benefit her efforts to move in on Cameron's job. She was also stupid enough to tell Drew that she was the source of all the leaks about Cameron and Zach, starting with the interview tape that just happened to get uploaded to YouTube.

Zach had a few things to say to Kacee. It might be smart for her to stay away from him until he settled down. Zach also realized that there was a pretty good chance that Cameron was now so pissed at him she wasn't talking to him at all. He'd thought he was helping her by spilling the beans to her dad about her boss's being such a dick to her. He should have realized her dad would make things worse. He would be infuriated if she did the same thing to him, too: Nobody messed with his career. Why did he think she'd welcome it?

He texted Cameron again: I NEED TO TALK WITH YOU. I SCREWED UP. FORGIVE ME? He waited impatiently for an answer. Five minutes later, he still hadn't heard from her. She must be tied up somewhere. He'd talk with her later.

THE ONLY PLACE these days where Cameron could have any expectation of privacy to make a phone call was her dorm room. She had about half an hour before she needed to be downstairs to cover today's practice. She'd have to talk fast. She locked the dorm room door behind her, and moved across the room so her voice wouldn't carry into the hallway.

She hit "dial" on her agent's cell number. Laurie picked up on the third ring.

"It's Cameron. I need to talk with you."

"This isn't a great time," Laurie said. "How about calling me back in an hour?"

"I have to cover practice in an hour. Do you have five minutes?"

"Five minutes will work. By the way, PSN is thrilled with the ratings for *Third and Long*. The ratings for *NFL Confidential* have gone through the roof, too. Good job.

Maybe they'll show their appreciation with a bonus. How about it? Want me to start the negotiations?"

Cameron allowed herself an epic eyeroll. "Laurie, question. Remember when you told me FOX Sports wanted to make me an offer?"

"Yes. Why? Is there a problem there?"

"You could say that."

Laurie let out a sigh. "They love you right now."

"Well, Laurie, they sure have one hell of a way of showing it. They're using a new on-air personality as of this morning." Cameron heard Laurie gasp. "Will you call FOX Sports at your earliest convenience and ask them if that offer is still on the table at all?"

"Are you sure?" Laurie asked. "You'll have to observe your non-compete if you go anywhere else. I'm not sure it would be a good career move, either."

Hmm. Moving from a cable network to a Big Four job was always a good move, but Laurie seemed willing to overlook that. "I'd like to know if they are an option for me at all. Please call me back right away when you hear from them."

"I will do that, but Cameron, again, do you really want to go there? I'd like to talk more about this."

"I'm positive. Please make the call. I'll be happy to talk with you about why I'm exploring the option when you have a little more time. Thanks for doing this for me, and I hope you're having a good day."

"Sure. I'll talk with you when I hear from them."

"Great. See you later. Bye."

Cameron ended the call and let out the breath she'd been holding. The next call was going to be even riskier, if that was possible. She scrolled through her contacts list, clicked on the number, and listened to it ring. She heard her father's voice.

"Ondine."

IT DIDN'T TAKE long to figure out why Zach hadn't been especially eager to talk with her about what he'd said to her dad, especially when her dad told her he'd put Walter Doyle, owner of PSN, on blast over the phone shortly afterward.

"Dad, that wasn't a great thing to do."

"Cameron Bennett Ondine, nobody treats my daughter like that," he boomed into the phone.

"Okay, Dad. Thanks. I think. I'll talk with you later."

She expected her father to act like he had, but she was pretty upset with Zach, too. She understood why he'd done what he did, but she was hurt that he didn't think more of her ability to take care of herself. She wouldn't interfere in his professional life. Why did he think he could do the same to her?

Cameron ended the call and pulled up an airline site on her iPad. She wasn't going to be able to fix these problems remotely, and she needed to take control of her life and her career. The only way to do that was to go back to New York for a couple of days. She also dialed Zach's number on her cell. He was getting ready for practice. He wouldn't hear the message for quite some time afterward, but she'd leave one anyway. "Zach, there's some things I need to take care of. I'll be back in a couple of days. I think we need to talk."

She ended the call. She booked a flight to New York, texted her producer that she'd be back in two days, and called a cab to pick her up in front of the facility in an hour and a half.

TWO HOURS LATER, Zach realized he hadn't seen Cameron in the facility during practice. She and the Earphones were nowhere to be found. Logan walked by a few minutes later; Zach grabbed his arm.

"Hey. Where's Cameron?"

"I saw her getting into a cab a few minutes ago," Logan said. "I'll let her know you're looking for her when I see her again."

"Thanks."

Zach walked away from him into the locker room and stripped out of his uniform and pads to take a shower. The voicemail light on his phone was blinking. Maybe one of his sisters called or something. He toed off his cleats and sat down on the bench in front of his locker while he punched in the password to his voicemail.

Thirty seconds later, his heart dropped. "We need to talk"? Cameron was a lot more than pissed: She'd left. Her voice sounded strained and unhappy. He'd lost her again. It was all he could do to hold it together while surrounded by his talking, laughing teammates.

Chapter Twenty-Four

AFTER THE RAIN-WASHED fresh air and relative quiet of Seattle's suburbs, the bustling sidewalks, acres of neon overhead and perma-honking motorists of New York City was like landing on another planet. Cameron swiped her credit card through the cab's backseat card reader. She grabbed her Birkin bag off the seat, thanked the cabbie, and launched herself onto the crowded sidewalk in front of Pro Sports Network's corporate offices.

The only time Cameron had visited this part of PSN's executive offices before was when she signed her contract. The room was crowded with network execs and on-air talent at the time. She remembered shaking a hundred hands, scrawling her name in a couple of places on the pa-perwork, and being whisked out for a press conference with Ben, where she announced her signing. She knew she'd met Walter Doyle, owner of PSN, but she didn't remember a lot about him except that she was taller than he was.

She'd spent the past couple of days since her flight landed in New York City getting her ducks in a row for this meeting. She didn't need to run to her father for help like a child who'd skinned a knee; she needed to handle her career problems and opportunities herself. Laurie continued to act evasive and refused to make a phone call to FOX Sports to explore the previous job offer, so Cameron dug out the business card their director of programming pressed into her hand at an industry gathering several months before and called the guy herself.

She'd hired the best attorney money could buy to review her contract with PSN. He'd found something interesting in the paperwork, which she looked forward to sharing with the owner of the network. She'd decided what the best case scenario would be for her and her career. If Mr. Doyle wasn't willing to offer her what she wanted, it was time to take a page out of her dad's book and go to the mattresses.

Cameron approached the executive assistant's desk outside of Mr. Doyle's office.

"Hi, I have a nine o' clock appointment with Walter Doyle. I'm Cameron Ondine."

"He's expecting you," the impeccably dressed young man behind the desk said. "Follow me, please."

Cameron was shown into a corner office that was bigger than her apartment. Two walls were windows looking out over Central Park. The décor was modern, featuring chrome and leather. The owner of PSN stood up from his chair and extended his hand to her. "Ms. Ondine, it's a pleasure."

"Thank you, Mr. Doyle."

"May I offer you anything? There's coffee, still or sparkling water, or soda. I can ask my assistant to get whatever you might like."

"No, thank you."

He gestured for her to sit down, and he sat down as well. Cameron took two deep breaths while she refreshed her memory on the talking points she'd memorized before she fell asleep last night. She crossed her legs and leaned forward slightly in her chair.

"I appreciate your making time to meet with me this morning," she said to him. "I realize it was last-minute."

"We're very happy with your ratings and the amount of advertising money *Third and Long* and *NFL Confidential* is making for the network. Your concerns are my concerns. What is it that we can do for you?"

He looked like someone's indulgent grandfather, but she was aware that he was as cutthroat in business as her father was. The only reason he'd agreed to this meeting in the first place was because she was making him money.

"Well, Mr. Doyle, I'm glad you asked me that. I'd like to move to Seattle for family reasons. I wonder if there's a mutually beneficial solution to this problem."

He stared at her for a moment. "What exactly are you proposing?"

"I'd like to film my show in the Seattle area. I will still be traveling to games during football season, but I will be living there the rest of the year."

He tapped his chin with one finger. "Why do you believe I'm going to agree to this? We sank significant resources into obtaining your services from ESPN, Ms. Ondine. We're based in New York City. You knew this when you took the job."

"Speaking of *Third and Long*, my contract was specific on my responsibilities with PSN. There should have been a separate negotiation for my appearance on the show, especially since my private life was exploited as part of it. My contract with your organization says that I'm allowed to leave without penalty if I agree to observe the non-compete in it." She recrossed her legs. "I have a job offer from another sports network that's willing to wait it out. They will be featuring me on their Sunday morning pregame show and another half-hour show during the week year-round. They're offering a significant increase in compensation as well."

He lifted an eyebrow. "So, you want to move to Seattle and you want a raise. Is that it?"

"The money is important, but moving to Seattle is what I want most. I'd also like to work for an organization that treats me as a professional and doesn't exploit my private life for ratings. I'm not sure PSN is willing to do that moving forward after *Third and Long*."

They stared at each other for a minute.

His lips curved up slightly. "No."

She smiled in response. "No?"

"That's right. You'll either work in New York City, or you'll leave PSN and deal with the non-compete."

She wasn't surprised at all that he ignored her comments about being treated as a professional. He appeared to be an amiable, agreeable older man, but she knew Ben would have checked out every decision he'd made on what to feature on *Third and Long* before he did so. She was a commodity to these guys, and they believed she and her work didn't deserve their respect.

She'd be off the air during most of football season, but she could work behind the scenes at her new employer's and hit the ground running before the NFL draft next year. She'd already discussed it with the executive that would be her new boss. It was an easy decision.

She got up from her chair, extended her hand to him, and said, "Thank you for the opportunity, Mr. Doyle. I wish you and your network well."

He shook his head. "You'll regret this, Ms. Ondine."

"I don't think so," she said. "Again, thank you." She turned to walk to the office door.

"Wait," he said as she reached out for the doorknob. She heard the chair he'd been sitting in creak a little as he got to his feet.

"Who made you the offer, and how much of a raise?" he said.

She turned to face him again. "FOX Sports. They also offered to double my yearly salary. They'd like to increase their female viewership and hiring a female football analyst is a priority for them." She kept the pleasant smile on her face as she gave him a nod. "It was nice to have met you. Please give my best to your family."

She looped her handbag over her arm and turned the doorknob as he said, "I suppose you'd want to sit at the desk for our pregame, too."

"I'd like to advance in my career, as I told you when I was hired. Why would I bother with anything less? Plus, I really don't want to work sixteen Sundays a year with Kevin Adkins."

They stared at each other for a minute or so. "So, you want me to get rid of Adkins, too."

"I didn't say that. I said I didn't want to work with him. There's a difference." She shrugged.

His eyes narrowed. "What do I get out of all of this?"

"You were just telling me how pleased you were with the ratings and the increased advertising dollars I generated for your organization."

He rubbed one hand over his face in exasperation.

"Did your father teach you how to negotiate?" he said.

"I learned that all by myself."

A FEW MINUTES later Cameron walked out of the PSN offices and onto the bustling New York City sidewalk for the last time. She took a deep breath of the humidity, the car exhaust, the food smells—she'd miss living here, but she had a new life waiting for her across the country. She hit "redial" on her phone and waited for her new boss at FOX Sports to pick up the phone.

"It's official: I've terminated my employment with PSN. I accept your offer," she said.

She heard him laugh a little. "We're glad to have you on board, Cameron. We'll see you in Los Angeles next week, and we'll schedule a press conference to announce your deal then."

"I look forward to it. Thank you again."

She had one more phone call to make, and there was no time like the present.

She stepped into the seating area of a sidewalk café and asked a server for an iced tea. "Coming right up," the guy told her.

"Thanks." She hit a number on her cell phone and waited for her agent to pick up. "Hi, Laurie. Yes, I understand you're busy. This shouldn't take long. I've lost faith in your representation. I've made other arrangements." She waited a beat. "You're fired."

CAMERON HOPPED OUT of another cab half an hour later.

"Here goes nothing," she muttered to herself.

She managed to get through the revolving front door at her father's office building without incident. She had an elevator car to herself, too. When the doors opened, she strolled up to the reception desk like she didn't have a care in the world.

The lobby of her father's office resembled a gentleman's club, with its dark wood paneling, wainscoting, and thick and priceless antique woven wool rugs lying over hardwood floors. The four chairs she saw were wingbacked tufted leather, facing each other in front of a five-foot-tall gas fireplace with an ornately carved mantel. The nineteenth-century British landscape painting that hung over the fireplace was worth more than her parents' apartment on the Upper West Side. The reception desk wasn't the modern wraparound most companies featured. It looked like an antique library table, which meant it probably was.

The woman sitting behind the desk looked like she'd just walked off the cover of the *Sports Illustrated* swimsuit issue, except she had more clothes on.

"I'm Cameron Ondine. I'd like to see my father, please."

"Do you have an appointment?" Ms. Swimsuit Issue didn't smile. Cameron was fairly sure that kind of thing was reserved for guys, specifically those with a high eight-figure balance in their checking account. "He doesn't see anyone he doesn't already have an appointment with. Let me take a look at his schedule."

"He'll see me. Please let him know I am here," Cameron said.

The woman picked up her desk phone, dialed a number, and said, "There's a woman here who claims to be Mr. Ondine's daughter. She'd like to see him." Cameron wondered if her father knew how rude his receptionist was. Maybe he didn't care.

The woman nodded several times, hung the phone up, and said to Cameron. "I'm sorry. He's not available today. You'll need to make an appointment and come back another time."

"I flew in here specifically to talk with him," Cameron said. She pulled out her iPhone and dialed her father's number.

"Ondine," he barked three rings later. She hit the speaker phone function for the hell of it.

"This is Cameron. I'm standing in your lobby. Your employees won't let me talk to you."

"You're here?"

The receptionist turned pale. Cameron resisted the impulse to laugh out loud.

"Yes, I am. And it's almost noon. Would you like to get some lunch?"

"Of course. I'll be right out." He ended the call.

Cameron put her phone back in her bag. Her father rounded the corner to the lobby two minutes later. He looked the same as he always did: He was tall; his dark hair was trimmed every three weeks; he was impeccably dressed in a handmade, tailored dark suit, and designer tie. He raised an eyebrow as he glanced at her.

He didn't have to say a word. She knew what he was thinking: *What the hell is she doing here?*

She could count the number of times she'd actually visited her father's company on the fingers of one hand. His workplace was sacrosanct. Whatever it was, it would wait until he came home from Wall Street.

Her father was also followed by a frantic-looking female assistant.

"Mr. Ondine, what would you like me to do about your one o'clock?"

"Reschedule my appointments for the rest of the afternoon," he said. The assistant was tapping away on her iPad. "I'm available on cell phone for emergencies." Her father thought any financial news constituted an "emergency," so it might be an interesting lunch.

To Cameron's surprise he reached out to give her an awkward hug. He wasn't a big fan of public displays of affection, either. Maybe he wasn't feeling well.

"If you would have told me you wanted to visit, I would have sent the jet, Cameron."

"That's really nice of you. The flight here wasn't too bad."

He didn't roll his eyes. Maybe it was trained out of him at Amherst. He gave a nod. "Shall we?"

She turned to look back at the receptionist. "Thank you so much for your help," she said. The woman stared at her.

"How are you, Dad?" Cameron asked as they waited in front of the elevator banks.

"I'm fine. Your mother has a slight cold, though. Will you stay for dinner? She'd like to see you."

"I'd like to see her too, Dad, but my flight back to Seattle is at seven pm tonight."

He held the door so she could step onto the elevator.

"I'll call my pilot and ask if he can take you home this evening. You can avoid the two-hours-in-advance check-in at the airport."

"It might be an inconvenience for him—"

"Cameron, let me take care of this for you." He pulled his phone out of his pocket, tapped in a text, and waited for a response as the elevator descended. "Your mother will ask the chef for an early dinner. My pilot will have the jet ready at seven PM our time, which should get you back to Seattle at nine PM their time. Will that work?"

"Of course, Dad. Thank you." If the flight was on time, she'd manage to make it back to the dorm before lights out, too.

The elevator stopped in the lobby, and they walked

outside. Her father held out his arm for her to take. "Where would you like to eat?"

"I know you have your favorites," Cameron said. "How about something a bit more casual?"

"What did you have in mind?"

She nodded at the food truck parked on the curb, one block down. "Greek food sounds good."

Her father was not a casual kind of guy. He preferred restaurants, specifically expensive, exclusive ones. He especially liked restaurants which provided a private room to conduct business in. She was willing to bet he'd asked his assistant to make a reservation at PJ Clarke's Sidecar before he came out to the front desk to meet her, but he didn't say so. He gave her another nod. "My assistant says their food is very good. Shall we try it?"

"We can take our lunch to the park and visit while we eat," Cameron said.

Twenty minutes later, she was fairly convinced that her father's body had been taken over by pod people. He ordered from a food truck like he'd been doing it his entire life. He asked the older gentleman dishing up their lunch if he could possibly double-wrap their food and drinks so they would make it to the park without incident. Cameron scrabbled in her bag for cash. Her father handed the guy a hundred-dollar bill and said, "Keep the change."

She'd never heard her father use the words "Keep the change" in her entire life. When the man and wife operating the cart thanked him, he smiled and said, "It's a special day. I'm having lunch with my daughter." He graciously accepted the small bag of baklava the woman pressed on them in response.

They made their way across the street to Central Park and managed to find an empty park bench, which was a miracle of some kind as well. It was possible her dad's security detail had been sitting on the bench ten seconds before they walked up to it, but she wasn't going to think about that today.

Maybe she'd hit her head on the overhead bin on the commercial jet or something. Maybe she was hallucinating. She waited for her father to do something rude, selfish, or thoughtless; it wasn't happening.

"I know you didn't fly twenty-five hundred miles to visit a food truck with me," he said.

"We might have to go to one more often," she said. She took a bite of excellent Greek salad. "Do you like your gyro?"

"Yes. It's very good," he said. She handed him another napkin to protect his tie from yogurt sauce.

"So, Dad, I'm not sure how to start this, so here goes."

She took a huge lungful of air. Her palms were sweaty. Her dad wasn't a yeller. He'd managed to keep her in line over the years with much more subtle and effective strategies, like disapproving of most of her life choices and asking why she'd earned a master's in art and antiquities if she had no intention of using her education. It was easier to give in to her parents' pressure as far as a major, but she knew she wanted to work in broadcasting from her teenage years, especially sports broadcasting. She'd learned a few things during afternoons spent running around a lacrosse field or on the intramural basketball court: There were stories in every antique, but the stories of athletes—amateur to professional, and their struggles and triumphs—were the ones that captivated her most.

She knew most people had challenges with their parents as they were growing up. She and her father didn't have the shared history of laughter and fun in her childhood to buffer the frustration and anger at their disagreements in later years, though. She knew he loved her, but she would have liked to make a snowman with him on Christmas Day instead of getting a notice from his lawyers that he had added funds to her annuity.

"I appreciate the fact that you took time out of your schedule to come to Seattle and check on my safety. I know you wanted to make sure I was okay, and I appreciate that, too." She put her container of salad down on the bench between them and turned to face him. "Dad, I'm pretty angry with you for what you said to Zach when you saw him. Maybe we should also discuss what you did to Zach and his family when he and I were married ten years ago. You weren't truthful with me for a long time, and I'm unhappy about that as well." She let out a breath. "I know that you detest Zach, but I am in love with him. If you and Mom would give him a chance, you might like—"

Her father half-turned to face her, too. "Eugene is a much better match for you, Cameron."

"No, he's not. He's a social climber who would make me miserable. I don't want that life, and Eugene and I have nothing in common."

"Yes, you do. His family is similar to ours. You both

went to the finest schools and know a lot of the same people. Eugene has the net worth to take care of you and the children you'll have together. He wants your family to continue our path of philanthropy as well."

"Path of philanthropy"? It was more like charitable donations as a tax write-off and to make others think her parents were generous, but she had bigger points she'd like to make with him first.

"Dad, this isn't the British regency, and I don't want my future to feature a mission statement. I have my own money. I can take care of myself."

"Eugene will fit into our lives. Zach Anderson won't."

"Dad, again: You don't even know Zach. You can't say whether or not he will fit into our lives. What if I want to fit into his?" She concentrated on keeping her voice down. The park was full of people on the beautiful August afternoon. "Why do you hate him so much?"

Her father's expression froze into a polite mask. "I don't hate him, Cameron. I don't hate anyone." He picked up his gyro and took another bite.

"You say that, but you tried to destroy him and his family ten years ago. You filed a restraining order against him? Maybe you could explain to me how in the world you got a judge to sign off on that in the first place, too. You threatened Zach again when you saw him at the Sharks' training camp. Why?"

Her father concentrated on smoothing out the paper bag they'd received their food in and using it as a place-mat for his gyro.

"Cameron, all I have ever wanted for you was the best

in everything. Women still derive most of their happiness from a husband and a family. I knew you wanted a career when you were younger, so we steered you into the arts and antiquities major. You could have that career without sacrificing your home life to do so. If you marry Eugene, you'll stay on the East Coast, which your mother and I believe is best for you as well. You'd be close to your family, close to your in-laws, and there are more career options here." He took a sip of the iced tea he'd ordered. "It's the best decision for your future. Look how happy Paige is."

"Dad, I'm not Paige." Cameron loved her sister, but she'd lose her mind going to Fashion Week, Mommy and Me yoga classes, and three-hour lunches. "I'm never going to be Paige. Will you still love me if I make a different choice?"

"That's ridiculous," he snapped.

She waited for him to say he would love her anyhow, but he didn't. She knew she was expecting a lot from a man who was obviously trying to understand her, but just once she'd like to hear him say the words.

"Will you come to my wedding if Zach and I get married again?"

The question hung in the air between them for a seemingly endless minute.

"Why, do you want to remarry him?" he asked.

The Greek salad tasted like the best thing she'd ever eaten in her life, but she put the container down in her lap again. "I'm in love with him. I know we'd be happy together."

"He can't offer you what Eugene can."

She looked into her father's eyes. "Zach offers me more than I could ever explain to you."

She heard her father's phone ringing in his suit pocket. He ignored it. She almost fell off the park bench in astonishment when the call went to voicemail.

"Try me," he said.

"Dad, Zach has some money of his own, but he doesn't use it to exclude other people. He enjoys things like playing with his dog in his backyard and going on a picnic or a bike ride. Simple things. He's getting a job when his NFL career is over, for instance. I've spent time with his family. They're good, hardworking people. If all of Zach's money went away tomorrow morning, they might have to move to a smaller place, but they would still be happy. He also says he's forgiven you for the things you did to him and his family ten years ago, which stuns me. I'm not sure I'd be able to do so." She hauled in a breath. Her father pressed his lips together so hard they formed a bloodless slash in his face. "You and Mom have done everything for me. I don't want you to think I am ungrateful for all the things and experiences you've showered on me, but what Zach offers is something I really want. I love my job, I love New York City, but I want to come home to someone who loves me no matter what I do for a living."

"What exactly does he offer, besides an inexpensive lifestyle and limited career choices?"

She almost rolled her eyes, but she knew the only way to get through this conversation was to remain calm and focused. "A family. I can be myself with him," she said.

"Do you think that we don't love you, too?"

"Dad, it's not that you, Mom, and Paige mean less to me. It's—I can live without a lot of other things, but I can't live without him."

"You'll miss New York City. What about this career you value so much? I'm guessing he doesn't want to leave the Seattle area. If he loves you, maybe he should be willing to relocate."

"Asking Zach to relocate isn't going to happen," she said. "It's not fair to his family."

"Why is it fair to *your* family?"

She flopped back against the bench in frustration. Her impatient, arrogant father was back. He wasn't asking questions because he wanted her to think about what she was doing. He was bent on undermining her decisions. She needed to get things back on track and focus on what she came here to do: call a truce with him, but tell him she was making her own decisions from now on. He wasn't going to give Zach or their relationship a chance until she grew the backbone to stand up to him, either.

"I love New York. I thought I'd live here the rest of my life. I value my career, but I can work somewhere else," Cameron said.

"Not a national broadcasting job. Not in Seattle," her dad said.

She let out the breath she was holding and gulped another.

"Dad, it's not a concern right now."

"It should be—"

She cut him off, just the way he'd cut her off a thousand times over the years. "I just resigned my job with PSN. I'm now at FOX Sports. They're happy to allow me to tape my show in Seattle—I have it in writing already."

He stared at her in amazement.

"Your agent did this?"

"No, I did it. I'd appreciate it if you would keep that confidential until the official announcement next week. In the meantime, I'm not sure what I can say to you to help you understand why I made the decisions I did, but I am sticking with them. I hope you'll respect them."

He took another bite of his gyro.

Trying to explain to her father why she would choose to marry a man who thought a fun Friday night was hanging out with his grandma and sisters in Seattle's suburbs instead of New York City's glittering, frenetic social scene was like attempting to explain a smart phone to someone who'd never seen a computer before. It wasn't part of his frame of reference.

"Dad, I have another question."

His phone rang again. He flinched a little.

"Go ahead and answer it," she told him.

He pulled the phone out of his pocket, hit the button, and said, "Ondine." He listened for a few minutes. "Okay. Tell him I'll meet with him at his convenience, but not this afternoon. I'll be in tomorrow morning."

Cameron hoped he wasn't blowing off the Fed or someone in the current Presidential administration for lunch in the park with her. It was entirely possible.

He hung up and stuck the phone back into his pocket. She watched children running and playing on the grass, people strolling or jogging on the path in front of them, and felt the humidity of a New York summer afternoon. She would miss this and so much more when she moved away. She couldn't stand thinking about the rest of her life without Zach, though.

"We got off on the wrong foot a long time ago. Could we talk about that a little?" she said.

"I don't know what you're talking about, Cameron. Maybe you should explain." Her father polished off his gyro and reached for his untouched container of Greek salad. She handed him another fork while she made the extra effort to think of something to say that might make him understand how she felt.

"I didn't spend a lot of time with you growing up."

"I was home at dinner every night. I made sure you, your sister, and your mother were provided for. Are we starting this again?"

"Dad, I'm not saying that you weren't a good provider. I know you've worked very hard to make sure we had everything we needed over the years. I told you I'm thankful for all the things you and Mom have done for me. I wish we'd spent more time together, though." She sipped her iced tea. "You might have known I was a lot more interested in sports broadcasting than art and antiquities if you talked to me about the things I enjoyed doing when I was in school, for instance. The nanny was still escorting Paige and me to lacrosse and basketball until we were old enough to take a cab there ourselves, for instance."

"So, you're mad because we didn't 'hang out.' Is that

it?" To say she was surprised to see her dad making air quotes was an understatement. She had to smile.

"You say you don't want me to leave, but I don't get to spend a lot of time with you, and you don't understand why I might want something else in life besides what you and Mom wanted for me. If we spent more time together, we might get to know each other a little better. That's what I'd really like. I might not be living in the same place, but I could visit, you could visit me, and we could at least try. I also want you to get to know Zach. Please." She let out a breath. "Maybe you'd have more in common with him than you might think."

Her dad slung one arm around the back of the bench. They were each lost in their own thoughts.

He cleared his throat. "I heard there's a food truck here that specializes in toasted cheese sandwiches. Maybe we should go and find it next time you visit," he said.

There was an instantaneous lump in her throat. She nodded.

They cleaned up the remainders of their lunch and dropped the trash into a nearby can.

"There are food trucks in Seattle, too, Dad."

"Good," he said.

Chapter Twenty-Five

AFTER BUYING HIM a microbrew—or four—at the dumpy bar across the freeway from the Sharks practice facility, Logan filled Zach in on Cameron's whereabouts: Cameron had been in New York for the past forty-eight hours, and she was due back tonight. The forty-eight hours she'd been gone felt like forty-eight months to Zach. He'd gotten one text from her since she left, too: TRUST ME. This time, he would. He wasn't giving up. He loved her, he wanted to spend the rest of his life with her, and he was going to do whatever it took to make that happen. If groveling over the argument they had the other day was involved, so be it. He might even beg.

Hell, who was he kidding? He'd beg. He'd plead. He'd kiss her breathless and promise her the world. He was in love with her. The next time he saw her, he'd say so. If he wasn't still in camp, he would have been on the first flight out to her.

Zach had to have something to do while he waited for her. If the groveling and begging worked and she forgave him, he would propose. He had no idea when and where he was going to ask Cameron to marry him, but he knew he was going to, and he wanted to be prepared. To that end, he'd spent two hours at a local jeweler's yesterday picking out a ring. The jeweler somehow managed to discover Cameron's ring size. He'd delivered the finished ring to Zach half an hour ago. The seven-carat diamond ring was now burning a hole in Zach's shorts pocket.

Adding to Zach's stress, three of his teammates had invited themselves into his dorm room for a chit-chat on what they believed was his impending proposal. He needed to make sure she accepted his apology before he proposed, but he wasn't sharing that with the knuckleheads. He felt like he was at one of Whitney's middle school slumber parties. There was no nail polish, makeup tips, or Flamin' Hot Cheetos here, though. And he was fairly sure the middle school girls his little sister invited over back in the day weren't quite as entranced with the F-word as a method of self-expression.

"You fucked up, Anderson. Women want romance and magic. You should have asked her at sunrise. You had a whole lake all to yourself out there. She's not going to be impressed if you get down on one knee in the cafeteria or something," Derrick told him.

The team had picked up a defensive end cap casualty, Julian Jones, who was flopped out in Zach's desk chair and watching the proceedings with a half-smile on his face.

"I've seen how that girl looks at you," Julian said. "She doesn't have a reason to say no, dawg."

Zach rubbed a hand across his face. "I asked her at sunrise last time. I have to come up with something better this time," he said. "Everything I can think of someone else has already done, and I'm not hiring a flash mob, either."

"Did you call her dad already to ask for his blessing? Women *love* that," Drew said.

That would have to wait, considering Cameron was probably still pissed over his last conversation with her dad.

Zach's dorm room door banged against the wall as the Sharks' starting secondary invited themselves in.

"Heard you got a delivery from Alvin Goldfarb Jewelers, guy," Conroy said.

"Does she need another security guard? You buy a ring for that girl, it better have as many carats as possible. Lemme see it." Antoine stretched out a hand for the box.

"I bought a ring for my wife there last year. Nice people. I still had money when I was done, too," Jasha said. He slapped Zach on the back. "I got myself a little somethin-somethin before I walked outta there." He displayed a Rolex on his wrist.

Terrell stared at the other three men. "You're wack. How you going to ask her, Z?"

Zach shook his head. "I have no idea. I've been thinking about it for days now. I—I still don't know."

"You could always take her to dinner, order champagne, and ask the server to put the ring in her dessert,"

Drew said. His comments were met with a cacophony of laughter and jeering.

"Everyone does that."

"Fuckin' boring."

"Remember McKenna? He asked HIS wife after the Super Bowl. How you gonna top something like that?"

"She doesn't really eat dessert," Zach said. "Then again, she does like brownies."

He saw a mysterious little smile playing around Derrick's lips and a few looks between some of his teammates. They were up to something, and it had better not involve anyone getting duct taped to the goal posts or thrown into the locker room showers and covered with shaving cream.

"If you assholes think there's a better way to ask, maybe you'd better tell him quick," Drew retorted.

Zach felt the phone in his pocket vibrate. I'M DOWNSTAIRS, Cameron texted. WANT TO GO FOR A WALK WITH ME?

His heart skipped a beat and then sped up. He couldn't stop the grin that spread over his face. He couldn't wait to see her again.

"She's back," he said. "I've gotta bounce."

"Huddle up," Derrick barked. Eight men formed a circle and threw their arms around each other's shoulders.

"She's going to say yes no matter what," Conroy said. "That girl's in love with you."

"Tell her you love her. Tell her you can't live without her. Get down on one knee," Drew said.

"Go get your ass engaged," Derrick said. "We'll see you later."

All Zach had to do now was get downstairs, find the love of his life, and ask her to marry him. Again.

THE SHARKS' LOBBY was dark. The team's employees had gone home for the night, so it was the perfect place to get a few minutes alone with Zach. Cameron rooted through her gigantic handbag for the little plastic container of Tic Tacs she knew was in there. She should have brushed her teeth, combed her hair, and freshened up her makeup before she saw Zach again. He'd made it clear he didn't care about that stuff, but all she could think about for the past five and a half hours was how much she wanted to see him again, and she wanted to be at her best when that happened. No matter how irritated with him she'd been when she left Seattle, she couldn't stay mad. She couldn't wait to be in his arms again.

She shook the entire bag, heard the tell-tale rattling of the breath mints, and redoubled her efforts.

Cameron heard heavy footsteps on the staircase, and Zach appeared seconds later. She dropped her bag on the lobby couch, ran up to him, and threw her arms around him. He picked her up off the floor and swung her around in response.

"I missed you so much," she said, covering his face with kisses. She couldn't get him close enough, either.

"I missed you, too." He squeezed her so tightly it took her breath away. "How did it go?"

"It went really well. I have stuff to tell you, but right now, all I want is you," she said.

"I want you, too." He tugged her over to the lobby couch, and sat down next to her. "I need to talk to you." He cradled her cheek in one of his hands and looked into her eyes. "I really fucked up, darlin'. I'm sorry. I should never have told your dad what I did, and I didn't think that he'd actually call the big boss, either—"

"I was a little upset about it at the time, but the more I thought about it, I couldn't stay mad at you. You're not my dad, and I know you didn't do it to hurt me," she said. "I was afraid you thought I couldn't handle it on my own."

He was shaking his head before she finished speaking. "No. No. Not at all. I—I don't know what the hell I was thinking, but it was wrong. I thought I could help, but it was a stupid thing to do. I won't do it again." He leaned his forehead against hers. "Please tell me you'll forgive me."

She relished the feeling of his warmth against hers, his scent, and the puffs of his breath against her cheek. "Right after you forgive me for not even telling you where I was going and not talking to you for two days," she murmured.

"You sent me a text."

"It wasn't enough. I had to go fix it all, and I couldn't do it from here." She sat up and looked into his eyes. "I have some news. Would you like the good news or the bad news first?"

"We'll face it together, darlin'." He reached out to pull her close. "What's the bad news?"

"I fired Laurie."

"*That's* the bad news?" She saw his huge grin. "Really?"

"Oh, there's more." She took a deep breath. "You'll have to get used to having me around more often, Zach Anderson. I quit my job at PSN. I took a job with FOX Sports instead. They agreed to let me work from Seattle."

"What? Really? You're moving here?"

"Of course I'm moving here. I can't leave you here all alone, can I?" she teased.

He pulled her up off the couch and twirled her around in his arms, over and over. His mouth covered hers, and she slid her fingers into his hair. His tongue slipped into her mouth. She could never describe how he tasted to anyone else, but she craved him, and that taste, more than anything else she'd ever known. He lowered her feet to the floor again, but she didn't let go. In a little less than twenty-four hours, they could be alone. She couldn't wait.

She had to be back in New York in three days. She'd be back in Seattle as soon as she wrapped up some details and moved out of her apartment. In the meantime, she was enjoying as much of him as she could possibly get.

"Won't you miss New York City?"

"I can live without New York," she told him. "I can't live without you."

"There's nobody in the training room right now," he whispered into her ear. He leaned his forehead against hers again. She let out a laugh.

"Sounds romantic. Maybe I can tie you to a training table with some gauze strips or something."

"There's a hot tub in there."

"It's more like a cold tub, isn't it?"

His smile flashed in the dimness of the Sharks' lobby. "We'd warm it up in a hurry, darlin'."

Zach tugged on her hand again. "Let's go. I want to show you something."

They exited the building, and Zach made a sharp right onto the path that ran alongside the practice field.

"Where are we going?"

"Let's dip our toes in the lake and look at the stars," he said.

The Sharks owned a dock on their lakefront property. It was convenient when the ownership wanted to fly a coveted free agent player in via seaplane to see the facility, or when one or more of the players wanted to show up at practice by boat in the summertime. It was a perfect summer night: cloudless, warm enough to be comfortable, and the stars were already brilliant in a dark periwinkle sky.

"Don't you have to be back in the dorm in an hour?"

"We've got plenty of time," he assured her.

They stepped out onto the dock, and he let out an "I'm going to kill those guys" seconds before she noticed a picnic basket sitting beside a bench that hadn't been on the dock two days ago. It looked just like one of the benches the Sharks' VIPs sat on in the covered area during practices.

"Is something wrong?"

He still held her hand, but she noticed his hand had grown a little sweaty in the past thirty seconds or so. She also noticed that the bulge she felt in his shorts pocket earlier when she plastered herself against him wasn't necessarily just him, and her heart rate sped up a little, too.

Her mouth went dry. She felt herself trembling. She hoped the thing she wished for most was about to happen.

She knew she loved him, and she knew he loved her, too. Did he love her enough to try it again, to propose one more time and to go through the work involved in making their crazy schedules mesh? Maybe he thought she should do the asking. She couldn't imagine that, though. Zach was still pretty traditional. He'd want to be the one doing the proposing.

His voice broke into her frantic, excited thoughts. "Of course not. Want to sit down? Let's see what they left for us," he said.

"Should we be worried about this?"

"Oh, hell, no. This is from my meddling teammates. They must have moved ass to get it out here . . ." He sat down next to her, sliding one arm around her shoulders as he swung the basket onto his lap. "Take a peek."

She flipped open the top and peered inside. "There's a bottle of champagne and a couple of plastic cups." She reached inside the basket to move the champagne bottle aside. "Oh, wow. There's some huge strawberries, too." She saw a sealed container of brownies from the local grocery store's bakery below the strawberries. "It's really nice of them." She tried to pretend like she was calm. It wasn't working well, especially when he lowered the basket to the deck again, turned to look into her eyes, and took her hands in both of his. "I thought we were having a toast."

She could hear her voice shaking. She was surprised he didn't comment on it. He raised both hands to his lips, and kissed her knuckles.

"We need something to drink to first."

"I got a new job," she burst out.

A huge smile spread over his face. "That's right. You did, and you handled it yourself. That's incredible, darlin'. I am so proud of you."

She beamed. Her already thumping heart went into overdrive when he got to his feet and sank to one knee next to her. She let out a gasp.

"This is really happening. Really? I should have—I should have brushed my hair and I—I—oh. I should have dressed up a little, too. I—" She pulled one of her hands out of his and slapped it over her mouth. It was the only way she was going to stop talking. He waited until she stopped jabbering.

Her nerves seemed to steady his.

"I could have rented a marching band or written it on the sky or made a big banner to hang on the 405 overpass, but maybe something simple is best right now. The words would still be the same," he said. "I love you with all my heart, Cameron. I want to spend the rest of my life with you." He reached into his shorts pocket and pulled out a small black velvet box. "Will you marry me?"

Her hand was still over her mouth. She was nodding, but it might have been nice if she could speak. She didn't want to let go of his hand, but her arm wasn't obeying the "down, down!" signal from her brain. Finally she managed to get her hand to move. It didn't help matters that she was insta-crying, too.

"Yes. Yes. I love you so much. Yes." She threw her arms around him and managed to choke out, "I hoped you would ask me. I was afraid you wouldn't, and I wondered if I needed to ask you, and then I wondered if you needed a ring, too—"

His voice was quiet. "You were going to propose to me?"

"You asked me last time. It was only fair."

His mouth touched hers, sweet and soft. Adrenaline and adoration surged through her. There was so much to say to him, but the worries about their families, their careers, and everything else could wait. Right now, it was just them, and it was perfect. She'd remember the rain-washed air, the waves lapping the dock, the twinkling stars overhead, and the tender look in his eyes for the rest of her life.

"I'd ask you every day for the rest of my life if you wanted me to," he said.

She wished she could respond, but the happy tears came even faster. He took her left hand in both of his and slid the ring on. He got up off his knee, drew her to her feet, and wrapped his arms around her. "Don't cry," he soothed. "Everything's fine."

"I—I'm so happy," was all she could get out.

He brushed her tears away with his fingertips. She hiccupped a few times, but she finally managed to get control of herself. He kissed her again. Her knees knocked, her heart pounded, her head was spinning, but she had him to hang onto.

They heard whistles and applause in the distance.

"I think we have an audience," he said into her ear.

"I don't care." She leaned her head against his shoulder and felt the unfamiliar weight on the third finger of

her left hand. "I haven't even looked at my new ring yet."
She brought her hand in front of her face, and her mouth
dropped open. His lips curved into a smile.

The large, round, radiant-cut diamond was surrounded
by a halo of smaller diamonds, set into a thin platinum
band. The diamonds sparkled in stray light as if they were
afire. She looked, and then she stared.

"Oh, God, it's gorgeous. It's gorgeous! It fits perfectly,
too. Thank you so much!"

This brought on another round of excited kisses and a
few more tears, and they heard more applause, wolf whistles, and someone shouted, "Get a room!"

"Here's our choice. Should we sit out here and enjoy
the champagne and treats by ourselves as God intended,
or should we take them inside and invite the knuckleheads to celebrate with us?" He rolled his eyes, but he was
still smiling. "It's like having fifty-two brothers," he con-
fessed.

"They're not going to leave us alone."

"No, they probably won't." He slid one arm around
her waist, leaned down to pick up the basket, and they
moved around the bench to head up the path toward the
dorm. Their forever started right now.

Epilogue

Fifteen months later

CAMERON ONDINE ANDERSON tied an apron on over her clothing and stared at the turkey she'd put into the kitchen sink. She'd managed to buy it without incident. She'd left it to thaw in the refrigerator like the butcher had told her to. She'd pulled off the netting and the plastic surrounding it. *Now what?*

She'd read the directions. It really didn't matter if she had a master's degree. They might as well have been written in Sanskrit—she couldn't figure them out. What the hell was a "giblet"? She could see ice crystals still in the turkey's breast area and in the drumsticks. She was doing it wrong. Everyone would be so disappointed. She should have bought the ready-made kind, but Zach had said it would be easy.

Zach was enjoying a little more sleep before he had to go

to practice for a couple of hours, and before the entire family descended on them later this morning. Butter had crawled in next to him shortly after Cameron got out of bed, too. She couldn't stand to wake them up. Watching their ninety-pound dog cuddle with her husband was adorable.

Zach didn't have to play again until Sunday, and the team was in town this week. She asked the FOX Sports brass if she could have their first Thanksgiving as a married couple at home, and they agreed on one condition: A pretaped few minutes of the Andersons would be shown on the network this afternoon. Ever since Cameron and Zach's romance was featured on PSN's *Third and Long*, football fans couldn't seem to get enough of their love story. Logan had also made the jump to FOX Sports; he'd be one of their dinner guests today as well.

Cameron pulled out the well-worn Betty Crocker cookbook Zach's grandma had pressed into her hands last night, flipped to the "poultry" tab, and started reading. A few minutes later, she pulled on the plastic gloves with frilly fabric on one end her sister had sent her as a joke, and rinsed off the turkey. According to the cookbook, she was going to have to stick her hand inside it and pull out the neck—eww—and the giblets, which should be in a bag of some sort.

She heaved a long sigh. "I must be out of my mind."

She heard heavy footsteps behind her and a big dog's nails on the hardwood floor.

"No, you're not. You're doing just fine," her husband reassured her. He wrapped his arms around her waist. "Why didn't you wake me up?"

"You and Butter looked so peaceful—"

"I didn't want to miss this," he said. "I don't want to miss a minute with you."

The dog put two massive paws on the kitchen counter and eyed the turkey. Cameron and Zach both said, "No. Down," and Butter lay down on the kitchen floor.

Zach kissed the side of her neck. She wished they could go back to bed for a couple of hours, but he had to leave soon for the team facilities. Maybe it wasn't too late to call the grocery store and get one of those premade turkey dinners.

"You just want to make sure I'm not going to screw up the dinner," she teased.

"We'll be fine," he reassured. "Let's see here."

Ten minutes later, Zach had washed his hands, preheated the oven, pulled out the turkey neck and giblets bag, rinsed the rest of the ice crystals from the turkey, and directed Cameron to grab the roasting pan and the "oven bags" he'd bought from the pantry. A few minutes later, the unstuffed turkey was smeared with butter and in the roasting bag, placed into the pan, and Zach lowered it into the oven. He set the oven timer.

She knew Zach was handy in the kitchen—in more ways than one—but she was a bit surprised to note his calm mastery of a situation that kept the Butterball Turkey Hotline in business each year.

"Voila," he said. "It'll cook on its own." He washed his hands again. "Grandma and the girls are making most of the side dishes when they get here. We can set the table later."

"So, I can learn how to do this myself for Christmas?"

"Why would you want to do it yourself when I'm here?" He kissed and nuzzled the back of her neck. "We'll work together."

"But you have a game! We won't both be here. I—"

He wrapped his arms around her waist again. She leaned back against him and closed her eyes.

"Everything will be fine," he soothed. "I promise it will."

Butter dozed on the kitchen floor. Their house was silent around them. Cameron felt the warm puffs of Zach's breath on the side of her neck, the security of his arms, and the gentleness of his touch. He laced his fingers through hers.

"Zach," she whispered.

"Yes, darlin'?"

"I'm thankful for you."

A SHORT TIME later, Zach was on his way to practice, and Cameron stepped out of the shower. She heard voices and laughter. Zach's sisters must have let themselves in. His grandma lived in a little cottage in their backyard. She said she would be over as soon as "her shows" were done.

Zach and Cameron had offered Grandma their ground-floor master bedroom suite shortly before their wedding. The empty carriage house over their three-car garage would be a perfect love nest for the newly married. By taking the master suite, she wouldn't have to climb stairs.

"No, no, no," she'd said. "You kids are so sweet to offer, but that's your room. Newlyweds need their privacy." It seemed that Grandma longed for a little place to call her own. Zach hired an architect and had plans drawn the next week.

Grandma's place looked like a dollhouse nestled in a grove of trees. She was about fifty feet from the back door of Zach's house. She loved listening to the rain on the roof, hearing the wind whistling through the trees, and puttering in the little garden they'd helped her put in around her front door. Zach made sure she had a driver/ companion in case she wanted to go somewhere when he and Cameron were traveling or at work. Cameron had a standing coffee date with Grandma most mornings, too.

Nobody in Zach's family cared if Cameron's hair was a mess or if she was wearing last season's clothes. They laughed a lot, and she laughed with them.

She heard a knock at the bedroom door. "Come in," she called out.

All four of Zach's sisters piled inside. Whitney hurried over to throw her arms around Cameron. "I've missed you," she said.

"I missed you, too. How's school?"

"Great." Her sister-in-law's face glowed with joy. "I brought someone home for dinner with me."

"You did? I know some of the girls at the sorority probably didn't go home. It's nice of you to invite a friend."

Cameron hugged Ashley. Courtney threw her arms around both of them. Cameron reached to kiss Shelby's cheek. Having four younger sisters was a whole new world for her, but she loved it. They were all out of the house and on their own now. They visited frequently, though. There were daily phone conversations, shopping trips, and all the fun of family members who couldn't wait to spend time together.

"She didn't bring home a sorority sister," Ashley said.

"It's a guy," Courtney said. "He's in the family room. Plus, your parents are here."

Seconds later, Cameron heard another tap on the bedroom door, and her mother's voice. "Honey, are you in there?"

"Come on in, Mom."

Olivia Ondine, dressed in head-to-toe vintage Chanel complete with seven ropes of Chanel-logo pearls in varying lengths, glanced around at five women in casual clothing. "I'm overdressed again, aren't I?"

"Mom, don't worry about it," Cameron assured her. "You look gorgeous. If you want me to, I'll dress up. We didn't want to wreck our clothes working in the kitchen."

Cameron noted the sadness in her mother's eyes. She wanted to fit in, too, it seemed. She just wasn't sure how. Zach's sisters must have noticed Olivia's crestfallen expression as well.

Shelby smiled at Olivia. "That suit is beautiful. Want to hang out in the kitchen with us? We'd better find you an apron first." She patted Olivia on the back. "We're planning on making a huge mess. Want to help?"

"Don't fuss," Olivia said. "I'll be fine."

Ashley reached out for the doorknob leading to Cameron's closet and glanced at Cameron with one raised eyebrow. Cameron gave her a quick nod.

"C'mon, Olivia. Let's see what she's got."

Several minutes later they'd coaxed Olivia into a pair of Cameron's jeans and a plum cotton v-necked sweater. They replaced the high heels she wore with a pair of slipper socks.

"I can't remember the last time I didn't wear high heels on a holiday," Olivia said, but Cameron was touched to see her mom smiling. The sisters clustered around her. "These are definitely more comfortable."

Ashley nodded at the Chanel pearls. "Those are perfect with that sweater."

To Cameron's surprise, Olivia took a strand of them off and draped them around Ashley's neck. "They're yours, if you'd like them," she said. Ashley responded with a hug. Olivia glanced over at Courtney. "You need something pretty to wear with your lab coat," she said, and pulled off the diamond-studded bangle she wore. She slid it onto Courtney's wrist.

"But this belongs to you," Courtney said.

"I want you to have it," Olivia insisted.

Shelby and Whitney both got a strand of pearls, too.

"Olivia, these are so expensive, and your daughters might be upset—" Ashley protested.

"They already have some."

Cameron hurried across her and Zach's room to grab her own strand of Chanel pearls out of the jewelry box and looped them over her head.

"Now we all look stunning," Olivia said, looking satisfied.

"We don't cook in anything but Chanel," Cameron

told her sisters-in-law and her mother. Talking and laughing, the six women descended on the kitchen.

ZACH ARRIVED HOME from practice to find a houseful of guests. He could hear the women in the kitchen from the front door. Butter ran up to him, tail wagging, and tried to knock him over.

"Down, boy. Where is everybody?"

His wife hurried toward him and threw her arms around his neck. She had a little flour on one of her cheeks, too. They must have opened a bottle of wine, because he tasted it when he kissed her.

"My dad's in the family room. He's behaving himself so far."

"Good. It'll be fine, darlin'," he reassured.

"Wait until you see who else arrived a few minutes ago," she said into his ear. She tugged him past the formal living room that nobody used and into the family room.

His father-in-law got to his feet and stuck out one hand. "Happy Thanksgiving, Anderson."

"Happy Thanksgiving to you, too, Mr. Ondine. Would you like something to drink or a snack while you're waiting for dinner? Let's flip the game on. I like the Lions this year."

"Call me Preston," he said.

Cameron's dad didn't quite meet his eyes. They'd mended fences enough that Cameron's family had attended their small and private wedding, but Zach and his father-in-law's relationship was still a bit dicey. Surprisingly enough, his mother-in-law was at Zach and Cameron's every chance she could get. He was shocked to learn that she and Grandma shared the same addiction to daytime TV, for instance. She'd coaxed his grandma into shopping and mani-pedis and lunches out, too. He had to admit he loved it. It was time for Grandma to enjoy herself.

"I'll do that, Preston. Again, do you need anything?"

"Your wife got me a scotch on the rocks, so I'm fine. Thank you for asking." He sat down again on the couch and nodded toward Zach.

Zach felt the air behind them shift a bit, and Caleb walked into the family room.

"Hey, Z."

"Caleb." The two men embraced, slapping each other on the back. "What the hell are you doing here?"

"Your sister invited me."

"She did? That's great," Zach said. "Which sister?"

"Whitney." Preston took the club chair, so Caleb settled himself onto the couch in front of the TV.

"How'd you meet her?" Zach tried to keep his voice casual. Since when did his little sister start hanging around with his teammates?

"She was at Family Day." In other words, Caleb met her the last day of training camp, when the Sharks were encouraged to invite family and friends for a not-especially-professional game of flag football and barbecue. "You're not mad, are you, bro?"

"Have you been dating her?"

"Yeah. We've had coffee or lunch a few times."

Preston watched the two men like he was sitting in center court at the US Open. For once, he didn't say a word. He took another sip of his scotch and observed.

"When were you going to tell me about this?" Zach said.

"Now's a good time." Caleb rested his forearms on his massive thighs. "I've really enjoyed spending time with your sister. I care for her, and I treat her with respect. I'd like to keep dating her. I hope you won't object."

Zach tried to come up with a reason why he should tell Caleb no, and he didn't have one. Caleb's upbringing was almost as rough as his own, but the younger man had managed to stay out of trouble, graduate from college, and take care of his mother and grandmother. If he had to pick anyone for Whitney to end up with, she could have brought home a hell of a lot worse. He wagged his finger at Caleb, though. "Her schooling comes first."

"Always," Caleb said.

"You'll bring her home on time, even if she's not living here anymore."

"Every time."

"She needs to finish school before she gets serious with anyone."

Caleb met his eyes. "I will ask for your blessing before I propose to your sister."

Preston put his scotch glass down on the end table next to him and studied Caleb. "You mean it."

"Absolutely," Caleb said. He glanced up at Zach again. He squared his shoulders and sat up straight. "If anyone wanted to date my little sister, I'd expect the same things."

To Zach's surprise, Preston extended his hand to Caleb. The two men shook. Caleb gave him a nod, and settled back on the couch. Zach couldn't imagine the prep school and Ivy League–educated hedge fund owner and the product of an inner-city high school and state college raised by a single parent who cleaned houses for a living having anything to say to each other. They seemed comfortable together, though.

Zach crossed the room, and stuck his hand out to Caleb as well.

"Let's watch some football before we start talking about our feelings and shit," he muttered.

Caleb laughed out loud. Even Preston smiled.

CAMERON GLANCED AROUND the new expandable dining room table she'd talked Zach into a couple of weeks ago. The table he'd bought from Ikea a few years ago made a great sideboard for the overflow of side dishes and desserts to feed the Andersons, the Ondines, Caleb, Logan, and a few of the girls' friends from school and work. The candles were lit, and the china and crystal at each place setting sparkled as twilight fell outside. Butter lay in the corner of the dining room gnawing on an extra-special bone they'd obtained from the butcher for him.

She set the platter holding the perfectly-done turkey down in front of Zach's place at the table. He got to his feet and slipped his arm around her waist, lifting his wine glass with the other hand. The conversation and laughter around the table quieted.

He opened his mouth and shut it again. His brows knit. He seemed to be struggling for words. Cameron saw tears rise in his eyes, and she gave him a squeeze.

"There are so many things to be thankful for today," he rasped.

Caleb's voice was soft. "Amen."

Zach swallowed hard. "Let's drink to health, happiness, and life's greatest blessing—loving, and being loved."

Zach and Cameron touched glasses.

MORE LOVE AND FOOTBALL!
Can't get enough of Julie Brannagh's Love
and Football series?
Great news, there is so much more to come!
Next up, golden-haired hottie and Sharks linebacker
Drew McCoy meets his match . . .
and she's not at all what he expected.
And in case you are not yet caught up with all
things Seattle Sharks,
take a look at where the series began . . .

BLITZING EMILY

LOVE AND FOOTBALL, BOOK ONE

Emily Hamilton doesn't trust men. She's much more comfortable playing the romantic lead on stage in front of a packed house than in her own life. So, when NFL star and irresistible ladies' man Brandon McKenna acts as her personal white knight, she has no illusions he'll stick around. However, a misunderstanding with the press throws them together in a fake engagement that yields unexpected (and breathtaking) benefits. Every time Brandon calls her "Sugar," Emily almost believes Brandon's playing for keeps, not just to score. Can she let down her defenses and get her own Happily Ever After?

RUSHING AMY

LOVE AND FOOTBALL, BOOK TWO

For Amy Hamilton, only three F's matter:
Family, Football, and Flowers.
It might be nice to find someone to share Forever
with too, but right now she's working double overtime
while she gets her flower shop off the ground. The last
thing she needs or wants is a distraction . . . or help,
for that matter. Especially in the form of gorgeous and
aggravatingly arrogant ex-NFL star Matt Stephens.
Matt lives by a playbook—*his* playbook. He never
thought his toughest opponent would come in the
form of a stunning florist with a stubborn streak to
match his own. Since meeting her in the bar after
her sister's wedding, he's known there's something
between them. When she refuses, again and again,
to go out with him, Matt will do anything to win
her heart . . . But will Amy, who has everything to
lose, let the clock run out on the one-yard line?

About the Author

Julie Brannagh has been writing since she was old enough to hold a pencil. She lives in a small town near Seattle, where she once served as a city council member and owned a yarn shop. She shares her home with a wonderful husband, two uncivilized Maine Coons and a rambunctious chocolate Lab.

Julie hasn't quite achieved the goal of owning a pro football team, so she created a fictional one: The Seattle Sharks. When she's not writing, she's reading, or armchair-quarterbacking her beloved Seattle Seahawks from the comfort of the family room couch. Julie is a Golden Heart finalist and the author of four contemporary sports romances.

Visit www.AuthorTracker.com for exclusive information on your favorite HarperCollins authors.

Give in to your impulses . . .
Read on for a sneak peek at two brand-new
e-book original tales of romance
from Avon Books.
Available now wherever e-books are sold.

FALLING FOR OWEN
Book Two: The McBrides
By Jennifer Ryan

GOOD GIRLS DON'T
DATE ROCK STARS
By Codi Gary

An Excerpt from

FALLING FOR OWEN
Book Two: The McBrides

by Jennifer Ryan

From *New York Times* bestselling author
Jennifer Ryan comes the second book in an
unforgettable series about the sexy McBride
men of Fallbrook, Colorado. Reformed bad boy
Owen McBride will do anything to protect his
beautiful neighbor when she gets caught in the
crossfire between his client and her abusive ex.

Claire woke out of a sound sleep with a gasp and held her breath, trying to figure out what had startled her. She listened to the quiet night. Nothing but crickets and the breeze rustling the trees outside. A twig snapped on the ground below her window. Her heart hammered faster, and she sucked in a breath, trying not to panic. Living in the country lent itself to overactive imaginings about things that go bump in the dark night. The noise could be anything from a stray dog or cat to a raccoon on a midnight raid of her garbage cans, even an opossum looking for a little action.

Settled back into her pillow and the thick blankets, she closed her eyes, but opened them wide when something big brushed against the side of the house. Freaked out, she got up from the bed and went to the window. She pulled the curtain back with one finger and peeked through the crack, scanning the moonlit yard below for wayward critters. Not so easy to see with the quarter moon, but she watched the shadows for anything suspicious. Nothing moved.

Not satisfied, and certainly not able to sleep without a more thorough investigation, she padded down the scarred wooden stairs to the living room. She skirted packing boxes and the sofa and went to the window overlooking the front yard. Nothing moved. Still not satisfied, she walked to the dining room, opened the blinds, and stared out into the cold night. Something banged one flower pot into another on the back patio, drawing her away from the dining room, through the kitchen, and to the counter. She grabbed the phone off the charger, went around the island, and tiptoed along the breakfast bar to the sliding glass door. She peeked out, hiding most of her body behind the wall and ducking her head out to see if someone was trying to break into her house. Like she thought, the small pot filled with marigolds had been knocked over and broken against the pot of geraniums beside it. Upset that her pretty pot and flowers were ruined, she moved away from the wall and stood in the center of the glass door to get a better look.

With her gaze cast down on the pots, she didn't see the man step out from the other side of the patio until his shadow fell over her. Their gazes collided, his eyes going as wide as hers.

"You're not him," he said, stumbling back, knocking over a potted pink miniature rose bush, and falling on his ass, breaking the pot and the rose with his legs. She hoped he got stuck a dozen times, but the tiny thorns probably wouldn't go through his dirt-smudged jeans.

In a rage, she opened the door, but held tight to the handle so she could close it again if he came too close. She yelled, "What the hell are you doing?"

"I'll get him for this and for sleeping with my wife," the guy slurred. Drunk and ranting, he gained his feet but stumbled again. "Where is he?" The man turned every which way, looking past her and into her dark house.

"Who?"

"Your lying, cheating, no-good husband."

"How the hell should I know? I haven't seen or heard from him in six months."

"Liar. I saw him drive this way tonight after he fucked my wife at his office and filled her head with more bullshit lies."

"Listen, I'm sorry if my *ex* is messing with your wife. I left him almost two years ago for cheating on me. Believe me, I know how you feel, but he doesn't live here."

"You're lying. He drove his truck this way and stopped just outside."

"He doesn't drive a truck."

"Stop lying, bitch."

"I'm not. You have the wrong person."

"You tell that no-good McBride he better stop seeing my wife. If he thinks a bunch of papers will ever set her free from me, he doesn't know what I'm capable of, what we have. He'll be one sorry son of a bitch. She's mine. I keep what's mine."

"You don't understand."

"No. You don't understand," he said, almost like a whining child. "You tell him, or I'll make him pay with what's his." He pointed an ominous finger at her. "You tell him if he doesn't leave my wife alone and let her come back to me like she wants, I'm going to hurt you before I come after him."

An Excerpt from

GOOD GIRLS DON'T DATE ROCK STARS

by Codi Gary

Gemma Carlson didn't plan on waking up married to her old flame—and her son's father-turned-country rock star—Travis Bowers, following a night of drunken dares. So she does the only sane thing: she runs!

Travis finally has a second chance, and he doesn't plan on losing Gemma again—or the son he didn't know he had. He's in this for the long haul. Even if it means chasing his long-lost love all over again . . .

"What are you doing here, Travis?"

The rage and frustration that had been simmering below the surface of his skin started to burn. "Why wouldn't I come here?" He turned around and faced her, crossing his arms over his chest. "You're my wife. We spent a magical night together, and I just happen to have a break in my tour that allows me to spend several weeks with you."

"I thought you would—"

"What, Gemma?" His voice was low and dark as he approached her. Grabbing her shoulders, he gave her a gentle shake. "What? You thought I'd just read your letter and be grateful? That I'd think, 'you know what, she's right' and leave you alone, just disappear from your life again?"

She stopped struggling, and he could tell by her expression that was exactly what she'd been thinking.

"This is my home, Travis. You can't just show up here and disrupt my life," she hissed.

"I'm not trying to disrupt your life. I just want to know why you left without talking to me. At least trying to work out what happened," he said.

"What happened is we got drunk and did something stupid. End of story," she said.

"No, that's not the end of it, sweetheart," he snapped before he could rein in his temper. "Like it or not, we're married. It wasn't something I planned, but that's the way things are, and you could have at least given me the courtesy of waking me up and talking about it."

"What's there to talk about, Travis? We haven't seen each other for ten years, and yes, I had fun with you, but we want totally different things," she said, sounding almost disappointed. "You and I . . . we don't work anymore. We're too different. Our worlds are too different."

He took a calming breath and thought about her words. It was true that their lives were different, but that wasn't a kill switch for a future. People called alcohol "truth serum," and if he'd stood up and pledged himself to Gemma legally, deep down he must have wanted it. Which led to a whole new line of crazy he could sift through later, but right now, he needed to make her understand that he took what they'd done seriously. He wasn't going to let her just sweep it under the rug as a drunken mistake.

Especially since it took two to say "I do."

He had been developing his strategy the whole drive, and he'd come up with an idea he was going to propose—before he'd lost his cool. He needed to prove that there was more to what happened than a wild weekend gone wrong. Gemma had said he didn't know her; well, what better way to get to know someone than to date them?

She'd never agree to it, though, until she got over whatever had her in a panic. He needed to show her that it wasn't over, not just like that. There was too much left between them for "closure" or whatever her letter had said.

And he would prove it to her.

"I thought we were working really well together," he said softly, his tone seductive. He took her hand, holding it gently when she tried to pull away and caressing the back of it with his thumb. He saw her shiver and smiled as he brought her fingers up to his mouth, his lips hovering above the knuckles as he spoke. "When we were in your hotel room, and I had my hands on your body, running them over your skin . . . you felt so good." She licked her lips and closed her eyes. He pulled her closer, trailing his lips from her wrist to her elbow. "And the taste of your skin . . . all the little sounds you made when I played with your breasts . . . or when I was deep inside you."

He wrapped his arms around her, his large hands splaying across the curve of her ass, using it to pull her against him. Her breath whooshed out as he pushed himself against her, knowing she could feel every inch of his erection between them. He felt her relax into him, and her hand held onto his bicep, her eyes opening slowly, meeting his. He saw the matching desire in those mossy depths and dropped his lips to her temple, traveling over her skin until his mouth reached her ear. He nipped the small shell teasingly, and her body tightened against his, making him smile as he added, "I can show you again, if you don't remember."